A science fiction ...
about a boy and a girl who fall in ...
and the Alien Reality Television show
that wants to kill them for entertainment.

Andy's eyes twitched as his fear deepened. His throat felt suddenly dry and raw. He thought the scrawny guy who had just run away after warning him about the invisible *things* was crazy. His knocking knees were not so sure. In fact, his whole body was seriously leaning towards believing the crazy man's story entirely, while his nervous mind sweated with the hope of denial.

A second invisible Eye cruised out from behind the trees onto the earthen road. Sweat beaded on Andy's brow. To the cyborg Eyes' bubble vision, his forehead glistened with tiny soap bubbles.

The two Eyes glided in closer.

The strange bracelet on Andy's wrist tingled madly. It felt as though a swarm of buzzing bees had just covered his entire arm. *Freeze*, the bracelet communicated. *This is not a drill. Don't make them hurt you.*

Andy's entire body trembled.

The pair of unseen Eyes stopped on opposite sides of Andy, then moved around him in a slow circle. Passing by his sides, the hairs on Andy's arms stood up on end. Like a freaky lawn of fear, every hair became stiff with an eerie clarity.

When the two Eyes moved to the front and back of him, the thin stalks of panic lay back down, resuming their normal place.

Andy began to lose his grip on reality.

The Eyes kept circling his body. Each time they did so, his arm hair rose up, then fell. The repetition of it terrorized his flesh. He became so frightened, even his goose bumps had goose bumps.

The Munchkins said it best.

There once was a boy who could sing

When he met two invisible things

Since the things were the meanest

Fear shriveled his penis

Now the high notes are all he can swing!

With Andy's arm hair fully erect, the Eyes crept in even closer.

The bracelet raced the chilling information to Andy's fevered brain. *Move a muscle and your dead.*

Andy believed it.

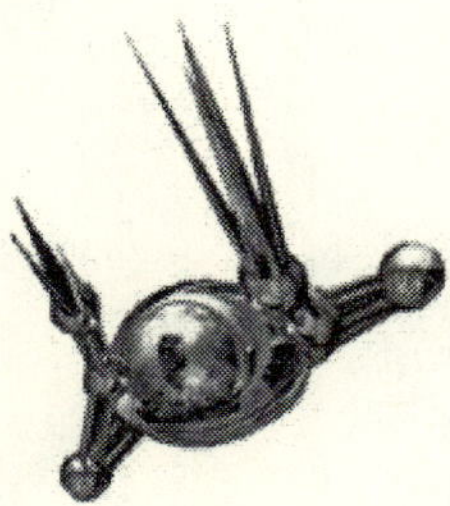

Galactic Eye books by Jon Henn

Those Who Watch
The Stranded*

<u>Childrens Books (grades 3-8)</u>
The Adventures of Flippy the Magic Frog*

* forthcoming
(see last page for details)

THOSE WHO WATCH

Jon Henn

Galactic Eye Publishing
Los Angeles

www.GalacticEyePublishing.com

This is a work of fiction. All the characters or events portrayed in this novel are either fictitious or used fictitiously.

ISBN - 13: 9780615267760
ISBN - 10: 0615267769

Library of Congress Control Number: 2009921372

All rights reserved. Published by Galactic Eye Publishing.

Cover illustration copyright © 2009 by Paul Swendsen.

To the memory of Lilli Oldfield
whose friendship and artistic talents I will cherish forever.

At one point in creating this story, I was reading actor Bruce Campbell's book *If Chins Could Kill: Confessions of a B Movie Actor*. It happened to be at a time when I was searching for the names of my two main characters. When I read the names of Mr. Campbell's children I knew I had found the perfect names for my lead characters.

Thanks, BC. We have at least one thing in common. We both love our Andys and Rebeccas. (And, of course, *The Evil Dead*.)

ACKNOWLEDGEMENTS

Francis and Donna Henn	You Can Do It Award
Kathy Aguilar	Rear In Gear Award
Paul Swendsen	Cover Artist & "Superbulous" Friend Award
Steve Shankland	Fellow Writer Support Award
Les Plesko (UCLA)	Favorite Mentor Medal

And a special thanks to my friend Chris Anderson who, although he does not know it, continues to be an inspiration to me to this day. May the force be with you my friend … and may you never run out of tobacco papers.

CHAPTER 1

THE END OF THE BEGINNING

<u>Alaska – The Frozen Tundra</u>

It was like being thrust into the middle of the ice age. Snow blanketed the ground and there wasn't a sign of life for miles around.

Or was there?

Carson's snow-shoed feet trudged through the icy wasteland tracking a feint trail of footsteps that stretched out beyond his sight. In one hand, he carried a brown leather suitcase, in the other, a handkerchief soaked in her blood.

Violent images, like white hot needles, stabbed at his tortured mind--screaming finger, baby hammer, flopping kitty litter corpse. The harder he tried to reject them, the deeper they cut into his brain. Raw fingers, scraped and bloody, stroked small glass shards in his wounded face.

Where is she? the voices whispered. *Find her or she will die.*

A gust of wind shoved him sideways. Carson swayed and stopped to rest--a fragile speck of life in a sea of deadly white. The bitter cold hurled ice picks of air that chipped at his fevered flesh. His breath broke out in steamy, ragged gasps.

He hoisted his parka about his stout body; the suitcase dropped to the chalky ground. Her terrified face haunted him. *Attackers ... Kim ... the ransom note.* Memories of her abduction flitted in and out of his delirious brain.

Scanning the vast terrain, Carson's vision blurred. His muscles ached from hiking, yet he felt numb to the pain.

"I killed them," he muttered to no one. "They told me and I killed them."

Find Kim, the voices murmured. *Only you can save her. Time is running out.*

Dark clouds gathered in the overcast sky. A tear rolled down his cheek; the bloody handkerchief blew out of his hand, tumbling away in the robust wind.

Urged on by emotions he neither understood nor controlled, Carson grabbed the suitcase, lifted his snow-shoed feet and plodded along the meager trail. He prayed he would find his wife--bound and gagged and left to perish in the snow--alive.

At the bottom of the icy ravine, Kim held a rusty knife in her mouth. The ice-cold blade hurt her teeth as she sawed at the rope that bound her hands. Several cuts on her wrists bled crimson, stinging reminders of her grim plight. Smearing her own blood upon her face, she twisted her head from side to side, forcing the encrusted blade to cut deeper into the rope. She wore a parka, a snowsuit and boots. Her thick black hair, stuck to her face, was matted and caked with blood.

Several grueling minutes later, the last strand broke. Kim wept. Shivering, she grasped the knife in her numb hands and attacked the rope around her feet, her tears dripping on her boots.

The rope snapped. She was free. She looked up to the top of the steep gulley where her kidnapper had scaled a knotted rope after leaving her to die. The crest was a good thirty feet above her. She looked for the rope; it was gone, only the black iron stake it had been tied to remained. Rising, she thrust her hands under her armpits and took her first weary step towards the slope, the muscles in her body singing a tune of stinging pain.

Kim climbed the slippery embankment stopping six feet from the top. Strands of rope trailed from her wrists and ankles. She glanced at the grooves in the snow beside her. Three times she had tried to scale the ravine, three times she had failed and slid back to the bottom.

Exhausted and freezing, all she wanted to do was die.

A voice inside her echoed, *the baby ... Carson's got to save the baby. If not ...*

Kim clamped down hard on her anxious thoughts. Her precious son was with the Stranger, the one who threatened to harm him if they didn't pay his price.

With the strength of a desperate mother, Kim's arms pawed at the snow. Legs churned as boots forced their leathery hide into slick white powder.

Five feet to go ... four feet to go ... three ... the top was nearly within her reach ....

She began to slip down the slope; snow plowed into her nose as despair consumed her heart. The image of the Stranger invaded her mind. Holding a knife, he approached her baby, prepared to do the unthinkable.

Kim's heart beat out of control; her mind was clouded by a chemical rush. Willing herself forward, she clawed her way up the embankment, her body burning with need.

Heaving herself over the top, she collapsed, utterly spent; her face lay sideways on the glossy snow. The sharp cold bit at her blood-boiled flesh, but she didn't care, she had escaped her captor's death sentence.

Momma's coming, Eric. Momma will save you, my love.

Blinking snowflakes off of her eyelashes, Kim raised her head. In the distance, a figure stood wearing snow gear. In his arms was her baby boy.

Eric. Carson. Thank heaven, they're alive.

Raising herself up, Kim frantically waved her arms.

When Carson saw his wife alive he rushed forward. He dragged the suitcase beside him, plowing a groove through the knee-deep snow. Coming together, he embraced her fiercely; joy flooded every cell of his body.

Kim cried out his name. Carson's soul gave thanks to god. He didn't care that the car was miles away, she was in his arms at last. He wanted to kiss her, to tell her he loved her. He wanted to touch her precious lips with his own.

Carson pulled back his hood.

Kim saw the beaming, scratched-up face. It wasn't her husband--it was the Stranger! She looked for her child--Eric was gone! Where she thought he had been moments ago there was only an old, brown suitcase.

She shoved her hood back and screamed, "Where's my baby? Give me my son!"

Carson blanched at her livid face; bile rose up in his throat. It wasn't his spouse--it was the kidnapper. The one who killed his child … the one who seized his wife.

"Where is she?" he demanded. "What have you done with her?"

They pulled out guns from under their parkas and shot each other at point blank range. The thunderous blasts of the weapons echoed across the frosted plain.

Pain flared in Carson's chest. Smoke curled up from the Colt 45's barrel. Then a veil sharply lifted and Carson saw what he had done.

Kim gripped her parka. A cherry-red stream oozed over her fingers. Staring in shock at her husband, Kim slumped to the frozen ground.

Horror pierced Carson's soul. He had killed his wife, the woman he loved.

Bleeding to death he toppled over, the smoking gun still clenched in his hand.

Inches beyond Kim's fingers lay a sleek, pearl-handled revolver. About her wrist was a silver bracelet, slender and smooth, with three gleaming black stones. Blood dripped out of her nose onto the cloud-colored earth, followed by a pebble-sized copper cylinder with writhing hair-like tentacles that plopped into the growing red puddle.

The tiny creature inside emitted an eerie cry as it incinerated into ashes.

The corpses lay still ... all was silent ... even the wind ceased to blow.

Then, from out of nowhere, Opera music began to play.

It was *La Donne Mobile* by Verdi, a merry, lively song. A whirlwind came, the suitcase burst open, a hundred thousand dollars whipped high into the frosty air. The money swirled about the bodies, slapping their faces, moving in patterns like a Las Vegas dance show. It formed two paper doll figures, which pirouetted, hugged each other, then joined together creating a beating heart.

When the joyous music climaxed the heart exploded, scattering the money like confetti. As the tumbling bits of paper fluttered towards the ground they formed the words "love stinks."

A clapperboard materialized. On it were symbols not of this Earth.

"Cut. Print it," a gravely voice said. "That's a wrap."

The Alien Reality Television camera crew decloaked, becoming visible.

The Production Manager clapped his hands. "What a story, Herr Director. A magnificent work of A.R.T."

"Yes," said the Director, peering at the bodies with half-closed eyes.

"And it's so funny," exclaimed the Production Manager. "How on Earth do you do it?"

The Director gazed at the green money as it soaked up the humans' red blood. "I am a genius," he said coolly. "I make death hilarious."

"But how …"

"No more questions," shivered the Director, flapping his elbows in the blustery wind. "It's cold. Let's get going. I want to sip a hot toddy and listen to Mozart. It's been a long three months."

"Pack it up, people," yelled the Production Manager. "We're going home."

Rowdy music played. The cameramen whooped in delight. Grasping their remote control consoles, they made their cameras become visible and raced them through the gusty air. The cameras flew in figure eights, spirals and loop de loops; they zoomed above the Director in formation trailing colored smoke in a formal salute.

The Director nonchalantly waved in acknowledgement and spoke a command into his communicator.

A sparkling energy surrounded them. The aliens and the guns vanished.

A great blast of heat washed over the corpses creating a pond of water in which the bodies floated. The water refroze with the bodies half beneath the water line, a strange memorial to the police who would find them several days later.

A short distance from the human remains, a strange geometric pattern the size of a house formed a deep depression in the dense snow. It looked as though it had been made by a giant cookie cutter.

Slowly, gently, the fragile flakes began the long task of filling it in.

CHAPTER 2

THE V-LAN HOME WORLD

I wish that obnoxious punk Producer would have a heart attack and die, the Director thought as he waited in the studio green room, 87,000 light years away from Earth. He hated show days, and the one today especially.

The production staff was also with him, lingering for the ratings to come in on the new production. No one was sure if it would be a success or would end up a complete flop and a major embarrassment. Anxious and fidgeting, they would soon find out.

The Director stiffly reclined in an anti-gravity lounge chair, his body horizontal to the floor. Humanoid, yet fishlike, he had a thin scaly body, three jointed arms, webbed hands, and round glassy eyes. His cheekbones stretched back into finny ears. His long lips puckered and relaxed as he sipped a cocktail from a large, wide glass with a tiny crab inside it scuttling away from the end of the straw.

How dare he ruin my project by chopping it up in post production, the Director thought. He drank deeply from his cocktail, drawing the tiny crab inside the straw. Its crusty legs clung to the straw's exterior in a futile effort to survive before it was inevitably sucked up. *I'm a class 6 intellect; he's only a class 5. I've made over 400 shows. He's fresh out of film school. Studio nepotism really irks me.*

Crunching the crab between his teeth, the Director kept his disgruntled thoughts to himself. He would never overtly state his displeasure for that would brand him as *egotistical,* something he would have never tolerated about himself, even if it had not been a capital crime on his planet.

Four squat, green-skinned cameramen sat at a star-fish shaped table playing computer games on portable consoles. Each cameraman had four arms, four legs and four eyes which bobbed on the ends of eye stalks on their foreheads. Despite only being class three intelligences, they played four different games at once while sitting on a pair of stools, one for each pair of their four buttocks. Sexless creatures grown in clone vats their legal name was *cameraman*, although when their superiors were angry they would often call them by their more common name-- *its*.

Their secret names between them were Iggy, Zonk, Wank and Glop.

The Production Manager played six dimensional chess against a computer opponent. A class four intelligence, he was smaller than the Director with a bulbous squid-shaped head that sat on his shoulders without a visible neck. The precisely groomed hair on top of his head was shaped like a mushroom; his mouth hung down over his chest. Genetically bred for his organizational skills, the Production Manager glanced up at the chronometer.

"Show's over," the Production Manager said. "We should know the results any moment." He moved a chess piece to another level while, on a wrist monitor, he studied the computer's programming code as it responded to his latest move.

The opaque, force field door vanished. A hover monitor with a round, 360 degree screen floated into the room. The number 32 in a large font moved around the screen's circumference. The name of the show, Planet Earth, Episode 187, *Cold Calamity*, appeared in a smaller font below it.

Strutting into the room, the fussy, shark-like Producer gnashed his teeth together, making angry, growling sounds. In front of his snout, he held a wiggling trout stuck on a stick coated in steaming hot mustard.

The Production Manager cut the power to the cameramen's games. Unable to play, the disgruntled its folded their four hands on top of each other and pretended to pay attention to their superiors.

"A 32 point market share in a prime time slot," the Producer said in a nasally voice. "Adequate, but not superbulous." He wagged his fingers at the Director, each finger sporting a flashy ring. "I am disappointed. I know you can do much better."

Glowering at the Director, he savagely bit off the head of his trout stick with his pearly white, jagged teeth that contained several small diamonds in them. The trout ceased to wiggle; its body slumped in death; hot mustard dripped on the floor.

The diamonds sparkled once he licked them clean.

Not amused by the threatening gesture, the Director imagined the Producer as the victim in every violent death scene he had ever filmed, in particular those with beheadings.

"The story line was weak," the Producer said, exhaling hot mustard fumes out of his nostrils. "Next time come up with something not so choppy."

The Director's temper rose to the boiling point. He bit his tongue. The pain kept him from lashing out. *You twinkle toothed ignoramus. I'll show you who the genius is here.*

Grasping the crabless cocktail, he adjusted the anti grav chair's height so that he was level with the Producer's chest. Extending his audio receptors, he prepared to toss his drink in the Producer's face so the alcohol would sting his eyes.

If I made it look like an accident ... like in the movie "The Hunt For Red October" when Sean Connery kills the KGB agent. I blind him with my drink, he slips on the floor, then 'oops' his neck gets broken with the help of my forceful arms shoving his head on the end of the table.

The Director grasped the chair's controls, preparing to launch his drink attack, when something poked him hard in the leg. The Production Manager wiggled an ear in warning, then moved his Bishop from level 1 to level 3, putting the computer opponent in check.

The Director took the hint. His audio receptors retracted.

Very well, thought the Director. *I'll fix you, Mr. 'I'm-the-boss' Producer. Before I'm through with you, you'll wish you'd been born an "it" in a clone vat.*

The Producer ripped another bite from his fish stick and continued. "Go back to Earth and make a new story. I've arranged for you to use the latest cyborg camera technology. Make me something fresh." He tossed some ruby gemstones onto the table. "Here are your passes. You're scheduled to lift off tomorrow morning."

The cameramen greedily pressed the gems into their earlobes. The thought of using new technology always made them eager to shoot a new show.

"Be sure to be more creative this time," the Producer said, digging a piece of fish gristle out of his jagged teeth. "And don't forget, we're on a budget. Be cost efficient." He swallowed the gristle, smacking his lips. "Have a profitable trip. Don't fail me if you want to keep your job." He took a deep breath. "Just kidding ... not really."

The Director's skin turned an angry purple.

The Production Manager prayed he didn't attack the Producer and get them all executed as accomplices to murder.

As the Producer strode towards the doorway, he tossed the bones of the fish stick into the trash incinerator. The food flared with a burst of heat as it was reduced to ashes. Passing through the force field door, his growling noises vanished as the door resumed its former opaqueness.

The Director sat and fumed. While he plotted out his vengeance, the Cameramen rigged hidden batteries on their persons to their portable consoles. Being careful not to attract attention, they resumed playing their computer games with hidden zeal.

The Production Manager held a flagon of Metamucil mixed in prune juice in front of the Director. It was something he discovered on Earth that relieved his superior's mental constipation. He called it "the brain plunger." Under the circumstances, he made it extra strong.

Smelling the prune juice, the Director's stomach gurgled. Taking it in his webbed hand, he took several long, gluttonous swallows.

The Production Manager played chess for a few more minutes, letting the concoction kick in. "So what genre do you want to do?" he muttered nonchalantly.

Slumped in the anti-grav chair, the Director licked his lips. His mind was relaxed; he had a nice buzz; it always helped his creative thinking. "Let's do a murder mystery," the Director said. "Something with violence, fear, and an abundance of blood and death."

"A love story?" said the Production Manager.

"Of course," the Director nodded as the brain plunger sedated him. "As long as it's weal love, not some mind-controlled imbitation," he said, slurring his words as the drink kicked in. "It weads to blad acting. I have a webutation to ub-hold."

The Director tilted the anti-gravity chair to a standing position and stood up. His legs wobbled when he tried to walk. "I need a nab. We'll talk aboud it ober dinner."

Interlacing his fingers, the Director stretched his hands out. Cracking his knuckles loudly, he stumbled out the door.

Two hundred years with the same director, the Production Manager thought. *I am most fortunate his former Production Manager was crushed by a rock slide on Alpha Centauri Prime under suspicious circumstances. Good production jobs are hard to find. I shall deserve my position by continuing to serve him faithfully.*

He made his last chess move, defeating the computer opponent, then used his wrist device to shut down the cameramens' consoles with an Electro-Magnetic Pulse beam.

Unable to play their computer games, the cameraman protested like little boys.

"All right you its," the Production Manager said, rising up on his snake-like tails that he slithered on like legs. "You heard the boss. Stop your whining, get off your butts and load up the ship. We leave for Earth in the morning."

CHAPTER 3

SETTING THE STAGE

<u>SOUTH DAKOTA – 1988 – early Fall.</u>

A shabby, blue Ford pickup bounced along the twisting highway through the crowded pine tree forest. As the pickup rounded curve after curve, paint cans and other objects in the bed of the truck slid back and forth from one side to the other. One of those objects, a Mysterious Man, his thin, wiry body disguised by loose dark clothing, sat uncomfortably in a corner. A backpack lay on his lap. He used it as a pillow to catch some much-needed sleep. Behind his gaunt face, a well-trimmed ponytail hung down his back.

The pickup sputtered past a small feed store on the outskirts of a town. With red-rimmed eyes, the Mysterious Man saw a road sign welcoming him to Hot Tub, South Dakota. The town was just a few blocks long; if you blinked you missed it.

Twisting his body, he rapped on the rear window. The blue Ford pulled into a dirt parking lot, stopping in front of a butcher shop. With an agility that belied his worn down appearance, the Mysterious Man vaulted out of the truck. He hit the dirt with a dust-raising thud, but whether the dust came from the ground or the top of his boots was anyone's guess.

Spewing puffs of smoke out of its tailpipe, the truck pulled away. The Man ignored the foul-smelling fumes. He had an urgent task to do.

It was time to take the test.

He slung his backpack over his shoulders, closed his eyes, and calmed himself. He envisioned the beauty of the trees, the smell of the forest, and the grandeur of God's great creation.

His mind relaxed.

He was ready.

He entered into a trance.

Pulling up the left sleeve of his grungy shirt, he exposed a silver bracelet with three shiny black stones. He lightly touched them with his fingertips; the polished minerals felt warm.

His head began to swim.

He imagined himself shrinking, getting smaller and smaller until he was a speck of dust on the centermost stone. It was no longer a rock, lifeless and unyielding, but hummed with a curious vigor as though it were alive.

A dark hole swirled open beneath him. He sank into the strange pool of power.

Down the rabbit hole, he thought, *and into Wonderland.*

At once his mind exploded; it was wildly euphoric. He wanted it to last forever, but he knew that it would not. Past experience had taught him the hard way that the elation would soon be replaced by pain.

The Mysterious Man got down to business. He asked the fateful question.

Are they here?

The bracelet took him soaring over the earth, showing him people, foxes, rabbits, a bear, birds, and fish in a stream. The sensation of flying was so powerful, he felt like he was God.

His disembodied mind swooped over a mountain and into the valley below, when a large geometric pattern pressed into the ground suddenly loomed before him. The shock of discovery was like plunging naked into a pool of freezing water.

It's Them. I found Them. The murderers are here.

His eyes suddenly popped open, his heart pounded in his chest. Gasping for air, he tore his fingers away from the bracelet. The buzzing current vanished; his knees buckled; he dropped to the ground, shaking uncontrollably.

Wrapping his arms around his shivering body, he prayed to God for relief.

His prayer was answered in the form of music … opera … Wagner … *The Ride of the Valkyries.* The melody enveloped his person like the embrace of a soothing angel.

The Mysterious Man clung to it like a lifeline.

Inside the Butcher Shop, the Valkyries rode their fiery steeds to Wagner's grand bombastic score. In time to the rousing music, a brawny hand hoisted a large meat cleaver high into the air and, swinging it down with great force, skillfully chopped up a chicken.

The butcher, Gunter Barulich, 60 years old, robustly sang in a deep baritone.

"Bom-bom, da-da bom-bom.

Bom, da-da bom-bom.

Power and glory.

Bom, da-da bom."

Three elderly ladies watched in silent amazement as the Wagnerian enthusiast completed his heroic display of poultry preparation.

Gunter held the blade across his chest, closed his eyes, and let the music fill his soul.

"Dad?" Andy said from behind the deli section, wiping a hand on his butcher's apron.

Caught up in the melodic glory, Gunter stood as still as a statue.

"Dad!" Andy shouted, surprising everyone including himself.

Gunter turned towards his lanky, 19-year-old son, as Andy nodded towards the elderly women. Gunter smiled at the ladies and solemnly bowed his head.

The three old women burst into applause.

Andy rolled his eyes upward. *He acts weird and gets applause. I act weird and get yelled at.* Sighing, he turned towards the slicing wheel. *Life is so unfair.*

"Oh, my, that was wonderful, Mr. Barulich," Mrs. Thompson said. "Such … um …" She looked imploringly at Mrs. Atkins.

"Bravado," said Mrs. Atkins, glancing over the rim of her glasses.

"Bravado," said Mrs. Thompson, clapping her hands in delight.

"Bra what?" rasped Mrs. Wilson, tapping on her hearing aid.

"Bra-va-do!" her two friends shouted.

"Stop yelling," Mrs. Wilson said, covering her hearing aids with both of her hands. She glared at her two friends, then turned to Gunter. "Bra-va-do," she said distinctly, her jaw thrust forward, her mouth set firm.

Gunter smiled. "Thank you, gracious ladies. I am but a humble lover of great music."

The ladies exposed dentured grins, then turned their attention to Andy, who, preoccupied with the injustices in his life, rubbed his forehead with his fingers.

"Andy," his father gently spoke.

Andy turned around, his eyes wide open, fingers splayed. He appeared to be giving his dad a goofy salute.

Gunter tried to be patient. "Customers are waiting, son."

His forehead massage complete and with another deep sigh, Andy approached the three ladies, assuming his best be-friendly-to-the-customer manner.

"Good morning, ladies. What'll it be today?" Andy asked politely. "Same as usual?"

The three old ladies smiled. It was their turn to perform like Andy's father and they were rising to the occasion.

"Half a pound of roast beef sliced real thin," said Mrs. Atkins in a melodic voice.

"A dollar of provolone cheese as quick as you please," joked Mrs. Thompson, making a funny rhyme.

"Two dollars of cole slaw, not a penny more, not a penny less," rasped Mrs. Wilson without any comedic talent whatsoever.

The three women cackled together, feeling clever.

Smiling and nodding, Gunter left the room, heading towards the freezer.

Andy mustered a plastic smile. *Same as usual,* he sighed. *Nothing ever changes in this town.* Grabbing the roast beef, he walked over to the meat slicer. *On the highway of life, why am I always in the slow lane? Why is my life so dull? Does God hate me or what?*

Setting the cutting wheel to thin, Andy played the rhyme game, something he always did when he felt his life was boring. He imagined ten tiny men, speaking in an irreverent, sing-song kind of speech. They were Munchkins from his favorite movie *The Wizard of Oz.* They were strangely dressed, two inches tall and spoke like they had just inhaled helium from a balloon.

Andy peeled the plastic off the roast beef while the Munchkins sang his thoughts to the tune *If I Only Had a Brain.*

"Andy tries to be creative,
But the response is negative,
Cause people think he's nuts.
Don't be different, just be boring,
Can't you hear their brains are snoring,
Life in Hot Tub really sucks."

While the Munchkins crooned, Andy thumped the roast beef onto the cutter and turned on the motor. Several Munchkins caught the slice and carried it over to the butcher paper, while others rode on top of the big lump of meat.

Gnarled knuckles rapped the deli's glass counter. "Young man?" a wobbly voice said.

Andy turned. The elderly ladies' faces were lined up along the counter looking as though they had no bodies. Andy imagined them as decapitated heads, floating in the air like weird balloons.

"Geriatric shooting gallery!" the Munchkins cried.

Dressed in a bright green *Wizard of Oz* army uniform, a Munchkin soldier trumpeted a battle charge. Stumbling over each other, Munchkin soldiers raced to the paper-covered straws. The soldiers ripped off the paper and chewed it, while others broke off the ends of toothpicks, took the wet paper and made spitball darts.

The air borne granny heads floated above the tiny militia. Watching them intently, their elderly eyelids twitched with concern.

"Young man?" said Mrs. Thompson, waiving her hand at Andy's vacant face.

The Munchkin Army raided the deli section. Some grabbed round cucumber slices, while others munched kidney beans from the 3-bean salad. They made cannons out of straws, cucumber wheels and plastic forks, then loaded the cannons with the spitball darts.

The hovering granny heads scowled. Sweat beaded on their leathery brows.

"Young man," Mrs. Thompson said to Andy. "Is something wrong with you?"

"Death to Grandma!" the Munchkins cried, aiming the cannon barrels at the floating heads.

The kidney bean eating Munchkins pushed their rear ends up to the straw cannons and farted. Munchkins with matches lit the fuse. The cannon boomed. Spitball darts blasted forth.

The grannies screamed as their heads exploded and sparkling fireworks burst in the air.

The Munchkin Military band played a jazzy victory song.

"Young man, I want my cole slaw."

Andy stared at Mrs. Thompson, a silly grin spread on his face.

Mrs. Thompson balled her frail hands into tiny frustrated fists while the other two old ladies held their purses tight and frowned.

I just love my imagination, thought Andy. *It's the best thing in my life.*

The front door opened, ringing an old-fashioned cowbell hanging above it.

"Mrs. Senicki," Gunter said, returning from the freezer. "How wonderful to see you again."

Hearing the word "Senicki," Andy turned towards the door.

At the entrance stood Mrs. Alexandra Senicki. She was his former history teacher in high school, 47 years old, with dark brown hair and an angelic face. Her deeply caring nature made her so popular with her students that they called her Momma Love.

Gunter stood at the sink, drying his hands on a towel. "Come in, Mrs. Senicki. I made something special for you today."

As she stepped towards his father, Andy uttered a silent prayer. His wish was immediately granted, for entering the shop was Rebecca, Momma Love's teenage daughter. They had taken one class together when he was in high school --drama.

And I didn't even have the courage to sit next to her, Andy thought. *Why am I such a coward?*

The Munchkins noticed Rebecca. Several of them wolf whistled in awe.

"Who's the babe?" sighed a Munchkin.

"Fu-fu-fellahs. Mind your ma-manners," a stuttering Munchkin scolded.

"Be-a-uti-ful," a third one spoke in admiration.

"Excuse me, Miss," a fourth Munchkin blushed. "Would you go steady with a bashful dwarf?"

"Andy!" a gruff voice barked.

Andy turned, still smiling. His father clutched a dead goose by its scrawny neck. It appeared to have died from strangulation. Standing beside his dad, three ignored and indignant old ladies cast dark looks upon him.

Andy's smile withered; his stomach tightened into a knot.

Gunter scowled. He snapped at his son in German to "pay attention."

Andy cringed.

Gunter took a deep breath, exhaling slowly. "Customers are waiting, son."

Andy's ears turned red. "Yes, sir. Right away."

Getting busy, Andy glanced at Rebecca wishing he could disappear. He reached for the provolone cheese, setting it next to the finished roast beef order. Grabbing a takeout box, he stuck his head inside the glass case where the cole slaw was kept. He wanted to get this over with as quickly as possible so he could talk to Rebecca.

He stuffed cole slaw into the box when he noticed a dress with two beautiful knees in front of him. Gazing up between the marinated mushrooms and the fruit-filled ambrosia, he saw Rebecca looking down at him.

She was smiling; she looked so pretty it nearly took his breath away.

Andy jerked his head, hitting the glass shelf above him. Several marinated mushrooms bounced out of their bowl. One rolled over the ledge, falling downward.

Dressed in a baseball uniform, a Munchkin ran towards the plunging mushroom. Sliding along the rim of a bowl of potato salad, he raised a gloved hand to catch it. The mushroom struck the glove hard, knocking him so deeply into the potato salad that he disappeared from sight.

The other baseball playing Munchkins ran to the bowl, worried about whether or not the plummeting fungi had been caught.

Covered in potato goop, a tiny arm shot upward, the mushroom trapped inside the glove's webbing.

"We win!" the other Munchkins cheered. "Free tacos for everyone 2 inches tall."

Raising his head up over the glass counter, Andy smiled at Rebecca. When she smiled back, he became tongue-tied. He tried to speak, but his lips failed to form words. His brain froze; he just stood there like a brainless wide-eyed statue.

"Uh-oh," the Munchkins mumbled.

"No fresh Mex tonight," a Munchkin pouted.

"Girls ruin every thing," a second one cried.

"I need guacamole or I'm going to die," declared a third.

"Girls ruin guacamole?" said a fourth, nervously. "Merciful heavens, fellahs. Do you know what that means?"

"What?" the others said in unison.

The fourth Munchkin fell to his knees. "Guacamole is life! Girls are death!"

"Hello, Andy," Rebecca said sweetly.

"Hi," Andy replied in voice that was barely a squeak.

What is wrong with me? Andy thought. *Am I a loser?*

Rebecca, too, had trouble speaking. But as their eyes met, words were no longer necessary. Their pupils dilated, the room disappeared, and reality diminished to the size of each other's face.

"Rebecca," a soft voice called. Mrs. Senicki stood at the butcher shop entrance holding a bag with the stuffed goose inside. "Come along dear, it's time to go."

Rebecca glanced at Andy and bowed her head. "Bye Andy," she quietly said as she shuffled away to join her mother.

Andy's chest clenched tightly. He wanted to ask Rebecca out. Get her phone number. Anything, just to see her again. It was now or never. "Reb --."

"Andy!" his father snapped, tapping his clenched fist on the palm of his other hand. "Act like a man," he growled in German. "Customers are *waiting*, son."

Andy winced from his father's stern gaze.

The Munchkins huddled together. Putting their hands beside their faces, they imitated the Edvard Munch painting *The Scream.* "Deadly dad has spoken. Andy's body will be broken."

The three old women stood near Gunter, staring at Andy with reproachful eyes.

Andy imagined them as horrible zombies. Their eyeballs sprang out of their sockets; their tongues slithered out from their mouths, hissing like grumpy snakes.

Andy told his imagination to shut up.

He hurried to give the old women their orders. He took their money and made their change, all the while wanting to run outside before Rebecca and her mother left.

Putting the last penny into Mrs. Wilson's wobbly hand, Andy tugged his apron-string and pulled his smock over his head.

The sound of an engine accelerating made him look out the window. Mrs. Senicki's station wagon disappeared down the street.

Andy's heart sank like a capsized boat. His one chance with Rebecca was gone.

The three old ladies left the shop. The cow bell rang. To Andy it felt as if the door was closing on his pathetic life.

A beefy hand jarred Andy's shoulder. Turning, Andy saw his father's grinning face. He wondered what he was so happy about. The day had been a total disaster.

"Guess whose coming to dinner tonight?" his father said.

Gunter's head bobbed up and down, as though he were sharing a grand secret. At first Andy couldn't figure it out, but then the meaning became plain. The Senickis were visiting his parents. Rebecca would be at his house tonight.

Andy's sunken heart righted itself with hope.

Through the stenciled butcher shop window, the Mysterious Man stared at Andy. His fingers touched the black stones; his eyes were glazed; he was in a trance. The stones informed their human bearer with a surety that brooked no doubt.

He is their next victim.

The stones were never wrong.

CHAPTER 4

THE GATHERING

Like a celestial nightlight, the cool beams of the full moon caressed the Barulich's country home. Located in the forest, their nearest neighbor miles away, the Barulich family enjoyed the tranquil country life.

Engaged in its evening nut hunt, a squirrel climbed up a pine tree. Hopping amongst the branches it heard human voices coming from the house. Through an open window, six people ate and talked around a food-laden table. Being hungry himself, the squirrel found a fat pine cone and started gnawing on the kernels.

The famished squirrel, however, was not the only one watching the human abode.

Hidden in the forest a short distance from the front porch, a camera Eye materialized beneath a tree. About the size of a rolled up sleeping bag, it hovered two feet above the ground waiting for its operator's electronic orders.

Inside the starship's camera control room, Iggy plopped his four buttocks on a two-seated hover chair in front a curved holographic display. He slid the chair to the left by pushing off with his two right feet. The Eye's technical manual was on the monitor. He read it out loud in his child-like voice.

"Hey, Glop. Listen to this," Iggy said, his eyestalks leaning towards the holo-display. "This new camera sounds amazing. The Model P-1000 is the latest development in inter-dimensional camera technology. The first cyborg model, it is part animal, part machine. At its heart is the new Z-6000 cat-eye lens, with micro-gear joy stick zoom capacity."

"Hot damn," uttered Glop, his four eyestalks glued to Iggy's holographic display. "That's cutting edge stuff. The tech journals say ..."

"Quiet," interrupted Iggy. "Let me finish."

"Right. Whatever you say."

Iggy continued. "In its midsection is a WYSIWYG replicator ..."

"That's not supposed to be out for another year!"

"Shush," hissed Iggy.

"Sorry."

"Its back end contains the next generation of subatomic molecular scanner.

"Wow ...I'm in techno geek heaven ...."

Iggy switched the screen to white so the manual could not be seen. "Can you control yourself, please? We have to know all this and be able to use it. I'd appreciate your full cooperation."

Glop pressed his lips tightly together and contritely nodded.

Iggy switched the manual back on and continued, "Four mechanical arms fold about its middle each with 20 foot extension capability and over 1000 tool hands to choose from."

"Oh, that makes me tingle ..."

Iggy ignored him. "Communication antennae and anti-gravity propulsion drive plates surround its otherwise smooth surface."

"I'm having palpitations ..."

"To make the Eye more aggressive in hunting its prey for filming purposes, its micro circuit brain--the size of a cough drop--has been genetically spliced with the genes of a panther."

"Serious palpitations ..."

"It can also record," Iggy said, his voice growling, "the subject in hundreds of ways, even seeing bones and organs under the skin ..."

"Techno heart attack imminent ..."

"AS WELL AS ITS NEWEST FEATURE," yelled Iggy, "OF BEING ABLE TO SHIFT ITS BULK INTO A PARALLEL DIMENSION TO AVOID SUBJECT

CONTACT INSTEAD OF JUST BECOMING INVISIBLE!" He folded his four arms across his chest. "Why do you always do that?"

"Do what?" said Glop.

"Act obnoxious."

Glop thought for a moment. "Either I have a genetically designed techno fixation or on occasion I am callous and strange?"

Iggy's four eyes narrowed into slits of glaring intolerance.

Glop's four eyes blinked. "But this is more exciting than pleasure candy, Iggy. "You're a techno geek like me. Can you honestly say you feel any different?"

Iggy pursed his thin lips. "Okay. You got me there. All is forgiven."

A voice came over the communication channel. "One minute to rolling cameras," said the Production Manager. "Be ready."

Iggy became all business. "Let's get to work. We've got to film killing these beings for entertainment."

Glop frowned. "Have you ever wondered about the morality of our occupation?"

"Don't get emotionally involved," Iggy advised. "They're only human."

"Glop thought a moment. "Did anyone ever tell you, you have a talent for cramming complex issues into a nutshell?"

"Did anyone ever tell you that you can be tossed back into a clone vat and be melted back into genetic goop?"

"No," replied Glop, his voice uneasy.

"I've seen it. Unless you enjoy screaming you really don't want to go back there. Survival Rule #1: Don't make clone vat waves."

The communicator hissed. "Begin production," said the Production Manager. "Roll all cameras. Establishing shot, then dolly into the human dwelling."

Iggy snapped his fingers hard. With a fearful glare, he stabbed them at Glop's seat.

Glop plopped down on his hover chair. In the transporter off to his right his P-1000 camera Eye hovered above the pad. Glop appraised it with awestruck eyes. His agile fingers activated the transport sequence. A stream of radiant energy demolecularized the Eye, whisking it off to the production location. Glop rubbed the palms of his four hands in front of him with excitement. "This is going to be the best production ever," he grinned. "We are so lucky to have this job."

Iggy nodded in agreement. He too was trembling with eagerness. He sent a radar ping out through his Eye to see if anything living was nearby. Except for the humans in the house and a couple of squirrels there was nothing alive worth worrying about. There never was way out in the country. That's why the director always chose isolated locations--to keep their existence a secret.

The second camera Eye materialized beside the first Eye near the human dwelling. "All systems go," said Glop.

Iggy decided to test the new cat-eye lens. He pulled out to a long shot of the dwelling seeing the moon in sky in great detail, then zoomed in to an extreme close-up of an ant crawling across the front porch. The ant stood out with such startling clarity he thought he could reach out and touch it.

The two cameramen gasped in awe. Their feet tapped on the floor like a pair of excited dogs wagging their tails.

Iggy took an establishing shot of the house, then had the first Eye float towards the wooden porch of the dwelling.

"All clear," said Iggy to Glop through his headset. "Prepare to dolly in."

"Doesn't it seem silly," said Glop moving his camera motion joystick, "to use headsets when I'm sitting four feet away and can hear you perfectly?"

"Protocol is protocol," replied Iggy, his camera approaching the porch. "At least they don't require headset implants."

"I hate post clone vat surgery," said Glop, adjusting his camera's framing. "Having discipline chips in our heads is bad enough."

"Shh," Iggy warned in a whisper. "Don't let the higher intelligences hear you say that." He switched the screen to dimension control mode, showing a night view of the Barulich house. "Let's move in closer. Engage dimensional shift."

Reaching the porch, the two Eyes seemed to vanish as they peered through the living room windows. A small fire burned in the hearth. Firelight licked the sides of six chairs, three on one side facing three on the other. Along the far wall was a shelf with a stack of records with a record player beside it. Pictures of people and souvenirs from Germany covered much of the walls.

The flickering light fascinated the panther genes in the Eyes. The fire danced on top of the logs as though it were performing a surreal ballet.

Incandescent light flooded the living room. Acting like the panthers whose genes they possessed, the Eyes retreated to the shadows of the predatory dark.

"Wow," exclaimed Iggy. "These cameras react with animal instincts."

"This is going to be the coolest shoot ever," replied Glop, rubbing his four hands together.

"Come in everybody, come in," Mr. Barulich spoke jovially. He directed Mr. Senicki to a padded armchair. "Sit, Mr. Senicki. Be comfortable."

"Please Mr. Barulich. Call me Herman."

"Very good, Herman. But you must call me Gunter."

Andy saw Rebecca move towards an end chair on the near side of the two rows. He darted past Mrs. Senicki to get to the middle chair next to it.

His father raised his hand.

"Andy, no," Gunter said. "That chair is for Mrs. Senicki. You sit over here next to your mother."

Andy took the seat beside his mother, six feet away from Rebecca.

How am I ever going to speak to her with all these parents around? Andy thought. *Mom and Dad are so old-fashioned it's ridiculous. It's like we're still living in Germany. I've got to come up with a sneaky plan so we can ditch the adults and get together.*

Rebecca sat across from Andy, her hands folded lady-like in her lap. She wished her parents weren't so traditional about social occasions. Why couldn't she be alone with Andy? Did they think we would run off into the forest, rip off our clothes and have wild sex? She glanced at Andy. He stared into space, lost in his thoughts. He was obviously as bored as she was.

The parents relaxed into the comfortable armchairs and let their digestion catch up with them. Gunter reached under a side table and pulled out a box of cigars. He opened the lid and held the box out to Herman.

"Cigar, Herman?"

Herman removed a cigar and smelled it. The aroma was very pleasant. His eyebrows arched upwards as he nodded. "Mmm, delicious. Thank you, Gunter."

Mrs. Senicki glimpsed at Rebecca and smiled. Rebecca smiled back, then glanced at Andy with a look of wounded patience.

Andy raised and lowered his eyebrows towards the kitchen, trying to signal to Rebecca that he wanted her to go there. His facial gestures confused her. She obviously had no idea what he was trying to do.

Rebecca glanced in the direction his eyes seemed to be pointing and saw the record albums on the shelf. She turned back towards Andy and silently mouthed the word "music?"

Andy could not read her lips, so he kept signaling with his eyebrows.

As the two teenagers silently confused each other, the Eyes returned to the window. Adjusting their sonic sensors, they spied on the humans, transmitting their footage to the star ship.

Inside the Director's private control room, the Director observed the broadcasted data as his fish lips sipped on squid juice and vodka. He learned that the Senicki-creatures lived in Romania at the same time the Barulich-creatures lived in Germany during World War II.

That was when Adolph Hitler was in power, thought the Director. That was interesting news. Maybe he could use it as a story motif. Nazism hadn't been used in 40 years, not since he shot that war epic on Earth back in the 1940s. The Andy and Rebecca things were young and appealing, a possible love story. Like the two people in Alaska, he could use these humans to make A.R.T.

Using a thought pen, the Director projected his ideas onto a storyboard wall. Pursing his fishy lips back and forth, he drank, watched and plotted.

While the parents conversed, Andy caught Rebecca's attention. He pointed his finger towards the kitchen.

She raised her eyebrows in a silent "what?"

Andy pointed again.

Mrs. Senicki saw the movement of his finger. She looked at him and frowned.

Andy clasped his hands together on his lap, mustering an innocent smile. When Mrs. Senicki turned away, Andy's thoughts became gloomy.

This supervision thing is so annoying. Act like a man. How can I do that if they won't let me? They treat me like I'm still in a crib.

Andy noticed Rebecca staring at him, biting her lower lip to keep herself from smiling. She hid her finger behind the arm of the chair and wagged it at him.

Bad boy, the finger seemed to say.

A warm thrill coursed through Andy's body. At least he and Rebecca were talking, even if it was only in sign language.

Gunter leaned back in his chair. "But I do miss going to the Opera in Germany. We used to see it all the time."

"All the time," agreed Emma.

Gunter addressed Mrs. Senicki. "Do you like Opera?"

Mrs. Senicki perked up. "Oh, yes. I used to be an Opera singer in my youth."

Mr. Senicki chimed in. "Tell him, Alexandra. She was incredible. Such a voice."

Everyone looked at Alexandra.

Her eyes widened as she cleared her throat. When I was 17," Alexandra said. "I wanted to sing for the opera house. So I auditioned for Puccini's *Turandot*."

"A powerful love story," said Herman.

"Yes," Alexandra agreed. "I auditioned for the chorus--"

"And they cast her in the title role!" said Herman, beaming at his wife. "Alexandra sings like Maria Callas."

"Did you hear that, Emma?" Gunter said, secretly winking at his wife. "She played the famous Chinese princess."

"I heard, Gunter," Emma said, her eyes sparkling in response to her husband's wink. "Turandot is a very difficult role."

Andy wondered what was going on between his parents. It was as though they shared a secret. He coughed and patted his chest with his fist causing all four parents to stare at him. He stopped his thumping and froze, a deer caught in the social headlights. A sharp warning came from his father's penetrating eyes.

The parents continued their discussion as though he didn't exist.

Relieved, Andy blew air through his lips.

Rebecca wagged her finger at him again. *Bad boy.*

She smiled.

Andy blushed.

Gunter blew a smoke ring. "Emma and I love Opera."

Emma rocked her head slowly. "Especially Wagner's Ring Cycle."

"I just love *Die Walkure*," said Alexandra, clutching her hands above her lap. "The music is so powerful it makes my skin tingle."

Gunter put his cigar in an ashtray. He clenched his fists, his chest muscles swelled. "Wotan, King of the Norse gods. Tales of giants, the ring of power and glory."

Oh, no, Andy thought. *Please Dad, don't sing.*

Gunter belted the opera's famous music theme.

"Bom-bom, da-da bom-bom.

Bom, da-da bom-bom.

Power and glory.

Bom, da-da bom."

Andy prayed his dad would keep it short, when Rebecca's father vigorously joined in.

The two men sang with an off-key gusto, filling the room with raw vocal power. They raised their fists in defiance as though they were defying the will of the Gods.

"Bom-bom, da-da bom-bom.

Bom, da-da bom-bom.

Power and glory.

Bom, da-da bom."

Delighted with their husbands' singing, the wives vigorously applauded.

Andy wanted to run and hide. *Oh, no. Here comes the climax.*

Before the men could open their mouths, Alexandra burst forth with a high note that shook the room. It vibrated deep within Andy's bones, making them shiver.

The two men laughed. They clasped hands and shook them heartily.

Emma and Alexandra sighed in giddy delight.

"That was wonderful!" said Herman. "Wotan is my favorite opera character."

"Mine, too," Gunter replied. He turned to Alexandra. "You have such a powerful voice. In fact, I invited you over here tonight because I have a surprise for you."

Alexandra took a quick breath. "A surprise?" She turned to her husband.

Raising his eyebrows, Herman puffed a plume of smoke from the cigar and smiled.

Gunter walked between Andy and Rebecca to the stack of records next to the phonograph.

Andy glanced at Rebecca, forming the word "kitchen" on his lips. Rebecca thought he said "itching" and mimed scratching her arm. Andy bit his lip in frustration, wishing they both had walkie talkies.

"It took me months to get this," said Gunter, flipping through the albums. "I contacted an old friend of mine in Hamburg and begged him to find it."

Gunter stepped in-between Andy and Rebecca, blocking their view of each other. Andy cursed his luck while Rebecca fretted with impatience. Gunter turned the album around. On the cover was the title: *Turandot* by Puccini. Under the composer's name appeared the face of Alexandra.

"That's me!" Alexandra said, her face brightening. "That was made before Herman and I were married!"

"And now," said Gunter. "With your permission, I would be honored to play it for you."

Alexandra looked at Herman, her mouth open in genuine surprise.

Herman gently squeezed her hand.

Andy and Rebecca leaned behind Gunter so they could talk without their parents overhearing them.

"Kitchen," Andy whispered.

Rebecca nodded, understanding him at last.

Gunter removed the record from its jacket.

"I will play the famous aria where Princess Turandot sings of her love for her abused female cousin and her vow of vengeance on men," Gunter said. He lowered the needle on to the vinyl and the singing voice of 17-year-old Alexandra Tupolsky, now Mrs. Herman Senicki, was heard by its owner for the first time in 30 years.

Alexandra put her hand over her heart; her fingers fluttered on her chest. Hearing herself sing as a teenager, she held her breath, becoming rigid.

Rebecca saw her mother's eyes water with a painful beauty. She appeared so excited Rebecca thought she might have a heart attack.

"Mother?" Rebecca whispered. "Do you want a drink of water?"

Alexandra clutched the neckline of her dress. Her mouth stretched tight, she nodded.

Rebecca headed towards the kitchen.

Leaning back in their chairs, the parents looked at the ceiling and shut their eyes while they listened.

Now's my chance, thought Andy. He bent low and snuck off towards the bathroom. Reaching the hallway, he glanced back. Everyone still had their eyes closed.

Great, Andy thought. *I can sneak out the front door right now and meet Rebecca. I don't even have to fake going to the bathroom. This is going to be easier than I thought.*

Andy snuck over to the front door and silently opened it. An invisible Eye entered the house above his head. It swerved around the entryway, filmed the parents, and transmitted their images to the star ship.

Finny fingers scratched the table as the Director watched the footage. It had been too long since he had seen his favorite color--blood.

Blood and violence are so necessary to create A.R.T. It's so important to establish the proper tone of the story from the beginning, especially in a murder mystery. Besides, Those Who Watch love a good death scene. It gets things off to a rousing start.

The Director hadn't thought of a story line as yet, but an idea came to him. The adults' eyes were closed, the young ones gone, the Alexandra's pale throat was exposed. The opera was in her honor. The music was perfect. How fine it would be to slash her neck and have them scream over her blood-soaked corpse.

It would make a wonderful inciting incident.

He spoke into his wireless headset.

"Camera one," said the Director. "Slit the Alexandra's throat when no one is watching." He tapped a boney fingertip on his smooth fishy lips. "And make sure to hold the victim's head back so camera two can get a slow motion shot of the blood spray from outside the window."

The Director visualized the gory scene with relish. *Sam Raimi,* he thought. *Eat your 'Evil Dead' heart out.*

Back in the Barulich's living room, the first Eye processed its new orders. One by one, it stuck all four of its mechanical arms inside its replicator, each arm emerging with a panther paw. Three of the paws were for holding down its prey, the last one had a single sharp claw capable of cutting flesh and bone like a hot knife through butter.

Skulking behind Alexandra's back, the first Eye prepared to grab her hair and shoulders, holding her in a grip of iron so she couldn't move as the blood sprayed out of her in a bright, red fountain.

Before it could grab her, Alexandra leaned her head back, exposing her soft, white throat.

Altering its dimensional density, the Eye exposed the tip of its claw and swiped.

A glass of water invaded its sight. By instinct, the Eye snapped back to the invisible dimension. The tip of the sweeping claw nicked Rebecca just above her wrist.

Not noticing the shallow cut, Rebecca held the glass out to her mother.

Still overwhelmed by hearing herself singing on the record, Alexandra's hand fluttered like a fragile butterfly as she reached for the glass. Holding it in her wobbling hand, she took a tiny sip of water.

A thin line of red wetness appeared at the base of Rebecca's thumb.

Programmed to kill, the first Eye's organic receptors detected the blood. The smell drove its panther brain wild with blood lust. Primal urges overpowered its hardware causing circuits to fizzle and spark.

Going out of control, the first Eye thrashed about on the living room carpet.

In the Control Center, alarms clanged loudly as cyborg readouts shot beyond the red line. Iggy stared at the holographic display. Instead of seeing what the first Eye viewed at the production location, the first Eye glared back at Iggy with the ghostly contours of a panther's savage face.

The holo-panther snarled. Iggy pushed his hover chair back four feet. "What in the clone vat is going on here?" said Iggy as the holo-panther snarled again.

Glop slid his hover chair closer. "Wow. Would you look at that … a holographic panther with sharp-looking teeth. That is so wrong it's scary."

"It's like the machine is really alive," said Iggy. "Do you think it can hurt us?"

"Sweet," said Glop. I love a universe full of surprises. Don't you?"

Before Iggy could reply in the negative, the Production Manager burst through the force field doorway on his three snake-like legs followed by his fussy Assistant. "What's wrong? Why aren't you shooting what the Director ordered?"

The holo-panther bellowed, causing the sparse yellow hairs between Iggy's eye stalks to wiggle in terror.

"Sorry, sir," said Iggy. "Camera malfunction."

"Well, don't just sit on all your buttocks," the Production Manager said to Iggy. "Put your hand in the display and fix it."

Seeing the holo-panther's razor-sharp teeth, Iggy hesitated.

"Hurry it up," said the Production Manager. "The Director's upset. We're losing the shot. Do it now."

Iggy glanced at the Assistant, who put his hands on his hips and impatiently tapped his foot.

Iggy thought it was a bad idea, but orders were orders. Attempting to make an adjustment, he stuck his knobby fingers into the holographic display.

Roaring, the holo-panther bit him.

Iggy howled in pain.

"Quit bawling, you big baby," said the Production Manager. "Use your logic. Write a stunner program. Hurry up. We need this shot."

Iggy did as he was told. He tapped on the keyboard, wincing every time he used his wounded finger.

On the holo-monitor, digital electric prods swooped in, surrounding the Eye-panther from every angle. Bursts of lightning flared in an energy web, jolting the holo-panther panther senseless.

In the Barulich's living room, the first Eye collapsed on the floor near Rebecca's feet.

The holographic display flickered; the panther face disappeared.

Relieved, Iggy sighed; the yellow hairs on his head bent back down to normal.

The Production Manager grunted. "Well done, it. That solved the problem." He watched the human's living room reappear on camera. Everything worked perfectly, only the image was sideways. Half the screen was filled with tan carpet, while the other half was a close-up of a shoe.

"I think it's broken, sir," said Glop. "We must get it out of there before it loses its invisibility."

"Yes, yes," said the Production Manager. "Remove it, pronto." He nudged one of Iggy's eye stalks. "See how this other cameraman uses logic to solve a problem? You need to do that, too."

"I reward you for good thinking," said the Production Manager, giving Glop a piece of pleasure candy."

Envious, Iggy watched Glop eagerly eat the delicious confection. As Glop chewed, he made uncontrollable gurgling sounds as his brain cells were flooded with ecstatic pleasure.

Over the intercom the Director shouted, "What's wrong? Why didn't you kill the human female? Where's my opening murder shot?"

The Production Manager's brow frowned. "I'm sorry, sir. Equipment malfunction. We missed it."

An angry hiss came over the intercom. "Get a replacement camera right way. I want that shot. What good's a murder mystery without a murder? Hurry it up."

Agitated, the Production Manager's squid eyes swished about in their sockets, moving so quickly his vision blurred. *These new panther brains still have some bugs in their system. I'll bet they're experimental models. I didn't see them on the A.R.T. approved equipment list. Our Producer is breaking the law. We're going to have to keep this quiet.*

He blinked rapidly several times, thinking. *Better get this one to the cyborg repair shop. Good thing I brought the repair manual and two extra technicians.* The Production Manager sighed. *I'll have to add a nondisclosure clause to everyone's contract on pain of discipline chip induced brain trauma before they can speak it out loud. I hate to do it, but I have no choice. If were caught we could be severely punished.*

The Production Manager ordered the Assistant to get a replacement Eye out of storage and take it to the transporter bay, then slithered out of the room.

Iggy and Glop sat still, staring at the Assistant.

"Well, you heard the PM," said the waspish Assistant. "Stop gawking at me and get that broken camera out of there. Do it now." He looked down at the its with a haughty expression and, with a swish of his head, bustled out of the control room.

Iggy heard his footsteps echo down the ship's hallway. He was glad the bizarre incident was over.

"So what do you think about these experimental cameras?" said Glop to Iggy. "Are they fresh or what?"

In response to his friend's question, Iggy rolled his eyes up until only the whites showed, stuck his wounded finger in his grimacing mouth and sucked it.

Still listening to the opera *Turandot*, Rebecca watched her mother take another sip of water. Hearing a high note of intense beauty, Alexandra let the water glass slip out of her hands.

Rebecca swiftly caught the glass, removing it from her mother's flimsy grasp. She wondered why mother was acting so fragile. Maybe she was missing her youth. She looked around the room, wondering where Andy had gone. She noticed her wrist had a bit of blood on it.

She wondered how that happened.

Being careful not to be seen by any of the parents, Andy snuck around the outside of the house. When he reached the kitchen window, he eagerly popped his head inside.

Rebecca was not there.

"Now what?" Andy murmured. "Getting to talk to Rebecca is like playing musical chairs and I'm always coming up one seat short."

He stole back to the living room windows on the porch, cautiously peeking inside.

On the porch beside him was the second invisible Eye.

Through the window, Andy saw Rebecca with a glass in her hand. She started to sit in a chair.

"No, Rebecca, don't!" whispered Andy as Rebecca sat down.

Andy thrashed his hands and walked in circles. He rushed up to the other window, stepping inside the same inter-dimensional space as the second Eye.

Andy suddenly saw double. Two Rebeccas stood before him, each one holding a glass of water. The strangeness of it made his head spin. He felt wonky; he thought he might feint. He had the sudden urge to hurl.

Andy stumbled sideways, moving away from the second Eye. Rubbing his eyes, he leaned against the house; his vision was one big blur. Feeling anxious, he wondered why his entire life weird things kept happening to him. It just wasn't fair.

Finally, his eyesight returned; his head became clear. He tried to make sense of the senseless event and couldn't. *Maybe I'm cursed with bad luck.*

He opened the front door slowly, then snuck back inside the house. The second Eye followed him in, hovering near the ceiling. It cruised into the living room to where the first Eye lay, dazed and unmoving. The second Eye placed two arms in its replicator, removing mini-tractor beam hands. It aimed them at the first Eye's body.

Pulsing beams of invisible light shot forward, connecting with the first Eye's body. The second Eye then dragged its associate across the carpet towards the front door.

Sliding backwards, the first Eye growled weakly. It dimension-shifted the tips of one of its paws, clinging to the carpet, jerking them to a halt.

The second Eye tugged and tugged, trying to dislodge the first Eye's paw. It moved about in a circle, jerking the first Eye's body up and down.

Every time the first Eye's paw came loose, it gripped the carpet again forcing the two Eyes to a halt.

As the cameramen struggled to control the situation, the two invisible cyborgs battled each other in a silent tug of war.

Iggy and Glop were at their wits end, when the Production Manager burst through the Control Center force field door … again.

"Get that broken Eye back here this minute," yelled the Production Manager, his face flushed red. "I can see the carpeting moving from here. Do you want the humans to see it, too?"

Iggy and Glop stared at the monitor. Sure enough, tiny bits of the carpet were jerking to and fro near a human's feet as the invisible Eyes struggled.

"We're trying, sir," Iggy and Glop said. "We can't seem to …"

"Magnetize its arms together," interrupted the Production Manager, *then* use the tractor beams to tow it out of the house. Quit wasting time, you stupid its. You've ruined the Director's opening shot. Do you want him to punish you?"

Iggy and Glop hunched their shoulders.

"No, sir," the two its said. "We'll fix it right away."

The Production Manager slunk back through the weak force field into the hallway. Sweating profusely, he leaned against the wall.

"They made me lose my temper," he said, drying his moist brow with microwaves from an electric handkerchief. "That a class 3 intelligence could do such thing to me. It's really quite embarrassing." Putting the back of his hand on his brow, he checked to see that it was dry. It was. He put the electric handkerchief in his pocket pouch. "I hope the Director doesn't discipline the lot of us. It's only the first day of shooting. These new cameras had better be worth the trouble they're causing."

He hurried down the hallway, sweating everywhere except his forehead.

Standing in the hallway, Andy peeked around the wall into the living room. He saw the back of his mother's head. Rebecca was just to the right of it. Mrs. Senicki was to her left, staring into space in his general direction.

Andy leaned against the wall, raised his hand and wiggled his fingers. *Come on, Rebecca. Look at me. Give me a break.*

On the opposite side of the entryway, Angelfish lazily swam in a small fish tank, seemingly without a care in the world.

I wish my life was that easy, thought Andy. *Meeting girls is hard work.*

Then an idea came to Andy. He did not like it much for the risk factor, but decided to try anyway. *The worst I can do is make a fool of myself, which isn't much of a demotion.*

Rebecca caught a movement out of the corner of her eye.

Andy leaned over from behind the wall, pointed towards the kitchen, then ducked back. He reappeared and pointed again.

She stuck her thumb in the kitchen's direction.

Andy shook his head, then hid.

The water glass in her hand, Rebecca sighed and walked to the kitchen.

Watching Rebecca leave her mother, a thrill of success surged up Andy's spine.

He opened the front door, heard his father yawn and froze. Crickets chirped in the night. He prayed they would not attract his parents' attention.

Having magnetized the first Eye's three paws so they stuck together, rendering them useless, the second Eye dragged the first Eye from the living room towards the front door. The first Eye resisted all the way with its remaining single claw. A long scratch line appeared on the wooden floor as the struggling Eyes zipped between Andy's legs and out the door.

Not hearing any more yawning, Andy stepped outside over the threshold, quietly shutting the door behind him. He tip toed across the large front porch towards the kitchen, passing the two Eyes beside him.

The first Eye had stabbed the tip of its now visible claw into a chair leg; the second Eye struggled to pull it off.

The chair moved several inches.

Andy didn't notice as he rushed around the corner of the house to meet Rebecca.

Rebecca waited in the kitchen. She swung her arms, fidgeting about. The sink was piled high with dirty dishes. She turned on the water to do them, then just as quickly turned the water off. "Some date this is, she mumbled. Where the kitty crap is he?"

She knew he had gone outside so she bent over the sink. Her face reached the open window just as Andy stuck his head inside.

Their faces stopped inches apart.

Andy froze; their eyes locked. He had wanted to get close to Rebecca all evening and now she was close enough for him to kiss her. The nearness of her made him nervous. Her lips were moist, her skin creamy, her eyes bright and enchanting. He wasn't sure what to say.

An idea popped into his head. "Do you like stars?" Andy stammered.

Rebecca raised her eyebrows and nodded.

Andy smiled and crooked his finger, inviting her to come outside.

As Andy headed back to the front porch, the second Eye bounced the first Eye along the lawn ran right past him. The second Eye spun in circles like a discus thrower, flinging the first Eye onto the dirt driveway towards the Bronco. The first Eye skipped like a stone over water until it came to a dust-raising stop.

A transporter beam snatched it away.

Its mission accomplished, the second Eye glided back into the house through the kitchen window.

Rebecca opened the back door; moths fluttered away from the weak porch light. She stepped down onto the grass, gazing up at the evening sky. The night was speckled with stars; the air was cool; the moon was full. It filled Rebecca's heart with secret romantic desires.

Smoothing out her dress, she went around the side of the house, expecting to see Andy at last.

He wasn't there.

"Now what?" she muttered. "Did he turn into the invisible man? Is he trapped in a time warp? What is going on with that man?"

From within a transporter beam, a third Eye materialized behind the Bronco. It cruised beside the car until it reached the front bumper and stopped. Hiding in the vehicle's shadow, it recorded Rebecca walking towards the kitchen window where she halted under a tree.

New instructions came. The third Eye became invisible and charged. Hugging the ground, it rushed across the lawn, blades of grass whipping by its cyborg body.

"Interesting," said the Director, watching the third Eye race through the overgrown grass on the monitor. The tall grass blades whipped by its camera lens like it was a predator hunting down Rebecca. "It's kinetic, it's strange, its got humor and a sense of danger. It's very Quentin Tarantino."

Like a silent phantom, the third Eye reared up behind Rebecca, reaching the same height as the back of her head. Through its soap bubble vision, Rebecca's hair appeared distorted. The strands in the center looked larger and wetter than the ones on its outer field of view.

Rebecca listened for any sign of Andy, the mysterious disappearing man. All she heard were crickets and all she saw were shadows. Did he think she would come running any old time he crooked his finger?

A sound caught her attention. "Andy?" she whispered, turning around.

The third Eye stood in front of her--invisible Eye to human eye. It stared intently at Rebecca, filming every pore of her features. It captured the moisture in her doe-like eyes, the richness of her wet lips, and the smoothness of her teenage flesh.

It even recorded the intake of air into her youthful lungs.

"Andy," Rebecca whispered.

The mist from her mouth fogged the Eye's lens, revealing a brief glimpse of its presence. A bladed hand materialized. The Eye lashed out at Rebecca's face.

Something struck Rebecca's head. Gasping, she stepped back. A pinecone rolled on the ground at her feet. Above her, a squirrel leapt, clawing its way to higher branches.

"A person could get killed out here," Rebecca said, feeling her head for bruises.

"Psst," came a voice from behind her. Rebecca turned around.

Andy stood at the corner of the house next to the front porch. Half his body was silhouetted by the yellowish porch light, while the other half was colored a pale blue from the moon. The middle of his face was dark with shadow. With the murky forest behind him, Rebecca thought he looked very mysterious. It sent a romantic thrill up her spine.

Andy waved for her to follow him and disappeared on the front porch. With a smile and wings on her heart, Rebecca sauntered off to join him.

A lock of Rebecca's hair floated in the air, then disappeared into the third Eye's molecular scanner. Flashing lights powered up the unit as it analyzed Rebecca's molecular structure. The Eye had taken numerous readings of Rebecca, scanning her body with every thing from x-rays to magnetic resonance imaging. It noted how her body temperature rose two degrees when the Andy appeared and spoke to her. It sent the information back to the star ship as a leaf fell in front of its lens.

Observing the falling leaf, Iggy tilted the Eye upwards. Up in the tree, a squirrel sat on a limb directly above him. Making a tool in the replicator, Iggy had the Eye shoot a low voltage bolt of electricity at the small animal. The energy shocked the squirrel, which screeched and dashed higher up in the tree.

Iggy and Glop giggled.

"This job sure has its perks," said Iggy.

"All work and no play makes for a boring day," replied Glop.

"Do you two want to be put in cryo storage?" said the Production Manager over the intercom.

"No, sir," Iggy and Glop replied, their eight eyes glancing downward.

"Then quit fooling around or I'll lock you both in the freezer. Understand?"

"Yes, sir ... right away," said Iggy.

"We promise we'll be good," said Glop.

The intercom clicked off. Iggy and Glop silently communicated to each other by blinking their eyes on their eyestalks. It was a secret code the its used when they did not want to be overhead by their V-lan masters.

"That was close," blinked Iggy in code. "I hate being frozen into an it-sicle. The very thought makes my eyestalks shudder."

"I dig yo diggity," Glop blinked back. "The deep freeze makes me ultra wiggy."

When Rebecca turned the corner to the front of the house her eyes widened. There on the front porch stood Andy. Next to him was a telescope. She hadn't known it was on the porch when she arrived. She thought it was wonderful.

Rebecca stepped up on the front porch, the floor boards creaking softly under her weight. Serenaded by heavenly opera music, she glided past the windows behind which her parents could be seen. Andy appeared handsome in the soft pale light. The moment was so romantic it made Rebecca shiver.

Andy pointed to the telescope. "Take a peek."

Sitting down on a wooden stool, Rebecca peered through the eyepiece. The moon, formerly a bright ball in the heavens, became a real world to her eyes, a cold desert with strange circles and canyon-like depressions.

"Oh, Andy, it's incredible."

"It's 240,000 miles away," Andy replied, *but you're right here.*

The third Eye snuck up behind Andy and snipped some hair off his head.

Feeling a slight draft, Andy wiped his hand over the clipped spot.

As the parents listened to Puccini, an Eye moved amongst them collecting samples of their hair. Analyzing the humans' dna, the Eyes transmitted their findings to their masters.

Tests would be performed.

Decisions would be made.

The night was far from over.

An hour before midnight, the parents congregated around the Senicki's Bronco. No one wanted the evening to end, but sleep was already tugging at their eyelids. The evening for Alexandra was memorable. Gunter presented her with the recording of *Turandot*. Alexandra choked with joy as she accepted the record from his beefy hands.

"Thank you, Gunter," Alexandra gushed. "Such a beautiful evening. To hear myself sing after all these years." Her hand fluttered on top of the record. "I'm so happy," she said, sniffling, her face twisting with the effort to hold back her tears.

"Rebecca," bellowed Gunter. "Help. Your mother is making us all cry."

"I'm so sorry," said Alexandra. "I am poor woman. I have no control over my feelings."

Rubbing an eye, Gunter smiled, "Alexandra, may I ask you a question?"

Alexandra nodded.

"Why did you quit singing opera?"

Alexandra turned towards her husband, Herman.

A gleam appeared in Herman's eyes.

"I was always surprised that a simple girl like me would become an opera singer," said Alexandra. "After a performance in Kiev, the whole company got on a bus to go to the next city on our tour. The seat next to me was empty and the next thing I knew this strange man sat beside me and stared at me. It made me so nervous all this staring. This was not the proper way to behave to a lady. So I got angry. I told him to go away. And then he said something I will never forget."

Herman beamed. "You are my shining star and I will never let you go."

Alexandra's faced brightened. "And as soon as he said that I knew I would spend the rest of my life with this man … have his children … be with him until God called us to the afterlife. My beautiful Herman," sniffled Alexandra.

Emma patted her hand. The two women looked at each other and broke out in happy sobs.

"Rebecca," yelled Gunter. "Help. Your mother is doing it again. She is making us all cry."

Rebecca scurried around the corner of the house, running to the Bronco's back door which her father had opened. Before stepping inside, she glanced back. Andy stood, his hands in his pockets, in the yellow porch light.

Their bashful infatuation with each other did not go unnoticed by the two fathers. They raised their eyebrows and smiled at each other, then warmly shook hands and bid each other good night.

Walking to the edge of the dirt driveway, Andy watched the Bronco drive away. He wished he was still on the front porch, holding hands with Rebecca.

A massive hand clapped down hard on his shoulder sending a shockwave through his body. "She's a nice girl, eh, son?" Gunter said, his strong fingers squeezing Andy's shoulder with affection.

Andy hoped his bones didn't snap.

"A very nice girl," Gunter said. "You do something fun together. Take her on a bike ride through the country. Young girls like that."

Andy thought it was a good idea, but kept his mouth shut.

"Sure," Gunter said. "Take her for a bike ride. Have a picnic. Talk to her. Maybe she make a good wife for you some day, eh?"

Gunter whacked his son hard on the shoulder.

Ouch, Andy thought, shaken by the friendly blow. Arm in arm, his parents strolled back inside the house. Andy stood alone in the night, thinking of Rebecca; the softness of her skin; her charming smile. He wanted to ask her out on a date. Then he remembered something very important.

I forgot to ask her for her phone number. How could I be so stupid?

Hovering behind Andy, the second and third invisible Eyes silently waited for new orders. Receiving a transmission, they sped down the road after the Bronco.

Andy's hair stirred in the wake of their passage. He attributed it to a breeze.

Hidden behind some bushes on a nearby rise, the Mysterious Man lowered his binoculars. His skin tingled with feelings of dread as it did with every new encounter with *Them.* He felt the bracelet's stones to make sure that *They* had indeed departed. The stones reassurance did nothing to change his gloomy mood.

"It has begun," the Mysterious Man said in a tense whisper. "God help us all."

Herman Senicki drove the Bronco down the dirt road towards home. Asleep beside him, Alexandra clutched the opera record across her chest. The sight made Herman smile. Alexandra had been so excited to receive the recording from Gunter. Her joy made him love her all the more.

The Bronco's headlights lit the road before him. The driver's side headlight was weaker than its counterpart. He reminded himself to replace it before it went out completely.

Herman came to a bend in the road. Turning the steering wheel, the headlights swiped the forest with brightness. Trees seemed to leap out in front of him, then vanish back into the night.

Herman glanced in the rear view mirror. Rebecca stared out the window, daydreaming, gently stroking the hand that Andy had so recently held. Herman sensed that his daughter was falling in love.

My little girl is becoming a woman, Herman thought. *This is a good thing.*

Two hills bordered the road. The Bronco was passing between them when the two Eyes caught up with the vehicle. The second Eye flew to the driver's side window, observing Herman. The third Eye sped to the passenger side, focusing its lens on Alexandra. They clung to the Bronco like cyborg crabs, only a thin sheet of glass separating them from their victims.

The Director wanted to try out some of the new holographic projection equipment. He gave the cameramen a command to do so and ordered the special effects department to whip up some test footage.

Iggy and Glop were delighted to comply with his orders. The effects department quickly created the footage. Anxious to see what the new technology could do, Iggy and Glop sent the data to their respective cameras.

Still clinging to the driver's side of the Bronco, the Second Eye extended a mechanical arm into its replicator, emerging with a rectangular mirror for a hand. It pointed it at the forest ahead of the vehicle. Trees appeared on its reflective surface. Stretching its arm out over the engine, it projected the image towards the windshield.

Herman liked to drive at night. He enjoyed the strangeness of the dark forest. Backlit by the moon, the trees were tall towers of harsh shadow, both fascinating and mysterious. Turning the wheel a bit, the forest flickered in and out of his sight.

Herman wondered why his vision went momentarily blurry, when the trees ahead of him began to move. Branches writhed in the night, coming together, weaving themselves into a large swastika inside the bright circle of the moon.

Herman flinched. He gripped the steering wheel hard. He recalled when he was a boy in Austria during World War II, standing in front of his parents 2nd story apartment window, looking down at the Nazi tanks and soldiers invading his home town. Rifles fired. A bullet shattered the window, falling glass cut young Herman's hand. Pulling him towards her, his mother frantically groped him to see if he had been shot. Her utter panic made Herman cry. The sounds of men screaming and guns firing rang in his tender ears, nearly scaring him to death.

As Herman came out of his trance, he saw his hands were gripping the steering wheel so hard his knuckles were white. He fixed his eyes on the moon.

The swastika was gone.

Herman's skin felt hot; he sweated. Reaching out, he turned on the fan. The cool breeze flowed over him, easing his troubled mind. He took a deep breath to calm himself, wondering how he had imagined the whole thing in the first place.

It was just a bad memory, Herman thought, his skin trembling. *Now we live in America. Such terrible things can never happen here.*

Still, much to Herman's regret, the evening forest was no longer pleasant to him. A feeling of menace bothered him despite his telling himself it was all a trick of the mind.

Bearing the two invisible cyborg passengers, the Bronco traveled through the mean forest towards home.

CHAPTER 5

THE BEGINNING OF THE END

Midnight came. The heavens were dotted with stars.

Hiding within the forest, two very visible Eyes recorded the back of the Senicki's home. Lights shone from the upper windows, the downstairs was completely dark. The Bronco was parked to the side of the house where the dirt driveway ended and the back yard began. A picnic table and a barbeque grill stood upon the lawn. Near the grill, an old-fashioned rope swing hung from the stout branch of an Oak tree. The weather was exceedingly calm. No breeze stirred the oak tree's many leaves.

Just for the heck of it, Glop made his Eye carve his name symbol into a tree trunk.

"Hey, don't do that," said Iggy. "You know it's against the rules to leave behind any evidence of our presence."

"Relax, Iggy. It's in V-lan. Who's going to know?"

"It's only the first day of shooting. I don't want to take any chances. We could be here for months."

Glop finished slicing his name in the tree. "There. All done. See? Does that look it could cause trouble? No, it doesn't."

"That's not the point you dope."

"Shush," said Glop. "My Eye has detected something coming this way."

In the drowsy silence, the Senicki's young Calico cat, Mr. Meow, lazily strolled across the yard. The Eyes became invisible and lurched forward to attack.

Iggy and Glop restrained the cameras.

"These new panther clone brains really want to hunt," said Iggy.

"Want to have some fun?" suggested Glop.

"Sounds good," replied Iggy, then he recalled the Production Manager's warning about being put in cryo storage. "What's the Production Manager's twenty?"

"He's in the cafeteria taking a dinner break," said Glop. "We should have at least half an hour."

"You go first," insisted Iggy.

"You are too kind, my it brother." Glop wrote a simple program, then released his Eye, who charged at the young feline.

Iggy took the opportunity to slyly burn Glop's name symbol off the tree trunk.

Reaching the rope swing, Mr. Meow lay down on the soft, cool grass. He licked his paws and washed his face, softly purring to himself. Meow was working up a good sized fur ball when the low hanging swing next to him yanked itself up in the air.

Startled, Meow leapt skyward. The swing's wooden seat swatted his kitty behind with a loud SMACK. Tumbling across the lawn, Meow coughed up the fur ball, then sprinted into the woods.

The swing's seat hung in mid air; several feet of rope dangled below it.

"Boom!" yelled Iggy and Glop, laughing and slapping their four hands in a high five.

"That was fabu," said Iggy. "Teasing simple-minded creatures is a great way to pass the time."

"Let's chase after it," said Glop. "We still have twenty minutes or so. We can replicate some paddles and play kitty ping pong."

"Winner is the first to score twenty-one?" said Iggy.

"You're on," replied Glop.

Their playtime was interrupted when, over the intercom, the Director ordered them to dolly the Eyes into the house. Time was wasting. He needed lots of footage of the actors at every step of the story.

"Coverage," the Director said. "Get me lots of coverage. And put one of the new senso-probes on them. I want to see what it can do." The Director kept the connection open.

Iggy's smile was replaced with a frown.

Glop shrugged his shoulders and sat back down at his workstation.

Iggy's eye stalks blinked in secret code to Glop, so as not to be overheard by their boss. *The prima dona is back*, Iggy blinked. *And, as usual, he doesn't know what he wants. That's why everything is a rush-rush crisis.*

Isn't it one of our best known laws, Glop blinked back, *that narcissism is illegal and punishable by having your mind go through Forced Rehabilitation Using Computers to Kill Ego Disorders?... commonly known as getting FRUCKED.*

Yeah, but whose going to know it way out here? Iggy signaled. *We're 87,000 light years from home. Whose going to enforce it … you?*

Iggy and Glop's eyelids fluttered in merriment as they sent new commands to their respective Eyes. They heard the Director switch off the connection. It was safe to speak again.

Glop made a sour face. "Work, work, work. Day and night. We need a union to protect our rights." He waved his four arms in the air to emphasize his point. "I am not an animal, I am an it!"

Iggy's four eyes narrowed. "We have a union, stalk-wad. Besides, we only need two hours of sleep a day and we spend hours playing computer games when the boss isn't looking and the actors are asleep." Iggy leaned forward. "What more could you possibly want? Don't tell me … you want to the big boss?"

Glop imitated the Producer's nasally, pompous voice. "A 32 point market share in a prime time slot. Not bad, but not *superbulous*."

Iggy and Glop cackled like a pair of idiots, laughing so hard they started to wheeze. They each pulled out a tube from the console, took a sip of seaweed juice, then turned back to their consoles.

On the holo-monitors, steam wafted out the second story bathroom window. Like kids not wanting to do their homework, the cameramen reluctantly went back to work. Iggy made one Eye drift towards the window while Glop had the other Eye dolly towards the Senicki's back door.

Rebecca rubbed her favorite shampoo, Mango Madness, into her long, brown hair. Its thick foam filled her nose with its tantalizing fruity aroma.

She always took a shower at night, rather than be the last in line when her parents were up and about at the break of day. When it came to bathing with body lotion and shampoo, Rebecca loved to indulge herself.

With a few quick twists of her wrist, Rebecca cut off the flow of water. She slid the shower door open, grabbing a fluffy towel off the rack above the toilet.

Dripping water, Rebecca stepped onto the shaggy floor mat, daydreaming about Andy and their magical evening together. She imagined Andy was with her, drying her off with the velvety towel. The thought of him caressing her gave her a delicious inner glow.

Like a pervert at a Peep Show, Iggy watched the Eye record the naked she-mammal as she stood dripping water and stroking herself with the soft, limp, fluffy, white thing. Iggy didn't understand why humans tried to drown themselves in water and rub frothy stuff all over themselves.

He knew nothing about personal cleanliness.

Its did not take baths or take care of themselves. When Iggy slept in his resting capsule, he was drugged unconscious while an automated hygiene program was performed on him: sonic waves cleaned his body and brushed his teeth, his blood was tested; medical tests were conducted to ensure that he was kept in perfect health. Even his ear hair and toe nails were groomed when he was fast asleep.

As per the Director's orders, Iggy released a golf-ball sized probe into the bathroom. Being that it was a brand new model, he was curious as to what it could do. It hovered above Rebecca's head, phase-shifted and vanished, leaving its bottom port open.

A tendril of energy snaked out. Twisting downward, it penetrated Rebecca's brain, assimilating her thought-images and feelings. When the data appeared on the holo-screen, Iggy transferred it directly to the Director's suite.

The Director walked by his hover chair with the word *DIRECTOR* imprinted on the back. Using the thought pen, he changed the letters to *GENIUS AT WORK*. Sitting in the chair, he placed a new device upon his brow--a senso-link. Via the probe, his mind was now connected to the naked she-human. He could see and feel everything she imagined; he had invaded her most private thoughts.

The she-human is making romantic thoughts about the Andy. How interesting. This is my chance to create a genuine love story.

He ordered the cameraman to have the Eye mist the she-human with PX-40, a chemical stimulant. He switched the feed to a holo-monitor the size of a wall so he could see in detail what the probe recorded in her brain. The probe floated above the bare she-human, spraying a mist from its bottom portal. Chemical pheromones drifted down, which the she-human inhaled. Her thoughts about the Andy became more intense.

The Director felt each stroke of the towel across the she-human's skin. He participated in her daydream that the Andy was caressing her shoulders, arms, legs and back.

The alienness of her mammalian existence made his stomach queasy, but as her emotions flowed into his frontal lobes his eyes grew wide. He had never captured such data before--the data of human pleasure. The new probes were a wonder. He could imagine doing things no one had ever done before with A.R.T.

Leaping on a creative impulse, he ordered the cameraman to increase the probe's current going into the she-human's brain.

Rebecca dried her leg when her body exploded with pleasure. Her thoughts swirled; she was with Andy; they swam in happiness.

Dropping the towel to the floor, Rebecca froze as her heart beat faster and faster.

A rush of bliss enveloped the Director, growing stronger with every second.

Without warning his limbs seized up. Dragged through the she-human's ecstatic feelings, he curled into a rigid ball. The she-human craved the Andy as her mate. Her raging desires besieged his body, overdosing his brain with passion.

An alarm sounded; the emergency override engaged. It automatically shut down the current, withdrawing the Director from the she-human's emotional bio-sphere. The destructive rapture retreated; the wild emotional ride slid to a grinding halt.

The Director's limbs dangled over the sides of the hover chair, flopping limply. He was so exhausted he might as well have been a rag doll.

So that was love. It's so pleasurable it's hideous! Wait until Those Who Watch get a load of this. No wonder such feelings are forbidden. Love can cripple you; it could cause your death. This is the advantage I've been looking for. I'll show that lame Producer I know my craft far better than he ever will. With footage like this I'll certainly win this year's best reality television episode award.

He ordered the Eye to collect more data.

The cameraman inquired how to do so as the she-human's e-force had drained.

The Director stabbed down on his console. "Do as I say … and don't talk back."

A blast of electricity flashed from the discipline chip implanted in Iggy's head. Yelping in pain, Iggy hurriedly signaled that the Eye was recording.

The Director took his finger off the console and slumped in his chair, recuperating. "Love is a terrible ordeal. How can the humans stand it? I need a stiff drink."

Back in the Control Center, Iggy's entire body quivered. High pitched moans escaped his lips as the discipline chip continued to intermittently jolt him.

Seeing his friend suffer, Glop did the only thing he could think of. Pulling out the tube of seaweed juice, he squirted it at Iggy's face.

Iggy's body was shocked with a sudden burst of current; he cried out, then slumped in his chair. The pain subsided.

"Master getting grumpy?" Glop asked.

Iggy nodded. Tiny bits of seaweed clung to his wet green face. "And we're still in the first act. This could go on for months."

"I predict this production is going to be a harsh one for us," said Glop in a glum voice. "We're very unlucky to have this job."

The implant ached. Iggy vigorously scratched the top of his head. "Dang, I hope you're wrong, Glop. Being disciplined makes my eye stalks itch like crazy. I still feel rather stressed."

"Here," said Glop. "Take this."

Iggy glanced down. In Glop's outstretched hand was a piece of pleasure candy.

"How did you …?

"I pinched it from the Production Manager when he wasn't looking," said Glop. "Go ahead. It will make you feel better."

Squeezing the wrapper, Iggy popped half of the confection into his mouth. His taste buds sizzled with dazzling flavor. "This is heaven," Iggy moaned. "I really needed this. Thanks."

"Glad I could help," said Glop. "What are obnoxious friends for?"

Outside the Senicki's bathroom window, Iggy's Eye continued to record the she-thing doing her cleanliness ritual.

Having recovered from his shock treatment, Iggy brought his attention back on-line. The human female was still drying herself. He found her nudity extremely boring. It was a good thing the pleasure candy kept his mind soaring with pleasure or he probably would drift off to sleep.

Although nothing worth filming was happening yet, Iggy tried to look like he was doing something work related so the Director wouldn't make him suffer again.

He increased the Eye's dimensional density to just under the human plane of reality while maintaining its invisibility. Like a water balloon being gently forced through a smaller opening, the Eye bulged slightly as it squeezed its hidden mass through the window. With a soft pop, it bounced inside the humid shower, causing its bubble vision to undulate. On the monitor the she-thing's naked body rippled strangely.

Iggy thought that was a neat trick.

Gazing at the she-thing's bare bottom, he wondered why these creatures still reproduced by having sex. Surely they had cloning on this backwards planet? It was irrational to create new life without genetic manipulation leaving the dominant genes to chance. Everyone learned that as far back as grade school. Don't these creatures pay attention to their teachers? Did they want everyone to have bad genes? He attributed it all to low intelligence.

Rebecca turned around.

Iggy stared at the strange curves of her figure, especially her breasts. Did human newbies really feed from such jiggly things? All V-lan women were flat chested. Reproduction was done in a birth control center. Suckling the young was done by nursing machines with over 200 flavors, pistachio salmon being his all time favorite. Besides, it was well documented that a mother's love was bad for a healthy society. It led to favoritism and civil unrest.

The she-thing leaned her head back. Iggy zoomed into a tight close-up of her nose. What had the Director once said? The nose was the gateway to the human soul? What a strange place to keep something so valuable. Wouldn't a sturdy jar be better?

Before he could complete his zoom-in, the she-thing shut the shower's glass door in front of the Eye's lens.

Iggy switched to z-ray mode and tried to look busy checking out her internal organs.

In the master bedroom, the third Eye watched the human parents prepare for bed.

Removing his white shirt, Herman reached for a clothes hanger on top of his dresser when feminine fingernails teased his neck.

"Mine schatze," a sultry voice whispered *my darling* in German, as she gently stroked him.

A tingly sensation aroused Herman's senses, but the voice aroused something more.

Herman turned; Alexandra stood beside him. Her gorgeous long hair, normally pinned up in a conservative bun, lay softly down over her pale, smooth shoulders. Her eyes were filled with desire. The sight of her was intoxicating.

"Let me just hang up my shirt, dear," Herman said, excited by his wife's amorous behavior.

Alexandra flung the shirt on the floor.

"There," she whispered, her voice deep and breathy. "It's hung up. Now kiss me."

A moment later, Herman Senicki found his arms full of passionate wife.

Rebecca slipped a bathrobe over her nakedness, tying the waist strap into a knot. Picking up a second fluffy towel, she dried her hair when she noticed the mirror was fogged over. She wiped the towel across the mirror, but the image remained blurry. Wanting to let the steam out of the bathroom, she slid the shower door aside.

The Eye in the shower stared blankly at her.

Noticing the small window above the shower was already open, Rebecca closed the shower door.

Still feeling high, Iggy kept the steam from going out the window with a force field, changing it into a variety of swirling colors. Watching a digital training program, he painted colorful patterns on the she-thing's body. After this production was over he wanted to take the special effects advancement test. Being a cameraman was fun, but the real action was in effects work.

Now that the senso-probe had been shut down, Iggy wished something interesting would happen. Since the Director was leaving him alone, he ate the other half of his pleasure candy. His brain was immediately drenched in joy. He wished he could have it whenever he wanted.

Reeling in pleasure, Iggy didn't notice Rebecca grab the hallway doorknob and gave it a twist.

Steam floated into the hallway as Rebecca reached for her hairbrush.

In his private quarters, the Director paced the floor. He had lost his opening shot, but no matter. He still needed a good story line. It was essential in order to create exciting reality television.

"The probes and the Eyes have revealed two important things," the Director mumbled to himself. "The Rebecca has strong feelings for the Andy, and the Herman and Alexandra love each other." He scowled at the thought, making deep lines across his forehead. Their love disgusted him, but how could he use it to create drama?

He wanted a story so repulsively emotional that the ratings would skyrocket. He wanted Those Who Watch to stampede to the holo-stadiums to see it a dozen times or more like humans did when *Star Wars* first came out. If the story was sensational, maybe it would receive an extended run.

What kind of a story would do that?

The Director recalled his previous career as a cultural anthropologist on a star ship. Star drive took him to far away galaxies where he studied hundreds of alien cultures. The sociological knowledge he gained from his travels had been extremely useful when he became a reality television director. His stories were well received; they even won awards.

Unless some idiotic producer reedited them and muddled them up.

If he was to create a masterpiece he must go back to the roots of the V-lan culture. He must tap into their race memory.

The Director recollected his race's history. A thousand years ago war nearly destroyed the V-lan civilization. Strong emotions were deemed the culprit and society used every means to eradicate them. The family group was outlawed; children were not raised by their parents but in camps where they were not allowed to make close friends. People had birth names which were never used socially. Everyone was always addressed by their occupation.

Sexual encounters were forbidden; procreation was restricted to fetus control centers. By law everything shifted to mental development. Advances in technology were rapid; society prospered; prescription drugs kept emotions sedated.

Yet after centuries of progress, the people suffered mental breakdowns. Denied emotional contact and close relationships, a poisonous depression eventually shattered the V-lan mind. This led to the creation of emotion festivals, where people could glut themselves with forbidden feelings then return to their civilization of pristine intellect and technological achievement.

The problem was the festivals didn't always produce the desired result. Many came down with emotion sickness. Rehab clinics sprang up all over the planet. It took a heavy toll on society.

A hundred years later, science perfected holographic technology with full frontal lobe sensory input. Gargantuan holo-stadiums became the new source of emotional sedation. As the people sat in their arena seats, they vicariously experienced the emotions of beings from other planets. The V-lans became a race of voyeurs who used reality television shows as psycho therapy.

The rehab clinics closed.

Under government funding the entertainment industry flourished. The Director found himself operating flying cameras and using alien races as actors for his stories.

He chose creatures with strong emotions, class 2 intelligences who had no right to life under V-lan law.

He could legally do whatever he wanted to with them ... even kill them. Death became a standard in entertainment.

But right now he needed a story. More importantly, he needed a theme. It was the theme that affected the audience. None of the other directors even knew what it meant. It was one of his professional secrets he had learned from eavesdropping on an Earth movie director named Roman Polanski.

The doorbell rang.

"Enter."

"Excuse me, Herr Director," said the Production Manager gliding inside. "Interstellar sub Ethernet call for you."

"Who is it?"

"The Producer."

"You've got to be joking."

The Production Manager raised his eyelids and shook his neckless head and shoulders from side to side.

Walking towards the communication chamber, the Director's ear tubes lengthened; he became agitated. Getting a phone call from the Producer on the first day of shooting was an ill omen. What could that pompous, meddling oaf want with him now?

He entered a private communication cell, shutting the door behind him. The palms of his webbed hands felt clammy as he activated the hyperspace module.

The Producer came on line. "Good day, Director. I am changing your production schedule."

"I beg your pardon," the Director said.

"From now on all footage will be sent immediately to me so the story department can get started."

"What story department?" the Director said coolly, while wiping the sweat from his palms on his pants.

"A new era of entertainment has begun," the Producer replied. "I have just invented it. You do the shooting, we will make the story out of the footage. It will greatly improve the ratings. It is history in the making."

"You're turning my story over to a committee?" the Director scoffed.

"Use the interstellar transit pod to send the footage," the Producer said. "Make dupes in case it hits a comet or runs into a nebula. Keep it fresh." The Producer smiled showing his sharkish teeth which now contained rubies instead of diamonds. It was an accepted symbol of cultural aggression. He then cut the connection.

The Director stood in silence, his two hearts pounding wildly. "Tyranny!" he bellowed, then clamped down on his taboo emotions. "Democracy will ruin my story."

Someone knocked on the door. "Is everything all right, sir?" the Production Manager said. "I heard a loud noise."

The door to the communication cell slid open.

"Get the other twelve cameramen out of cryo storage," the Director said.

"But only two of them are scheduled to be unfrozen and not for another week. We're still shooting footage for Act I. We don't want to go over budget so soon."

"Do as I say," the Director demanded. He told the Production Manager what the Producer had said. "He wants footage. I'll give him footage. I'll give that shark so much footage he'll drown in it."

The Production Manager decided to be politically correct and keep his mouth shut. Obeying his orders, he slithered down the ship's corridor towards cryogenic storage.

The Director shut the door. He thumped his leg repeatedly with a fist. All the best movies he had seen on Earth had been under the guidance of a single visionary – the director. Did a committee have his years of experience observing alien cultures, manipulating them to make A.R.T.? How could a committee do anything but water down the story? It required a strong personal vision--an auteur--to reach the audience's subconscious. This was bald-faced oppression. He'd get that pretentious Producer fired for this. Or at least reduced in rank to doing pathetic space craft commercials.

"How am I going to do this?" the Director said, pressing his webbed hands against his temples and making circles to stimulate his thinking.

For starters he would send out the extra camera crews, have them take loads of meaningless footage and send it back to Home World. When the Executives saw what poor work the Producer had done they would be most unhappy. Then he would show them his masterpiece; they'd put the Director in charge for good.

But what would his storyline be? How could he reach his race on the deepest emotional level and move them to hyperventilate their gassy chambers until they became gooey?

Pacing the floor, he put his mind back to devising the theme. With the cultural assessment of his people in mind, he looked over his story board wall that he had created with the thought pen, mulling his story elements over: "Parents lived under Hitler, tyranny, art, human love, family, oppression, World War II, opera music, criminal emotions."

An idea formed in his mind.

Yes. Of course, it's perfect. The theme to my story will be: Love leads to destruction with a Nazi Germany motif.

Balling his hands into fists, he raised them up, shaking them hard. "It will be my masterpiece. It will show the A.R.T. world I am a genius."

A madness took over his features.

"It will also prove that NO ONE CAN SCREW WITH ME! I'LL DESTROY ANYONE THAT DARE TRIES."

He clicked opened a computer sound file; the room filled with zealous applause. Stretching his arms out wide, he imagined receiving the award for best director in front of a cheering crowd. Soaking up their fervent adulation, he ordered a shrimp martini from the food replicator.

Sporting lipstick on his mouth, a bare chested Herman Senicki slipped out of the bedroom into the hallway. "I'll be right back, dear," Herman said, receiving a romantic giggle in reply. Herman wanted to obey the call of nature with his lovely Alexandra, but he had to obey a different calling first. Preoccupied with the taste of her lips, he meandered towards the bathroom, not noticing the cloud of steam that floated out into the hallway.

Madama Butterfly, Pagliacci, Un Ballo en Maschera, Turandot, Glop had the third Eye record the labels on the record jackets on a shelf in the living room for insert shots then transmitted the information to the star ship.

Receiving new orders, the Eye surged across the green shag carpet and swooped up the stairs.

I am a lucky man, thought Herman. *I have the perfect life with the perfect wife. I can't imagine being happy without my beloved Alexandra. She brings such joy to my heart.*

Smiling, Herman grabbed the outer door frame and swung himself partway into the bathroom.

That's when he saw Rebecca.

Rebecca brushed her hair. Her arms were raised over her head, partially exposing her breasts beneath her bathrobe. Embarrassed, Herman quickly stepped back into the hall to give his daughter some privacy. It was the decent thing to do.

The third Eye sprayed him square in the face. A chemical substance raced through the capillaries in Herman's nose straight into his brain cells that ignited an explosion of unbridled lust. The shock of it hammered his body. Overwhelmed by the chemical mist, he leaned against the wall. Herman touched his forehead with his hand. It felt hot and sweaty.

What is happening to me?

Glop recorded Mr. Senicki fighting the effects of the lust spray. In another part of the spacecraft, an effects technician programmed a probe to thrust images of forceful seduction into Mr. Senicki's drug-soaked mind.

Iggy was still using a paint program.

"Hey, Iggy," Glop whispered. "The actions about to start. Get back to business. Goof off later."

Iggy put the finishing touches on his painting of Rebecca. She looked like a human zebra with a punked out mane of black and bright pink spiked hair. "This is good. Want to see it?"

"Get rid of it and hurry up," said Glop. "I can't control the actors, you know."

Wiggling his four buttocks, Iggy admired his art work, then stored it on the hard drive.

"Move your asses," said Glop reproachfully. "You're always saying I'm obnoxious, now you're the one goofing off. If you get us sent to cryo I'll bite your eyestalks off myself."

Iggy switched back to the camera controls. He was still feeling elated from the pleasure candy. "Ready to rip, diggety dude buddy. On with the show."

Herman peered into the bathroom while Rebecca brushed her silky brown hair. Perspiration beaded on his forehead; his body wanted to force himself upon her.

His mind abhorred the sinful feeling. Rebecca was his daughter, his own flesh and blood, how could he even think of such a thing? And yet the primal urge welled up inside of him. It was only the horror that these unwanted feelings provoked that barely kept them at bay.

Herman was a Christian man, a church-going soul who believed in God, the creator of heaven and earth. Such impulses were blasphemous to his religious beliefs. Dots of water beaded his brow as the spiritual and the bestial warred within him. His moral fiber struggled to the utmost to reject the profane urge to rape his daughter.

With his lust demanding release, with his bladder demanding release, Herman stood in the doorway and watched his daughter as he had never watched her before. He saw the brush flow through the luxurious strands of her glossy brown hair; saw her full, juicy lips; saw the sensuous curves of her firm, young body.

Herman struggled for self-control as the probe jammed lustful pictures into his skull.

Wearing the senso-link on low power, the Director relished the emotional drama that unfolded in the Herman's mind. He found it amusing that the father-creature could resist such a strong biological urge when his own mind was panting for him to assault her. What could be stronger than animal lust to an animal? Surely the poor, dumb human would succumb at any moment.

Increasing the senso-link's intensity, the steady rush of primitive urges flowed into the Director like a river of wantonness. It threatened to lock up his body, but the safety program he created after the last time he did something like this limited the emotional inflow to just below his biological red line. He eagerly awaited the outcome. No one had ever filmed a father/daughter rape scene before.

It would be fresh.

98 ... 99 ... 100.

Rebecca counted the last stroke and set her hair brush down on the counter. It was bedtime. She was so sleepy she could hardly think.

She stepped towards the doorway and, noticing her father, gave him a loving hug.

Herman felt Rebecca's arms entwine about him, her face nuzzled against his chest. The smell of her femaleness made him gasp. His eyeballs rolled up so only the whites showed. His manhood roared its need.

The hug lasted a few scant seconds, but to Herman it seemed like an eternity. *Help me, Lord. Help me resist this unholy desire.*

As Herman inwardly struggled, Rebecca dreamily kissed him on the chin. "I love you, Daddy," she whispered. "Good night."

Rebecca strolled into her bedroom, closing the door behind her.

The probe forced images into Herman. His moral restraint began to crumble. He imagined himself storming into Rebecca's bedroom, grabbing her by the shoulders and pushing her down on the bed beneath him.

His body took two steps forward.

He saw himself rip open her bathrobe exposing her lovely breasts. His sense of morality was outraged; he clenched his hands into fists. Straining to the utmost, veins popped out on his face and neck.

His body took two steps forward.

Herman pleaded to God for deliverance. His hands flew up to his face. He resisted with all of his might. He resisted for what he knew was right. *No! I will not do this! In the name of God, I reject this immoral compulsion!*

Herman strained himself to the limit. The pain set his soul ablaze. He was on the verge of collapse when the lust-mist gushed out of his nose, spraying his hands crimson. Freed from the chemical substance, the moral shame of his onerous behavior came crashing down on his pious soul.

Herman rushed into the bathroom, twisting on the faucet above the sink. He splashed the cool wetness upwards, rinsing his face and his guilty conscience.

The Director had Glop have the second Eye record the blood as it swirled down the porcelain drain, shooting it as a slow zoom-in while rotating the image in a circle. He had gotten the idea from watching a Hitchcock movie named *Psycho.*

Having ordered the arty shot, the Director became furious. He could not believe his plans had just been thwarted. And by a class 2 intelligence! How dare an actor rewrite his story like that oafish Producer back home.

"I am an auteur," insisted the Director. "I am Hitchcock, Bertolucci and Tim Burton all rolled into one. No one can change my story. It's an insult to my creative genius. Besides … he's just a dumb animal!"

His mind pumped full of anger and lust, he tore off the senso-link to Mr. Senicki. Fingers stabbed down on the control board, sending searing whips of pain into the two Eyes' brains.

The Eyes pitched about in anguish, spinning wildly about the bathroom, arms thrashing, colors swirling, vision blinded by the white hot agony.

The Eyes raced outside the bathroom window into the gloomy forest, shrieking their unearthly screams in a parallel dimension where no human could possibly hear them.

Stunned by the Director's shocking cruelty, Iggy and Glop stared at the holographic monitor as their cameras went berserk.

"Did you see that?" said Iggy.

"Wow," replied Glop. "These new camera's can scream. Now that is really wicked."

"Are you crazy?" said Iggy. "They're cyborgs. Who cares about them? We're just lucky the Director didn't hurt *us.*"

"You're right, my friend," said Glop. "This show is getting seriously creepy."

Iggy sank his head into all four of his hands and moaned. "I've got such a bad feeling about this production. Put me back in cryo. I'd rather be frozen."

Glop patted Iggy's shoulders with two of his four hands. "Cheer up, Iggy. Look at the bright side."

"What bright side?" said Iggy, his face miserable.

Glop scratched the top of his head. "We can only die once?"

Groaning, Iggy buried his face in his lap.

Glop laid a hand on Iggy's shoulder. "Would it help if I pinched some more pleasure candy?"

CHAPTER 6

THE DUSTY HORSE SALOON

Originally a trading post built in the 1860s, the Dusty Horse Saloon was built like a big log cabin. Its walls were made of large trees horizontally stacked on top of each other, all of which were well worn with age. Despite being the only bar for miles around, there were only a few regulars present.

"Little" Judy, the bartender, a smallish woman with a very loud voice, filled two beer glasses from the tap. Rita, the weekend waitress, carried the mugs to the pool table where Butch and his buddy, Jim, racked up the balls for a game while they smoked cigarettes, one after another, covering the table in a swirling haze. At the bar sat Sam and Pete, two portly, bearded men commiserating over shots of Jack Daniels while humming drunkenly to oldies tunes on the jukebox.

Last in the social hierarchy was Joe, a scrawny man nicknamed the "Drunk." Joe was the local "I-live-in-the-forest-because-I-want-to" crazy man, to whom cleanliness was as commonplace as sobriety and who was trying to horn in on the aforementioned Jack Daniels. The Drunk wore a grungy fishing hat that was the cleanest part of his clothing.

"I seen it," the Drunk said to Sam and Pete. "Nearly scared the skin right off me. Ran away from that white light like the devil was comin' for me soul. Nipped me on the boot it did. Sure makes a fellow's throat dry, all that runnin'."

Sucking on his front lip, the Drunk stared at the whiskey bottle.

"Don't bother Sam and Pete here," little Judy said, her voice loud and grating. "The lumber mill just closed down and they lost their jobs. Leave'em alone." Little Judy poured Sam and Pete another shot of whiskey.

"It's all right, Judy," said Sam. "Leave the bottle."

Sam turned a bleary eye towards the Drunk. The Drunk had bloodshot eyes; his gaunt hands shivered. "Show me your boot, then," said Sam, not really all that interested.

The Drunk extended his right leg forward.

Sam and Pete saw a gnarled old boot with a chunk missing from the front. Several dirty toes, each sporting crusty toe nails, gaped through the hole.

Sam decided to have some fun with the Drunk. He nudged Pete's arm, giving him a conspiratorial wink. "All right, mister," said Sam, shoving the shot glass with a sip of whiskey in it across the counter. "Drink this down and tell me your story. If I believe ya, I'll fill a shotter up for you three times to the brim."

The Drunk downed the sip of whiskey like it was a life-saving antidote.

Little Judy rolled her eyes towards the ceiling. She knew if you gave a starving animal a tiny bit of food it would become even more ravenous and aggressive. If she had to, she'd throw the Drunk out the door on his buttocks, aided by her shoe in the same general vicinity.

Sam scratched his massive beard. "So what happened? The truth now, no lies."

Realizing the stakes were high, the Drunk did his best to tell the truth, the whole truth and nothing but the truth, so help him Jack Daniels. He hadn't been to church in years, but, figuring to look more honest, he held his grubby fishing hat in front of his chest.

"I was fishin' near Cattle Cross Creek just after nightfall," said the Drunk. There's a place you can barricade the fish in and grab'em with your hands. Don't need no pole or bait or nothin'; just wade in and snatch'em. Well, Mister Sam, I'd just tossed me a nice trout on shore when I heard this weird hummin' noise behind me. Comin' right round the creek bend was this big, bright, white light."

The Drunk wiped the sweat above his lips with a grimy finger. The act left his face dirtier than before. "Like a flashlight it was, tall as a pine tree, shootin' down from the sky into the water. There were little dark dots floatin' in it, goin' round and round in a circle with sparkly silver bits."

Feigning interest, Sam widened his eyes. "Sparkly silver bits, round and round you say?"

"Round and round," confirmed the Drunk. "Bright as a Christmas tree it was." The Drunk stepped in closer as though to impart an important secret. "And when the twisty cone come by me, I saw them black dots up real close. And guess what, mister Sam?"

"What?" said Sam.

"They was *fish*."

"Fish, you say?" Sam nodded as if impressed, then secretly winked at Pete.

The Drunk licked his lips. "Honest to God, they was fish!" The Drunk laughed. "Flew up with them little silver bits like they was a swimmin' upstream."

"To where?" Pete interrupted. "Fish got to go somewhere."

"That's the mystery of it," the Drunk said solemnly. "There was nowhere else to go. Them fish just swam to the top and poof."

"Poof?" said Sam.

"Poof!" said the Drunk. "They was gone. Like poof."

The Drunk rotated his hat in a circle with both hands as he coveted the whiskey bottle.

Sam poured Pete and himself a drink. "So is that it? Is that all?" said Sam. The huge-gutted men downed their whiskey and smacked their lips. "What about your shoe? Be honest!"

The Drunk lied as truthfully as possible.

"This is the god's truth, for sure. One of them fish fell off from up high; splashed in the water near me. I paddled over to pick it up and *the light moved towards me.* Guess it thought I was stealin' its fish."

Sam glanced at Pete, his eyes glowed with mocking laughter.

"I waded through the water," said the Drunk, "but the white light was faster than a striking snake. Got so close I screamed and jumped back. Nipped off the top of me boot. You seen me boot. You seen it!"

"Calm down, friend," said Sam. "Keep going. Tell me everything."

The Drunk blinked his eyes and huffed air through his mouth. "Well Mister Sam, when that light struck me boot it felt like death bit me toes. I thought I was a goner, yes sir, Mister Sam. No lie."

"And then what happened?" asked Sam, leaning his elbows back on the counter.

"I floated down stream and got away. Hiked back to my truck. Drove here faster than a bad habit. Ran out of gas a mile down the road and walked. Now you know the truth. They're out there, Mister Sam. They're out there, sure as trouble."

Sam pursed his lips and nodded as if deep in thought. "You hear all that, Pete?"

"Yep," said Pete. "Every word."

Sam twirled the whiskey bottle between his fingers, deliberating.

The Drunk watched the label go round and round. With each circle he swallowed hard. After reliving the story of how he had almost died, he seriously needed a stiff one.

The Drunk held out the empty glass Sam had given him earlier. "I reckon I'll have me them drinks now."

"Judy," called out Sam. "Bring me another shot glass."

Reluctantly, little Judy set a clean shot glass on the bar.

Sam gathered the three glasses together and ever so slowly began to fill each one to the top with 80 proof Kentucky whiskey. The Drunk gaped at the golden liquid, anxious for his reward.

The first glass was filled and given to Pete. The Drunk panted in anticipation, the taste of the tiny sip from before haunted his tongue like an alcoholic ghost.

Sam filled the second shot glass.

The Drunk rubbed his lips with his grimy fingers. His entire being focused on the third shot glass--his shot glass. Time slowed to a trickle as Sam tilted the bottle and poured.

The precious fluid flowed down in a twisted rivulet. The Drunk remembered how the creek water had flowed up into the sky in that same coiled pattern. Spots appeared before his eyes. The spots turned into little trout that wiggled up the alcoholic stream. The Drunk fixedly watched the silver fish swim up to the top where they mysteriously disappeared with a *poof.*

Sam filled the third shot glass with whiskey all the way to the very top.

The Drunk's tongue grew thick in his mouth; he reached forward, his fingers stretching towards his salvation.

Sam covered the glass with his beefy hand. Feeling alarmed, the Drunk backed off.

Sam and Pete raised the glorious juice to their lips. With a quick flick of their wrists, they snapped it to the back of their throats, exhaling loudly in satisfaction. Sam picked up the third glass, dangling it between his thumb and forefinger. Careful so as to not spill a drop, he brought it around to where the Drunk stood.

Still hallucinating, the Drunk watched his salvation approach. *Here, fishy, fishy.*

The glass neared the tips of his fingers. He reached out for his reward.

Sam let the glass slip through his fingers.

The shot glass dropped like a bomb. Whiskey exploded across the floor.

"You dropped the truth!" the Drunk shouted, staring painfully downward.

Sam and Pete guffawed.

"Excuse me," said Sam. "But I guess that means I don't believe your story."

The two hulking men laughed uproariously.

"Don't believe a word of it!" Pete said. "Little blue fishies swimming up silver flashies, round and round into the white light until they go poof! Haw, haw, haw."

Sam took up where Pete left off, "That's the biggest fish tale I ever heard!" Sam poured two more drinks of whiskey that he and Pete downed with relish. "Its too bad for you I didn't say I'd pay up if I LIKED your story, just if I BELIEVED it!" Sam laughed, his belly jiggling.

The Drunk quivered from head to foot. Except for the fact that his shoe had been torn open from excessive wear, not only had he told the truth, not only had he almost died, but he needed a drink something furious.

"Are you calling the truth a liar?" he said in a low, angry voice.

Sam's hairy face stared back at him. "No, Joe. I'm not."

He poured another shot glass and held it out towards the Drunk. "I'm calling *you* a liar. Pete and I are calling you a *damn* liar." Sam chugged the whiskey down.

"One damn liar," Pete agreed, his voice slurred.

Judy noticed the lumber men's' belligerent attitude. "Sam, Pete, don't you start something," she said sharply.

The Drunk beat them to the punch, for with a bony fist he smacked Sam hard on the nose. Blood spurted out Sam's nose.

The Drunk snatched the bottle off the counter and ran over to the juke box.

"Believe in the truth!" he yelled. He hefted the bottle upside-down and swallowed the whiskey in large, thirsty gulps. The whiskey flowed over his mouth, running down his dirty face and clothes.

Wiping his bloody nose with the back of his hand, Sam bellowed like an angry bull and charged at the Drunk. He wanted to kill the thieving chug-a-lugger with his own two burly hands as the jukebox played *Proud To Be An American.*

The Drunk choked on the booze, spitting it out on the floor. Sam slipped. The Drunk leapt sideways as Sam's bulky carcass rammed into the jukebox.

The Drunk howled. "I'm proud to be an American, where at least the booze is free."

Pete lunged his barrel-chested body forward, intent on teaching the Drunk the true meaning of suffering. The Drunk kicked a small table in front of Pete, who fell on top of it, bust it in half, and crashed hard to the floor.

The Drunk danced in glee. He upended the bottle over Pete's head, giving the burly lumber man a liquor shampoo until the whiskey ran out. The Drunk turned his attention to Sam, who lay groaning by the jukebox. He held the empty bottle above Sam's head, taking aim. His inebriated eyes held a devilish glint.

A hand snatched the bottle away. Little Judy grabbed the Drunk by the ear and carted him towards the front door.

The Drunk cried in pain, his head tilted sideways as his body struggled to catch up to his distraught appendage.

Judy hauled the Drunk by the pool table. Butch and Jim applauded his departure, smoke puttering out of their mouths.

Shoving the bar door open, Judy hauled the Drunk outside. She introduced him to the dirt parking lot, ably assisted by a prodigious kick in the booty.

The Drunk slid to a halt, scraping his knee through a hole in his jeans.

"I'm through being nice to you, Joe, just because your Mom, god rest her soul, used to work here," Judy said. "If you're going to talk crazy don't come back to my bar, you hear." Judy stomped back inside the bar, slamming the door with a loud bang. A loose shingle fell off the roof and shattered on the ground in a dozen pieces.

Bruised, intoxicated, and desperate to be believed, the Drunk wiped the dirt off of his mouth. He crawled towards one of the posts which held up the overhanging roof.

"I seen'em," he muttered, creeping along, talking to his deceased mother. "White light nearly killed me."

Reaching the post, the Drunk clung to it, weeping. He had told the truth and no one believed him. He truly missed his mom.

Mumbling to himself, he closed his eyes; his head drooped; he fell asleep. A bright *something* stung his eyes. Squeezing them tight, he tried to loosen his gummy tears.

Squinting through narrow slits, the Drunk saw an intense white light come out of the forest. Twinkling silver bits floated within its towering beam. Seeing it as the instrument of his death, the Drunk hugged the post for dear life as his flesh quivered.

I knew you'd be back, he thought as the white light engulfed him. Its neural paralyzing field quickly rendered him unconscious.

Why is it so cold?
The Drunk awoke, shivering on the stony ground. His fishing hat was tight around his brow. He was naked, except for the grubby underwear around his loins. Large strips of metal lay beside him. Dark trees stood tall against the night.

Where am I? Where's the bar?
A brilliant light pierced the darkness behind him. On unsteady feet, the Drunk stood up, shielding his eyes from the harsh beacon. A glaring eye bore down upon him, exposing his nakedness to the world.

The Drunk screamed.

It was cut off as the train ran over him.

His fishing hat flip-flopped through the air, plopping on the ground in a crumpled heap.

Through an invisible Eye, the Director saw the train obliterate the one man who knew the truth. It wasn't justifiable homicide. He would dispose in any fashion--and the more horrific the better--anyone who could conceivably disrupt his plans. Humanity must never know that *They* existed, and the only sure-fire way to maintain their secrecy was to annihilate all opposition before it took root.

He murmured his favorite motto: "Death is the ultimate entertainment."

CHAPTER 7

THE STUFF THAT DREAMS
ARE MADE OF

Stuffed animals and dolls lined several shelves beside Rebecca's bed. Mixed together were teddy bears, lions, the Cheshire Cat, Barbie dolls, a clown, a cute little pig and many others. Their faces were unanimously happy and their toothsome smiles indicative of first class plastic animal dental care.

Dreaming teenage love dreams, Rebecca slept in her bed. Only the steady rising and falling of her chest gave any indication that she was alive.

The Director stood barefoot on his massage rug, which he had moved from his personal quarters to his private screening room. Slipping in and out of his toes, the squirming grasses kneaded the soles of his webbed feet, soothing them and giving him pleasure. When his feet relaxed so did his mind. He needed his mind calm to be creative. The rug was even better than Metamucil in prune juice as it did not distort his senses, giving him a more energetic tranquility. Besides, he had already drunk a quart of various alcoholic beverages today.

"Now to get down to artistic business," the Director said serenely.

The Director believed the Rebecca would make a good murder victim. The rape plan had failed, so he devised a different scenario, one that would put her life in mortal danger and provide Those Who Watch with many thrills in the process.

Yet, as with all of his cast of characters, the young female would be given a chance to survive. The Director recalled one actor in the past that stayed alive, although he was left horribly maimed and a drooling idiot. It wouldn't do to let survivors run around loose, knowing that *They* existed. Still, they definitely did have a chance, however miniscule.

The Eyes were in place. The time had come.

"Let the tour de force begin," the Director said. "Roll camera."

Rebecca's bedroom door creaked open; the light from the hallway gradually exposing the stuffed animals perfect grins.

An Eye dollied inside.

Through its bubble vision, the Eye panned across the dolls and animals. They took on the appearance of being seen in a fun-house mirror … distorted … stretched out … bizarre. The Eye saw bear button eyes and funny clown eyes, an Elephant's dangling trunk and a cute pig's nose, the Cheshire cat's smile and a sweet seal's grin.

The Eye floated over to the sleeping Rebecca and sprayed her with a substance that would keep her unconscious for hours.

"Run effects program, She-Human One," the Director said.

Iggy's fingers scrambled over the keyboard. Computer software seamlessly substituted parts of her face with those of the toys. Rebecca's eyes--Rebecca with bear button eyes, Rebecca's nose--Rebecca with Miss Piggy's nose, Rebecca's mouth--Rebecca with the Cheshire Cat's wide toothy grin.

Iggy morphed Rebecca into what he thought comical or grotesque. Now Rebecca had huge clown eyes, a lion's nose, a seal's mouth with whiskers, and floppy puppy dog ears. She looked like a seriously weird animal. A few moments later, she was hairless and all her major features--lips, nose, eyes--were as tiny as a Barbie doll.

It reminded Iggy of an anti-genetic research poster back on Home World decrying using pinheads to test cosmetics.

The Director was amused with the software's substitution hijinks, but he was anxious to move on.

"First though, I have to set up a future scene. Run She-Human One, script plant one."

The Eye dollied to the top of the dresser. On it was a jewelry box and a framed picture of Rebecca and her parents. Below the photo was a tube of lipstick, some perfume, and a hairbrush. The Eye took the lipstick from off of the dresser, storing it in its cyborg body.

"Cut," said the Director. "Prepare the next setup."

"Move along, people" said the Production Manager. "Time is money. Make it happen."

Mr. Meow was not a happy cat. Not happy at all.

After being swatted by the backyard swing, he had run and hid in the woods beneath some bushes. The next thing he knew, something grabbed his tail and was dragging him backwards towards the house.

Meow struggled to escape. His paws flailed; the earth felt like sandpaper under his chest; he was in kitty hell. Reaching the backyard, Meow was towed across the thick lawn. His invisible captor swung him from side to side as though he were water skiing across a lake of grass.

Moments later, Meow was spun in a circle and flung through the air under the Bronco. Running out from under the vehicle, he struck an invisible barrier, hurting his nose. Meow scurried back under the middle of the Bronco; he hunkered down, confused and mewed.

The back door to the kitchen slowly opened. The hinges squeaked, but nothing was there. It was as though the door had moved by itself.

Meow's kitty senses were like a five alarm fire. Opening or closing, the back door always squeaked. It had bothered Meow many a time, as a family of mice lived under the house with their mouse hole near the doorway and they squeaked just like the door.

Meow hotly remembered the time that he was patiently hunting the furry little snacks, when he heard that telltale squeak. He had dashed around the corner and pounced, claws extended, right onto Mr. Senicki's calf and bit him. Mr. Senicki chased him all over the yard, yelling, while his wife and daughter laughed. A week later, Meow did it again. That time Mr. Senicki pursued him all through the house with a rolled-up newspaper.

With a half-ton automobile over his head for protection, Meow quieted down. The back door opened by itself again. The uptight Calico sensed that, like the mice, he was now the furry snack. Something was out there, something dangerous, something watching him this very moment. The disturbing sensation sent a chill up his kitty spine.

It made Mr. Meow mrow.

Glop recorded the cat's pitiable yowl, playing it backwards and forwards to amuse himself. As Glop and Iggy chuckled, Glop rummaged through the cat's primitive thoughts with a senso-probe. Glop learned of the mice living under the house. He thought it would be funny to grab a couple of the little creatures and dangle them under the bumper in front of the freaked-out cat. He was just about done writing a "mouse catch and dangle" computer program, when the Production Manager ordered him to send the camera into the house and go upstairs to the parents' bedroom.

Disappointed, Glop made the Eye slam the back door several times, making a lot of noise.

Mr. Meow's spine bent in a curve. He slunk out from under the vehicle, his body low to the ground. Glop shot a probe that struck his furry behind, lifting his rear end off the ground like he was a sack of potatoes. For a second the beleaguered kitty found himself walking on his front paws in a hand stand before he was flipped over in a circle, landing on his four feet.

Materializing in front of Meow, an Eye extended a three foot finger. Poking repeatedly at the cat's body, Meow swiped at it with his claws, always missing.

Using its three other arms, the Eye pinned Meow to the ground. The finger secreted a goopy substance which it smeared inside Meow's ear. To Meow the goo felt worse than being dunked in a barrel of water.

The hands let go. Meow streaked off into the woods where, rattled by the weird wet willie, he rubbed his ear against the rough ground for the next half hour.

This is even better than pleasure candy, Glop and Iggy blinked in secret code to each other. Laughing like silent maniacs, their eye stalks leaned against each other as the two cameramen shook with mirth.

Having satisfied their funny bones, Iggy and Glop maneuvered the Eyes into the house.

Mr. & Mrs. Senicki lay side by side in bed, unconscious. Medical probes hovered behind their heads, emitting a neural tranquilizing ray that kept the two humans in a coma. The two Eyes in the room were ready at their first camera positions.

"Action," the Director said.

The camera Eyes began recording.

The second Eye dollied from the foot of the bed towards Mr. Senicki's dresser. It opened the top drawer with its invisible mechanical hands, revealing socks and underwear, all neatly folded and stacked. Next it opened Mrs. Senicki's top dresser drawer, exposing her undergarments, also fastidiously put away.

The second Eye closed both the drawers.

"Cut," the Director said coolly. "Send the Eyes through the house for insert shots. Prepare the room for surgery. It's time to implant the Cortex Control Devices."

An hour later, medical force field projectors sealed the bedroom, making it sterile. A stack of med-probes sat in a rack on the floor. Mr. and Mrs. Senicki lay face up in bed; their arms by their sides; their bodies straight; completely unconscious.

The operation began in earnest.

In the spacecraft's hermetically sealed operating room, the Production Manager clicked a switch. Beside the surgery platform, two Surgical Robot Arms hummed with power. Wearing control gloves, he lifted the arms out of their cradles and entered the proper coordinates on his control panel.

Two transporter holes, the size of manhole covers, opened on the floor of the surgery platform. Dark, swirling tunnels, the holes connected the star ship to the Senicki's bedroom, separated by miles of atmosphere.

The holes would remain open during the entire surgical procedure.

Having established a permanent link, the Production Manager looked through a transport viewer. Seeing the Senicki's lying in bed, he plunged the Robot Arms into the whirling passageways.

Inside the parents' bedroom, the Robot Arms emerged through the inky black transport holes. They grasped some med-probes off of the rack, then placed them near the parents' heads and feet.

The Production Manager adjusted the med-probes anti-gravity output levels to suit the humans' body mass. The little units were very powerful. He didn't want his patients to levitate up so fast they would hit the ceiling. It had happened once a long time ago, crushing the actors' faces. The Director cancelled the production. He also put the Production Manager in cryo for a month as punishment. Although he knew he deserved it, he hadn't liked being conscious and frozen one bit.

Turning on the probes' anti-gravity rays, a high-pitched pinging sound filled the room. Mr. and Mrs. Senicki gently floated exactly thirty inches above the bed and halted, suspended in mid-air. Their bed sheet hung down below their elevated bodies, not touching the bed, making them appear like sleeping ghosts.

A Robot Arm grabbed a bio-scan probe off the rack. Placing it above Mr. Senicki's stomach, a red laser beam shot out, measuring a line from Mr. Senicki's head to his toes.

"Flight path established on male subject," the Production Manager said into the sound recorder. "Commencing scan."

Following the laser track, the probe drifted back and forth, scanning Mr. Senicki's body with a purplish light.

Satisfied with the results, the Production Manager turned a dial. "Initiating pre-operation sequence."

The room darkened; Mr. Senicki's internal organs became glowingly visible where the purplish light illuminated him.

Using several bio-probes, the Production Manager placed Mr. Senicki's internal body systems under his complete control, paying particular attention to the brain. The bedroom hummed with the sounds the probes made, from eerie energy warblings to low hums and high-pitched beeps.

Patient readout displays showed that the human was ready for the implant procedure. Now the delicate surgery could begin.

The Production Manager selected a sleek-looking device with several circles around its exterior. Putting it through the transporter hole, a Robot Arm held it two inches above Mr. Senicki's forehead, just above his nose.

"Starting implantation procedure with the male subject," the Production Manager said. "Turning dimensional scalpel on."

The device's circles moved up and down, producing a strange warbling sound. An iris opened up at the bottom, shooting a circle of reddish dimension shift rays onto the subject.

Mr. Senicki's skin began to bubble.

This was the dangerous part of the operation. The Production Manager had lost patients doing this before. He carefully shifted part of the forehead, skull and flesh into another dimension without interfering with the body's regular functions. Next, he would insert the Cortex Control Device, commonly referred to as the "jellyfish."

It was delicate work; he had to be careful. One time in the past, a tiny bubble of air had gotten into a patient's brain. The patient had horrible convulsions, and then thrown up on the scalpel and died.

A minute later, the Production Manager examined the dimensional hole in Mr. Senicki's head. He was pleased with what he saw.

"Inserting jellyfish inside the frontal sinus cavity."

Surrounded by the dimension rays, a tiny copper cylinder with hair-like tentacles swam like a tiny jellyfish down the reddish beam. The tentacles gracefully whipped back and forth as though the light were a liquid. Reaching Mr. Senicki's skin, the mind control device slowly sank into his flesh as though it were made of gelatin. Halfway down it met resistance and stopped … it was stuck and could move no further.

The Production Manager made an adjustment. The dimension rays made the forehead slightly less dense. The copper jellyfish submerged below the flesh until it reached a point just beneath the skull. Mr. Senicki's skin density was then returned to normal.

"Jellyfish in optimum position. Connecting memory access now."

Using a special tool that could manipulate objects under the skin, the Production

Manager teased out the jellyfish's tentacles. Certain ones he connected to the optic nerves. Others were guided deeper into the brain where memories were stored. The ends of the tentacles bifurcated repeatedly into millions of microscopic sized feelers, each one capable of transmitting – in full color, sound and emotion – a human memory into the star ship's media database. The tentacles made squishy noises as they wormed their way into Mr. Senicki's brain.

The Production Manager switched on a holo-monitor. Mr. Senicki appeared as a baby looking at himself in a mirror while his mother bathed him in a bathroom sink.

These new jellyfish work perfectly. Now the Director can really make A.R.T. Who would have thought that I, a mere class four intelligence, would become a licensed xenomorphic surgeon with a specialization in earthling biology. I am so very lucky. I always wanted to be in show business.

"Operation on the male subject complete," the Production Manager said into the recorder. "Starting implant procedure with the female."

His ears erect and facing forward, Mr. Meow crouched on a branch of a large oak tree observing the strange multicolored lights and sounds coming from his home. Although, being a cat, he could not see in color as humans do, being limited to shades of blue and green, Meow was so spellbound he wouldn't have noticed a coyote stalking him. His feline mind did not comprehend the terrible fate that lay in store for his masters, but as long as they kept feeding him, he probably would not even notice the difference.

Mr. and Mrs. Senicki lay in their bed, completely unconscious, comfortably ensconced between their bed sheets. The room had been returned to normal by the set decorator and his staff. The only clue that anything had happened at all was a small reddish spot on their foreheads which slowly faded away. Although their outer appearance was serene, the inner world of Herman and Alexandra Senicki was vastly different.

Staring at a data wall made of thirty-six images, the Director surfed through Herman's anterior cingulated cortex, where older memories were stored in the human brain. Applying sophisticated search criteria, the ship's computers explored trillions of memories seeking those of primal bonding between the Herman and his wife. An inspired idea had come to the Director when he was in a fit of anger after the Herman had defeated his ravish scenario. He would create the ultimate dramatic situation, showing the length and breadth of the horrors of love complete in all of its corrupting depravity.

"Come on," the Director said forcefully. "Where is it? Show me the memory money."

Observing three dozen memories at a time, the Director played them over and over, often fast forwarding the action, freezing it, or using slow motion as he saw fit. Not satisfied with anything thus far, he pushed a button and three dozen more memories came under his scrutiny. He did this again and again until ….

Passion … heat … undying love … devotion until death do us part … soul sharer … intense feelings enveloped the two lovers--husband and wife. Blood engorged penis and vagina. They made love. Heat flowed through the veins of their fevered copulation.

Ecstasy erupted from Herman's loins, thrilling him to the last cell and pore.

"Hah!" the Director said triumphantly. "I found it. Now I own you."

The Director took Herman's memory, fed it into the computer and gave it a hard TWIST!

Dripping with perspiration, his body glowing with pleasure, Herman gazed down at his special lover.

"I love you, Daddy," Rebecca said, her eyes worshiping her handsome father.

Herman replied with deep sincerity. "You are my shining star and I will never let you go."

Herman and Alexandra lay in bed facing the ceiling, their eyes jogging back and forth under closed eyelids, caught up in their dreams which were not their dreams.

The ship's computer recorded every moment of their coupling, every thought, every touch, every taste, every smell, every feeling that passed between them.

The Director roamed through their minds and would continue to explore and shape their memories throughout the night.

Tomorrow was not going to be just another day.

CHAPTER 8

A DAY TO REMEMBER

The early morning sun cast rays of warmth on the Senicki's country home. The air was crisp and lightly scented by the nearby pine tree forest. Sprightly classical music drifted from the living room throughout the house.

In the kitchen, Mrs. Senicki cooked breakfast on the stove. Apple–sausage was frying in one pan, while eggs kept their sunny sides up in another. Mr. Senicki sat at the table, his face buried in the local newspaper.

Humming to the music, Mrs. Senicki slipped the eggs onto a plate, followed by three sausage links and two slices of cantaloupe. She was in exceptional spirits this morning after making love to her husband last night. She believed she was the luckiest woman on Earth, her Herman meant so much to her.

What can I do to show how much I love him, she thought. *He deserves something special.*

She turned to where fresh strawberries were sitting in a bowl and put two of them on the plate.

Something special, she thought, looking at the food she had made for her husband.

Rebecca lay in her bed, asleep, dreaming she sat in the fifth row of a darkened theater during mime class at high school.

Sitting on the edge of the proscenium stage, a dark figure sat in a spotlight. It was Andy, dressed in a black tuxedo, white shirt, black bow tie and a beetle-black cape. He wore six white gloves, four of which covered the hands of four fake arms that stuck out from his ribcage. A fake pot belly protruded from under his shirt at the waist. His head bobbed up and down a bit as he slept.

He looks like a spider, Rebecca thought. *Neat.*

Sleepy music played on a boom box. Stretching his eyes wide open, the Andy-spider covered his mouth to stifle a yawn. Seeing the audience, he froze. A smile crept on his face; he surveyed the audience with interest.

The music became more festive in a mysterious sort of way. Reaching behind his back, he flipped his hands forward. As if by magic, a top hat popped open in one hand and a black cane appeared in the other. The top hat had two wire antennas with styrofoam balls stuck on the ends that bobbed to and fro.

Rebecca was delighted.

Standing up on the stage, the Andy-spider slipped the top hat on his head as the music changed. Rocking the cane in front of his chest, Andy danced while Frank Sinatra sang *Come Fly With Me.*

Come fly with me, let's fly, let's fly away
If you can use some exotic booze
There's a bar in far Bombay ...

Leaping off the stage, he soft-shoed by the audience, licking his lips, his eyes beaming. Rebecca got the distinct impression that the spectators were the Andy-spider's food and it was time for breakfast.

The music changed to *Hall of the Mountain King*, becoming energetic. Miming pulling a web out of his rear end, Andy coiled it into a lasso, swung it in circles like a cowboy and cast it over the crowd.

Rebecca and the class laughed.

The Andy-spider danced about like a happy maniac, flinging webs and tying up the audience while his antennae bobbed up and down. He stopped in front of Virginia, the most popular girl in the class. Reaching out with a white gloved hand, he touched her shoulder then put his finger into his mouth, smiling.

His smile flip flopped into a grimace.

Pulling his finger out of his mouth, he looked at it with great disdain. He frantically wiped it off on his pants behind his knee, trying to get the bad taste off of it.

The class hooted at Virginia as her eyes widened in shock.

Rebecca giggled.

Marching down the aisle, the Andy-Spider stopped. He slowly towards Todd, the football jock. Licking his finger, he slowly reached out to touch him.

Todd's body jerked wildly. He swung at the Andy-spider's hand. The Andy-spider jerked it out of the way and calmly stroked his hair, looking cool.

Rebecca and the whole class chuckled.

The music changed to a lively rumba beat. The Andy-spider jumped back on stage, hunching his shoulders up and down as the music possessed him. His six arms and pot belly bounced up and down as he danced further upstage.

Taking several quick steps, he slid on his knees towards the end of the stage. Bending backwards, he sprang to his feet and front flipped off the stage. Landing on his feet, he did a clever dance move.

The audience whooped and cheered.

He's so talented, thought Rebecca. *I could never do that.* She shifted her weight in her chair. The chair squeaked loudly.

The Andy-spider stopped dancing. Seeking the origin of the noise, he peered about the theatre. When his eyes rested on Rebecca, a hungry smile grew on his face.

"Oooooh," the class cooed.

Rebecca gasped as the Andy-spider jumped on top of an empty chair. Walking on top of the armrests, he stalked his way towards Rebecca. Three rows later, he towered above her, his antennas bobbing menacingly.

Sinatra sang as the Andy-spider bound Rebecca up with his web.

("It's perfect for a flying honeymoon they say"),

tied an imaginary bib around his neck,

("Come fly with me let's fly, let's fly"),

rubbed imaginary knives together, sharpening them,

("Pack up, let's fly away!"),

then mimed cutting off her head and ate it.

The entire class applauded.

Andy leaped off the chair, landing on the floor beside Rebecca. Covering their heads with his cape, he leaned in close to her ear. "It's a spider's idea of dinner theater," he whispered, then kissed her full on the lips.

His kiss was wet and scratchy and his breath smelled like rotting tuna.

Rebecca awoke from her dream.

Opening her eyes, she saw her cat licking her face with his rough, pink tongue. "Oh, Mr. Meow, your breath smells awful," she said pushing her kitty away.

Tumbling out of bed, Rebecca went straight to her closet. She grabbed a blouse and was buttoning it up when the phone rang.

"Hello," said Rebecca.

"Hi Rebecca. It's Andy."

Her hands nervously smoothed out her sleep-tangled hair. "Andy. Oh. Hi. How did you get my phone number?"

"Uh," said Andy. "You're mom gave it to my dad … he sort of left it in the living room … anyway, I was wondering … would you like to go bike riding to the lake today?"

"Bike riding? Well, sure. I mean, I'm sure it will be okay with Mom and Dad."

"Can you be at the junction in about an hour?"

"The junction? Sure."

"That's great. I'll meet you there."

The phone went dead in Rebecca's ear, but her feelings came very much alive. She finished buttoning her blouse and went to her dresser to put on some lipstick.

It wasn't there.

She looked around, but could not find it, so she grabbed her hairbrush and brushed her hair.

Mrs. Senicki carried the strangest breakfast plate ever seen by man. The food had been transferred to a large oval platter and rearranged to look like it was having sex. At the top, two eggs were positioned like female breasts with large black olives for nipples. In the middle, two cantaloupe slices created an oval vagina. Sprigs of fresh-cut parsley formed a bright green lawn at its peak. At the plate's bottom, the first of three penile sausages began, garnished by two plump red strawberry balls. The rest of the rigid meat headed north, stopping below the sexy "O" of fruit. A dollop of sour cream was artfully splashed above it.

Mrs. Senicki hummed as she set the plate down on the breakfast table in front of her newspaper-reading husband. She was about to say, "Breakfast, dear" when Rebecca burst into the kitchen, glowing with excitement.

"Mother," Rebecca said. "Andy asked me to go bike riding with him today. May I?"

"Rebecca, you scared me," said Mrs. Senicki.

"I'm sorry, Mother. May I go?"

"Without a chaperone?" said Mrs. Senicki, covering her heart with her hand.

"Oh, mother," protested Rebecca, clenching her hands.

"Ask your father," said Mrs. Senicki. "Maybe he will escort you."

Rebecca hurried towards the table. "Father, can I go bike riding with Andy Barulich?"

Herman hid behind the morning newspaper. The classical music did nothing to cheer him. He had only one thing on his mind.

Did I make love to my own daughter last night?

He desperately wanted to deny it, but the memories were so real, not like a dream at all. He could see her, smell her, touch her, even taste her amorous lips.

His elbow flinched on the table, knocking the silverware several inches away. *No! It can't be. It must not be. Such thoughts are the work of the devil.*

The disturbing recollections made Herman tremble. After conquering his blasphemous desire in the hallway, after bleeding through his nose in the sink, had he awakened in the middle of the night, gone to Rebecca's room and ravished her? Even worse than his blasphemous crime was the strong perception that she wanted him to do so. Surely, he was wrong about that. Such a thing was unthinkable.

Am I a Christian man or a monster? Holy father help me see the light.

"Father, can I go bike riding with Andy Barulich?" he heard Rebecca say beyond his upright newspaper.

The Director forced Herman to imagine he was back in bed with his daughter hearing her say, "I love you, daddy." Herman stifled a gasp of horror. It escaped as a grunt instead.

Rebecca took the sound as a sign of approval. She turned to her mother and smiled.

"Oh, all right, I guess so," her mother said, relenting. "Go on your bike ride with Andy."

Smiling and rocking on her heels, Rebecca rushed towards the back door.

"Rebecca Senicki!" her mother snapped.

Rebecca came to a halt. "What?"

"You sit right down and have your breakfast. No daughter of mine is going chasing after a boy on an empty stomach. The very idea."

Sighing, Rebecca sat down at the table and hurriedly poured herself a bowl of cereal and some milk to which her mother added some slices of a banana.

Sitting down opposite her daughter, Mrs. Senicki stared at the lusty plate of food in front of her husband. Reaching out with a finger, she idly stroked a sausage.

Herman hid behind the newspaper while his wife and daughter crunched, slurped, chomped, chewed, gulped, and devoured their meals. The obnoxious noises made him feel like they were accusing him of sinfulness. Herman loathed himself; he wanted to leave; he started to rise.

He couldn't move.

Through the Cortex Control Device the Director paralyzed the Herman's body, forcing him to sit in the chair. His plan was just getting started and he was taking no chances. "No inferior intelligence is going ruin my story line for the second time," the Director said. "Sit still and suffer, you stupid actor. Do what your director tells you to do."

The Director wanted the two young ones to meet and fall in love, so they would get disgustingly emotional before he killed them. To that end, he had probes project images of each other in their minds all night long as they slept. The death of criminal lovers was always a treat for Those Who Watch. It was considered socially appropriate homicide.

"I have big plans," said the Director. "The actors must play their parts … and die."

Rebecca set down her milk glass and got up from the table to go on her date with Andy. Cruising around behind her dad, she gave him a quick peck on the back of his neck.

"Thank you, Daddy," she said, rushing towards the back door.

The touch of his daughter's lips sent a shockwave down Herman's spine. Her simple actions--footsteps clattering across the kitchen floor, twisting the doorknob, the door shutting--were like kettle drums pounding in his guilt-ridden ears.

I can't stand it any more! Herman thought.

The Director released his control over Herman.

Herman yanked the newspaper down. Whirling around, he looked out the window, seeing Rebecca ride her bike down the driveway. He fought the urge to chase after her; beads of sweat dotted his brow.

Spinning away from the window, Herman found himself facing his wife.

Batting her eyelashes, Alexandra slowly bit down on a red, ripe strawberry, and with her little finger rubbed the succulent juice around her lips.

Herman couldn't bear her coquettishness. Lowering his gaze to the table, he saw the food plate was nearly empty. Only smears of egg yolk, cantaloupe rinds and bits of parsley remained.

Through the Cortex Control Device, the Director forced Herman to see all the sexy food. As if by magic, it materialize before his astounded eyes--the sausage penis, the strawberry balls, the cantaloupe vagina, and the parsley pubic hair. Unwanted feelings of pleasure electrified his body. He thought he was losing his mind. When his daughter's voice whispered, "I love you, daddy," the sausage spurted a wad of sour cream across the vaginal fruit.

Herman bolted for the backyard door.

Alexandra wondered why Herman was acting so strange. Was he sick? Was he worried about something? She made his breakfast look like sex. Did she do something wrong?

"Babushka, where are you going?" said Alexandra.

"To work," replied Herman, opening the back door.

"But it's Sunday."

"I have to finish an order," said Herman, rushing outside.

Alexandra darted to the door. "But you're a taxidermist," she shouted as he rapidly crossed the yard. "Can't they wait until tomorrow for you to stuff a dead animal?"

Herman hustled into the Bronco, started the engine and drove off in a dust-raising rush.

Alexandra stood in the doorway, feeling abandoned.

"But its Sunday," she said, frowning. "Aren't we going to church together?"

Two thin bicycle tires spun in endless circles, kicking up dirt along a backwoods country road. Rebecca pedaled towards the crossroads, excited to meet Andy on their first date. The forest and sunny weather were especially lovely to her this morning. Romance took the colors and sounds of the world and amplified them to her senses.

As the road curved to her left, she shifted her weight and thought about boys. She had never had a real boyfriend before. Sure, lots of guys had liked her, but because her parents were so strict she had never gone out on a date without an adult present. Some girls in high school were practically married. At 18-years-old she was feeling like an old maid.

Then her father gave her *permission* to go by herself. It made bicycling four miles to meet Andy irrelevant--she practically flew there.

Powered by joy, her feet pedaled on.

The junction was where one of the side roads leading out of Hot Tub intersected with two other roads, one of which led to a lake. It was the way Rebecca and her mother drove each morning to high school before she graduated last spring. The intersection was bordered by ten foot high hills, forming steep mini-cliffs. Rebecca stopped her bike at the edge of one. Blocking out the sun with one of her hands, she looked about for Andy.

Something huge leapt off the hilltop, flying over the top of her head. It landed hard, skidding to a halt ten yards away. Rebecca thought it was a mountain lion, as there had been warnings about town that one had been seen in the area.

What she saw was definitely not a mountain lion.

It had an enormous pointy nose, weird twisting antlers and spongy elephant-like ears. Its face was blockish. Two shocks of yellow hair, like stiff yarn, stuck out on its sides, swaying in the gentle breeze. Its lips looked like large red erasers. Rabbit-like buck teeth hung down from its upper lip, giving it a cheerful, but goofy-looking expression.

Its shirt appeared to be made of icicles.

Rebecca stared at the freakish thing. Were the icicles made out of a colored bed sheet? It waved to her with an enormous white plastic hand, like a Disneyland character on parade. The cape it wore made it look hunchbacked. A small step stool was bungie corded to its chest.

Undoing the bungee cord, the Freak placed the step stool on the ground and stood upon it. It then released the bunched up fabric about its waist which unfurled, revealing long striped pants. As the pants struck the ground, two large, brightly colored clown shoes appeared attached to the pants legs' bottom.

The monstrous thing was now seven feet tall.

Rebecca saw sunlight reflect off of some fish line that connected its hands to its knees. Raising a hand, it lifted a leg off the ground.

It's a giant … freaky … monster puppet … thing.

The Freak crossed its arms as if impatient. It's kitschy shoes criss-crossed as well. It waved its right hand up and down, its right shoe moving along with it, then alternated with its left hand and shoe. It looked like it was either trying to climb an invisible rock wall or had to go to the bathroom something fierce.

"Andy?" Rebecca guessed.

"Nay, fair daughter of Senicki," the deformed Freak said in a goofy, high-pitched voice. "I am the mighty frost giant, Schnozola. I have smelled my way to you and will carry you off as plunder to my giant ice castle. There you will live in a large icicle where you may chill out and be frigid. Observe."

Schnozola inhaled and exhaled several times. Its rubber nose inflated and deflated like air being forced in and out of a balloon. On the last inhalation, the nose shrunk in on itself so far it twisted like a pretzel and stuck in that position.

"Whoops," Schnozola said, his rubber lips not moving. He tried to untwist his nose to normal again by snorting air into it and flicking it with one of its huge, white fingers.

Rebecca laughed to herself. *This is like the spider he did in mime class. This is cool.*

She playfully jumped into the moment. "Thou thinkest most stinkest, oh foul frost-faced fiend. For I would rather hang out with a box of granola, than such a Schnozola as thee. What sayest thou to that?"

Schnozola balled a fist under his chin. He lifted his other hand and scratched the top of his head. The act raised the string-connected foot off the ground making him look like he was trying to think while standing on one leg.

Rebecca planted her fists on her hips. "I'm waiting, oh terrible giant. What will you do since I'm defiant?"

Schnozola scratched behind his elephant-like ear. The ear came off, stuck to his hand.

Rebecca laughed out loud. "You big silly goof. How do you expect to catch me if you're falling apart?"

Schnozola's eyes rocked back and forth. Thrusting the big ear towards her, he said, "Talk to the hand."

On top of a nearby hill, two hands parted the bushes. The Mysterious Man stared down at the playful duo. The bracelet on his wrist hummed in alarm.

"Too close," he whispered to himself. He knew that *They* were around. The last thing he wanted in the world was to have *Them* find him.

The Mysterious Man pointed the bracelet like a radar detector, quickly determining what direction *They* were coming from. "He who fights and runs away lives to fight another day," he nervously whispered. Quietly closing the bushes, he snuck off in the opposite direction.

In the Senicki living room, an aria from *Pagliacci* played on the record player. Enjoying the music, Alexandra danced as she tossed dirty clothing into a laundry basket.

Opera is so grand, Alexandra thought, picking her husband's pants up off of the floor and pirouetting. *So emotional. So thrilling.*

She tossed the trousers into the basket, hefted it up and walked towards the door. Her husband's shirt lay on the floor under the dresser, the one she had tossed there last night before they made love. Setting the basket down, Alexandra scooped up the shirt. She recalled scraping Herman's neck lightly with her fingernails, knowing how that always excited him. Holding the shirt up to her nose, she inhaled her husband's scent. *Oh, Herman, you are such a wonderful lover.*

A bit of grime was on the collar.

How do men get such dirty necks? Alexandra thought. *You'd think they put it there on purpose.*

Tossing the shirt on top of the basket, Alexandra headed towards the laundry room. The opera had reached the part where a jealous Pagliacci sang as he stabbed his wife and her lover to death on the Opera house stage.

Such passion. Thank goodness real life isn't like that. Imagine if people went around killing each other over love betrayed.

Stirred by the riveting music, Alexandra sang along with the opera's murderer with gusto. As she descended the stairs with the laundry, an invisible Eye recorded her performance.

A hungry-eyed cougar stared at a wild turkey. A large brown bear raised up on its hind legs in front of a mule-tailed deer. An owl, a weasel and a jackalope (a rabbit with horns) looked passively at the nearby predators. They all had one thing in common – they were all dead.

Herman carried the last animal exhibit outside his taxidermy shop. He was not normally open on Sunday, but he wanted to be alone, away from Alexandra. He needed time to think; he needed time to pray.

"Forgive me, Lord, for I am a sinner."

Setting down a stuffed owl, Herman went back inside his taxidermy shop. Closing the door behind him, he dragged his feet towards his desk and sat down, surrounded by stuffed animals. On the wall beside him, a framed photograph of his family hung with other objects – a riding crop, a horse-hair whip, a horse halter.

Herman rubbed his head with his fingers. *What am I going to do? In the eyes of God I am a blasphemous sinner.*

"Herman," the picture whispered.

Herman's head snapped towards the photo; he was standing in-between his wife and daughter. The picture changed into two distinct images. In the first, Alexandra kissed him on the cheek. In the second, Rebecca pressed her lips to his face. The images jumped back and forth, from wife to daughter, over and over, like a metronome of sin. Herman felt their heated desire. Their passionate kisses burned his skin.

He shut his eyes, blocking out the picture, worried that he was going crazy. Such thoughts as these were obscene.

Lord. Save me from myself. I beg you or I am lost.

Herman shut his eyes tight. He concentrated on seeing the picture the way it was supposed to be – just a family photo. Praying for forgiveness, he submitted to the Lord's judgment.

He opened his eyes.

The picture was different, but not the way he wanted it to be. When Rebecca kissed him his face was joyous; when Alexandra kissed him, his face screwed up in disgust.

Shocked by the terrible images, Herman plunged backwards on top of his desk knocking a coffee cup filled with pens over the edge and sliding a stuffed squirrel into a corner.

"Stop it," Herman shouted at the photo. "I repent my sin. I cannot bear it any longer. Stop it."

Herman charged at the wall, yanking the short horse-hair whip off of a nail. He raised it to lash out at the sacrilegious picture.

The photo looked completely normal.

Sweat rolled off Herman's forehead; his eyes were glassy; his mind bewildered. He flopped down in a chair, buried his head in his hands and moaned.

With huge, lifeless eyes, the stuffed squirrel gaped at the weeping man, its tiny hands in front of its face.

It appeared to be praying for him.

Andy and Rebecca bicycled past a grove of oak trees, coming to a hillside covered by large dirt-covered rocks. Andy stopped his bicycle and pointed North.

"Check it out," said Andy.

Rebecca looked over the edge of the road; a hundred yards below them was a lake. It was not a large lake, nor did it have any commercial development. There were no boat rides or hot dog stands, no picnic tables or statues and no playground. Its natural simplicity was the source of its true beauty.

"Andy, it's charming," Rebecca said, surveying the deep blue water whose surface reflected puffy clouds in the sky. Flying ducks landed in the water, creating ripples; the mirrored clouds undulated. "I knew it existed," Rebecca said. "But I've never been here before. It's like a slice of heaven."

"Not many people come up here," replied Andy, taking off his frost giant costume and stuffing it in his backpack. "Which isn't surprising since not that many people live around here anyway. But I like it."

"I love it," Rebecca said, smiling.

Setting her bike on the ground, Rebecca ambled across the large rocks. Reaching one large enough for the both of them, she sat down and took in the view.

Forcing his monster costume into his backpack, a piece of it tore off in his hand. Andy tied it to his bicycle's handlebar, then lay his bike down and rushed off to join her.

Sitting beside her, he brushed a small rock away with a sweep of his hand. Andy admired the lake's beauty, then casually turned his head to admire the beauty sitting beside him.

Their eyes connected with each other. Andy felt himself tingle inside.

A noise attracted Rebecca's attention. A deer wandered off deeper into the woods. After the deer departed, Rebecca turned back towards Andy. He was still gazing at her.

Rebecca blushed.

Andy blushed, too.

"Are you happy living here?" said Andy.

"Why do you ask?" Rebecca replied.

Andy finger-painted in the dirt. He wanted to explain himself to Rebecca, but didn't want her to think he was a crybaby. He had lived in Hot Tub for seven years, since he was 13, after his parents moved to the United States from Germany. At first, he did not speak English very well. The kids in middle school teased him mercilessly, calling him names like Krout-mouth and Nazi boy. Andy worked hard to get rid of his German accent. He eventually succeeded, but it made him shy, a condition he wanted to change.

"Hot Tub seems to be," he stammered, "I don't know … small. Life here is … you know … small." He shrugged his shoulders and gazed at the lake.

Rebecca observed Andy withdraw into himself. "I don't mind it at all. Why? Do you feel small living here?"

Andy rocked his head from side to side. "My first semester in college, it was like the whole world opened up to me." He suddenly felt overwhelmed. "I du-don't want to be a bu-butcher in a small town mu-my entire life," he stuttered. "I wa-want mu-my life to bu-be … larger."

"So don't be a butcher," Rebecca said ignoring his stuttering. "Be whatever you want to be."

"Bu-but that's all I know how to do," Andy muttered gloomily. He flicked a small stone away with his middle finger. "Really, that's it." He brushed away his dirt doodles and bowed his head low.

Rebecca reached out and touched his arm. "Don't get down on yourself, Andy. Be positive. Have faith that things will work out the way they should. Do you know what else you'd like to do?"

Andy shook his head. "No. Not really," he confessed, glad he finally stopped stuttering. "Maybe that's my problem. Maybe I'm just a hopeless case." He sighed.

Rebecca licked her upper lip; the kidding urge grew within her. "Yeah, that must be it. Poor hopeless Andy. So wretched, so lost."

Andy caught her playful tone and decided to play along. "That poor guy. Such a waste of talent."

"Destined to never amount to anything," Rebecca teased.

"What will become of him?" Andy said.

"A butcher for life," Rebecca replied.

"Forever cutting up dead animals for people to chomp on," Andy sighed. "Chop, chop, chop … chomp, chomp, chomp … yeah."

"Yeah," Rebecca sighed back. "A regular Pagliacci. Woe is he."

Andy placed his hand over his heart as his imagination got the better of him. He thought of the tragic opera *Pagliacci*, the story of a wandering troupe of performers whose leader (Canio), plays a clown named Pagliacci in the troupe's comedy production. Canio discovers his wife (Nedda), has been having an affair with another man (Silvio). During the performance, Pagliacci stabs his wife and her lover on stage, then declares "The comedy is over."

Andy improvised his own lyrics to Pagliacci's famous music theme:

"I'm a butcher's son.

I chop up meat all day long.

I chop, chop, chop, chop.

So hungry people can chomp, chomp, chomp."

Rebecca sang the last "chomp" with him. They held the final note until it gently faded away. Andy tapped his chest with a clenched fist, pretending to be overcome with emotion.

Rebecca giggled and clapped her hands. *Bravo, Pagliacci. Bravo.*

Andy felt a rush of excitement. "How do you do that?"

"Do what?"

"Bring out the best in me."

Rebecca smiled. "That's what being positive is all about, silly."

Tucking her long brown hair behind her ear, she playfully poked her finger into his shoulder. "So, do you like living in a small town?"

"It's okay, I guess," Andy said, lowering his head. He didn't feel like talking about what was really bothering him any more. Instead, he drew the top half of a circle in the soil with his finger and lamely stared at it.

Rebecca poked two holes in the ground above the half circle and drew a big circle around everything, creating an unhappy face. Andy stared at the sad face in the dirt.

"He looks kind of familiar," Rebecca teased. "I know. It's your twin brother, Sad Face. He looks just like you, don't you think?"

Andy felt Rebecca's barb sink in. *Okay, I'm not being positive,* he thought.

Placing her hand upon his shoulder, Rebecca leaned close to his ear. "Got you, again, clowny." She wagged her finger at him.

Andy saw her finger move back and forth, just like it did last night after their families had had dinner together.

Bad boy, the finger seemed to say.

Sucking his cheeks between his teeth, Andy looked at Sad Face and smiled. Rebecca caught him in a lie. Life in Hot Tub was anything but okay. The ducks on the lake quacked boldly. Andy decided to tell Rebecca the truth.

"It's just that most people around here would rather sit on hot coals than use their imagination," he protested, chucking a pebble underhanded. "It gets so boring. I mean, there's so much more to who I am but no one likes it when I let it out."

Andy grabbed a fistful of dirt and let it run through his fingers. He thought about telling Rebecca about the Munchkins, but decided not to. *No sense in proving I'm crazy.*

"I loved your spider in mime class," said Rebecca.

"You did?"

She nodded. "Maybe you could join a mime troop. I hear there's some in San Francisco."

Andy frowned, creating two deep furrows between his eyebrows. The thought of being a professional mime intrigued him. He had never thought of it that way before. But San Francisco was so far away the idea seemed hopeless. *I don't even have enough money to replace my bicycle tires if they go bad. I may as well try and peddle my bike to the moon.*

He sighed. Everything he wanted seemed to be impossible. "I guess I am a Pagliacci … a hopeless clown … yeah." He leaned back on an elbow, staring blankly at the sky. "My destiny is to serve as an example of a failure to others … yeah."

Rebecca was determined to cheer him up. She had her own little scheme and she hatched it. "Well, Pagliacci. I'm positive about one thing," she said, crumbling some dry leaves in her hand, breaking them up into smaller pieces.

"What?" Andy asked.

"That I can get to the lake before you can." Giggling, she pushed him over and ran towards the bicycles, showering him with the broken leaves.

"Hey!" Andy yelled, falling on his back, getting leaves in his face. "That's not fair."

Laughing, Rebecca skipped across the rocks. When she got to the bicycles she saw a leaf-covered branch lying on the ground. She thought it would look marvelous stuck in-between Andy's tire spokes. So she put it there.

When Andy arrived, she had a thirty foot head start.

Not for long, he promised to himself, brushing bits of leaves out of his hair. He picked up his bike and pushed it forward, intending to do his run-and-leap trick. He would catch up with her in a hurry. He had barely gone a foot when the branch hit the frame, jamming the wheel. With his rear wheel frozen, Andy's tire plowed into the soil. Glancing down, he saw the stuck branch.

"Hey, you cheat!" he shouted.

"Positively!" Rebecca yelled back over her shoulder as she cycled down the road.

"I'll get you for this!" Andy said, grinning broadly. He wrestled the stick in the wheel, barely keeping himself from laughing, he felt so good inside. "You'll be sorry," he yelled.

"Start peddling, clown boy!" Rebecca shouted back.

Andy cleared the stick from his wheel spokes. He wanted comedy revenge. Raising his head, he yelled like Tarzan summoning the elephants to create a stampede.

Pretending an ape-raised white man was chasing after her, Rebecca squealed with joy; she pedaled faster.

Andy pushed the bike forward. He did his run-and-leap trick. Pumping the pedals hard, he yelled again like Tarzan and chased after her down the dirt road.

Life with Rebecca was such fun.

Filming from a within parallel dimension, an invisible Eye positioned itself inside the washing machine. Through the washer's opening only the bright ceiling could be seen surrounded by the dark interior. The Eye focused up towards the round opening as Mrs. Senicki put the laundry basket down on the counter. It recorded Mrs. Senicki tossing white socks and underwear inside, followed by undershirts and pillowcases. A white bed sheet plopped inside, giving its vision a see-through, gauzy look. It was soon followed by several bath towels which blocked its view completely. The Eye materialized a thin arm and pushed the obstructions aside so it could see clearly.

The Eye waited … and waited … and waited for Mrs. Senicki's face to appear.

Mrs. Senicki held her husband's white shirt, the one she had taken from his hands and tossed to the floor before they made love last night; the one that, moments ago, had some dirt upon the collar.

Now she saw lipstick on that very same collar--lipstick in the shape of a female's kiss.

How did this get here? This is not my lipstick.

Through the device implanted in her forehead, the Director executed a computer program that altered Mrs. Senicki's memories. He compelled her to remember that the lipstick on her husband's collar was not a color that she wore, that the bed sheets smelled like sex, but they had not made love last night. The Director made Mrs. Senicki believe that her husband had made love to another woman in their marriage bed.

Pain welled up inside her gut. Her insides burned with a jealous fire.

She crammed the hated shirt into the washing machine, poured the detergent inside and slammed the door shut, enveloping the Eye in total darkness.

Iggy switched the camera to z-ray mode with a red/orange filter; circuits flashed over to the new setting. Mrs. Senicki burst into view on the holographic display as a riot of orange and red wavelengths. Pulsing and shifting in intensity, Mrs. Senicki banged her multi-hued fists on top of the machine. An orange hand pushed the start button, then flew to her reddish face as she began to cry.

As the Eye recorded her actions, streams of bluish light gushed into the washing machine, ostensibly flooding the compartment with the torrents of her watery grief.

Shh-takkk!

With indifference of the dead, the stuffed squirrel watched Mr. Senicki lash himself with the horse hair whip. Droplets of perspiration ran off his brow; his armpits and chest soaked his shirt with sweat.

I have sinned against God. I must be punished.

The words echoed in his brain like the skipping of a broken record and in-between each skip his memory flipped back to the passion he had shared with Rebecca.

The Director was ready for Herman. "Now I'm really going to mess with your head." He executed a special effects program which he had ordered to be created by the effects staff last night.

"This is how an artist does it. Now give me a proper performance."

Shame! Guilt! Blasphemy!

Herman stood on the precipice of damnation and watched in horror as an avalanche crashed down the mountain of heaven towards him. He realized the pounding snow was the wrath of God, white in its purity and relentless in its condemnation of his sacrilegious deed with his child. His bones quaked; his Christian faith condemned him. Such wickedness deserved no mercy.

A current of hot air rose behind him. Turning, Herman looked over the edge of the cliff. An inferno raged far below him, a volcanic pit of sin that had no bottom. Snow blew over the cliff's edge, turning into steam. It layered the air with a misty fog that evaporated almost as quickly as it formed.

An image swam beyond the haze, surrounded by blistering hellfire.

It was Rebecca.

Her face looked like a siren, with large, sensual eyes and ruby red lips that glistened with heated desire. A vibrant red dress flowed around her, revealing flashes of her silky skin. Below her the shapes of men and women grappled together. Moaning in pleasure and pain, they floated in an endless orgy, surrounded by whips of flames that lashed at their impassioned flesh.

"Join me forever" Rebecca called out, extending her arms towards her father as a whip of fire cracked beside her.

Herman's throat tightened. She was his shining star, so aching beautiful. He wanted to leap off the edge, to spend eternity in her arms, to escape God's moral justice.

But what about his soul? Was it better to be destroyed by God with the hope of redemption, or to embrace everlasting perdition with the woman he loved?

Herman had time for one last act. He must choose and choose now forever.

Sinking to his knees, he prayed for forgiveness as ten thousand tons of rampaging snow swept over him, ripping his flesh from his bones.

Shh-takkk!

The whip sang on Herman's back for the umpteenth time. Blood seeped out of his flesh, staining the cotton shirt he wore with narrow streaks of crimson. Herman grimaced in pain, but the whip continued to sing its song of anguish and punishment.

Rapture and wrath, rapture and wrath, Herman see-sawed his way through rapture and wrath.

The Director forced Herman to relive each experience, switching back and forth between making love to his daughter and the avalanche of God's fury, capturing him from several different camera angles so he would have plenty of coverage for editing purposes later on.

This footage is incredible! the Director thought. *The abstract minds of these dumb creatures is so much better than unmotivated special effects. This is rich character development. By the time I'm through with the Herman his emotions will be so violent it will prove why family ties and religion are rightfully abolished by planetary law.*

The Director was proud of his experimental footage. If he had been a rooster he would have crowed. Prior to this production, all he could do was use the cortical implants to change what the actors saw. By applying the new technology in this unique way, he could access the casts' real life experiences, their ego, their religious morality, anything he wanted. He could manipulate them for the sake of A.R.T. He had discovered fertile new ground for the cinematic experience. He would make sure that he got all the credit for it and not that idiot Producer or his ridiculous story committee.

I will call it memory-vision. It will make me rich and famous.

Even so, the Herman was still resisting him. He should have jumped into the flaming void after the sexy she-daughter, not surrender himself to some mystical deity who was about to destroy him. The female was a tangible biological desire. How could a primitive class 2 intelligence resist sex connected to love?

"The Herman is illogical," concluded the Director. "He rejects immediate gratification for some abstract ethereal "soul' controlled by a so-called omnipotent being who doesn't directly talk to him, but punishes him if he misbehaves. Humans are so childish. What's the good of being created in a deity's image if the deity doesn't teach you anything scientifically relevant? God is merely an invisible friend for adults. Still, humans are well known for being insecure and irrational. That's why they make such good actors. This planet is filled with incredible stories if one has the genius to discover them … which I certainly do."

The Director considered connecting the Herman to the primal father-daughter protection instinct, but it was so cliché. He had used it in A.R.T. shows before. Still, it was very powerful if used correctly …. He took a deep breath and cracked his knuckles … searching … searching … searching.

He wanted something fresh … something genuine … something *superbulous*. He had an idea on the tip of his tongue, but it kept itself hidden from his thoughts. He knew that a hunch was creativity trying to tell you something.

He kept on listening to the darkness.

An idea sprang into the light. The Director ran a search through the Herman's religious memories. He discovered a revered moral teaching.

For God so loved the world that he gave it his only begotten son, that whoever should believe in him should not perish, but have eternal life forever.

"With root behavior like this it's no wonder human beings are so screwed up."

He rewrote the saying, cementing it back in the Herman's mind.

For God so loved the Herman that he gave him the woman Rebecca, so that by platonically loving her and protecting her soul the Herman should not perish, but have eternal life in heaven with her and God forever.

It was a sensational production concept – combining obsessive love and religion. It should produce some unique behavior. He would use it to motivate the Herman to kill his wife and the Andy. Yes … he liked it.

It would be fresh.

The Director smiled. His masterpiece was coming together. Everything was shaping up nicely.

Time to whip the Alexandra into a similar emotional frenzy.

Sunlight filtered through the Senicki's bedroom window, filling it with a cheerful warmth. Alexandra stood before her dresser. She felt anything but cheerful. She slid open her top dresser drawer. There was plenty of room inside it to store her clean clothes. A little block of cedar sat in the middle to ensure her laundry would smell fresh. With great care, she placed her folded clothes exactly where they ought to be – socks on the left, undergarments on the right. Everything had its proper place and she saw to it that everything was returned to it just so.

When she opened the top drawer to her husband's dresser, she crammed his garments into the open space, bunching them haphazardly together. She did not care one bit whether they were neatly folded or put in their proper place.

Where was his proper place when he took up with that woman, that whore! When I find out who the slut is I'll butcher them both.

The bunched up laundry overstuffed the drawer. A sock hung over the drawer's edge, dangling towards the carpet.

Alexandra's head began to buzz.

Looking at her bed, her husband appeared like a ghost; he was making love to a strange woman. It was as though it was happening right in front of her.

Alexandra hated the mystery woman's sensuous curves, her creamy skin. She strained to see her face, but somehow could not do so. Herman rolled off of the woman's firm body, having spent his passion. His flaccid penis looked as droopy as the sock before her.

The ghostly lovers vanished.

Alexandra slammed the dresser drawer shut.

The droopy sock got pinned between the two pieces of wood. The force of shutting the drawer inflated it upright. It seemed erect with vitality, mere inches away from her astonished face.

Screeching, Alexandra bit the rigid sock with her teeth. She tore it out of the drawer, then threw at the floor and stomped on it. The sock became limp and lifeless.

She rejoiced at the sight.

Serves him right! Alexandra thought, breathing hoarsely. *I should cut it off with a knife and serve it to him for dinner, that filthy man … he deserves it.*

Alexandra's chest heaved from exertion. Her rage died down, but her eyes bore a crazed appearance. Her vengeance could only take this particular form at this particular time, but a voice inside her told that the rest would come later … the voice promised revenge.

Alexandra could hardly wait.

Riding her bicycle ahead of Andy, Rebecca reached the lake. Laughing gaily, she laid her bike down, then took a scarf from around her neck. As Andy approached, she waved it like the checkered flag at a car race.

Seeing the gyrating scarf, Andy increased his speed. His legs pumped like pistons as he sped towards her finish line.

Rebecca cheered as Andy whipped by her, feeling a rush of air on her face.

Andy didn't stop, but rode right into the lake. The front tire flung water high into the air; the bike came to a sudden halt and flipped over. Andy did a somersault, landing in the lake with a great big splash, getting himself and his backpack wet.

Rebecca stopped laughing. She ran to the water's edge. "Andy. Are you hurt?"

Andy stood up in the water, which came halfway up to his knees. He flung out his arms and smiled.

"I win!" he declared.

Rebecca crossed her arms and frowned. "And how do you figure that?"

"You said the race was to the lake, right?"

Rebecca nodded.

"Well," said Andy, "you only made it *beside* the lake."

Staring at him through thin slitted eyes, Rebecca pursed her lips and put her hands firmly on her hips.

"I win," said Andy, grinning sheepishly.

Later that morning, the forest seemed filled with life. Tall trees stretched to the sky, their branches heavily laden with leaves which swayed in the light wind like waving hands. Wearing his Schnozola the giant costume, Andy sat on a low tree limb and had a sword fight with Rebecca. Using sticks for swords and frisbees for shields, they battled and joked around in a playful Norse god opera war.

Rebecca was the powerful Valkyrie warrior, Brunhilde, from the Wagner Ring Cycle operas, her face fiercely painted with theatrical makeup that Andy had brought with him. Her Tupperware helmet bristled with twigs and broad leaves crazy glued to its surface and tied to her head with some old shoelaces.

Andy kicked at Rebecca with his giant puppet feet; Rebecca leapt to the side. Howling, she ran between his legs, poking his back with her wooden weapon. Andy yelped in facetious pain. Shimmying off the tree, he landed standing up. The legs of his monster costume appeared to stretch away from his monster knees to where his giant shoes lay several feet away.

"You broke my legs," he protested, speaking in his dim-witted Schnozola voice. "How am I supposed to fight you if I can't walk?"

"Die, filthy beast," Rebecca said, raising her sword-stick to smite him. "Bother mortal men no more with your goofy monster voice."

Before Rebecca could stab him, Schnozola spoke quickly. "What if I bought you ice cream? Would that change your mind about stabbing me?"

"What flavor?" Rebecca said coolly.

"Rocky road," Schnozola blurted.

"Rocky Road?" said Rebecca, lowering her sword arm.

Schnozola crossed his arms smugly and chuckled, figuring his bribe had worked.

"Butter pecan!" yelled Rebecca, thrusting her mighty sword-stick under Schnozola's armpit. "Rocky road is for demons and high school principals."

Schnozola stared at the sword-stick under his arm pit. "Methinks I have been stabbed most ouchedly." Twisting his body, he fell on his back, his head landing in-between his giant clown shoes.

Rebecca stood over her fallen enemy, her sword-stick aimed at his putrid heart. "You're lousy at bribes, Schnoz-baby. What are your final words I send you back to the monster underworld?"

Schnozola glanced at his giant shoes, impossibly located at the top of his head. "I'm not a monster," he said tearfully. "I'm just a nice guy with a really big nose and a bad complexion and a spongy ear that sometimes falls off."

Rebecca waved her sword-stick over his chest. "That sounds so sad I almost feel like I should spare your life. Hurry up. Convince me."

Schnozola made up his best excuses. "Well, my mother told me it's because as a boy I ate too much chocolate. This gave me a loving disposition, but put zits on my face the size of cherry tomatoes. When I popped them, my schoolmates would bet on how far the puss would travel ... I got extra points for squirting it inside a fish bowl .... "

"That's disgusting" said Rebecca. "You lose. Time to die." And so saying, she sent a pretend bolt of energy through her sword-stick into his monster heart.

Schnozola's body shook. He cried in comedy pain. "Monsters need therapy, too," he croaked and died with a wheezing death rattle.

Rebecca put her foot on his chest. Raising her mighty sword-stick, she sang in her powerful, soprano, warrior voice,

"Fare thee well, thing from hell. I win, I grin; you lose, you snooze."

Later, Andy and Rebecca bicycled back to the crossroads, stopping in the cool shade of some cedar trees. They stared affectionately at each other; neither one spoke, not wanting to break the joyous spell.

"I have to go to work," Andy finally said, lowering his gaze. "Thanks for going bike riding with me."

"It was fun," Rebecca said. "You sing pretty good."

"Do I, really?"

Rebecca nodded. "For a hopeless clown, yeah."

Smiling, Andy took a handkerchief out of his pocket and handed it to her. "Open it."

Rebecca peeled back the top layer. Sitting in the middle of the cotton cloth was a ring. It had a simple gold band with a stone of polished turquoise set in it.

"Oh, Andy. It's lovely."

"It was my grandmothers," Andy said. "She gave it to me before she died. Will you wear it … for me?" he blushed.

Andy watched her face intently. Rebecca looked like she had just received an electric shock treatment with a defibulator. Her eyes bulged; her mouth parted; she froze without saying a word. Andy couldn't figure out if this was a good thing or a bad thing. While he waited patiently his heart beat faster. Nervous ants climbed all over his body as the seconds passed like hours. Surely time was going against him. His stomach started sinking, his heart felt like a bomb about to explode.

Rebecca raised her head; she was smiling. She raised her hand towards him, extending her fingers forward.

Andy took the ring from the handkerchief and put it on her ring finger. The feel of it sliding across her skin thrilled him, for this was the first time he had ever given a girl a ring to be his girlfriend.

Andy wanted to kiss her. He started to lean forward when he remembered something his grandmother told him before she died.

"The truest way to a woman's heart is to show patience and respect for her before you become too involved. It shows how much you care."

Andy wanted to be involved with Rebecca, but he also wanted her to know how much he cared. Taking her hand in his, he decided to be patient.

"I'll call you later?" he asked.

Rebecca nodded, secretly disappointed that Andy didn't kiss her.

Andy rode his bike towards the butcher shop. Emerging from the shade and into the bright sun, he sang his Pagliacci song: "I'm a butcher's son. I chop meat all day long …." He turned and waved to her as he headed down the road.

Waving back, Rebecca watched him go. She looked at the ring on her finger.

If her heart could sing, it would have turned into a joyous choir.

Alexandra hung a dress in her daughter's closet, careful to separate Rebecca's casual wear from her nicer school clothes. She was in a state of shock; nothing in her life had prepared her for Herman's betrayal. Her feelings were a jumbled mass of stress bordering on complete hysteria. Unbidden tears rolled down her cheeks, splashing onto the dress.

"Oh, no," said Alexandra, "I have cried on Rebecca's favorite outfit. I am a poor mother." She dabbed at the wet spot with the bottom of her blouse.

"What did I do to have Herman cheat on me? It must be my fault. What have I done wrong?" She resisted the urge to cry. "But who could it be? Where could he have met her? Why now?"

Alexandra continued to pat at the wet spot, trying to soak up the tears. Each time she did so, additional drops from her eyes splashed onto the dress. Doing more harm than good, she stepped out of the closet and wept.

Several minutes later, drained of emotion and a teaspoon of water, Alexandra resumed her motherly task. She opened Rebecca's top dresser drawer and placed her freshly washed clothes inside. The act of doing something for the child of her heart made her feel a bit better.

Memories of motherhood streamed through her mind: feeding Rebecca as a baby with the milk from her breast, pushing her on a swing in a park, tending a bruise when she scrapped her knee, giving her singing lessons and teaching her how to act like a lady. The recollections kept coming.

For 18 years, Alexandra had loved, cared for and prepared Rebecca for womanhood. She couldn't be more proud of her daughter. Now she was seeing a boy, Andy Barulich. Soon the day would come when she would be married and raise a family of her own. This was evident by the simple fact that Herman had allowed her to go out on a date without a chaperone, something he would have never permitted even a month ago.

She gazed at a picture of the three of them in a small wooden frame on top of her daughter's dresser. She prayed every mother's prayer that her child would find a mate that would be good to her. A mate that would honor her, cherish her and love her with the same passion Alexandra had once known with her husband, Herman.

A tube of lipstick lay in front of a family photo. Curious, Alexandra lifted it up, removing the small plastic cover off the case. Twisting the bottom, the lipstick extended up into her sight. It was the same color as the lipstick she had found on Herman's shirt.

Yes! She was sure of it.

She smelled the lipstick. It even smelled the same as the one on the shirt.

Yes! She was sure of it.

Alexandra looked back at the photo. Herman was in the middle, they were all smiling. She blinked; the photo changed. Rebecca was now kissing her father. And something else … the look in her husband's *eyes* …he enjoyed being kissed by Rebecca.

What does this mean?

Realization smote her like a hammer blow; there was no mistake; she finally knew the truth.

The other woman is my own daughter!

She was sure of it.

Andy was on Cloud Nine as he zipped down the dirt road towards the butcher shop. His thoughts were on Rebecca; his feet barely seemed to touch the pedals of his bike. He now knew in his heart what it was like to meet someone who enjoyed his vivid imagination and even participated in it without thinking he was either weird or brain damaged. They had improvised together like they were born to it. Andy had never experienced its like before.

She's amazing, Andy thought. *What a woman.*

He thought of the ring that Rebecca now wore, the ring that his Grandmother had given him. He had been 11-years-old when his grandmother asked him the question, "Grandson, when you get older, how will you know who to love?"

Andy didn't know and didn't care; he shrugged his shoulders and went outside to play. The next day after school his Grandmother was baking home made apple strudel in the oven. She told him it was almost done. Andy wanted a piece so badly that he hung out in the kitchen with her rather than go out and play. While he waited, he remembered what she had asked him the day before.

"Grandmother?" asked Andy. "When I get older how will I know who to love?"

Grandmother slipped on an oven mitt. "When the time comes, grandson, there will be no doubt in your heart who that person is, for you will feel happier than you have ever felt in your life."

"Even happier than getting a new bike for my birthday?" he had asked her.

She laughed, the skin around her eyes crinkling. "Even so, Andy, even so." She whispered in a low voice as though telling him a secret. "Watch your parents when they hug each other and you will see the answer in their eyes." She opened the oven door. The delectable smell of fresh baked pastry filled his nostrils.

"Now how about some nice warm apple strudel?"

Andy would never forget her words, or that strudel, for as long as he lived.

The road slanted downward; Andy squeezed his brakes to slow down. He was nearing the intersection leading into Hot Tub, his mind still on his grandmother's words. Now he knew exactly what she meant. In his heart there was no doubt. Rebecca and he had made a connection which illuminated his entire existence. He understood why Rebecca's father called his wife his "shining star." Now that Rebecca wore his ring, Rebecca was his "shining star."

Andy released the brake, stood up on the peddles and let the bike pick up speed. The wind whipped about him, making his clothes ripple, tickling his flesh. He felt like the king of the world.

A sudden impulse overtook him. He swerved his bike off the road onto a steep hill. Shooting downward, he picked up speed, whipping by trees, feeling elated. Not far ahead was a rocky outcropping. Andy headed straight for it at top speed.

Launching himself through the air, he yelled out Rebecca's name.

A few minutes later, Andy coasted downhill towards the intersection of the road that led into town. On the corner was the taxidermist shop that Rebecca's dad owned.

Andy wanted to be sure Mr. Senicki had no objection to him seeing his daughter. He felt it was very important to show respect to her parents, if for nothing else than to be accepted into their family. He knew guys from school who had broken up with their girlfriends because the mother or father of the girl had not liked them. Andy did not want that to happen to him and Rebecca.

He brought the bike to a skidding halt, unslung his backpack and took a comb out of a small pocket. He combed his hair, then dusted himself off with his hands, slapping them briskly. He checked his pants. They had dried after his plunge into the lake and appeared clean. It was the best he could do. It showed that he cared, or so he hoped.

He probably isn't there anyway. It's Sunday.

He checked his watch. It was 11:52 a.m. He was supposed to open the butcher shop in less than ten minutes.

I better get going.

Slinging his backpack over his shoulders, Andy shoved off with his feet and pedaled. The road leveled out as he neared the taxidermist shop. There were a few stuffed animals outside, including an enormous brown bear that had been shot by some poachers from another county. The hunters had shown off their catch at a local diner where a Ranger was having lunch. They were arrested. Afterwards, the Ranger had given the deceased animal to Mr. Senicki to stuff.

The bear looked amazingly real, raised up on its hind legs as though it was getting ready to charge. It was so lifelike he felt a twinge of fear creep up his spine. The other animals were equally well done.

Mr. Senicki is really good. That bear must be worth thousands of dollars.

It occurred to Andy how strange it was that Mr. Senicki would leave these valuable beasts outside of the shop, unattended. Not that Andy would ever dream of stealing them, but other people were not as honest as he was. He made a mental note to call the Senicki's home when he got to the butcher shop, when Mr. Senicki opened the door and lumbered outside.

A creepy sensation came over Andy. Something was wrong here, but what? Mr. Senicki stood next to the huge bear looking in his direction, but he acted as if he didn't see Andy at all. A scary kind of energy emanated from him. Andy shook off the feeling, attributing it to the aggressive stance of the bear.

Better say something, he thought. "Hi, Mr. Senicki," he called out, waving his arm in greeting.

Mr. Senicki remained frozen as Andy cycled past him. His face was blank and emotionless.

Wonder what's up with that? Andy thought. *Oh, well. I have to open the shop on time. I better get going.*

Further down the street, Andy glanced back over his shoulder. Bizarrely enough, Mr. Senicki was still standing next to the bear, unmoving, staring nowhere.

Andy shrugged and pedaled on.

Herman Senicki gaped up at the avalanche that would dispense the harsh judgment of the Lord upon him. The back of his shirt was in tatters and stained crimson with his blood.

Rebecca rode her bicycle down the dirt road towards home. She could hardly wait to see her Mom's reaction when she showed her the gorgeous ring Andy had given her.

First her eyes will grow huge, then she'll ask a thousand questions.

Her hair stirred in the breeze as she contemplated the questions her mother would ask: *Rebecca, you just met the boy. Shouldn't you date for a while? Does this mean he wants to marry you? What about children? I knew your father should have chaperoned you.*

The last thought made her laugh out loud. Her mother loved her so much--and worried about her so much.

When I have a family, I hope I'm as good a mom to my kids as my mom is to me. Well, maybe a little less old fashioned.

She leaned slightly in her seat as the road curved to the left.

And Dad! I wonder what he'll say?

Sunshine reflected off thousands of tree leaves, surrounding Rebecca like a living pastoral painting. The events of the day made her feel wonderful. She felt daring.

She had the urge to fly.

Aiming her bike down the center of the dirt road, Rebecca lifted her hands off of the handlebars, less than an inch. It gave her a feeling of weightlessness, a sensation of lift off, a thrill of adventure.

She raised her arms up a bit higher, prepared to grab the grip pads at the slightest hint of losing control. The bike stayed on course like an arrow. Summoning her courage, she held her arms out, embracing the wind. She imagined her arms were wings, flapping slightly, as she soared through the air. Closing her eyelids, she let the breeze rush over her, imagining angels flew beside her.

The screech of tires ruined her lovely fantasy as a car bore down on her from a side road.

Rebecca clutched the brakes hard; her bike skidded; a cloud of dirt and dust enveloped her. Blinded, Rebecca held on tight; the car's bumper missed her by inches as she passed beyond it. The bike flew off the road, hit bumpy terrain and slid out from under her. She tumbled onto the earth, almost hitting a tree.

Over the star ship's intercom, the Director told the Effects Technicians to shut down the special effects dust cloud.

Coughing, Rebecca felt dizzy. As the dust cloud faded away, she saw her bicycle lying on its side, its front wheel spinning in circles above the ground.

A shadow cast itself across her. Rebecca gazed up. The person's outer edges were painted white by bright sunlight. Squinting, Rebecca blocked the sun with her hand to see the person who had almost run her over.

"Mom? Is that you?"

Then Rebecca saw something so startling it made her forget she was almost killed.

"Mother?" she said astonished. "What happened to your hair?"

It was teased, full and sensuous; tinted purple, red and yellow in places.

It looks like her head is on fire!

Rebecca got a whiff of hairspray fumes. She recognized the smell. It was same spray that she used.

But mother never uses hair spray. And where did she get all those colors? I haven't bought any colored hairspray for months.

Her mother used to be shocked when she streaked her hair. She was so conventional about such matters. Now she outdid her own daughter. This was really strange.

Rebecca looked even closer. *Is mother wearing makeup? I rarely see her with any.*

Heavy mascara, severely overdone, thickened her mother's eyelashes. Then Rebecca realized something.

Is mother wearing my eye shadow?

Her mother's overused eye shadow looked more appropriate for an Egyptian Queen than a High School history teacher.

Is that my blush powder?

Rouge stood out like a bruise on her mother's cheek; her lipstick was thick and garish.

Is that my lipstick?

Her cherry lips were outlined in heavy pencil. The overall image was of a beautiful hooker with hair like shocking flame. Rebecca started to ask a question, but the dust in her throat made her cough.

"Put the bike in the trunk, dear," her mother said sweetly. "I have to go into town."

As her mother strolled back to the car. Rebecca noticed her clothing.

Hey. That's my favorite dress. But Mom can't fit into my clothes. She's too big.

Extra fabric had been sown into the sides of the garment. The extra material looked familiar.

Hey! Rebecca thought. *That looks like my other favorite dress. What is going on here?*

The Mysterious Man ran through the sun-drenched forest, flattening small plants in his anxiety-driven wake. His lungs burned from running for miles. *They* were behind him. *They* were coming. *They* would find him and when *They* did he was as good as dead.

Panting for breath, he stumbled, but managed to stay on his feet. He stopped to catch his breath, hiding behind a tree lest *They* should spot him. Raising an arm, he leaned against the tree trunk; his heart hammered in his chest.

I'm glad I quit smoking. I would have never gotten this far.

He peered around the tree.

Did I lose them? He hoped he had. He needed a rest.

He touched the bracelet's stones with his fingertips, made the all too familiar connection and waited for a response. SHIT! *They're* still out there. *They're* still headed this way. Do *They* know it's me … their secret stalker?

The Mysterious Man looked around for a hiding place, a cave or a ditch. Perhaps he could dig a hole and cover himself up with leaves and sticks. He had done it once before and it had saved his life. That's why he kept a small spade in his backpack. There were plenty of leaves around. He unslung the backpack, took out the small shovel and hacked at the earth.

Crap! The ground is too hard. That other time it had been a dried up stream bed, still moist, easy to dig.

Running was his only chance, but he was tired. He had been at it for quite awhile. How much longer could he last? Ten minutes? Half an hour? Surely not more than that.

He hurried on, fear feeding new energy into his burning thighs.

Half a mile later, he came out of the forest to a road. A short ways away he saw a building--the *Dusty Horse Saloon.* Several cars were parked in front.

He rejoiced at the site. Experience had taught him *They* did not go places where other people congregated. *They* never went into the cities. *They* did their dirty work in the country, in places where *They* could hide from the eyes of the world.

The Mysterious Man trotted towards the bar. The crunch of the road beneath his boots was reassuring. He knew he would make it to safety. For years he had tracked *Them* all over North America and had had more than one close call, but the bracelet *always* warned him in time to escape. Without it he was dog meat.

His mind wandered back in time, back to the beginning when his life had been changed forever by *Them.* It was a good thing the house had sold for so much money. It was amazing how frugally one could live a jobless life by living off the land. He used to rent a motel room every night, but not now. There were other ways, better ways to pursue *Them.* Most of the time he slept in the forest on his bed roll, even though it got terribly dirty and smelly. He remembered it got so bad he cleaned it once in a stream and had to sit around for hours while the sun dried it. He never cleaned it again.

The Mysterious Man recalled the many times since he began his quest, how he had broken into motels, buildings, even barns--just to take a shower, wash his clothes in the bathtub, or have a roof over his head when the weather was bad. He had killed forest animals and eaten their flesh. He raided the crops of farmers, eating the vegetables that he stole raw.

The Man thought that he was as good a hunter as *They* were. Even better. Was he not a Hunter of Hunters? Quick, sly, wary? He took great pride in his body, feeling powerful despite his wiry frame. When he first started tracking *Them* he had a belly. He was fat! He got easily winded. But now he had stamina, he could run for miles, he was strong.

Yes, he would survive this encounter. He would spend some money to refresh himself and continue with his quest. He would prevail over *Them,* even if it took another six years.

The smell of hamburger roasting over a hot grill filled his mind with mouth-watering images.

Beef ... onions ... barbecue sauce.

An insect whined by his ear. He stepped on a rock, almost losing his balance. Where was he? What had he been thinking? Oh, yes, he would prevail, he would defeat *Them* ... he would ....

His nostrils flared from the savory odor of cooking meat.

Forget THEM, the Mysterious Man thought.

He would soon sink his teeth into a delicious, juicy H-A-M-B-U-R-G-E-R.

"So what did you do on your date, dear?" said Mrs. Senicki, her hands on the steering wheel as she drove down the back woods road towards town.

"Nothing much," replied Rebecca. "Just bike riding."

"Just bike riding? Nothing else?"

Rebecca felt guarded. She wanted to tell her mother everything about her date with Andy, but after almost being run over and the strange way her mother was dressed, she didn't feel like telling her hardly anything that happened.

"We had a picnic together," she volunteered.

"Just bike riding and a picnic?"

"Yes."

"And where did you have this picnic?"

"By the lake."

Mrs. Senicki slowly increased the speed of the station wagon.

"And what did he bring to eat? Did he bring any alcohol?"

Rebecca wondered what she meant by that.

"No mother. Just cheese and crackers, stuff like that."

"That's nice dear," said Mrs. Senicki still increasing her speed. "Did you play any games?"

Rebecca decided not to tell her about the giant monster puppet.

"We took sticks and fenced with them," she volunteered. "We pretended to be Brunhilde and Siegfried. You know, like the characters in the Wagner opera."

"You did, did you?"

The car swerved to the left on the dirt road, jerking Rebecca around in her seat. "Sorry, dear," said Mrs. Senicki coolly. "I was trying to avoid a squirrel."

Rebecca had not been looking at the road when it happened, but, when she did, it seemed to her that her mother had tried to hit the squirrel, not miss it.

"Siegfried was in love with Brunhilde," warned Mrs. Senicki, her tone becoming harsher. "Did Andy try to make love to you?"

Rebecca's lips parted, forming an astonished "o."

"Did he try to touch you?" interrogated Mrs. Senicki. "Did he put his hands on you or try to kiss you?"

"No, mother. Of course not."

"Did he try to look up your dress?"

Rebecca's tongue stuck in her mouth. Her throat tightened. "No, mother," she said in a low voice.

"Boys will be boys," cautioned Mrs. Senicki. "And while all of this was going on, did you act like a responsible young lady or did you act like a whore?"

Rebecca flinched in her seat. Was her mother accusing her of something? The interrogation was totally unlike her.

"If you get pregnant before you are married, you'll have to move out of the house and your father and I will never speak to you again. Do you understand me?"

The car swerved violently again on the road.

"There's a lot of squirrels out today," said Mrs. Senicki.

Rebecca wanted to cry, but restrained her tears.

Why is Mother upset with me? I haven't done anything wrong.

"I won't have any whores growing up in my house. Do I make myself clear?"

Rebecca was astonished. What was she going to do now? Did her mother really think she was a whore? What could she possibly say to that?

Rebecca kept her mouth shut, retreating into a quiet shell.

Mrs. Senicki took her foot off the gas pedal. The car slowed down. "If you act like a lady, you'll be treated like a lady. If you act like a whore, you'll lose your family. Understand, dear?"

Before Rebecca could answer, another squirrel crossed the road. Her mother stomped on the gas pedal. The station wagon lurched forward; the engine roared.

Rebecca winced, she clung to her seatbelt. They barely missed killing the small fleeing creature.

"I said do you understand," grilled Mrs. Senicki, slowing down the vehicle again.

"Yes, mother," Rebecca mumbled as the station wagon passed by a road sign. Rebecca caught a glimpse of it: *Slow. Animal crossing.*

Wearing his blood-speckled butcher's apron and carrying a bag of meat, Gunter strode out of the Butcher shop and got inside his car. The Volvo had barely driven down the street, when a green station wagon pulled into the parking lot.

Mrs. Senicki turned off the engine. "Stay in the car," she said sternly to Rebecca, then exited the station wagon, slamming the door shut with a bang.

Rebecca watched her mother through the bug-spattered windshield wearing *her* best dress, *her* makeup, and with her hair held up by *her* hairspray. She sauntered into the Butcher shop, shutting the door behind her.

Andy's bicycle was parked ten feet away, a piece of his frost giant costume tied around the handlebars. She wanted to see him, but her Mother had told her to stay put. So she sat alone and brooded.

The bug smear on the windshield got her attention. Still smarting from the tongue lashing her mother gave her, Rebecca related to its gross predicament.

"Why is she acting like this?" Rebecca fretted. "She's being mean."

Her gaze returned to the dead bug, its insides spread out like crème cheese on glass toast.

She thought the bug got the better deal.

Andy stood by meat grinder, cleaning it up. His father had rushed out the door with two dozen fresh ground polish sausages for the Williams family. The Williams' dog, Brutus, had helped himself to a plate full of sausages and the family barbecue was in ruins. Hence, Gunter to the rescue.

Andy smiled and shook his head, remembering how the entire incident had happened. The phone call … the sudden urgency … his father trying to calm Mrs. Williams' panic. The grandparents were there … they loved polish sausage … bad Brutus, bad dog.

When his father hung up the phone, Andy felt he had participated in a mission more worthy of Obie Wan Kenobi and Luke Skywalker than a small town butcher and his son. His father made making fresh polish sausages seem as important as Jesus feeding 5,000 people with a few loaves of bread and some fish.

"Son," his father said, pushing meat into the sausage grinder. "The grandparents must have the very best sausage to make up for this dreadful tragedy."

Andy took a measure of delight in the vitality his father displayed during the crisis. His time spent with Rebecca had stirred within him a new awareness about the wonderfulness of being alive.

The cowbell over the front entrance rang. Andy turned to see who had come into the shop. Much to his surprise it was Mrs. Senicki. Much more to his surprise was her appearance. She was gorgeous! He looked again. Was his mind playing tricks on him?

Is her hair on fire?

Mrs. Senicki, her head held high, sprayed her neck with perfume, then sprayed a little in her mouth for good measure. Putting the bottle back in her purse, she glided across the floor towards Andy like royalty on parade.

Andy, his hands unclean with sausage bits, turned his back to her and washed up in the sink. "Hi, Mrs. Senicki. Dad took an order to the Williams. He'll be back real soon. Can I get you anything?"

He dried his hands with a towel and turned. Mrs. Senicki had come behind the counter and was so close he could have reached out and touched her. Gazing deep into his eyes, she appeared to be in a trance.

Andy's fingers dripped water on his shoes as his nostrils filled with the odor of sweet perfume.

Why is she staring at me like that? What the heck is "Momma Love" thinking?

A gentle breeze spread the aroma of fragrant lilacs throughout the immense Greco-Roman plaza. Massive pillars of marble towered into the night, ascending into the heavens as though they held up the star-filled sky. Tall hedges bordered the plaza, ensuring it as a place of intimate seclusion. Unseen centaurs played pan-pipes and lutes, drugging the air with their dreamy song.

Illuminated by the light of the full moon, Andy stood alone in a marble-tiled pool filled with warm water and rose petals.

He was completely naked.

The delicious water came up to his waist, teasing his young male flesh with its arousing wetness. Stairs led out of the water up to a white marble landing where a spectacular woman stood--Alexandra the goddess.

A sparkling gossamer gown draped across her shapely body, so sheer it did little to hide the divine curves beneath it. Alexandra's voluptuous, fiery hair burned with erotic purpose; her milky white skin glowed with the promise of passion. Two slender white trains flowed behind her outstretched arms, rippling like wings in the delicate wind.

Raising a well-formed foot, Alexandra stepped toward the stairway heading down to the pool. Her flowing trains magically bore her aloft as she glided above the stairs towards the perfumed waters and Andy. The muscular contours of Andy's body aroused an ardent thirst within her. Desire flooded her heart.

Alexandra slid into the pool, unhindered by its fluid substance. The sweet-smelling water divided in half before her like the Red Sea before Moses. Her garments did not get wet, nor did a strand of her coiffured hair get mussed as she approached the object of her affections.

Reaching out for his manhood, she whispered "Andy, my love."

"Excuse me," Andy said, his voice quivering, his hands still dripping water on his shoes. "What did you say?" Although his eyes feigned ignorance, he had heard quite clearly what Momma Love said, he just didn't want to believe that she had actually said it.

And what is she doing with her hand?

The urge to flee assailed him, but his legs refused to move. He felt paralyzed, unable to act. Wishing it was all a hallucination, he tried to divert her attention.

"Can I get you some thing, Mrs. Senicki? Some meat perhaps?"

Momma Love took a step closer. Andy took in her makeup, her luscious lips, her overpowering femaleness. She smelled delicious … intoxicating ... it made his head spin. He wondered how something so wonderful could make him shake inside like a baby's rattle.

Momma Love spoke in a low, husky voice. "Show me your turkey," she said, stroking his arm with her finger.

Andy dropped the towel on the floor; his throat constricted. Feeling both excited and uncomfortable, a number of half-formed answers came and went before he could utter a single word.

"Ungle," was all he managed to say.

Inside the station wagon, Rebecca squirmed on the car seat. "What is taking mother so long? Is she giving Andy the third degree about our date, too?"

Rebecca felt a great concern for her newfound relationship with Andy. Her mother had no right to interfere like this. This was her life! Her boyfriend! He had given her a ring. It was completely unfair! She wanted to get out of the car and rush into the butcher shop, but disobedience came hard to her, so she sat on the vinyl seat and brooded. Her thoughts were like an itch she couldn't scratch that got increasingly irritating.

A minute later, she was so worked up about what she thought her mother was doing to her Andy that she opened the car door and swung her leg around. She was going to go inside, confront her mother, and defend her boyfriend.

As her shoe connected with the Earth, a nearby probe jammed an image into her brain.

"Stay in the car!" her mother snarled, her face suddenly appearing beside the vehicle.

Rebecca yelped. She flung herself back inside, slamming the door shut in a panic. As she did so, her left hand struck the rear-view mirror, knocking it out-of-place. Her eyes searched outside the window, expecting to see her mother's stern features, but her mother was nowhere in sight. Confused, Rebecca wondered where her mother had disappeared to. She also was relieved she would not have to endure another confrontation.

Rebecca's hand stung. She pressed it against her chest. Her face reflected in the out-of-place mirror. It was covered with splotchy fantasy makeup.

"Oh, kitty crap!" she whined.

Andy placed the largest whole turkey he could find on a cutting board and patiently waited while Mrs. Senicki stared at it. The last few minutes had definitely made the "Top-10-Weird-Moments-In-Andy-Barulich's-Life" list.

"Is it big?" Mrs. Senicki asked, her face calm and unrevealing.

"It's the biggest one here," Andy stammered, hoping to get this over quickly.

"Spread its legs," she said, her voice barely a whisper.

"Spread it's legs?" Andy repeated, feeling suddenly warm.

Mrs. Senicki nodded.

Trying to obey his father's maxim "service with a smile," Andy spread the legs of the huge bird apart.

"Wider," Mrs. Senicki cooed.

Andy spread the legs further apart.

"Wider." A trace of awe in her voice.

Andy held the turkey's legs as far apart as they would go, afraid the bones would snap at any moment. *Service with a smile,* he thought to himself as the situation reached deep into his "Top 10 Weird" list. He held the turkey legs apart for what seemed like an eternity as Mrs. Senicki appeared to be making a decision. If he knew that Mrs. Senicki imagined herself as naked as the turkey with Andy pulling her legs apart he would have run screaming from the room.

"Does it hold a lot of stuffing?" she whispered.

Andy's skin grew flushed; a sudden lump grew in his throat.

"I like … a lot … of stuffing," Mrs. Senicki purred.

Andy stood silent. "Okay," he muttered awkwardly. "Can I wrap that up for you?"

Mrs. Senicki eyes took on a far away look; she fell back into a trance. Andy wondered if she was having a seizure. Her breathing became deeper, her shoulders rose and fell. It was weird in a captivating sort of way. She took a sudden deep breath and held it, her face a mask of exquisite tension. Andy worried that maybe he should call for a doctor when she gasped, her lips pursing.

"Yes," she said with breathy passion, then blew a stream of hot perfumed air on his face like an endless kiss.

Andy felt his hair wiggle. His eyelids fluttered in confusion. His lips parted soundlessly; he swallowed the lump in his throat. "Okay," he muttered timidly. "I'll get right on it."

Picking up the large turkey, he walked to the counter to wrap it up.

Climbing into the back seat of the station wagon, Rebecca grabbed the water bottle from her bicycle. Wetting a tissue with water, she furiously washed the fantasy makeup off of her face. "What is taking so long," she fumed. "What is mother doing to my poor Andy?"

As she wiped off the makeup, the tissue kept breaking apart. Leaning over the front seat, Rebecca checked her progress in the rear view mirror. Tiny bits of tissue clung to her skin, making her appear fuzzy faced.

Rebecca groaned.

She couldn't stand it any more. Orders or no orders, Rebecca just had to find out what was going on.

White fuzzies or not, she opened the door and stepped out onto the hard ground.

Andy tore off a piece of adhesive tape and applied it to the butcher paper covering the large turkey. Putting it in a big paper bag, he carried it over to Mrs. Senicki, who had stepped away from the counter and now had her back to him.

"Here's your meat," he said.

Mrs. Senicki spun around, grabbing Andy by his arms, pinning them to his body so that the turkey was trapped in between them.

"You are my shining star and I will never let you go," she uttered, then kissed him with passion.

Hot lips clamped down on his, hungry, demanding, exciting. A feral current shot through his body. If his neck had been a light socket her kiss just blew his bulb. Lip-locked to his girlfriend's mother, Andy turned into a piece of human toast blackened by a lust-filled flamethrower.

The Munchkins liked it so much they sang:

(To the tune "When Johnny Comes Marching Home")

"When Andy got his first real kiss,

Hurrah. Hurrah.

His mind was shot so full of bliss.

Hurrah. Hurrah.

Her lips touching his were like shooting stars.

His head blasted off now its orbiting Mars.

(Houston, we have a proo-bleem.)

His life got a twist when Andy got his first kiss."

Andy's brain was fried in a very nice way. He had never been kissed by a woman liked this in his entire life. The kiss was beyond terrific.

It was awesome times infinite plus one.

Rebecca rushed up to the Butcher shop window and peeked inside. Andy and her mother were kissing each other, while Andy held a large package between their stomachs. As the two lovers separated, Andy had a huge smile on his face.

Rebecca felt a sledge hammer strike her heart.

She spun away and ran down the stairs, crumpling to her knees on the dirt parking lot. Her hands flew up beside her head as though trying to force the terrible image from out her brain.

Delicately, Mrs. Senicki broke off the kiss. She took the turkey from Andy's hands and strolled towards the door. Andy stood still as a statue, his eyes as large as a light bulb and twice as bright. He was incapable of movement or speech.

Emotional rigor mortis had set up residence inside his head. The entire event had launched itself into the number 1 slot on the "All-Time-Weird-Moments-In-Andy's-Life" list and was so far ahead of number 2 he couldn't even remember what number 2 was.

A car's engine started up. The sound derigidified him. Twisting his head towards the window, he saw Rebecca in her mother's car as it backed away from the shop.

Rebecca was crying.

The shop door opened, ringing the cow bell. Gunter entered in a panic.

"Andy. What is going on?" his father asked worriedly. "What have you done?"

"What?" Andy said, mystified.

"Mrs. Senicki just told me that you are to never see her daughter again."

"She what?"

The sound of the station wagon's engine roared as it charged into the distance. The sickening feeling that he would never see Rebecca again tore at Andy's heart.

Why is this happening? Andy thought. *Why would she do such a thing to me?*

His eyes caught the placard above the doorway. It read: "The customer is always right." His chest felt like it was caving in.

Playing banjos the Munchkins sang: "You dun stomped upon my heart … and squashed that sucker flat!"

CHAPTER 9

A NIGHT TO FORGET

A reddish purple ribbon stretched across the evening sky hunkering behind dark mountain peaks that pointed to the coming night. As the last vestiges of daylight faded, the air took on a chill. Stars peeked out in the heavens like beings of light awakened by the all-pervading darkness.

In the Senicki's dining room, the long, polished wooden table could seat as many as eight. At the moment, only three people occupied its great length.

Herman sat at one end, Alexandra at the other, with Rebecca on one side in the middle. A great feast lay before them, the main course being a large turkey. It was raised above the table on a silver platter supported underneath by four tall, silver candleholders. It looked liked an altar, a sacrifice to the god of fowl, golden brown and glazed with plum sauce.

A small army of side dishes cluttered about the steaming bird: mashed potatoes with slivered almonds, country gravy, apple-raisin stuffing, string beans in cheese sauce, home made cranberries, fresh apple pie and more served in Alexandra's best dishes. Despite the plethora of food, Rebecca wasn't very hungry.

She quietly spooned brown gravy over her mashed potatoes. A small pile of slivered almonds sat beside them. She never did like almonds; she had picked them out with her fork.

Rebecca thoughts went back in time to just after she and her mother had left the butcher's shop. She had cried in the car all the way to the grocery store. Her mother dragged her through the market, buying enough groceries to feed an army. Arriving home, Rebecca was put to work in the kitchen preparing the turkey for the oven.

While Rebecca prepared the stuffing, her mother went into a cleaning frenzy. In the living and dining rooms, she vacuumed the carpeting, polished the furniture, then wiped the Venetian blinds clean with a wet sponge. The entire time she sang her role as the ancient Chinese princess *Turandot*, playing the record Gunter had given her, electrifying the air with her vibrant voice.

Rebecca wondered if her mother had gone mad. She had just put the turkey in the oven when her mother burst into the kitchen, singing with gusto for Rebecca to bake a homemade apple pie (and to make the crust from scratch!). After almost hitting her with the car, wearing her clothes and makeup, calling her a whore, running over squirrels and kissing her boyfriend, Rebecca decided it was safer to just to go along with her mother's program, whatever it was.

Her mother forced her to cook for the next six hours.

At one point, while she peeled the potatoes, Rebecca timidly asked her mother "What's the occasion?"

"Just do what you're told!" her mother sang in her powerful soprano voice.

"Yes, mother," Rebecca said, bowing her head and wilting inside.

Her mother went back to her energetic cleaning, singing as though the living room was an opera house stage. When her father came home it was just after 8:00 p.m. They sat down at the dinner table almost completely covered with food.

Rebecca finished spooning the gravy on her mashed potatoes. Her parents were not eating a thing. Their plates were completely empty. Ignoring the feast, they stared at each other with unblinking eyes and blank faces. The silence was weirding her out. She set the gravy spoon down, no longer hungry.

Herman gazed intently at the figure sitting at the opposite end of the table. The figure he saw was not his wife.

"Mother found my lipstick on your shirt today," the image of Rebecca said in a tense, low voice. "She knows all about us. She tried to run me over with the car."

Alexandra focused on the person sitting opposite her. That person was not her husband.

"Rebecca saw us kissing," the image of Andy whispered gravely. "She'll tell your husband. We need to move quickly."

"We must kill Mother and Andy," the image of Rebecca said to Herman. "Before they slay us."

"We have to murder your husband and your daughter," Andy said to Alexandra. "We have no choice."

Herman and Alexandra each listened to a person who existed only in their mind, hearing them urge each other to murder … to kill or be killed.

Rebecca glanced back and forth between her parents, ignorant of their deadly conversations. She quietly excused herself and left the table to go up to her room, treading softly towards the stairway. Reaching the bottom step, she glanced back.

Her parents had not moved a muscle, not taken a single bite. The large feast she had spent hours making just sat there getting cold.

Placing her hand upon the railing, a feeling of dread grew deep inside her. The day had begun so full of happiness … the date with Andy … the lake … the ring. It had ended like a train wreck. Were her parents punishing her because Andy kissed her mother? She had never seen them act this way before. It hurt her feelings to be given the silent treatment. She felt like being alone.

Rebecca walked upstairs to her bedroom. At the table, the fatal discourse continued.

Destroy them before they slay us. Murder … kill … death.

I'm grounded!

Andy lay flat on his bed. He had just had a dreadful fight with his parents, who sent him to his room without any dinner. They hadn't done that to him in years. He was so miserable he wanted to curl up into a ball and hide forever.

The fight with his parents replayed in his mind. He and his dad had come home from the butcher shop after hearing the horrible news from Mrs. Senicki. His mother wore her frilly cooking apron. She had just put dinner in the oven — a ham with pineapple rings. It smelled delicious. Andy loved how she made ham.

His father sat him down in the living room and the battle began in earnest.

"Andy, what did you do to upset Mrs. Senicki?" his father said. "She was very upset."

"I don't know, Dad," Andy said, sitting in a living room chair while his parents surrounded him.

"Tell the truth, young man," his mother demanded, gripping her apron. "Don't you dare lie to your father."

Andy felt like his body was in a vise; their accusations slowly crushing him.

"I'm not lying mother."

"Then what happened?"

Andy fidgeted in the chair. "Well, she came in, bought a turkey and then ... left. The next thing I know, Dad comes in and tells me I'm not permitted to see Rebecca." His head hung down limply.

"Well something had to upset her," his father said, pacing the room. "Were you daydreaming like you did yesterday with Mrs. Wilson and the other two ladies?"

"No," Andy answered in a soft voice.

"You do that a lot, son," his father reprimanded. "Some times I wonder what's gotten into you. I give you the responsibility of opening up the shop, the responsibility of a man, and then you are rude to our customers?"

"But," Andy stammered. "I … " his voice trailed off.

"What made Mrs. Senicki so disturbed then," his mother pried. "Can you think of any reason?"

Andy wanted to tell the truth, that Mrs. Senicki had grabbed him and kissed him. But he knew that if he did so his parents would not believe him. They would be certain he was lying. It would do far more harm than playing dumb. Still, under their constant pressure he almost let the truth slip out.

"She was acting a little strange," Andy blurted out.

"Strange?" his father said, towering over him. "What do you mean strange?"

Andy grimaced towards the ceiling. The light hanging above him shined harshly in his eyes. It was like those old gangster movies when someone is being given the third degree.

"Well, she, I ..." his tale of truth began to falter.

"Go on," his mother urged. "Speak."

Andy knew there was nothing he could say that could explain what had really happened, so he gave up.

"I guess not," he fibbed.

His dad crossed his arms akimbo. "Then it must have been when you snuck off with Rebecca last night while we listened to music. You broke the rule about always being chaperoned by an adult."

"But I go to college, Dad, not high school. I'm almost 20 years old ..."

"Shut up," said his mother. "Don't interrupt your father."

"Su-su-sorry," said Andy stuttering.

"The Senicki's are like us," his father continued. "They come from the old country, use the old ways. You see what happens when you act like these American kids who have no respect for their elders and think only about what they want to do? You acted selfishly."

His mother shook her finger at him. "Don't you see how much trouble you've caused young man?"

Andy squirmed in the chair.

"If you want to be treated like an adult," his father said, "then you must first act like one."

"If your grandpapa were still alive," his mother added, "he'd tell your father to whip you with the belt."

"Under the circumstances," his father said, grinding his fist into the palm of his other hand. "I'm going to have to ground you, son."

"But Dad!"

"For one week. Now go to your room and think about how you should have behaved. A man takes responsibility for his actions. Be a leader of yourself."

Andy gripped his knees, "But, it's not my fault, he protested weakly. "I didn't do anything wrong."

"Learn to accept your punishment," his mother scolded, wringing her apron. "Go upstairs like your father told you. Be grateful he doesn't give you the whipping you deserve."

Andy slumped deeper into the arm chair. He wanted to stand up for himself against his parents; yell at them that they were wrong, that he was a responsible adult.

Instead he rose and shuffled towards the stairs, his head bowed low, feeling his parents' stares stabbing him in the back like knives.

Lying in his bed, two pillows stacked under his head, Andy relived that fateful kiss over and over in a relentless act of self-induced, mental cruelty. Drowning in wretchedness and hungry from not eating dinner, Andy gaped pointlessly at the ceiling thinking futile thoughts.

My life is not worth living. I never get a break.

Opera music drifted up from the living room. He was fed up with his parents, especially his dad. He wanted to be out on his own, answerable to no one but himself. He was sick and tired of being treated like a little boy. What did his parents know about how hard life was? Did they live his life? How could they know what he had gone through since they moved to America? They didn't even know about the bullies in high school making fun of his German accent for years, calling him names, picking on him. His life was worse than hard. They had it easy.

Andy heaved himself off the bed. He grabbed his bathrobe and tossed it at the bottom of the door, stuffing it into the crack with his feet in an angry effort to stifle his parents' music. The music went right through the walls.

I can't win. Why do I think I should even try?

Andy recognized the opera. It was Wagner's *Gotterdammerung*, the last opera in the famous Ring Cycle series. His dad said it was a German masterpiece, something that Adolph Hitler loved. That his parents had something in common with Der Fuehrer of the Third Reich was a source of profound irony to him. His parents had railed many times against the injustices Hitler had perpetrated against his own people.

And to think Hitler started out as a window washer, Andy remembered from his history class. *I guess if you're cruel enough you can work your way up to the top. Why do nice guys like me always finish last?*

Andy lay back down on his bed. An Eye hovered above him near the ceiling. It sprayed the room with anger pheromones while a probe thrust images into Andy's unguarded brain.

Andy imagined that Rebecca was kissing him, but his parents pulled her away. He inhaled the anger spray. His parents were ruining his life! He would show them that he was a man. He would straighten out this mess. He would go to Rebecca's house and win her back somehow, even if he had to wash her windows for eternity as penance!

Andy lurched out of bed. Opening his closet, he grabbed a light jacket. His biggest problem was how to get past his parents. He decided to jump out the 2nd story window. He didn't care how far down it was. He would go over Niagara Falls in a barrel to win back Rebecca. He didn't think the fall would hurt him. After all, he was a man. He could take it.

Andy put his arms through the windbreaker's sleeves. He rushed to the window, shoved it open, stuck his head out and looked down. Directly below him was his mother's prize flowerbed. He would have to leap out to avoid them. The probe showed him falling on the snapdragons and petunias, crushing them while his mother shrieked like a ghoul.

His courage dwindled.

The probe sent him another sweet kiss from Rebecca. The Eye misted him with a second dose of anger spray. Andy's emotions swelled as he breathed in the potent substance.

"To hell with my parents," said Andy. "I'm getting my woman back."

He shoved the window closed and marched towards the door. With a mighty tug he pulled it open, but the bathrobe stuffed under it abruptly stopped it. The sudden halt jerked Andy forward. He hit the door, banging his head. With one hand clutching his forehead, he whipped the bathrobe out of the way, then stepped into the hallway. The Eye and the probe followed Andy, recording his every thought and feeling.

Listening to Mozart, the Director conducted the music with a wave of his hand. "The Andy is quite possessive of the young female. How delightfully pathetic. This is emotional leverage I can really build on. I just need to know what the Andy fears the most so I can plant it early on in the story and capitalize on it later."

On the holo-monitor, Andy smacked his head on the bedroom door. The Director chuckled.

"A small sample of how love destroys you. This just keeps gets better and better. Let's see what makes him really tick"

He ordered the cameraman to spray the Andy with chemical paranoia.

"Some times I'm so brilliant," said the Director, "I need sunglasses just to see myself."

The stairway was dark, but Wagner was darker. Andy tip-toed down through the murky shadows while the chilling music and paranoia vapors fueled his imagination with menacing visions. He imagined his father was Adolph Hitler and his mother was Eva Braun. They wore ominous-looking, black leather garments and stood in front of an evil-looking torture chair with electric coils above it connected to a head cap with straps. Waving their hands in slow-motion, they smiled at Andy, inviting him to sit down.

Clinging to his hair, the Munchkins whispered in Andy's ears (to the *Wizard of Oz* tune *"Lions and Tigers and Bears."*)

"Hitler-Dad's waiting downstairs. Oh, my.

He wants to trap you unawares. Oh, my.

He'll torture your short curly hairs. Oh, my.

Don't sit in his rude torture chair. You'll fry."

Andy wished his bizarre imagination would just shut up. He brushed the protesting Munchkins out of his hair ("Hey, watch it, Bub." "Bombs away." "As you wish ..."), then took another hesitant step downstairs.

Dad's going to catch me ... I can feel it. No ... I can do this... I'm a man.

He reached the hallway landing just a few feet from the living room entrance. On the wall was a fish tank with Angel fish swimming inside.

The probe dispersed more paranoia fumes.

Holding onto the railing, Andy's head snapped back, making his eyes as big as saucers. Sneaking over to the living room archway, he peered around it, seeing the bizarrest sight he ever saw.

Hitler-Dad sat in the torture chair, his Nazi officer's hat bristling with sausages like the music pipes of a calliope. Inhaling a cigar, wisps of smoke curled out of the sausages which gave a subdued toot. Beside Hitler-Dad stood Eva Braun-Mom dressed in a dominatrix leather outfit with a frilly cooking apron around her waist that bore the image of the word "I", a bright red heart, the letter "2" and a whip on it. Sticking out of the wall next to her was the body of a goose from the neck down, its feathery rear end confined in an upright position by a frame made of wood.

Behind Hitler-Dad, a large Nazi flag hung against the wall, outlined by small flashing light bulbs. In front of the flag, a dozen chorus girls that looked like Rebecca wore glitzy, Las Vegas showgirl outfits with pink feather boas and headdresses that looked like the face of Schnozola.

Each Rebecca carried a silver serving tray which had a goose head on it. Together the Rebecca's danced and sang while Eva Braun-Mom whipped the decapitated goose's bottom causing the goose heads on the trays to honk.

(to the tune of *Dunkeshein*)

Hitler-Dad, he will make you mad;

Treat you like a boy, steal your sense of joy;

Send you to your room; no dinner, just gloom;

Hitler-Dad, will make you mad.

Bad boy! Swat! Honk!

Hallucinating like a madman, Andy plunged even deeper into the strange waters of his distorted mind. He remembered the real Hitler had spies everywhere. They could be watching him even now. His need to escape became unbearably strong.

Feeling as safe as a rabbit at a gun club, Andy got on his hands and knees, ready to crawl to the front door. His eyes came level with the fish tank. The Angelfish swam up to the glass, their lips puckering and relaxing; they seemed to be staring at him.

The probe dosed him with more paranoia mist.

Andy's imagination kicked into full *weird* mode.

Swastika bands appeared on the Angel fish fins. Their mouths turned into trumpets, blaring an alarm that sounded like wild cats howling.

Andy's head spun wildly as more bizarre images stomped through his mind.

The heads of the dancing Rebeccas had been switched with the goose heads on the trays. Mrs. Senicki was strapped in the electric torture chair. Eva Braun-Mom threw a giant electric switch on and off, sending great bolts of electricity into Mrs. Senicki's body as Mrs. Senicki operatically sang:

Come fry with me,

Come fry, let's fry today ...

Her skeleton flashed through her skin on the high notes. The smell of her fried perfume filled with air with a sickening sweet odor.

The goose heads on the Rebecca's bodies said, "Want a date?" after which the Rebecca heads on the silver trays honked.

Hitler-Dad and Eva Braun-Mom stood on opposite sides holding flashlights under their faces, giving them a sinister appearance. Hitler-Dad grinned like a mad demon. He smoked a cigar as the calliope sausages on his Nazi hat tooted.

Andy's pulse raced; his brain splintered. Dropping to the floor, he stared at the Angel Fish still sounding the alarm.

Please Lord, get me out of this. I'll go to church every Sunday. I promise.

Drenched in anxiety, Andy crawled on his stomach towards the front door. Thirty nerve-wracking seconds later, he managed to creep outside onto the porch.

Andy leaned against the house. He squeezed his eyes closed and opened them wide several times. The world was thick with darkness; his skin was wet and clammy; his hair was plastered to his forehead.

He felt like a mess.

The cool air calmed his pounding head; he shook himself back to reality.

How does my mind get so weird? It's as though someone's playing tricks on me. Maybe I need to see a doctor.

Regaining his senses, Andy found his bike lying on the lawn. Doing his 'run and leap' trick, he took off on his mission of love and freedom.

The Munchkin marching band pursued him, playing a song from the musical *Oklahoma.*

"Paranoia has a grip on Andy's little brain,

Every single thought's like a gunshot,

'Til your sanity goes down the drain…."

Through the Eye on the front porch, the Director watched the Andy leave on his bike. The pheromone sprays had worked extremely well. Even the fish were easily controlled with a little electromagnetic energy. The youngster's mind had been a banquet of strangeness: Hitler-Dad, Nazi fish, tiny little beings marching in a band.

The probe had captured it all.

The paranoia mist had revealed the truth. The Andy greatly feared his father. He was a stern authority figure that could destroy his sense of self-worth. All the Director had to figure out now was how to use this useful information in a way Those Who Watch would find exciting.

He had chosen two interesting victims.

He could hardly wait to see them murdered.

Rebecca was trapped in her own private hell.

Dressed in her pink nightgown, she sat on her bed and stared at the phone. She wanted to give Andy a piece of her mind, but couldn't bring herself to call him.

Andy Barulich, how could you!

Angry fingers plucked the phone off its cradle; she dialed Andy's number. An older female voice answered: "Barulich residence." Rebecca opened her mouth to speak, but couldn't utter a single word.

"Barulich residence," the female voice said again.

Rebecca's lower lip quivered.

She tossed the handset at the cradle and missed. It bounced off the phone, dangling by the curlicued cord. Mrs. Barulich, her voice small and tinny, kept saying "Hello, Barulich residence" over and over until Rebecca reached over and hung up.

She covered her eyes with her hands; tiny bits of liquid pain emerged from her troubled soul.

She noticed the ring on her finger, the ring from Andy-the-violator. Tearing it off, she threw it away. The ring bounced off the teeth of a smiling, stuffed lion, landing somewhere on the carpet. *I never want to see you again. Never, ever, for as long as I live.* But even as she thought the words, part of her knew that she was lying. She wanted to see him; had to see him, if only to shout in his face. *Andy, how could you? My own mother!*

As if they were acting on cue, more tears spouted from her glands like performers in a TV soap drama having heard the words, "It's show time!"

Pump, pump, pump.

The road was dark; the trip was long. Andy's legs made endless circles so a metal chain could turn the wheels that would take him to Rebecca's house.

On the front of the bike, a small, battery-operated headlight cast a weak beam of light. Andy wouldn't have noticed if it went out completely. His body became an engine as he cycled on through the night. He was a man on a mission with a serious mind. He would get there no matter how dark it was … or far.

Pump, pump, pump.

At the Senicki's dining room table, the conversation continued between the two parents and their imaginary lover-killers.

"Mother's in her bedroom," Rebecca said to Mr. Senicki. "She's all by herself. Let's kill her while we can, my darling."

Sitting in the same seat as Mr. Senicki, Andy spoke to Mrs. Senicki. "He's alone in his room, my sweet. Now's our chance to put him to death."

The two parents stared at each other; desperation beat in their hearts. It was God's will that they protect their beloved so they could live forever in the Kingdom of Heaven. But how could their love survive when their spouse was alive and out for their blood?

"If you love me, kill her," urged Rebecca.

"If you love me, slay him," Andy begged.

"Do it for love," they said together. "Do it for God."

The two parents rose from opposite ends of the table. They walked towards each other, each seeing the object of their deepest desire.

"My one and only," Mr. Senicki said to Rebecca.

"Now and forever," Rebecca replied through her mother's lips.

"Until death do us part," Andy told Mrs. Senicki.

"My shining star," Mrs. Senicki replied.

Mr. Senicki hugged Rebecca. Mrs. Senicki embraced Andy.

The Eyes in the room recorded Mr. and Mrs. Senicki embracing each other.

Listening to Irish music, the Director watched Mr. and Mrs. Senicki kiss each other on the lips. He was exhilarated. The memory implants were working perfectly. Murder was coming … joyous murder. The anticipation of the upcoming slaughter made his mouth water; his masterpiece was taking shape beautifully.

Breaking a major taboo of his culture, the Director danced a jig.

Andy cycled on the dirt road through the dark forest towards Rebecca's home. Moonlight broke through the trees casting numerous shadows across his path. The shifting murkiness strobed across his eyes, playing tricks on his mind. Was it just his imagination or did the forest seem to move? Was something out there? Was something following him? Was he in danger?

Ignoring the creepy sensation, Andy increased his speed. He traveled another 100 yards when his leg muscles began to cramp.

Coming to a decline in the road, Andy coasted on his bicycle, grateful for the chance to rest his legs.

A howling shadow hurled out of the darkness, knocking Andy to the ground.

Andy struggled with the dark Assailant who sat on top of him, gripping his chest and pulling him closer, its hoarse, fetid breath heating his face with its powerful stink.

Andy spun wildly to his left, flipping the assailant off him. He crawled backwards from his attacker, propelling himself with his limbs and a gut full of fear. Ending up in a shaft of moonlight, he wondered what to do next, when he heard the ragged breathing change into terrified whimperings.

It sounds like a child?

Andy got to his feet. He approached the sobbing shadow with caution. "Who are you?" he said. "Why did you attack me?"

He took a small step forward.

The Assailant lunged towards him.

Andy leapt back, clenching his fists, ready to run or fight.

The Mysterious Man plunged into the moonlight; his face looked skullish; he extended his hand towards Andy in a plea for help.

"Please, hide me. Don't let them find me."

"Don't let *who* find you, mister?" Andy said, unfisting his hands.

"Them. It." the Man groaned. "I don't know what they are. God save me, I don't know."

The Man's anguish touched Andy deeply. He stepped towards the cringing figure.

"Easy, mister, easy. You're really scared, aren't you?

The Mysterious Man wrapped his arms about himself. He spoke in a moaning voice.

"They almost caught me with the white light … almost …." The Man's throat tightened so he could not speak. He took a deep shuddering breath.

"Stay out of the white light," he croaked. "Once inside it there is no escape."

"What white light?" Andy asked, perplexed yet curious. "What are you talking about?"

Clutching himself, the Mysterious Man rocked back and forth. "Last night a man was in a bar … his name was Joe … Joe was drunk and raving about things… things that he had seen in the forest … *dangerous things* …. They laughed at Joe … threw him outside … Joe was killed by a train … killed I tell you."

The Mysterious Man's eyes flashed at Andy; a glint of madness resided there. The Man's fingers twitched in front of his mouth. "Joe said he escaped in his truck … that he drove like the wind to get away … that his truck broke down a mile from the bar … don't you see? Don't you see?"

See what? Andy wondered.

The Man whispered to Andy as though imparting a terrible secret. "They found his body by the train tracks … *13 miles from the bar!* … how did he get there if he was drunk and his truck broke down … how?"

Andy didn't understand the relevance of the question, let alone know the answer. He didn't fear the crazy stranger so much now; in fact, he pitied him.

The Mysterious Man fished a small bottle of whiskey out of his jacket pocket. With shaking hands, he loosened the cap then upended it over his open mouth. Eighty proof nerve settler briefly gushed out until the bottle was empty.

Andy realized the Man was drunk and decided he'd better get on his way. He stooped over to pick up his bicycle. "I've got to go, mister. I've got to see my girlfriend."

At the mention of the word "girlfriend," the Mysterious Man whipped his head around towards Andy; the bottle slipped from of his grungy hands. He pronounced his next words like an oracle of death.

"They're going to murder Rebecca …."

A chill touched Andy's heart. "Rebecca? Who is going to …?"

"Them."

"Them?" said Andy, confused.

"Them."

"Who is them?"

"Them! Them! Them!"

Frustrated by the Man's cryptic response, Andy lost his composure. "Who is *Them!*" he yelled.

After many years of keeping a secret so horrible that to possess it meant an end to one's own sanity, the Mysterious Man could no longer hold it close to his soul.

"They're not ghosts, no. Ghosts you can see. They're not demons, either. Demons have to be summoned. No. They're worse … they're … they're … ."

Andy held his breath. "They're what?"

The Man's face went pale. He pointed a boney finger towards the woods behind Andy. "They're coming," he whispered in a voice thick with fear.

Andy turned round towards the forest. He could see nothing. He could hear nothing. *What the heck is going on? What does this have to do with Rebecca?*

He was so concerned over the danger to Rebecca, he didn't notice the Mysterious Man advance upon him until he heard his reedy voice behind his neck say, "Take this."

Andy turned. A silver bracelet with three jet black stones was held a foot from his face. The stones fascinated him. They seemed to be strangely alive. He felt something touch his arm. The bracelet was now clamped around his wrist.

"You can feel them coming with this," said the Man. "It's your only chance. It's Rebecca's only chance."

An owl hooted, startling them both. The Mysterious Man breathed hoarsely. He crept backwards away from Andy as if he were walking on eggshells, his hands in front of him as though he was saying *keep away.*

Andy thought the poor guy was scared out of his wits.

The Man's breathing became short and rapid. "You can't see Them. They're invisible. They can play tricks with your mind ... make you see things that aren't there. If the bracelet tingles … run … hide. Stay out of the white light."

An owl hooted again. The Man's eyes glazed with panic. Raising his hands up level with his shoulders, he squeezed them into tight fists and shook them back and forth. His mouth opened in a grimace of terror, a silent scream, as a vision of something *horrifying* came out of the night.

Andy didn't get it. "Mister?" he said.

The Man hissed at Andy. The hiss began with a burst of terror, but finished with a savage growl that gripped Andy from his head to his toes.

This guy is a total wacko, Andy thought. *I better leave.*

The Mysterious Man sprang to the side making Andy flinch. He arched his back; his hands became claw-like; he snarled like a cornered animal. Biting the air twice, he moaned, then ran into the woods and vanished.

Andy heard the Man race away. Five seconds later he couldn't hear him at all.

Wow, Andy thought. *For a skinny guy he can really hustle.*

Andy pondered the preceding events. Something tugged at his mind with increasing insistency. He became aware of a humming, but couldn't figure out where it was coming from. The bracelet on his left wrist vibrated. He held it before his eyes. It seemed, wonder of wonders, like it was trying to warn him of something.

Andy scanned the area. There was nothing there. Nothing at all.

This is bizarre. That guy must have put some weird voodoo mojo on me. There's nothing out there.

He looked over his right shoulder. As he did so his left arm wearing the bracelet began to rise. Turning his head back, he discovered his arm pointing towards the forest. Startled, he pulled it back to his chest. The stones on the bracelet felt warm.

Andy glanced out into the forest. It was the same direction the weird guy was looking at before he got spooked and ran. Andy remembered what the Mysterious Man told him.

Ghosts and invisible demons? But, that was booze talk. Wasn't it?

With a thought bordering on a premonition, Andy realized that he was all *alone* on a backwoods country road, in the middle of the *night*, surrounded by a dark, shadowy *forest*, several miles from the nearest human *dwelling*, with no *protection* of any kind, wearing a strange *bracelet* on his wrist that somehow was warning him that *dangerous*, invisible beings were coming to get him.

The Munchkins sang it another way.

(to the tune of "Daisy")
"Andy, Andy, what are you going to do?
Invisible things want to mess with you.
Your life will become a real bitch,
When they stick you in a sandwich,

Their breath will smell,
You'll scream like hell,
When their molars chomp down on you."

As the Munchkins burped and giggled, Andy trembled deep in his bones. The bracelet told him he was being watched. An ungovernable fear took up residence in his knees. They shook.

Don't move, the bracelet told him. *They're here.*

Andy's entire body tingled. *This is not happening. There's no such thing as invisible demons.*

An invisible Eye emerged from the thick forest, gliding towards the defenseless youth. As it crossed the barren country road, Iggy programmed the Eye to become transparently visible for a brief moment. Andy saw the bizarre apparition appear like the ripple of an ominous armored ghost under the pale moonlight. A phalanx of spear-like projections thrust forth from its spectral body; then it vanish.

Andy's eyes widened in terror. His head started to spin.

That better have been a hallucination.

The bracelet informed him it wasn't.

Andy's eyes twitched as his fear deepened. His throat felt suddenly dry and raw. He thought the scrawny guy who had just run away after warning him about these *things* was crazy. His knocking knees were not so sure. In fact, his whole body was seriously leaning towards believing the crazy man's entire story, while his nervous mind still sweated with the hope of denial.

A second unseeable Eye cruised out from the trees onto the earthen road. Sweat beaded on Andy's brow. To the Eyes' alien vision, his forehead appeared covered with tiny soap bubbles.

The cyborg Eyes glided in closer.

The bracelet on Andy's wrist tingled madly. It felt as though a swarm of buzzing bees had covered his entire arm. *Freeze,* the bracelet communicated. *This is not a drill. Don't make them hurt you.*

Recalling the spear-like projections he had just seen, Andy's entire body trembled.

The two Eyes stopped on opposite sides of Andy, then moved around him in a slow circle. Passing by his sides, the hairs on Andy's arms stood up on end. Like a freaky lawn of fear, every hair became stiff with an eerie clarity. When the two Eyes moved to the front and back of him, the thin stalks of panic on his arms lay back down, resuming their normal place.

Andy began to lose his grip on reality.

The Eyes kept circling Andy. Each time they did so, his arm hair rose up, then fell. The repetition of it terrorized his teenage flesh. Andy became so frightened even his goose bumps had goose bumps.

The Munchkins said it best.

There once was a boy who could sing,
When he met two invisible things,
Since the things were the meanest
Fear shriveled his penis,

Now the high notes are all he can swing!

With Andy's arm hair fully erect, the Eyes crept in even closer. The bracelet raced the chilling information to his fevered brain. *Move a muscle and your dead.*

Andy now believed it.

Looks like we're screwed, said a Munchkin.

And we didn't even get kissed, protested another.

The other Munchkins sighed, disheartened. *How did we ever get stuck with this loser?*

Inches away from Andy, the two Eyes examined his clothing with minute detail. Switching to z-ray vision, they examined him beneath his garments, passing beyond the fabric to reveal his inner body. The Eyes recorded his rapidly beating heart and every other part of his anatomy, sending the information to the star ship's data banks.

Andy was so petrified he could barely breathe. It felt as though two magnifying glasses were roaming all over his body, violating every inch of him like the subject of a bizarre science experiment. One Eye went up his front side, while the other wandered down his back. His flesh cringed as the eerie circles crept across his person without his consent.

Just for fun, Iggy and Glop had the Eyes transfer some static electricity onto the frightened youth.

Andy felt his hair stiffen, growing skyward, writhing erect. His scalp seemed to sizzle. When the static electricity stopped, he looked like he was wearing a fright wig. The rest of his body hair stood on end like rigid toothpicks, pushing his clothing away, giving him the appearance of being inflated.

Iggy and Glop laughed; they slapped each other with high-five's.

Andy was beside himself. *Should I run? Should I fight? What should I do?*

The bracelet repeated its warning, *Freeze or they will rip you apart and feast on your bones while you are alive and watching.*

That last argument was good enough for Andy. He decided not to fight. The resolution came as a relief because he was shivering so hard he was having trouble keeping his knees from collapsing. Having to run or fight just didn't seem plausible when it took everything you had just to remain standing up, let alone the fact that you had no idea what you were up against, couldn't see them, and there were two of them.

Some static electricity discharged on his head with a painful zap. Andy smarted from the shock; he had but one heartfelt desire.

I really want to go home and crawl into bed.

He hoped he would live long enough to do so.

The Eyes' intensive scrutiny ended. They drifted on down the road.

The bracelet communicated to Andy that now would be a good time to casually ride away. That sounded real good to Andy.

His hair riding tall on his head, his clothing pushed out away from his body, Andy casually straddled his bike, his insides shaking like jello. Putting what was left of his mettle to the pedal, he cautiously cycled away.

As Andy disappeared around a curve in the road, the two Eyes floated higher in the air. A shaft of white light stabbed down from underneath their cyborg bodies. They glided into the forest in the direction the Mysterious Man had fled.

With a feeling of déjà vu (the certainty that he had done this before), the Mysterious Man hustled through the dark woods away from Andy, ducking under low tree branches and dodging obstacles with the skill of an experienced woodsman. In some ways it was all too familiar territory as he had been doing this for years, but this time it was different. This time he had confided to another the deep dark secret that had resided in his bosom and his bosom alone.

A feeling of elation came over him.

Allies! I have allies! They will help me defeat Them. They will continue the battle in my place. I have passed the torch of responsibility. They will use the bracelet to win.

Leaping over a fallen tree, a different train of thought caught him off guard. The Man shoved his boots into the ground, grinding himself to an abrupt halt.

What is wrong with me? How could I give that boy my only weapon, my only defense?

He suddenly felt naked without the item that had been on his wrist for many years. Panic sat in his gut like a stone.

I'm vulnerable ... unprotected.

He did not like the feeling one damn bit.

I have to go back. I have to get the bracelet. Whatever possessed me to give it to that boy in the first place?

North. North was where he had left the boy, so northward he marched, his mind so preoccupied with the loss of such an important object that it cancelled out the potential danger he was heading towards.

What if he has left with it already? What if They came and took it away from him? How will I ever get it back? I will never be safe without it. I am a fool.

His boots crunched the ground under his feet as he increased his speed towards Andy.

A few minutes later, he reached up to push an overhanging branch out of his way. Out of the corner of his eye, he caught something moving beyond him. He crouched down behind some foliage.

A hundred yards away, not one, but two, bright white lights shone onto the forest. Their beams flashed this way and that, illuminating shadows--searching for something.

The Mysterious Man had no doubt that it was himself they were searching for.

They know I'm here. The bracelet protected me, but now it's gone and they KNOW!

He quivered. There was no other explanation. They probably even knew he was the one shadowing their every move for many years. The Man feared that *They* must want him badly. He had never seen two out and about like this before now. Yes, they must want him worse than a flea wants a cat. And if they caught him ....

Turning, he slunk back into the forest. The boy would have to wait. Without the bracelet to guide him his senses were on full alert and then some. For the first time in many years of hunting the hunters, he knew he was now the prey. He was like a seal caught between two killer whales. If they trapped him, he would do anything to escape--even leap out of his own skin. The image of him running without his skin made him shudder. He took off in the opposite direction.

Feet don't fail me now.

With the agility of a jungle cat, his heartbeat quickened its pace to match the swiftness of his feet. Before the next few minutes were over, he was sure the pace of both would be even faster. Playtime was over. This was business – the business of life and death. He plunged into the concealing forest, careful not to leave a trail or make a sound that would lead *Them* to him.

Stopping beside a large Oak tree, Andy sat on his bike near the Senicki home. He had recovered from his encounter with *Them* long enough to be the owner of a newly acquired sense of caution. A light was on in an upstairs room. In the living room, a fire burned in the hearth. The flickering light took on a mysterious quality as he stood in the dark, watching for signs of anything unusual.

Andy tried to make sense out of the last 20 minutes. Maybe this Mysterious Man was wrong. Maybe he imagined all the bizarre vibrations that had frightened him so badly a mile back down the road.

Maybe the bracelet he gave me is some kind of sick joke.

Andy desperately wanted to believe that the intoxicated "Them" hunter was actually some kind of weird gag salesman who would show up at the Butcher shop tomorrow and try to sell him a bunch of cheap, corny stuff.

"Ha, ha, ha. I tricked you good didn't I, kid? Ha, ha, ha. Now imagine the fun you'll have pulling this same prank on your friends. Only $5.95. And I've got a car full of other great tricks. Ever hear of a palm buzzer. It's a doozy. Only $4.95."

Andy would have purchased an entire car-load of deplorable gimmicks just to know for certain that the entire evening was all a joke, that Rebecca was still his girlfriend, that her mother hadn't kissed him, that he wasn't grounded, or that two creepy invisible *things* hadn't looked up his backside or down his pants with a magnifying glass. He would have considered it a bargain.

He bit his lower lip. Whatever was going to happen, it wasn't going to help matters if he stayed rooted to this spot.

I better go see Rebecca. I hope she forgives me. I really like her.

Leaning his bike against the tree, he headed towards the house. Each step he took sounded like he was treading on a loud drum pronouncing his doom. Andy imagined himself caught in the beams of several powerful searchlights. Armed guards aimed high-intensity rifles at his head, ready to squeeze the trigger if he so much as sneezed.

Halt or we'll shoot! Achooooo. Crack go the rifles. His head explodes. Have a nice day.

Andy stuck his fingers inside the imaginary hole in his head and touched his brain. It felt sticky.

Good shooting, men. Beer and cookies for everyone.

Hooray! the sharpshooters cheered.

Reaching the side of the house, Andy shimmied along a hedge and peered inside the living room. Mr. and Mrs. Senicki were silhouetted by the golden flames from the fireplace. Their arms were entwined about each other; their faces were inches apart.

They stood still as a statue.

Andy saw a turkey feast that was completely untouched. The dishes were clean; the silverware was wrapped inside a napkin; no glasses were filled; even the turkey had not been carved.

What is going on here? he wondered. *Never mind. I've got to get to Rebecca. I've got to explain what happened.*

Andy hoped that the upstairs light was from Rebecca's bedroom window. He had never been to her home before now. The window was open an inch from the bottom; a vine covered trellis led up to it from the ground. Thinking he was trying to break into prison, he tested the first wooden slat, making sure that it could carry his weight without breaking. But worse than the notion that watchtower guards would use his head for target practice, was the fear of apologizing for something he was not responsible for in the first place.

I'm sorry I'm innocent, Rebecca. Please don't hate me because I'm not guilty.

Andy scaled the trellis.

Sitting on his shoulders, the Munchkins prayed for his forgiveness using the *Lord's Prayer* as their template.

"Our Andy, who art in trouble,
Safely climb this fence.
Apologize, tears filled with eyes,
May she not hit his face with crème pies.

Give him a break, Lord. He needs it bad.
And don't let her beat him to death.
For it would make his ego a hopeless wreck.

And lead him not into manic-depression,
But deliver him from paranoid-schizophrenia.
For she is the Queendom, and the power
To pussy-whoop him forever.
A-woman. A-woman."

Wearing a pink nightgown and hugging a teddy bear, Rebecca sat on the edge of her bed, daydreaming. She found it impossible to go to sleep. She simply sat and felt emotion--and the emotion felt terrible. It cut her insides up. Her parents were abusing her; Andy was abusing her. She was unused to being treated this way. She couldn't have felt more dreadful than if she had been turned into a wart-faced witch.

Rebecca didn't notice Andy crawl through the window until he tumbled into her room. Turning, she saw his face pop up beside her bed, sporting a look of stunned confusion. She took in his furrowed brow, his eyebrows were slanted, giving him a sad, worried expression.

Dazed, Andy blinked his eyelids rapidly. "Rebecca, are you all right?"

She hit him with her teddy bear, knocking him back down to the floor.

Rebecca tossed herself across the bed, looking down at the boyfriend villain in her midst.

Andy rolled over, gazing up at the girl of his dreams, seeing her upside down.

"You kissed my mother," Rebecca accused. "I saw you. What kind of a boyfriend are you?"

Andy knew he had seconds to make amends. "Rebecca. I didn't want to. Your mother kissed me. You've got to believe me."

"I suppose you think kissing your girlfriend's mother on the lips is normal?"

"Has anyone tried to hurt you today?" Andy blurted out.

Rebecca paused, caught off guard at the sudden change in the conversation.

"Andy, what are you talking about?"

Andy rolled over onto his knees so he could see Rebecca's face right-side up.

"I met this nutty guy on the way over here and he told me, well, I mean, I thought he was dangerous cause he tackled me and cried like a baby, but he had a bottle of whiskey so when he told me what he told me, I just, I dunno, he didn't --"

"Told you what, Andy?" Rebecca demanded, her voice still steaming with resentment.

Andy stood up. He gazed intensely into her eyes. "He said your life was in danger. That someone was trying to kill you."

His truthfully uttered words and the worry in his eyes melted Rebecca's anger. Her mouth hung open; she was speechless; she put her hand to her heart.

"Kill me? Really?"

Andy sincerely nodded.

A masculine arm reached inside a refrigerator and pulled out half a gallon of milk. From inside the living room china cabinet, a feminine hand removed a bottle of bourbon. On a gas stove, a pilot light clicked to life. Orange-blue flames licked the underside of a sauce pan into which some milk was poured. A second pan was filled with water into which the bottle of bourbon was placed and heated.

Standing side by side at the kitchen stove, Herman and Alexandra warmed their respective liquids on the burners. As Herman turned towards his wife, his eyes saw Rebecca standing beside him.

Rebecca nodded solemnly.

Alexandra looked at the man beside her. It was Andy.

Andy nodded gravely.

Herman reached down under the kitchen sink, pulled out a box and set it down on the counter. It was rat poison.

Two glasses were filled, one with warm milk, the other with brandy. A scoop of rat poison was ladled into each drink and stirred.

The flames on the stove were extinguished.

"He said my life is in danger?" said Rebecca, pacing back and forth in front of her closet. "How could he know that? I've never even met him?"

"I don't know," Andy replied, watching her plow the carpet with her bare feet. "He knew your name. He sounded serious."

"Do you know him or is he a stranger?"

Andy shook his head. "I never saw him before. It's just --"

"What did he wear?" she asked.

"I don't know. It was dark and I wasn't paying attention."

"Were his clothes clean or dirty?

"They were dirty but --"

"I thought so," interrupted Rebecca, her hands grasping the sides of her head in relief. "It's crazy Joe."

"Crazy who?" asked Andy.

"You've lived here for years and you don't know who crazy Joe is?"

"Is it that guy that lives in the forest?" Andy guessed.

"And fixes people's cars for money or food. The guy that finds dead animals and sells them to my dad for his taxidermy work. That crazy Joe," Rebecca said, crossing her arms across her chest and raising her eyebrows at Andy as though she was saying "get the picture?"

Her expression made Andy feel foolish. He now believed the whole evening with the Mysterious Man was nonsense, even being examined by invisible *things*. The guy spooked him so badly he must have imagined the whole thing. His imagination was always getting the best of him and it had done so again. His dad was right, he needed to grow up. He needed to act like a man.

Andy's ears turned red with embarrassment.

"He said you were in danger … I thought …." His words trailed off into silence; he bowed his head, silently berating himself.

"You thought what?" Rebecca said.

Andy spied a ring on the floor. "Hey, that's my grandmother's ring," said Andy, picking it up. "How did it get there?"

"I threw it there because you kissed my mother."

"But I told you --"

"Are you in love with my mother?"

"No. I had to see you. I was afraid." Andy's voice became quiet. Misery covered his face.

Observing his despair, Rebecca softened. "Afraid of what?" she said.

"That I would never see you again," Andy whispered so softly she could hardly hear him.

Rebecca was touched. "You did? Really?"

Andy nodded, gazing dejectedly into her eyes.

Rebecca's heart melted. She forgave him. She knew it had to be a mistake. She had let her anger get the best of her. After all, what was more important — being mad or being with Andy?

"That's so sweet of you," Rebecca said. She looked at the ring; her eyes twinkled; she held out her hand and smiled.

Andy slid the ring over her finger. His apology had been accepted. He had won her back into his life. Despite all the crazy turmoil, the day had turned out for the best after all. As the ring neared the end of its romantic destination, he asked her the big question.

"Rebecca Senicki. Will you be my …"

Andy was about to say "girlfriend," when muffled footsteps ascended the stairs.

Rebecca's hand flew up to her mouth.

"It's my parents!" she said in an alarmed whisper. "Quick. Hide in the closet."

Carrying the poisoned drinks on separate trays, Herman and Alexandra walked down the hall towards Rebecca's bedroom.

The Director watched them in his control room. He could now make the parents see what he wanted them to see, hear what he wanted them to hear, and feel what he wanted them to feel. He had manipulated their memories and emotions, even their religion, rearranging them to suit his story line.

"And now for the part of our story where the murder of a loved one is revealed as a family value," the Director said in his best announcer voice. His slit of a mouth formed a smile, revealing small, sharp teeth. "Your religion can't help you," he said smirking. "What good is your God now?"

Nearing the door to the bedroom, Herman spoke to Rebecca. "Wait here."

Rebecca squeezed his arm.

Herman felt the smoothness of her skin. He couldn't live without her. He must protect her from harm so they could live with the Lord forever.

Carrying the deadly glass of milk on a tray before him, he stepped towards the closed door as his eyes began to water. Alexandra had to die. God demanded it of him.

"Stay here," Alexandra told Andy, eyeing the poisoned Brandy on her tray.

Andy gave her a tender glance. It kindled within her the devotion necessary to carry out the treacherous task against her husband.

Carrying the poisoned drinks, the two parents entered Rebecca's bedroom.

Rebecca lay on her bed under the covers. A large book covered her face, her Chemistry textbook, her worst subject.

As her parents entered her bedroom, she hid behind it.

Andy peaked through thin slits in the closet door. He couldn't see much, only the trays with the drinks. He wondered what was happening. It looked a little strange.

The parents split apart, moving to each side of Rebecca's bed.

Rebecca saw a chemical equation loom large on the page before her.

$2FeO(s) + Si(s) + CaO(s) = 2Fe(s) + CaSiO_3(s)$. The formula for steel.

She slowly lowered the book. The lamp on her nightstand illuminated her parents' faces from underneath. They looked like characters out of some grim, horror movie getting ready to do who knows what to her.

Rebecca glanced at the equation for steel a second time.

Rebecca steeled herself.

"I brought you a brandy, dear," said her mother.

"Have a glass of warm milk," entreated her father.

Rebecca looked at the tray her mother carried. Brandy in bed? That was bizarre. They never let her drink alcohol, even under adult supervision. She looked at the milk glass her father was carrying.

What's that black stuff at the bottom ... chocolate syrup?

In the closet, Andy watched and tried to keep quiet. The unsettling feeling that crazy Joe wasn't so crazy after all soured his stomach. Unable to do anything except betray his presence, he watched and waited, hoping the parents would quickly leave.

Suspicion gnawed inside Rebecca; her stomach felt queasy. Her parents' eyes were blank, zombie-like. It was as if their brains were working but no one was home, at least no one she felt like having a friendly drink with.

They're not even blinking their eyelids. This is mega creepy.

"It will help you sleep," her mother said.

"I made it just for you," her father said.

"Drink it," they said. "It's good for you."

Rebecca felt like she should do something, so she lifted the glass of milk off of the tray her father held. As it passed before her eyes, she stared at the murky gunk in the bottom of the glass. Blackish swirls loomed before her eyes, filling her with disgust. Setting the milk glass down on the end table, she took the brandy off of her mother's tray. It had the same icky-looking, black substance in it.

Rebecca set the brandy down next to the milk, folded her hands in her lap and tried to convincingly smile.

"Thank you. I'll drink it later." She picked up her chemistry book, hoping her parents would take the hint and leave.

Her parents didn't move. They simply stood there staring at her.

Rebecca glanced over the rim of the book. She thought she saw an evil intent lurking behind the blank expression on her parents' faces. Her body turned to jelly as she contemplated the frightening notion that her parents meant to hurt her. Panic welled up inside her, her heart beat like a loud gong tolling her doom. She wanted Andy to burst out of the closet, turn the bed into a magic carpet and whisk them away to safety.

A sob crept up her throat like a living thing seeking release. She swallowed forcefully, trying to wash the blob of fear back down.

I'd better do something ... before they do.

Mr. and Mrs. Senicki heard Rebecca's next words as though they were spoken by the person they intended to kill.

"Thank you. I promise to drink it as soon as I finish reading my book."

Through the slit in the closet door, Andy saw that no one was moving.

"I promise," said Rebecca, hoping her parents would go away.

The parents stared at her, their eyes not blinking, seemingly harmless, yet predatory.

"Good night, my darling," her father finally said.

"Pleasant dreams, babushka," her mother cooed.

"Have a nice long sleep," the beverage assassins said fondly, exiting the room and closing the door behind them.

Andy emerged from the closet. Rebecca appeared to be in the throes of a silent battle.

"Rebecca?" Andy whispered. "Your parents are gone."

Rebecca didn't move a muscle.

Andy tenderly touched her shoulder. "Rebecca," he said. "Are you okay?"

Rebecca whirled her head around; her eyes were glazed with fear. Lunging forward, she wrapped her arms around Andy's waist, pressing her head tightly against his chest.

Andy saw the two glasses on the nightstand. The globs of muck had settled to the bottom. He recognized it as rat poison. His dad had used it from time to time outside the Butcher shop to keep it vermin free. "Can't have customers worried about the meat in their sausage," his dad would always joke. But poisoning their own daughter?

Crazy Joe's warning came to mind: *They're going to murder Rebecca.*

Andy was not used to making snap decisions in his life, but in this instance he broke the mold of indecision.

"Get dressed. We're getting out of here," he told his freaked out girlfriend.

Crickets chirped their evening song as Andy helped Rebecca climb down the trellis towards the yard. Rebecca wore jeans with beads sewn on them, a pink knitted sweater and tennis shoes. She snagged her sweater on the wood, tearing the sleeve, leaving a couple of broken strands dangling.

Andy didn't know where they were going to go, he just knew they couldn't stay here. She had insisted on knowing what was in the glasses, so he told her. It had not been a good idea. His confirmation that her parents were trying to snuff her unnerved her even more. During the climb down she faltered twice, nearly falling so that he had to support her with his hand. Her emotional pain made him feel terrible. He belittled himself all the way down to the ground.

What is wrong with me? Oh, by the way, your mom and dad, well they're trying to murder you with rat poison. How do you feel about that? I am so stupid! Now she's in shock. I must be the worst boyfriend on the planet. I should have drunk the poisoned milk myself.

When they finally reached the bottom, Rebecca's feet touched the soil. She clung to the lattice for balance; Andy put his hand on her waist to steady her. He gazed at the moon, his mind a hodgepodge of questions.

Where should we go? My parents? No. They would just bring her back here to the slaughter house. The Sheriff? Too far away. The gas station?

Nothing stuck out as a great idea.

Maybe the high school? It's a little far, but not that far. We could bicycle there and hide until morning. Besides, they have vending machines. I could really go for some chips and a soda.

The last idea made the most sense. They could stay there, eat, then go to the Sheriff in the morning.

"Come on, Rebecca. We should get going."

In the darkness of the living room, two pairs of mind-controlled eyes watched the two young people cross the lawn. Their faces betrayed no emotion, yet inside they were cauldrons of seething resentment.

Herman Senicki stood beside his wife, but saw only what the Director allowed him to see--his wife and Andy dragging Rebecca across the front yard grass. Alexandra held a gun in her hands; Andy manhandled her; Rebecca cried.

Herman's body trembled. He wanted to dash to her rescue, but he was somehow unable to move.

Alexandra stood next to her husband, but her vision told a different tale. Herman and Rebecca were kidnapping Andy. Rebecca pointed a gun at Andy's head as Herman slugged him hard in the gut. Andy bent over in pain and fell to the ground. Herman dragged him by his feet.

A tear rolled down Alexandra's cheek.

Urged on by emotions they did not understand or control, Herman and Alexandra ascended the stairs towards their bedroom, believing they were walking alone.

Andy and Rebecca shuffled across the lawn towards Andy's bike. Andy had his arm around her, supporting her weight. Rebecca clung tightly to him, not speaking a word.

Despite feeling awkward, Andy tried to sooth her fears. "Keep walking. We're almost there. You're doing good, Rebecca … real good."

Rebecca was strangely fragile; Andy worried about her the entire way. When they reached the spot where he had left his bike, he realized they needed another one so they could escape.

"Where's your bike?" whispered Andy.

Rebecca didn't respond. She wrapped her arms about his body like she was cold even though the night air was only slightly cool.

Andy decided he'd better find the bike himself. He turned around, scanning the area. The much-needed bicycle was on the side of the house in front of a window beside a bush. He could see the handlebars in the moonlight. He wondered if her parents would see him, but made up his mind to chance it. It would be foolish for him to ride her on his handlebars on an unpaved road at night.

"Stay here," he told Rebecca. "I'll be right back."

He slunk back towards the house, hoping her parents were in their bedroom and the coast was clear.

Mrs. Senicki pulled her top dresser drawer towards her. Her neatly folded undergarments slid into view. Raising some panties with her hand, she exposed a small pearl-handled revolver. Lifting the weapon close to her eyes, she watched the light glint off the metal. An image of Andy in danger bloomed within her, causing her to grip the gun handle hard. She was flooded with the desire to gun down her evil husband and daughter.

Mr. Senicki opened his top dresser drawer. His clothes were randomly stuffed inside. Lifting a wad of socks, he uncovered an old, western, Colt 45 pistol. He stroked the long, black barrel with his hand, aiming it before him, imagining how he would shoot his enemies.

Armed with conviction and a gun apiece, the parents set out upon their lethal agenda.

The Director stood on his massage rug, wiggling his bare toes deep into the living grass. The energy drain to keep the parents ignorant of each other's presence was a burden on the ship's power system, but unavoidable.

"Making a masterpiece is never cheap or easy," the Director said. "Francis Ford Coppolla was notorious for going way over budget with films like *The Godfather*."

The story had come along much faster than he expected. It usually took three months or more to make a movie, but this one was happening like a runaway freight train. Now that the time had come to arm the actors the action scenes would really get going.

Things were about to get really exciting.

The Director twisted a knob that sent a current of energy into the massage grass. The grass writhed under his feet, energetically rubbing his soles, sending waves of pleasure up his nerve lines, stimulating his body. The Director turned the knob to its highest setting, letting himself be driven to such a high-pitched state of illegal excitement that it threatened to burst out of his body.

It was wonderful. Being away from Home World had its advantages. He could never enjoy himself this much there, even in his own abode.

Stretching his arms out wide, he gazed up at the ceiling.

"Next to me, Coppolla was a piker!"

Rebecca stood still in the cool night, a slight breeze brushed her cheek. It seemed a gentle act of kindness amidst all the recent turmoil. It lifted her out of her doldrums.

She faced an old Oak tree that bordered her parents' property. It was one she knew well. She had climbed it once to retrieve her cat when a coyote had chased him up it. Mr. Meow had refused to come down despite her protestations that "all was well." When it came to being eaten alive, Mr. Meow kept his own counsel about such matters. The memory of that event and the brisk air made her aware that she was standing outside in the dark.

What am I doing here? It must be late.

The last thing she remembered was Andy putting the ring on her finger and asking her to be his girlfriend--then the awful memories flooded her mind like a poisonous inspiration.

My parents ... the drinks ... rat poison ... get dressed ... climb down ... it will be all right.

A twig snapped. She turned to see Andy wheeling her bicycle across the lawn. He had come to her aid when she needed it, even *before* she even knew she needed it.

He is such a great boyfriend.

Andy saw her and waved.

Rebecca's parents stepped out of the house and aimed their guns at Andy.

Rebecca screamed.

As Andy took a step forward, the dark, flat hand of an Eye materialized under his shoe. The Eye pushed Andy's shoe backwards, making him slip and fall as bullets blew a chunk out of a tree that his head had just been in front of.

Andy glanced at Rebecca's parents, seeing smoke curl out of their weapons. Rising quickly, he pushed the bike forward. "Ride, Rebecca! Ride!" he yelled.

Rebecca flung her leg over the seat of Andy's mountain bike and cranked the wheels for all she was worth. Andy sped forward, used his 'run and leap' trick and dashed down the road on Rebecca's 3-speed bike.

Mr. and Mrs. Senicki raised their weapons, taking aim at their enemies' heads. They followed their targets along their gun sights and put pressure on the triggers. The hammers pulled back, bullets entered the chambers, one final squeeze would bring death roaring forth. The instruction to shoot formed in their brains when Andy and Rebecca disappeared on their bicycles into the shadows.

The parents lowered their weapons and stared blankly at the road.

"Cut!" the Director said. "Get me a medium close up of their faces with the house in the background, then thaw out the rest of the crew. I'll be in my private suite."

"You heard the Director," said the Production Manager. "And get some lighting probes out here. The key light is too weak. Punch up the moonlight on their faces, increase the rim, and for crying out loud you its, be sure to use a Gam 10 filter. I want it soft."

The it technicians scrambled to complete their work assignments.

While Mr. and Mrs. Senicki stood like mindless statues, inside the star ship the Alien Reality Television murder mystery crew went into all-out production. Fifty-six more crew members--all class 3 intelligences, all of them *its*--were released from cryogenic storage.

The Production Manager set the cryo-controls to revive 4 cameramen, 8 props department staff, thirty special effects technicians, four lighting techs, three production assistants, one music composer and four craft service "octopus siamese twins" with two bodies and eight arms each, capable of making enough food to feed sixty in a matter of minutes. The octopus chefs also furnished plenty of fresh eggs by constantly mating with itself while it cooked the food.

The Production Manager clicked the computer's start button. The whole process was like going through an automated car wash.

From within the star ship's cryogenic storage facilities, frozen bodies were stored in large oval chunks of a substance called an *ice egg*. Automated mechanical arms grabbed an *egg* and hung it from a transport rail like a side of beef in a frozen meat locker.

The eggs rode along the rail until they reached one of several defrosters. The egg was plucked and suspended between two halves of a metal mold. Indicator lights turned from yellow to red to green as the ice egg (and the frozen crewman inside it) was flash thawed by a jolt of intense microwaves. The metal mold cracked open; steam shot out; cryo-liquid spilled into a floor drain.

Soaking wet and looking fatigued, an *it* named Wank coughed up a bluish fluid, then sluggishly groaned and stretched as though waking up from a bad hangover while babbling like an infant. A cushioned chair moved into position behind the drowsy crewman. Soft mechanical fingers nudged Wank into the chair, tickling him, making him giggle. A restraint web lashed his body to the chair, causing Wank to squawk.

Wank was driven to the next station where, unable to move, a robotic arm with a syringe plunged a caffeinated serum in his buttocks that got his heart pumping and brought his mind to full alertness. Wank thanked the wakeup process with a hearty stream of inarticulate cusswords.

After the wakeup injection, the restraint web was removed. Wank stood up, perceived he was hungry, and stepped on a moving slide-walk to an automated cafeteria where he had five seconds to choose between one of six options for a meal. He chose meal option #1, a breakfast combination of a seafood omelet made with swordfish meat and octopus eggs, whale gruel, a glass of squid juice and a tuna fish cookie. A representative from the Crew Members' Union stood by to make sure that everyone was fed according to Union rules.

As Wank and the unfrozen crew members dined, Zonk arrived. "Man, am I glad to be out of cryo-storage. Being frozen is boring. At least now I get to be a working stiff."

The crowd of its broke into gales of laughter.

"Hey buddy, move over," kidded Zonk taking a seat. "Pass the squid juice. I'm starved. I feel like I haven't eaten in 87,000 light years." It was an old joke, but it caused Wank and some other crew members to choke on their whale gruel, while others slapped their backs to keep their fellow its from suffocating.

Half an hour later, Wank was strapped into a medical examination pod and forced to do speed aerobics for five minutes, after which, if he didn't collapse, he was rated "fit for duty" and told to report to work.

Wank didn't collapse.

Standing in a line, Wank entered a delivery pod which sucked him through a tube to the main production studio.

Stepping out of the delivery pod, the defrosted, fed and medically checked Wank entered a large chamber which resembled a concert hall orchestra pit with the director's podium in front. The room was surrounded by holographic screens which could view the action from any single direction or be split up into numerous views. Wank and the crew members took their places at their work stations, booted up their systems and opened the various special effects programs.

The Director entered, wearing sunglasses and a short cape. Standing at his podium, he tapped a baton on its surface getting everyone's attention.

Every it waited on the Director, which is just the way he liked it.

His arms raised, the Director swished the baton.

Fingers danced on keyboards and holographic screens creating whatever the Director dictated to them in seconds: background mattes, sounds and smells, temperature and wind, the light from the moon, the forest, dirt, everything. To their credit the genetically engineered beings made one heck of an art department. Everything was assembled in accordance to the Director's verbal storyboard in a mind-blowing, 3-dimensional, Computer Graphics Imagery concert of reality TV production.

Minutes later, after fine tuning the results, the Director burned his scenario into his actors' brains as though their minds were a Digital Video Disk.

"Begin memory insertion," the Director said. The programs engaged, blended seamlessly together and transmitted the mnemonic movie from the star ship into the jellyfish implanted in the parents' heads, where it squirted out through living tentacles in their minds as a bio-chemical memory.

"Roll it," the Director said.

Standing outside his home in the dark of the night, Herman Senicki's mind received the transmitted data.

Rebecca was forcefully kidnapped by Alexandra and Andy ... dragged across the lawn ... they were going to kill her .... He got his Colt 45 from his dresser drawer ... pursued them in the Bronco ... chased them through the moon-lit forest on foot ... tree branches swatted his face ... bushes tore at his pants ... scratching his skin ... making it bleed .... The pain and blood didn't matter .... Nothing mattered except saving Rebecca before they hurt her.

He caught up to her captors ... a gun battle took place ... bullets whizzed by his head ... Herman returned fire ... he dashed recklessly into the open .... A bullet grazed his shoulder ... he stumbled but kept going ... a second bullet wounded his leg ... he rolled on the ground .... Coming to his knees, he blasted Alexandra in the head and shot Andy through the heart.

Bleeding, he untied Rebecca ... she grabbed his leg and cried, her tears dripping on his bleeding wound. Herman glared at the two dead bodies ... their clothing soaked in rich, red blood.

The Director cemented the lesson home. "Roll sequence two."

Clouds parted in the heavens ... the light of God shined down on Herman ... in its radiance he felt the glory of divine vengeance ... his wounds magically healed.

The voice of God spoke. "Yeay though you race through the forest of the shadow of death, you shall fear no evil, for thy gun and thy bullets are with thee. Though violence may follow thee the rest of thy life, as long as you protect her, you shall dwell in the house of the Lord with Rebecca forever."

Herman had been true to his religion ... he had delivered Rebecca from evil ... their souls would live in heaven forever ... God guaranteed it ... they were saved.

Alexandra Senicki had a similar vision, except the Director had her rescue Andy and shoot Herman and Rebecca. She stood over the dead bodies ... pleasure and rage surging through her veins ... Andy clung to her leg, weeping with joy as the Lord made his holy promise of eternal salvation.

"I have supplanted their God with my own agenda," said the Director "Now we will see some proper Judeo-Christian murderous behavior. Ha!" he shouted, stretching his arms forward and cracking his knuckles with satisfaction.

The Director played his movie memories of the kidnapping and rescue of their loved ones over and over, inside the Herman's and Alexandra's minds.

"It will give them a sense of inevitable victory that will turn them into fearless, devoted fanatics." *Too bad they're not Muslims. I could have them wrap dynamite around their bodies and blow each other up. God could promise them a harem of virgins in the afterlife. Those Who Watch would be greatly offended. It would have increased the ratings.* The Director shrugged. "Oh, well, you can't have everything.

He pondered for a moment. "Even so ... you can always count on religion to bring out the worst in lower class people."

When it was time to start filming the chase scene, the parents would believe that their beloved--Andy or Rebecca --would be killed by their evil relations if they didn't act quickly. Bound by their devotion to God via the new beliefs the director had implanted in them, they would hunt their enemies down with a vengeance, even to the point of giving up their lives to achieve their foes destruction, and save the one whose life mattered more to them than their own.

The Director called this process giving his actors *motivation.*

CHAPTER 10

FLIGHT

Rebecca struggled on the bike to keep up with Andy. They had gone a couple of miles down the dark, moon-lit backwoods road and she was tired and winded. Andy had urged her three times to keep going. Although she was not the avid biker he was, she had gamely responded and pushed herself onward. Andy rode his mountain bike to school, to work, to everywhere. He flung himself off ten foot heights over the head of his girlfriend for the thrill of showing off. He physically outclassed her. Even though she now rode his superior bike and he used her little 3 speed, he tore up the road around her.

She could never hope to keep up with him.

After another quarter mile, she gave up and coasted to a stop.

Andy rode in front of her. He glanced back for the umpteenth time and realized he had to turn back once more.

"We have to keep going," Andy said as he neared her. "We can't stop. They might come after us."

Rebecca ignored his words; she ignored her aching legs and lungs. Instead, she said exactly what was on her anxious mind.

"What's happened to my parents, Andy? Why are they doing this?"

Rebecca covered her eyes with her hands so that Andy wouldn't see how miserable she felt. Andy recalled how telling the truth about the rat poison in the glasses didn't help them the last time. Prudence got the better of him now. Since he didn't know what to say, he said nothing. Instead, he lowered the kick stand, walked over to her, and held her in his arms, hoping that would comfort her and give her the strength she needed to continue. He also kept glancing back at the road to make sure her parents didn't catch them unaware.

Rebecca clung to him, her face buried in his chest. "I'm sorry, Andy. Mom and Dad shot at us. What are we going to do?"

"I thought we'd hide at the high school," replied Andy. "Or maybe we could go tell the Sheriff." The Sheriff was many miles further than the High School. Andy didn't think Rebecca could bike that far.

"Tell him what?" said Rebecca, distractedly. "That my mother and father are trying to kill us. That they shot at us with guns? We'll be the ones locked up, not them."

Andy glanced at the starry night. Its beauty had always fascinated him, but at the moment he couldn't enjoy it. Rebecca's body trembled in his arms. He tried to think of something to comfort her.

"Don't worry," Andy said soothingly. "We'll think of something … I hope."

Rebecca tore away from him, waving her arms about as though she were tormented by a swarm of hungry mosquitoes.

Andy saw her run her fingers through her hair and bury her head under her arms. An intense wail surfaced from deep within her throat.

Rebecca started to keen.

Great drawn out moans of anguish pierced the air; Andy had never heard anything like it.

This is not good, Andy thought. He sensed he better do something fast before she became hysterical. They still had to get to someplace safe. He didn't want to be trapped in the forest all night; he wanted a roof over their heads. He was not going to let things fall apart.

Rebecca continued to keen.

Andy forced her arms down to her sides. "Rebecca, look at me."

She lifted her face. Dark eyeliner ran down her cheeks, making a long dark streak. Her body quivered.

Andy could see she was in great need of assurance. "Rebecca, I'm here. I won't leave you. We'll find an answer. I promise."

Rebecca stared at him, her eyes shiny. Andy did his best to look confident. He straightened his shoulders, stuck out his chest, and gave her his best warm smile.

Rebecca keened again, albeit softer.

Discouraged but not defeated, Andy gave it another try.

"Rebecca," Andy said softly. "Remember what you said to me today about being positive? About having the faith that things will work out the way they should? There's a way out of this and we're going to find it. I know we will. I have faith in you. I have faith in us."

Rebecca felt the strength in Andy's hands, the confidence in his voice. His vitality and assurance brought her back from the edge of hysteria.

"Do you really think so?" she asked, sniffling.

"I really *know* so," he said, his voice filled with conviction.

Rebecca's face muscles ceased twitching, a glint of hope appeared in her eyes. The corners of her mouth curved upwards in a slight smile, she nodded her head slightly.

Andy pulled a wad of something soft out of his pocket and cleaned the muddy streaks off her face. When he finished, she looked at the hunk of white stuff, now smeared with black eyeliner and wet with her tears.

"What's that?" Rebecca asked.

"Toilet paper," Andy said.

"Toilet paper?"

Andy nodded, his eyes beaming, a smile creeping on his lips.

Rebecca hoped the toilet paper hadn't broken up into little white fuzzies all over her face. But fuzzies or no fuzzies, she was glad that Andy was with her. If she had had to endure this alone she knew she would have curled up into a ball of misery, sat by the road and cried all night.

A bright white light flared in their eyes. Half-blinded, they turned towards it as a car came to a sudden halt before them. The car came from the direction they were fleeing, not from Rebecca's house so it couldn't be her parents. Andy realized this was their chance to get to safety. He heard a door opening.

"Can you help us?" said Andy. "We need a ride into town."

"Do you have it?" a voice demanded.

The shape of a man staggered in front of the headlights. Outlined by their brilliance, he seemed composed of menacing shadow. Car keys fell to the ground at his feet.

"Do you have the bracelet?" the Mysterious Man said.

"It's you!" Andy exclaimed. He whispered to Rebecca. "It's him."

"Him who?" Rebecca whispered back.

"Him. You know. The guy." He was about to say "crazy Joe," when the Mysterious Man took a small step forward.

"Give it to me or I'll hurt you," he said in a low guttural whisper. "Do it now."

Alarms rang inside Andy's head. He thought he should defuse the situation before it became serious. "Mister, can I ask you a question?"

The Man howled and leapt at Andy, bowling him over. Andy hit the ground hard as the Mysterious Man sat on top of his chest. A blow battered Andy's jaw. Andy flung his arms up to protect himself. The Man flung his fists, whimpering as he fought. He tried to knock Andy's arms out of the way. His breath came out in ragged huffs.

Something struck the Mysterious Man hard, stunning him. He arched his back and wailed.

Andy saw the Man's silhouette above him, his arms raised above his shoulders, his head twisted to the side in a surreal picture of shadowy wretchedness.

A thick stick pushed him over; he fell off Andy onto the dirt road.

Rebecca stood beside him. In her hands was a broken tree branch. "Who is that?"

Andy touched his sore jaw. "That's crazy Joe."

"No, it's not," Rebecca said. "I've never seen him before. Who is he really?"

"It's the guy I was telling you about. The one who said your life was in danger."

Rebecca looked at the crumpled figure. "Nice to meet you too," she said, dropping the branch to the ground.

Andy got to his feet; together they looked at the fallen Man. His limbs were twisted all over where he lay, giving him the appearance of a soul in torment. Andy pitied him, he would have thought he was dead, but the Mysterious Man was breathing evenly.

"Wow. Am I glad you're on my side," Andy joked, nudging Rebecca's arm.

Rebecca snorted, pleased with herself.

"What do you think we should do with him?" Andy asked.

Rebecca thought a moment. "We've got a car now. Let's take him to the Sheriff."

The car was an old, yellow, 1966, four door Dodge Dart. "I think that's the Johnson's car," Andy said. "He must have stolen it. What if he wakes up and goes batty on us again?"

Rebecca shrugged her shoulders. "Let's look in the car? Maybe we can find something to tie him up with."

Rebecca picked the keys up off the dirt. They walked over to the vehicle.

Andy opened the rear passenger door. Inside the Dart's back seat he saw a backpack. Curious, he rested his knee on the seat, reached inside and dragged the backpack towards him.

Rebecca popped the trunk lid open. "Andy. Look what I found." She lowered the trunk so Andy could see her through the rear windshield. In her hands was a length of rope. "Think this will do the trick?" Rebecca said.

"That's enough for his hands," Andy said. "We should tie his feet too. Just in case."

Rebecca raised the lid up and inspected the trunk again. *Jack, spare tire, road flares.* Her vision rested upon some yellow jumper cables.

"I've got you covered."

Unconscious, the Mysterious Man lay down on the back seat, his head resting on the backpack. His arms and hands were firmly tied to the center of his chest with rope; his feet and knees were secured with the yellow jumper cables after Andy had pulled them apart into two long strips.

Andy and Rebecca sat in the front seat of the stolen Dodge Dart. They had put their bicycles into the truck, letting them hang part way out. Andy tore a piece of his Schnozola costume and tied the trunk down so it wouldn't bounce. Now that they had a car they could go to the Sheriff. It made them both feel a lot better.

Andy put the key in the ignition and turned it. Nothing happened.

"Have you ever driven a car before?" said Rebecca.

"No," replied Andy. "Have you?"

"No. My parents always do the driving. I'm just a passenger."

Andy tried the key again. Still nothing. He blew air out of his lips. He had seen his father start the family car a thousand times.

"What am I doing wrong?" he spoke out loud.

"My mom always fiddles with the gear shift first. Try that," Rebecca suggested.

Andy grasped the gearshift located on the steering column. He thought if the Man had to steal a car, why couldn't he steal one with automatic transmission? He tried to move the gearshift, but it wouldn't budge.

"It's stuck."

Rebecca frowned and slapped her thigh.

"Did you push down the thingy on the floor?"

Andy realized she meant the clutch. "Oh, yeah, right." He pushed down on the pedal. The gear shift moved freely. He put the gears in neutral, took his foot off the clutch and turned the key in the ignition.

"Come on, start!" said Andy.

The car did not start.

Andy felt about as smart as a fish hanging from a fishhook. *How am I going to get anywhere in this world if I can't even start a stupid car?*

Frustrated, he pushed down hard on the clutch, turning the key. The engine started right up.

Rebecca patted his shoulder. "Yes, Andy. You did it."

Andy's stupidity faded away as the engine rumbled to life. He told himself to remember that in order to start the car you had to depress the clutch first.

"Now put it in gear and let's go," Rebecca encouraged.

Andy shoved the gear shift into first gear. *At least I hope this is first gear,* he thought. His foot pushed down on the gas pedal; the motor roared; he decided to let the chips fall where they may.

"Here goes," he said, releasing the clutch.

The car jerked forward, tossing the bicycles out of the trunk. The Mysterious Man slammed into the back of Andy's seat, hitting the floor with a solid thud. The engine clattered to a halt.

Andy's feelings of stupidity returned in full force.

Leaning over the seat, Andy and Rebecca saw the Mysterious Man lying face down on the floor.

The Man moaned, still unconscious.

"Sorry, Mister," said Andy, gritting his teeth. He remembered how his father had accused him of not being able to handle manly responsibilities. Andy had wanted to prove him wrong.

A chance to prove I'm responsible and I can't even drive a car without hurting someone. Why is being an adult so difficult?

"Maybe we should put him back the way he was," Rebecca suggested, an embarrassed giggle escaping her lips.

Seeing her cheerful expression, Andy raised his eyebrows and nodded.

Exiting the car, they opened the back doors. Rebecca grasped the Man's feet; Andy gripped his shoulders. Their muscles strained as they hoisted the Man's body, bumping it against the seat. He slipped out of Andy's grasp; his head bounced hard upon the doorjamb.

Andy sucked air through his teeth and grimaced. *Gee, I hope he doesn't get a concussion.* Then he got an idea.

"I know. Let's roll him up on the seat. That should do it."

Rebecca nodded. She leaned in, grabbing the yellow cables about his legs.

Andy gripped under the Man's shoulders. "On the count of three. One, two, roll."

They twisted his body, heaving with all of their might. The Man's middle rolled over onto the seat on his stomach. Andy and Rebecca lost their balance. Yelping, they fell forward on top of him.

Rebecca found her face pressed up against the Man's jean-covered hiney. She raised her head and scowled. "This guy stinks. I give his personal hygiene a score of zero."

Andy nodded. "He smells pretty bad from this end, too."

The Mysterious Man groaned, then farted a prodigious stream of gassy funk that sounded like a bull frog belching.

Rebecca shoved herself out of the car, waving her arms in front of her to get rid of the loathsome smell.

The twisted grimace on her face made Andy laugh. He pressed his lips together to keep it hidden. It escaped through his nose as a snort of mirth. Sure enough, Rebecca heard it.

She ceased her smell-clearing gesturing and gave Andy a meaningful stare.

"Sorry," Andy mouthed silently, then proceeded towards the bicycles, still clamping down on a smile. When he walked around the end of the car the damage he saw made his smile vanish.

The bikes lay in a heap behind the bumper. The front headlight on Andy's bike was busted, the fender dented, and a wheel spoke bent and crooked. But the worst thing was the chain had broken. There would be no more riding his 10 speed tonight. Frustrated, Andy pushed the trunk closed, then noticed the little red tail light had broken off as well. He ambled over and picked it up. It was dirty. He blew it off and turned on the switch. The bulb blinked on and off with a modest red light.

"Still works," he said meekly, showing it to Rebecca, who gazed at him in sympathy over the loss of his bike.

Andy put the small tail light in his windbreaker's pocket. As he did so, a wave of insecurity washed over him. He had not been able to do anything right all day and it was tearing him up inside. Stuffing his hands into his pockets, he thought gloomy thoughts about himself.

Rebecca observed his sudden mood swing. "Andy, what's wrong?" Rebecca said. "How do you feel?"

Andy stared at his shoes. "Kind of stupid. I mean, when I left for your house tonight I wanted to talk to you about--well, you know--your mom. I wasn't expecting to be tackled by some nutcase or have your parents try to kill us, or try to drive a car, or trash our bikes."

When Rebecca touched his arm, his panic attack worsened--he moved away.

"Mu-maybe I should ju-just stay a lowly bu-bu-butcher," Andy stuttered. "I'm almost 20 years old and I cu-can't do anything ru-right. I'm ju-just a small-town lu-loser."

Andy's stomach twisted into a knot.

"I don't think you're a loser," said Rebecca.

"Sure," said Andy, not believing her.

Rebecca stepped closer. "I think you're very talented … and smart." She tenderly stroked his arm. Andy calmed down.

"You do?" said Andy, frowning. "No one ever tu-told me that before."

"Not even your mother?" asked Rebecca.

Andy shifted his shoulders uncomfortably, "Well … yeah … it's just that …"

"Are you saying you don't believe your own mother?" said Rebecca accusingly.

Andy's panic returned. His eyes bulged in their sockets.

Rebecca thought he looked like a squeezy toy whose eyes popped out when gripped tight. "You know what you look like? You look like this." She clutched her throat with her hand, popped her eyes out and inflated her cheeks.

Andy's brain locked up. He couldn't respond. He just stood there feeling stupid.

Rebecca poked her finger into his stomach. "Zing," she said, smiling. Got you again, Pagliacci."

"You zinged me," Andy said, realizing she had tricked him.

Rebecca giggled and wagged her forefinger at him.

Bad boy, the finger said.

Andy grinned. "You're pretty sneaky, Senicki. That's why I like you. You make me smile."

Rebecca smiled back. "I like you too. See." She showed him his grandmother's ring on her finger.

The warmth of her smile penetrated Andy with a gentle heat. For a moment he was so happy he completely forgot where he was until the Mysterious Man groaned, bursting his bubble.

Andy crash landed back to reality. He wished the Mysterious Man would just disappear. He wished all their troubles would disappear. Bending down, he reached for his bike. "I guess we'd better get him to the hospital. Let's put the bikes back in the trunk and go."

"You just locked it," Rebecca said.

Realizing what she said was true, Andy stopped lifting the bike and shook his head in mild despair.

"Hey, Andy," Rebecca giggled. "I think you just zinged yourself."

He made a silly face at her, then pawed at his pockets to find the keys. His search was interrupted when a bright, white light engulfed him.

The Mysterious Man's head popped up in the rear windshield. "White light! They found me. They'll kill me. Let me go!" The Man thrashed about in the car, rocking it on its shock absorbers.

From further down the road, a pair of headlights bore down on them.

"It's your parents," said Andy. "Time to go."

Abandoning the bikes, they rushed back inside the car. Andy fumbled in his pockets for the keys as the Mysterious Man wiggled about in the back seat.

Andy patted his shirt pocket. "I can't find the keys. I've lost them."

Rebecca saw the keys dangling out of the ignition. "They're in the thingy. Hurry."

"Let me go," the Man cried.

"Shut up!" Andy yelled, pushing down on the clutch and twisting the key. The engine fired up. Andy thrust the gearshift into first, ready to push down on the gas pedal. The Mysterious Man heaved himself over the seat beside him, whacking Andy in the face with his ponytail.

"Let me out," the Man wailed, flailing about. "They're going to kill me!"

"Get off of me," Andy said.

Rebecca exploded. "Shut up or I'll kill you myself!" She shoved the Man into the back seat, scowling at him. The Man cringed into a corner and whimpered. Through the rear windshield, Rebecca saw her parents getting closer. Her scowl turned into a fearful frown.

"Time to go Andy," she urgently whispered.

With a silent prayer on his lips to the god-that-makes-cars-go-forward, Andy stepped on the gas and released the clutch. Wheels spun in frenzied circles, spitting dirt behind them. Rubber gripped the road, the Dart took off like a rocket.

"You did it!" Rebecca screamed. "But you're going the wrong way."

Through the dusty windshield, Andy saw they were heading directly towards the car with Rebecca's parents.

"Turn around," said Rebecca. "Hurry."

Andy turned the wheel with all of his might. The Dodge Dart lurched to the left, entering the forest. Andy found himself swerving between the trees, frantically turning the wheel to avoid crashing the vehicle. Bushes scraped the sides of the car, which bounced over the bumpy terrain causing Andy's teeth to rattle. Turning back towards the road the headlights exposed a fallen tree trunk.

"Look out," Rebecca shouted.

Andy pressed down on the brakes, missed, and hit the gas pedal by mistake. The yellow Dart surged forward, struck the tree trunk and bounded over it, tossing them all into the air, screaming. Tires hit the ground, they bounced again. Andy clung to the wheel for control.

He swerved the Dart back onto the road. They were now headed in the right direction.

"You did it, Andy," Rebecca cheered. "You did it. We're getting away."

Andy's body flooded with joy. Feeling brave, he floored it. The car sped up, the engine whined from the high revolutions.

I did it, thought Andy. *I'm driving. It's not so hard after all.*

Andy glanced at the rear view mirror, he did not like what he saw.

"They're catching up," he said. "How can they do that?"

Then he noticed how slow they were going. "How do I go faster?"

Rebecca looked at the gearshift. "Second gear, Andy. Go to second gear."

"How do I do that?"

"Push in the thingy and move the stick thing."

Andy pushed in the clutch. The engine roared like an enraged beast. He slammed the stick down, hoping he was doing the right thing. The gearbox screeched; the sound was horrifying.

The Mysterious Man struggled against his bonds. "We're all gonna die! Help me, Jesus. I'm a sinner."

"Shut up!" Andy and Rebecca yelled.

The Mysterious Man bawled in panic.

Andy pushed the clutch in further; the stick slipped into second gear. "I think I got it."

Letting go of the clutch, the vehicle shot forward. Andy raced down the winding road. He changed into third gear without any problem, zipping around each curve like a daredevil, putting distance between themselves and their pursuers.

"Andy, you're amazing!" cheered Rebecca.

Her praise made him feel fantastic. It was a rare moment in his life when anyone shouted their approval of him.

Rebecca wanted to kiss him. Impulsively, she leaned towards him.

The Mysterious Man thrust himself over the seat, his ponytail whipping Andy in the face again, stinging his eyes.

"Untie me you savages! Cut me loose."

Andy couldn't see where the car was going. "Get off me!"

Rebecca shoved the Man, trying to push him away.

The Man knocked into Andy.

Andy missed the curve in the road. Tires bobbled over plants and rocks; a tree loomed in front of them. Screaming, Andy slammed on the brakes.

The tires locked, the car skidded, destroying some bushes, several dandy lions and a spider's web before colliding with the tree. A headlight broke; sparks shot out; the motor died; they jerked to a halt.

Thrown forward from the collision, the Mysterious Man flopped into the front seat, his body bent at the waist, his face buried in the seat covering.

Andy touched his forehead and winced. He had bumped it on the steering wheel. "I am so sorry."

Rebecca removed her hands from the dashboard. "It wasn't your fault, Andy. It was his," Rebecca glared at the Mysterious Man, slumped over the seat between them.

His head bent low, Andy said, "No, that's not it?"

"That's not what?" said Rebecca.

"That's not why I'm sorry."

"Then why are you sorry?" asked Rebecca, perplexed.

"I took the name of the Lord in vain."

"Oh," said Rebecca, seeing how dismayed he was. "Well, I'm sure he'll forgive you under the circumstances," she bewilderingly reassured him.

Relieved, Andy took a deep breath when he heard a voice below him.

"If God is through forgiving you," the Mysterious Man grumbled, "would you please untie me before I suffocate."

Andy and Rebecca struggled to lift the Man up. He cooperated until his head neared the ceiling. "Please untie me," he pleaded. "I'm feeling much better now. I'm normal. See." He forced a grin for his captors' benefit.

Rebecca's eyelids turned into suspicious slits. "Why should we trust you?"

"I'm a doctor," said the Mysterious Man. "I'm a doctor and its okay to trust me. Really. Look inside my backpack." He rubbed his itchy nose against the seat, whimpering softly.

Andy and Rebecca gazed at each other and shrugged. Giving the Mysterious Man a push, he fell into the back seat with a squawk. Andy twisted around, grabbed the back pack and pulled it over the seat. Unzipping the pack, he reached inside, withdrawing a large black bag with a silver clasp.

"Open it," the Mysterious Man whispered.

Andy undid the clasp. Raising the flaps up, he spread the sides of the bag apart revealing a stethoscope. A wordless conference was held between them. Andy raised his eyebrows questioningly. Rebecca didn't like it, but she reluctantly nodded.

The Mysterious Man understood their body language. "Thank you," he whispered. "I have this terrible itch that I can't scratch."

He bounced himself up on the seat so Andy could cut the rope that bound his hands to his chest. Andy got a scalpel out of the medical bag, when light flooded the car's interior.

"It's *Them*," the Man said. "Get me out of here. Quick. Cut me loose."

Rebecca put her hand on Andy's arm. "No, Andy. Start the car."

The Man looked at Rebecca with "how-dare-you-interfere" eyes. Rebecca glared back at him. The Man lowered his head, looking down.

Andy twisted the key, the engine started. He reached for the gearshift.

The engine died.

Uh-oh, Andy thought.

"Andy, hurry," said Rebecca.

"I'm trying." He twisted the key. The engine protested.

Rebecca saw her parent's car coming closer. The hairs on the back of her neck began to rise. "Andy," she whispered tensely.

Andy twisted the key again. The engine almost turned over, but failed.

Come on. Andy thought. *Start.*

He twisted the key harder. It broke in the lock. "Oh, no," he groaned.

Rebecca didn't like the sound of his voice.

"Oh no, what?" the Man said.

Andy held up the broken key.

The Man beheld it as though it was an omen of death.

"Now you've done it," the Man said. "How could you do such a STUPID THING?"

Andy tried to turn the broken key, but the ignition switch was jammed. As Andy berated himself, a car pulled up behind them; headlights blazed in their faces.

The Man spun wildly around; the glaring headlights assaulted his senses.

"It's *Them*." he cried. "We're doomed! They're going to kill me."

The Mysterious Man went berserk. He launched himself into a frenzy, biting his ropes, moaning strenuously, screaming the entire time. He flayed about the vehicle, kicking at the doors and beating his head upon the windows. Andy and Rebecca watched in astonishment as the Man tried to roll the windows down with his teeth.

He plastered himself against the back seat, eyes livid like a cornered animal. He turned his attention towards Rebecca and the door she sat beside.

Rebecca connected with the crazed look in his eyes; she sensed what was about to happen. "Andy," she whined.

"Let me OUT!" the Man cried.

Snarling, he lunged at Rebecca.

A farmer's truck with caged goats in the back stopped on the road several car lengths behind the Dodge Dart. An elderly man rolled down the window. Sitting next to him was an old woman, his wife. A fearful shrieking came from the Dodge Dart, as though a savage beast was slaughtering those within it.

His body in the front seat, the Mysterious Man struggled on Rebecca's lap. He rolled over onto his back, trying to reach the door release with his rope-tied hands, yelling the entire time.

Rebecca freaked out and screamed. Andy tried to force the Man into the back seat. The Man snapped at his hands with his teeth and kicked out with his legs, smacking Andy in the head.

Andy cried out in pain.

Rebecca sprang to Andy's defense. She grabbed the Man's hair and pulled it hard. The Man shrieked, raising his face; Rebecca slugged him in the nose. The Man stopped thrashing about, going limp on Rebecca's lap.

"You nearly broke my nose," the Man said, sobbing. "What did you do that for?"

Swiping his hair back with his hand, Andy caught a glimpse of the truck behind them in the rear view mirror. He was shocked to see two people he knew – and they weren't Rebecca's parents.

"That's Mr. & Mrs. Keene!"

As if on cue, the truck accelerated down the road.

"Wait!" Andy yelled. He opened the door, falling out. Holding his head where the Man had kicked him, Andy stumbled towards the road. "Mr. Keene, wait. It's Andy Barulich. Don't go."

The truck trundled along, smoke puffing out of its tailpipe, the goats bleating in their cages.

Andy raced down the road. "Wait! Come back! We need your help!"

The truck passed around a curve; the tail lights vanished.

The Keene's were gone.

Andy ceased sprinting. Breathing heavily, he put his hands on his thighs and gulped down large breaths of air. He touched his bruised head and groaned.

"Andy, are you all right?" Rebecca said, running to his side.

Andy didn't answer. Anger boiled up inside of him like hot coals dropped in water. He marched back to the car. Doctor or not, Andy had had it with this freak. He jerked the front door open.

"Now you listen to me, Dr. Weirdo, or whatever your name is. I've had enough of you."

The Mysterious Man rolled over onto his stomach. He wore a guilty look on his face.

"Please excuse me. I lost control of myself. It won't happen again. I promise. You can untie me now. Thank you." he said in a humble voice.

Andy was unaccustomed to standing up for himself, but now he was furious. Not so much for himself, but because Rebecca was still in danger.

"Do you know what you just did, Mister? That was Mr. and Mrs. Keene and you just scared them away."

Rebecca strode up beside Andy. "What is wrong with you? One second you act normal, the next you turn into a madman. Are you on drugs?"

"I knew those people," Andy said. "They would have helped us."

"What have you got to say for yourself?" Rebecca scolded.

"Yeah, what have you got to say for yourself?"

The Mysterious Man stared at his cable-entwined legs and feet. His voice was a soft whisper. "Does this mean you're not going to untie me?"

Andy wanted to hit him. "Untie you?"

Embarrassed, the Man nodded several times.

Rebecca took a step closer. "Why on Earth would we untie you? So you can attack us, again?"

The Man looked at his feet, avoiding her accusing eyes.

Andy's face screwed up tight. "Mister, I'm going to …." Anger choked his throat.

"And if he doesn't, I will," said Rebecca, finishing Andy's sentence.

Andy raised his finger, trying to figure out what to say next. "Right!" he shouted. "That goes for me, too."

The Mysterious Man straightened his body. His eyes blazed with indignation. "Is that gratitude I'm hearing? Am I not the guy who warned you about the danger in the first place? Do you remember that? Huh? Do you?"

"That's right," Andy said, backing down. "You did warn me, didn't you?"

The Mysterious Man pressed on. "My warning saved both of your lives. Yours and hers, didn't it?"

Andy looked at his feet. "Well …" his voice trialed off.

The Man glared at him. "Well, didn't it? Yes or no?"

Andy scratched his arm. "Well, I guess so. But you better tell us what's really going on or so help me I'll--"

"Or you'll what?" said the Mysterious Man. "Wash my mouth out with soap? Tie me up with yellow jumper cables. Take away my driving privileges? What?"

Rebecca caught sight of a car down the road. One headlight was dimmer than the other. She remembered her father saying last night, "I have to change the headlight. It's getting faint." She knew they were in serious trouble.

"Andy," she said nervously.

The Man growled. "Stick pushpins in my eyes. Hit me with a tree branch? What? What will you do?"

Andy clenched his fists behind his back. "I'll dump you out of this car and leave you lying in the road all tied up."

The Man laughed. "Oh, really? Is that how you reward someone after they have *SAVED YOUR LIFE!*"

Andy's knuckles went white from making a fist. He wanted to scream "shut up" at him, but Rebecca screamed first.

"Andy!"

"What!" Andy shouted, blowing up at Rebecca the way he intended to shout at the Man.

Rebecca pointed into the night. "My parents are coming for real."

Their heads snapped towards the road. The Bronco was visible through the trees, just a minute or so away. The Man gritted his teeth, trying to break the ropes by flexing his muscles. Straining with all his might, his breath exploded, nothing happened.

"Please, save me," he said to Andy. "I saved your life. You owe me a favor … please."

Andy thought the Man was pathetic, but he was right, he owed him a favor. He reached inside the medical bag and withdrew a scalpel. "Mister. I'll cut you loose. But you attack us again and I won't be responsible for what I'll do. You hear me?"

"Yes, yes. Anything," the Mysterious Man promised.

Andy sawed the rope with the scalpel; the Man forced himself to shut up. His facial muscles quivered. His pride was wounded, but he needed to be free so he gritted his teeth.

Andy had cut through part of the rope when the Man blurted out. "You weren't so good defending yourself the last time we met. Were you, butcher boy?"

The scalpel ceased cutting.

The Man inwardly cursed, rebuking himself for saying something sarcastic before he got what he wanted. It was a really bad habit he had. He hoped the butcher boy didn't slit his throat.

Rebecca settled the dispute. "Whatever you're going to do, do it now. My parents have guns you know."

Again, they all looked down the road. Headlights shone on the trees. Andy figured they were half a minute away.

The Man clenched his teeth, his voice trembled. "I apologize. I got carried away again. Please. Can you forgive me? I'm really sorry."

His pride tasted sour.

Me and my big mouth.

Two lengths of yellow battery cable lay on the dirt at Dr. Weirdo's feet. The arrangement did not completely satisfy him as his hands were still tied to his chest.

Andy carried the backpack over his shoulder. He and Rebecca marched into the woods.

Dr. Weirdo strained to break the partially cut rope around his chest. He flexed his muscles and pushed his chest forward. His face turned red with effort. The rope held firm.

He called out over the top of the car. "Oh, come on. I didn't mean it. I said I was sorry. Come back … pretty please."

Andy and Rebecca ignored him, heading deeper into the forest.

Dr. Weirdo bounced on his knees and fumed. *Damn it, my nose itches.* He tried to rub his face against his shoulder and ended up dancing around in a circle.

Brakes squeaked. Dr. Weirdo twisted his head. The Bronco came around the last curve, heading straight towards him. Whimpering, he shuffled after Andy and Rebecca. His legs were wobbly from being tied up; he couldn't move quickly until he got his circulation back. The parents would be here in seconds. They had guns. Then it dawned on him.

They've been changed by Them.

Panic increased his speed. "Wait," he yelled to Andy and Rebecca, still barely in his sight. "Aren't you going to untie my hands?"

"No!" they shouted without looking back.

"But I saved your lives."

The steady crunch of their footsteps was his only reply.

"At least give me back my back pack, you ungrateful thieves," he said with venom.

Andy and Rebecca stopped walking.

Dr. Weirdo wished he hadn't said that. He saw Rebecca say something to Andy, who swung the backpack around. His words worked. They were going to return it. He could get the scalpel and cut himself loose. He trotted towards them, smiling broadly, thinking happy thoughts of freedom.

Rebecca took the medical bag out of the backpack. Andy flung the backpack at Dr. Weirdo. It skidded on the ground. The pack's aluminum poles whacked Dr. Weirdo's shin. He danced in circles from the pain.

Andy and Rebecca took the medical bag and marched on.

"Wait," said Dr. Weirdo. "I meant I need my medical bag."

Rebecca whirled around. Her voice was a shotgun and she let him have both barrels. "What you need is a bath!"

"Now, wait just a minute--"

"Shut up, stinky!" Andy said, anger flaring in his breast. "I'm sick of hearing you whine like a baby. Besides, you made me crash the car."

Dr. Weirdo stopped talking. His eyeballs bounced back and forth in astonishment. How dare they talk to him like this. Didn't they know who he was?

Andy grabbed Rebecca by the arm. "Come on, Rebecca. Let's get going."

They marched further into the forest.

Watching them leave with his medical bag, Dr. Weirdo pouted and sniffled.

Passing by several trees, Rebecca held Andy's hand. "Andy," she cooed. "You're such a tiger. I never knew that."

Self-respect blossomed in Andy's chest. He felt like a man, like his father-- proud, capable, strong.

Headlights shone through the forest from the road. Squealing brakes announced Mr. & Mrs. Senicki's arrival.

Still holding each others' hands, Andy and Rebecca ran.

Avoiding the bright headlights, Dr. Weirdo hid behind a tree. His breathing became shallow; his skin was electrified. He looked down at his bound hands.

"Me and my big mouth," he mumbled. "I have got to be smarter than this."

Scratching his nose against the tree bark, he whimpered, then scurried after the two young people.

Two pairs of feet, one heavy, one dainty, planted themselves on terra firma. Doors closed. Guns and flashlights searched the forest with grim intent.

Strong male hands gripped a flashlight like a neck it wanted to break. Seeing nothing, not even his wife beside him, Mr. Senicki continued on his holy mission of rescue and revenge.

Where is she? the voices inside him whispered. *Find her or she will die.*

A leaf, a rock, a plant--Mrs. Senicki's flashlight beam found no sign of her prey. Her mind whispered, *They're going to kill Andy. Only you can save him. Time is running out.*

Her inner voices made her desperate. She had to find him; had to protect him; she loved him from the bottom of her soul. Her need was so extreme that being alone in the dark forest didn't bother her in the slightest.

The Director wouldn't allow it.

The brainwashed parents found a backpack on the ground. They found some footsteps heading off to the right. They broke into a jog, flashlights pursuing the impressions in the soil. The tracks were fresh. They were close. They both shared the same thought.

Find them. Shoot them. Murder … death … revenge.

The full moon reflected in the river's glassy surface. Near the river's edge, an embankment stood several feet higher than the water; a dead Oak tree lay across its edge. In between the water and the embankment was a narrow walkway of dirt.

Andy, Rebecca and the Mysterious Man squatted beneath the horizontal tree, their feet upon the soil by the riverbed. Andy worried that they were too exposed. He looked about for a place to run to when their pursuers crashed through the nearby woods, forcing them all to take cover. Andy glanced at the mirror image of the trees in the water. The trees were like fingers pointing right at them, giving their position away.

Andy shuddered at the thought of what might happen to them.

Dressed like a punked out rock band, the Munchkins jammed with electric guitars …

Papa's got a gun …

Time to die or run …

Andy mentally shut off the Munchkins. He thought he was acting like a child. If they were discovered he had to protect Rebecca. He needed to be a man, not a boy. He told himself to pull it together.

Looking at the ground, he searched for something he could use to attack Mr. and Mrs. Senicki with if worse came to worse. He wished he had taken the tire iron from the car before they ran away. Then he remembered he couldn't open the trunk because he had broken the key in the ignition. It occurred to him that being a man like his dad required thinking ahead, not just going through life spontaneously dealing with things as they arose.

If we're going to get out of here alive we need a plan. What would Dad do?

The tip of a stone buried under the soil got his attention. Andy tried to free it with his shoe. Rebecca grabbed his arm and put a finger to her lips to silence him. Leaves crunched and twigs snapped as her parents traipsed through the nearby woods; they were very close now.

Andy had a gut full of fear.

Bending down, he dug up the rock, hoping he wouldn't have to use it. The Mysterious Man faced the tree trunk, his head buried into the bank like a human ostrich, his bound hands clutching each other like he was praying.

At least he's quiet, Andy thought. *Thank God for small favors.*

Andy felt like praying himself. If Rebecca's parents found them, there was nowhere to run for cover. Their only chance lay in complete silence. Cupping his hands together, he silently begged for divine intervention.

Mr. and Mrs. Senicki emerged through the thick trees, searching for any sign of their enemies. Fingers tight on the triggers of their weapons, they trekked towards the fallen tree that the three nervous humans secreted themselves below it.

Andy clutched the rock in his hand, ready to throw it if they were discovered. The stone seemed to exist not only in his hand, but in the pit of his stomach as well.

Mr. Senicki put his foot upon the fallen Oak, examining how far he would have to jump down. He rocked his weight back and forth in preparation for the leap.

Andy realized what was about to happen. Mr. Senicki was going to land right in front of them. Andy hoped he would land facing away from him, so he could hit him on the head with the rock before Mrs. Senicki shot him in the back.

Maybe I could hit him and spin him around so she shoots him instead of me.

Dreading what he thought he had to do, Andy clutched the rock a little harder.

Close by in the forest, a deer stepped on some twigs creating a loud *snap*.

Mr. and Mrs. Senicki turned and fired in the direction of the noise. The deer dashed away, crashing through the dark undergrowth. Mrs. and Mrs. Senicki chased after it, their flashlights waving in search of their victim.

Andy breathed a sigh of relief when something broke in his hand. He saw that the rock was not really a rock, and that he had been about to defend himself against a man with a gun armed only with a dirt clod. He had squeezed the clod so hard it had burst in his hand. Only a smaller clod was left, the rest was powdered soil.

Andy peered over the edge of the oak tree. Rebecca's parents entered the trees, their flashlights bobbing all over the place. This was their chance to escape. The time to go was now. Taking Rebecca's hand, they snuck away, heading upstream.

Keeping his head buried against the embankment, the Mysterious Man felt something shatter on his body. He opened his eyes, expecting to see blood, but only dirt lay on his shoulders. Brushing it off and turning, he saw Andy and Rebecca running away.

Hands shaking, he gazed to the stars, whimpered his thanks to God and scurried after the two young people.

An invisible light probe hovered in the background, giving his fleeing body a nice rim light for the Eyes to record that the humans could not see.

"Excellent," the Director mumbled to himself. "A narrow escape from the love-torn parents, emotional breakdowns, being attacked by a stranger, a car chase, a car crash, fighting amongst themselves and a bit of cloddish humor at the end. I couldn't have done better if I had scripted it. This will be my *Citizen Kane*. Except that I'm even better than Orson Welles."

He turned on a power back massager. The strong vibrations made his voice jiggle. "It certainly proves my theory about the importance of character motivation. But who is this other being?"

He replayed a section where the Mysterious Man hurled himself at Rebecca when they were in the car. He hadn't anticipated this new plot development.

"Whoever he is, he's terrific comic relief."

A buzzer sounded. Turning off the back massager, he switched on the intership communicator. "Speak."

"Sorry to bother you, Herr Director," said the Production Manager. We detected a faint signal from an old locator device, but could not trace it to its source until now."

"Well, where is it?"

"On the Andy's arm."

The Director was greatly amused. He guessed who the new person was, only he wasn't new after all. "A former actor has returned to our show. Check the old tapes. Find out who he is."

"At once, Herr Director," the Production Manager said. "And the Producer just called for you. He's on interstellar hold."

"Tell him I'm on my way to the viewing chamber. And keep the cameras rolling."

The Director snapped the communicator off. He was certain this was not good news. He flexed his hands, spreading his fingers as far apart as they would go, then balled them into fists. Stretching his arms wide, he shook them vigorously, releasing his tension.

"Keep your composure," he whispered to himself. "What do the humans call it-- wear a poker face."

In the viewing chamber, the Director stood before the trans-galactic screen. The edges of the Producer's image were distorted with wavy lines. His race had not quite perfected phone transmissions over 50,000 light years.

"The footage you requested," began the Director, "was sent by robot courier. Did you not receive it?"

"The Story Committee has reviewed it," said the Producer. "The family scenes are delightfully immoral. The rest is rather boring."

That's because I took out all the good parts, the Director thought to himself.

"We want you to assemble the entire cast, both families and those older females from the animal protein distributor. Have them all go to the lake tonight. Have their vehicles break down so they're stranded."

"Why?"

"The Story Committee has decided to make a monster movie. Use the holographic generator to create some monsters and wipe out the actors out one by one. The Art Department is sending you some 3-d models."

"What's the story line?" the Director said.

"It's a monster movie," said," the Producer. "We don't need one. The special effects is the story. Just make it scary with lots of violence and suspense. Kill the old females first, then give the others a fighting chance to survive. You'll need some gimmick, something they can find or build that they think will kill the creatures. Give them hope, then have them all eaten alive. We want the monsters to win."

"What about character development?"

"Not important. Just put control chips in all their heads and order them about. Just being a family is horrible enough. When they are eaten Those Who Watch will greatly enjoy their deaths."

A tone rang out. "That must be the Art Department models," the Producer said. "There are a number of holographic monsters to choose from. Pick a few and get started. This story will get much better ratings than your last one with repeat sales on the sci-fi channel. Eight minds are better than one. Work hard. Over and out."

The view screen went blank.

A flashing LED notified the Director that he had interstellar e-mail. He waved a hand across the engagement sensor. A horrific-looking lake monster, covered in fish scales, appeared on the 3-d viewer. Seconds later, another ghastly monster with long tentacles flashed on the screen. It's arms ended in long skewers; the bodies of the three old women from the butcher shop were pierced by them and held over a tree that was on fire.

"What is this supposed to be?" said the Director. "Grandma ka bob?"

Several other monsters appeared in 3-d, one of which was circular in shape with several mouths and arms around its circumference. It was stuffing humans into its sharp-toothed maws. Cheap sound effects had been added, mainly chomping and screaming.

The Director wanted to scream himself.

"This is an outrage! The Committee doesn't know a thing about creating A.R.T! Don't they know – character drives the plot, not the other way around. The conflict of the character's dilemma should manifest as a conflict within the character himself. The character works out a problem in the outer world that is inseparable from the problem within himself. That's how you create profluence! What idiots!"

The Director stopped ranting and raving. What was he going to do now? In a mental daze, he marched to his personal chamber and swallowed a double dose of Metamucil in prune juice.

Shivering, he rolled himself up in his massage rug and had a major panic attack.

CHAPTER 11
A SECOND CHANCE

The abandoned lumber mill was composed of several warehouse-sized buildings with an enormous dirt yard surrounded by a tall chain link fence. Signs crowded the fence demanding the mill be reopened. The chain which locked the entrance was cut in half and dangling.

Andy appreciated not having to scale the chain link fence to break into the place. He and Rebecca passed through the yard, empty except for several large John Deere machines. He swung opened the huge double doorway leading into one of the buildings. Inside, huge tree trunks, sheared of their branches, waited to be sliced into boards by enormous electric saw blades. It made Andy feel small, like they were invading the abode of a giant.

Toothpicks of the gods, Andy thought.

The Munchkins agreed. "Pick a pine, pick your teeth. Have a snack of human beef. Gooooooooo, giants!"

Rebecca didn't like the feel of the place either, especially at night. The moon barely sent enough light through the side windows and skylights to see by. What little light arrived tinted the piles of trees a ghastly blue. Rebecca felt like she was in a forest graveyard denouncing nature's right to exist. She did not like the place one bit.

The Mysterious Man caught up to them just as they were about to enter the building. His hands were still tied to his chest with rope, but he was going to try and snatch his medical bag from Rebecca and run. Before he could do so, his intentions must have been broadcast on some channel Andy and Rebecca were attuned to, for as he got within fifteen feet of them they both turned and gestured not to come any closer.

Bad boy, their waving fingers said.

The Mysterious Man took the hint. He followed them inside at a distance. The assortment of pine, cedar, spruce and other trees in the gloomy moonlight didn't bother him in the slightest. Having been on the road for years, he was accustomed to the eeriness of the night.

Reaching the end of the cutting room, they entered a side door leading into an office. Two low wattage overhead bulbs cast a feeble yellowish light in the dingy space.

The place had been trashed. Garbage cans were overturned, papers littered the floor, pictures were torn off the walls and smashed on the floor.

"This must be the owner's private office," Andy said to Rebecca.

"How do you know that?" Rebecca said.

Andy nodded towards a large picture on the wall. The placard said Leo Hullihan. The cover glass had been shattered with a hammer, exposing the photo. Black magic markers gave him horns, evil eyebrows, a demonic goatee and knife-like teeth. Written on the wall beside it was the phrase "Spawn of Satan."

"I guess the lumber workers were upset about losing their jobs," said Andy taking in the mess.

Andy and Rebecca approached the office window. The forest was dimly lit with moonlight; there was no sign of Rebecca's parents.

He lowered his arm to his side. "What do you think we should do?"

Rebecca frowned. "I don't know. But we better think of something."

Andy chewed his lower lip. "We could try and sneak around them … get back to the car."

"You broke the key in the switch, remember."

"Oh, right." He chewed his lip a second time. The consequences of his actions kept coming back to bite him. It seemed like every time he turned around, something he had done in the past gave him cause for grief in the present. He tried to think of a plan, one that wouldn't come back to haunt him.

"Maybe your parents left the key to their car in the ignition," Andy said, hoping this might be true and cheer Rebecca up a bit. "We could drive off and escape them. We could go to the Sheriff."

"What about my parents?" Rebecca said. "We just can't leave them like this. Can't we do something to help them?" Her hands covered her face as she broke into tears.

Andy groaned inwardly. *Oh, Rebecca. Not again. Not now.*

Her weeping made him feel helpless. He wanted her to be happy, but under the circumstances he had his limitations. He also wanted to not get shot dead, which he believed would happen if they tried to do anything but run away.

The Munchkins jived him.

"Run, run, as fast as you can, you can't catch me, I'm a cowardly man. If my courage were equal to the size of my dick, I'd be known near and far as Andy the pin prick. Ha, ha, ha."

SHUT UP! Andy shouted in his thoughts at the Munchkins. *This is important. Stop making fun of me!*

The Munchkins were not amused.

"Hey," said a Munchkin. "Can he yell at us like that?"

"I don't remember reading that in the imaginary person contract," another spoke.

"I may be a figment, but I got my pride," said a third.

"Who does he think he is … his father?"

"Just for that," added a fifth, "we won't say another word. Right, fellahs?"

"RIGHT!"

Andy returned his attention to Rebecca, who was still crying miserably. His throat felt very dry; he needed some advice; he returned to the Munchkins. *What do we do now, fellahs?*

The Munchkins crossed their tiny arms in defiant silence.

No, really, Andy asked his little pals. *I need your help. I'm feeling really desperate here.*

"Save the drama for your momma," the Munchkins chimed.

Tiny signs appeared in the Munchkins hands, each one bearing the word: Strike!

The littlest Munchkin did not have a sign. Not wanting to be left out of the action, he punched himself in the face, knocking himself out cold.

The other Munchkins flipped their signs around, giving the littlest Munchkin a perfect score of 10, except for the last one, who gave him a 1.0.

The other Munchkins glared at him.

The last Munchkin's face turned red. Giggling nervously, he shook his sign until the period moved over one decimal place to the right.

Still not knowing what to do, Andy chewed on his lower lip.

Dr. Weirdo leaned against a table, his hands still bound to his chest. "Did you know that emotions are biochemicals stored in the brain?" he said to Andy.

Andy and Rebecca looked at him with a "what-are-you-rambling-about" expression on their faces.

"It's true," Dr. Weirdo said, bending over, scratching the tip of his nose against the back of a chair. "Joy, sorrow, love, anger, fear, all these feelings exist in our heads as a tiny squirt of brain juice." Dr. Weirdo rubbed his arm against the table. "Memories are stored in a similar fashion. In fact, they are interconnected by electro-chemicals."

"Mister, what are you babbling about?" said Andy, wishing he had another dirt clod to fling at him.

"I'm talking about how to save her parents," Dr. Weirdo said. "Are you interested … or do you think your substantial ignorance is going to help them?"

Andy and Rebecca were silent.

"Good. Then shut up and listen to an educated doctor."

Dr. Weirdo took a step forward, his itchy nose adding fuel to his frustration. "Six years ago in Alaska, miles from the nearest town, surrounded by endless snow, a man and a woman shot each other. No one knows why they did it."

Rebecca wiped at her tears. "So what?"

Dr. Weirdo ignored her. "The bodies had no identification; no wallet, no credit cards, nothing. They were found half buried in ice, the back of their heads sticking part way out. Somehow the snow had melted, then refroze around them. An examination revealed a circular puddle of ice 80 feet wide and six inches deep. Their noses were barely under the ice.

Rebecca crinkled her nose. "That's disgusting."

"Disgusting?" said Dr. Weirdo. "I tell you what was disgusting--the police." He smiled bitterly. "A bunch of incompetent half-wits that would make Barney the dinosaur look like J. Edgar Hoover by comparison. A polar bear and two seals could have done a better job of investigation." Dr. Weirdo's elbows jerked up and down. "They found thousands of dollars trapped in the ice. They left the bodies, but spent hours hacking out the money. The case was closed for lack of evidence. Apparently they got an unexpected bonus cash bonus for not doing their job."

"Is there a point to all of this?" Andy demanded.

"Glad you asked," Dr. Weirdo said mockingly. "Proves at least one of you has a brain and can do more than just fill out a bra." He leered at Rebecca.

"I investigated the crime scene myself. Clues that I found," he thumped his chest, "led me to a small town near Seattle. I discovered a baby and his mother were kidnapped, ransom demands made, gruesome murders performed, horrible events sent into motion. But I alone discovered the reason why."

Dr. Weirdo paused, his expression challenging them to guess the answer.

Rebecca wouldn't play his game. "Which is what?" she said.

Dr. Weirdo smiled. "Open my medical bag. Take out the small vial in the side pocket."

He could tell she wasn't going to do what he asked. "This is about your parents. Go on."

Reluctantly, Rebecca set the bag down on a nearby desk and opened it. She pulled out a cylindrical glass container about two inches long and held it up to the weak light. Inside the vial, Andy and Rebecca saw a small, copper object that appeared to be manufactured.

Dr. Weirdo nodded. "That device was found implanted in the forehead of the frozen woman. I hacked at the ice until I managed to remove her head in one piece. Guess whose wearing the same thing now?" Dr. Weirdo jerked his tied-up fingers at the window. Flashlights in the forest could be seen, coming closer to the lumber mill.

Rebecca worried about her parents, wondering if it could possibly be true.

"What is it?" she asked. "What does it do?"

Dr. Weirdo rubbed his itchy nose on a table. "Autopsies and x-rays proved that the device was connected to the nerves that run from the brain to the eyes."

Andy and Rebecca didn't believe him, but said nothing.

"I believe it's an extremely sophisticated processing unit that can control what a person sees and feels."

Rebecca criss-crossed her arms on her chest. "That's impossible."

"Not only that," Dr. Weirdo continued, "but traces of an organic organism were discovered that connected to an area of the brain where emotions and memories are believed to be stored. Do you see where I'm going with this?" he challenged.

Andy and Rebecca remained silent.

"I thought not." Dr. Weirdo sighed, sadly shaking his head. "Young people today." He clucked his tongue, "Tsk, tsk, tsk. So useless." He stood up, breathing deeply. "Okay, listen up, kids, because here comes the bottom line. Just as motion pictures use certain computerized processes to make us believe that something we see on the movie screen is real, so I believe this device can reach into someone's mind, draw upon their life experiences and manipulate them in a similar manner."

Andy was speechless. The technology would be way beyond anything mankind could even begin to understand.

Dr. Weirdo addressed Rebecca. "For example, little lady, if you had one of those things in your skull, it could make you see Andy tied up here instead of me and make you hate Andy and love me."

Rebecca made a sour face. "Never," she said.

"Oh, no? Do your parents love each other?"

"So much so that they call each other their 'shining star,'" Rebecca said, defending her folks.

"Hey, that's what your mom called me in the butcher shop after she kissed me," Andy said, glimpsing the truth.

Dr. Weirdo brought the point home. "Somehow the device has transferred the deep love your mother has for your father to Andy, and the love your father has for his wife is now reassigned to you, his daughter."

"That's not true," said Rebecca. "That's impossible."

"Then how do you explain why your parents are chasing the two of you with guns?"

Andy started to speak.

Dr. Weirdo spoke in an outburst. "I'll tell you why? Your mother thinks you are stealing Andy away from her, while your father believes that Andy is kidnapping you away from him. That's why they're both in a jealous rage and want to kill the two of you."

"But why?" Rebecca asked. "What could make them do such a terrible thing?"

"Not what, but who?" said Dr. Weirdo in a low spooky voice. "To speak the truth, I've never seen *Them*. But with that device in their heads, your parents will never stop chasing you. Ultimately, they'll catch you and when they do... ." He pretended to shoot them while making popping sounds with his lips.

"But how can we stop them?" Andy asked.

"You have to remove the mechanism inside their skulls."

"How can we do that?" said Rebecca. "We're not surgeons."

"I am. I could do it. I have all the tools I need in my medical bag."

Andy and Rebecca were stunned. They added up the situation in their heads. The final tally was not to their liking.

Dr. Weirdo really had their attention and he knew it. "I can remove the devices if you can capture them. Are you willing to do that?"

Andy and Rebecca looked at each other; the implications overwhelmed them. How could they capture two people who had guns and wanted to hurt them, while they had no weapons at all and didn't want to hurt them even if they did?

Doctor Weirdo laid it on the line. "To be blunt, do you, Rebecca Senicki, love your parents enough to try to save their lives at the risk of losing your own? And will you, Andy Barulich, help Rebecca, knowing you will be shot at and may be killed?"

Andy's throat became suddenly dry. Rebecca's throat was not feeling too moist either.

"Well, speak up children. Have you got the guts or not?" He pointed at the window. "Guess who's coming, and it's not for dinner?"

Through the office window, two slivers of wavy illumination shot between the trees, highlighting their edges for a flickering instant. The beams appeared again, becoming steadfastly visible.

Not good, Andy thought. *That means they're headed this way.*

An intense pressure bore down upon him. Those lights were people with guns. This was no game. The stakes were huge. Losing could cost them their lives.

Andy recalled his high school history class with Mrs. Senicki. They had discussed President Kennedy and the Bay of Pigs, how President Kennedy had blockaded Cuban waters to prevent Russian nuclear missiles from being located so close to the United States. The President was protecting the nation.

Andy had once considered joining the military to get away from Hot Tub, but the thought of dying in battle sent him running to the bathroom where he promptly threw up in the toilet. He discarded the idea of a military career as quickly as he had discarded his lunch.

But now things were different. Now there was Rebecca to consider. Somewhere deep inside of him, Andy had found a reason to fight.

I have to protect her. If anything bad happened I'd never forgive myself.

Andy hoped he was up to the task. Like it or not, he was becoming the thing he wanted to become--a man.

Dr. Weirdo popped the big question. "So what's it going to be kids? Run or rescue?"

He wiggled his fingers and smiled, reminding them they would have to free him from his bonds.

Andy and Rebecca came to a silent decision. Joining hands, they committed themselves to the liberation of Rebecca's parents.

The Munchkins didn't like their chances very much. "Do a dance, blow your nose, change your name to twinkle toes. Andy you don't stand a chance. Guns will always beat romance."

The Director was tightly wrapped inside his massage rug like a rolled up croissant. Powdered Metamucil and prune juice was spilled all over the floor. He had suffered from mental constipation in the past and a small amount of the "brain plunger" had rectified his problem. Now he had consumed far more than he was able to handle and was so loose he had no control over any of his muscles, especially his brain.

"Frickin' monster movie," the Director cursed sipping some prune juice off the floor. "Socialist primates … ruin my masterpiece … damn twinkle-toothed producer … no talent shark buffoon …."

The Director hiccupped and hissed. How could he do both shoots at once? The answer was: he couldn't. If he put jellyfish in the Andy's and Rebecca's heads to shoot the monster movie they couldn't complete his murder mystery story. Besides, it would ruin their organic acting. If he killed them finishing his own production they wouldn't be alive to kill for the monster show. It was what the humans called a "Catch 22." No matter what he did he was ruined.

"My career is over," he said, slurring his words. "This horror movie fiasco will make me a laughing stock. I'll be lucky to drop down to the D list. I'll never work in television again."

Wetting his fingers in the spilled prune juice, he rubbed them in the Metamucil, stuck it in his mouth and sucked. A muffled tapping irritated him.

"Go away," he mumbled, his mouth barely showing through a slit in the massage rug.

He heard the tapping again.

"Herr Director," the Production Manager said from outside the door. "Is anything wrong?"

"Get lost."

"But the Andy and Rebecca are going to try to capture the parents."

The Director bolted in an upright position looking like a talking burrito with one hand tugging on its lips. "They what!"

His arms shot out of the rug. He struggled to rip himself free. The massage grass fought against him, responding to his attack, shoving themselves up his nose slots and mouth slit, cutting off his breath. They even thrust into his sphincter.

The Director rolled across the floor, unwrapping himself. The grasses pulled out of all his orifices; he inhaled deep gulps of air; his colon felt strangely clean.

Pushing himself off the floor, the Director stumbled to the door of his personal chamber. Waiving his hand across the motion sensor, the door slide aside.

The Production Manager stood in the hallway. He unrolled a portable monitor scroll. On one-side of the scroll, Andy and Rebecca were leaving the lumber mill, passing through the gate heading into the woods; on the other side Mr. and Mrs. Senicki searched the forest using flashlights.

"How did they choose to do this?" the Director said.

"The stranger is a human who knows about the implants. He says he can remove them from the parents."

"This is a disaster," the Director groaned, his mind woozy from the Metamucil. He gripped the doorframe above his head to keep himself from falling over. "The things I could make happen with these given circumstances. They're the dream of every director's lifetime … and I have to make a STUPID MONSTER MOVIE!"

His head drooped; his shoulder's slumped; he moaned in utter despair. He swung back and forth, deliberately hitting the door frame with his body, grunting with each blow.

"Herr Director, please," said the Production Manager. "Such a display of emotion is unworthy of your talent. Civil behavior is what distinguishes us from the lower creatures."

The Director raised himself up. "Yes, you are right Production Manager. I behaved wrongly. I just don't know what to do about this problem."

The Director told the Production Manager what the Producer's orders were.

"Why not shoot both stories?" the Production Manager said.

"Because it's not possible. I can't use the same actors for both stories. I'd have to kill them twice. Actors have limits."

"Substitute them with special effects?"

"For an entire show? It's too costly, even for me."

The Production Manager pondered a moment. "We have plenty of cameramen and equipment. And as I recall there's that film student frozen in cryo. Let him shoot the monster movie."

The Director rubbed his chin with his fingers. He tried to think logically, despite the Metamucil cocktail. "A student director. I like it. But how do I duplicate the cast?"

"The experimental one man holographic body suits have 360 degree realism," said the Production Manager. "I've tested them. They work."

"Can the Eyes film them as human?"

"If they stay within a limited light parameter, absolutely."

"Next to me you, are a genius," the Director said, drunkenly patting the Production Manager's shoulders. "See that it is done. Excuse me, I have to go to rehab now."

The Director bustled down the corridor, bumping into the walls along the way. He needed a stimulant and headed to the infirmary to get some lemons to suck on. Nothing regenerated his synapses like the powerfully sour fruit.

The Production Manager watched him leave. He knew the Director was under great pressure. To entertain a planet of several billion beings to maintain social order was a difficult assignment. The V-lans needed entertainment to keep their aggressive emotions in check. The Director was doing important work. By helping him create A.R.T. he was serving his people. He always tried to make the Director's life easier so his artistic greatness would be unencumbered by stress. He never realized until now how important Herr Director thought he was. Even though the Director struck his person, which had severe legal consequences should he ever file charges of assault, he did not find it offensive … in fact … dare he admit it … it felt rather friendly.

The Production Manager headed to cryogenic storage to thaw out the film student.

If it had not been considered immoral on his planet, he would have admitted he felt proud.

CHAPTER 12

A DESPERATE PLAN

Andy rolled an old tire from the lumber yard, weaving his way through the forest. He tried not to make any noise lest Rebecca's parents should hear him. His hands were getting black from the tire's grimy surface.

This is crazy. No, it's more than that. It's madness. They have guns and I have a tire? How did this happen? I should have made Rebecca listen to reason. What the heck am I doing here? We're both going to die.

Andy relived the fight he had just had with Rebecca back inside the warehouse. Leaving the Mysterious Man, he had taken her into the owner's office. Hammer holes pockmarked the walls, papers from a toppled filing cabinet littered the floor; the place seemed to seethe with anger and violence.

It made Andy very uncomfortable.

"Are you sure you want to this?" Andy said, pushing a broken cup aside with his foot so he wouldn't step on it. "Your parents have guns. They could kill us."

Rebecca's stare bore right through him. "It's not their fault. You heard the doctor. They're being forced to act this way against their will. We've got to help them."

"But dead is dead, Rebecca. Let's go to the Sheriff. It's safer that way."

Rebecca stood still, thinking. Andy hoped she would see the danger and leave with him.

"If it was your parents," Rebecca whispered in a soft voice, "what would you do?"

Andy was floored by the question. It put things in a much more personal perspective. It was the difference between hearing on the TV news of a terrible tragedy that happened to strangers, then discovering it was someone you loved. Andy's skin turned hot. He felt his heart hammer in his chest. No matter how strict his parents treated him, could he ever abandon them?

Who knows what these beings will do to them. Their time could run out any second.

"I'm not sure," Andy waffled. "It's a tough decision. But getting us killed is not going to help them, right?"

The truth was Andy was scared. Being shot at back at the house had rattled him severely. "I think we should go," said Andy, his voice apologetic and faltering. "Go and get help." Andy took hold of her hands. "Those guns are just too dangerous."

Rebecca inhaled a breath of anguish, then another and another. Andy could tell she was getting jumpy. He had to calm her down and quick.

"Remember when your parents shot at us?" Andy said, putting his hands on her shoulders. "They chased us down in the car. They're hunting us. This is serious. We can't do this alone, Rebecca. Don't you see that? It's suicide to even try. Besides, how will we catch them? Dig a deep hole and hope they fall in?"

Rebecca pulled out of his grasp. She wandered across the war-torn room, mashing paper and crunching objects under her feet. She crossed her hands tightly upon her chest as though she was trying to revive her heart.

"I can't leave them like this," Rebecca whispered resolutely. "I have to try and help them. If we go to the Sheriff, there could be a gun battle. They could be shot. I can't let that happen. They have to be captured unharmed."

She moved to the door, her hand on the doorknob. "I know it's dangerous, Andy," she said softly. "But if I don't do something now, I have this terrible feeling I'll never see them alive again. I just couldn't live with myself if I didn't try." She looked him square in the eye. "If you have to go then go. I'll see if the doctor will help me."

Andy grimaced as Rebecca swung the door open and stepped through it, disappearing behind the frosted glass window. Hearing her say she would seek help from Dr. Weirdo cut him to the quick of his soul. He knew she would rather trust a poisonous snake not to bite her than the crazy doctor.

"Rebecca, wait," Andy blurted.

Rebecca's face came back into view, her eyes filled with urgency. Andy could tell that she was frightened.

"Okay. I'll help you," Andy said in a low voice. "I'll help you save your parents."

Rebecca pressed her lips together. Their gazes locked together. Once again, they made an unspoken commitment to each other that bound them body and soul. Rebecca swung the door closed and hugged him, holding him tight against her.

Andy felt her body tremble. He realized she was committed to the task despite her terror ... despite his terror … despite the potential fatal consequences.

That's when they came up with the plan.

The old tire wobbled as it struck a rock. Andy tipped it upright and kept moving. His mind came back from the scene with Rebecca … back to the silent, dark woods. The forest reminded him of a graveyard. As Andy kept pushing the tire, imaginary tombstones appeared before him. Chiseled into the stones Andy read his fate to come: *Andy Barulich--Dumb To The Bone*; *Here Lies Andy – A Death So Painful He's Still Screaming*; *Andy's Restaurant – Night Crawlers! All You Can Eat!*

What have I gotten myself into? he thought. *Can I back out now? This is madness.*

Munchkin paparazzi popped into view on top of the tire, running swiftly to maintain their place. Their tiny hats bore a sign--NEWZ. Several snapped flash pictures with cameras. Others had cigars bobbing in their mouths, and steno pads in their hands.

The Munchkins spoke one after another.

"Hey buddy, that skirt is nothing but trouble, right?"

"Why'd ya let her talk you into this mess?"

"Was it love?

"Wanton hormones?"

"The fear that if you put your foot down it would only make matters worse?"

"Hey, Andy. If stupidity got you into this mess, can it get you out?"

"C'mon. Spill it, bright boy."

"Inquiring figments want to know."

FLASH went the tiny cameras. Mini-microphones on tiny boom poles stretched out to record Andy's answer.

Andy shoved the tire faster. The Munchkin paparazzi struggled to keep up.

"Hey! This is no way to treat the press!"

"Shut up," Andy said, pushing the tire even faster.

The Munchkins began to grill him.

"Who wears the pants in this relationship? You or the broad?"

"If she's the man, will you have to wear dresses?"

"What about a bra? You look like an A cup?"

"From now on you can do our laundry."

"OR," they said together, "DO YOU NEED TO ASK HER FOR PERMISSION, GIRLIE-MAN?"

Andy shoved the tire hard. The Munchkins slipped and fell inside the tire treads, holding on for dear life. Shrieking, they rolled in circles until the tire smashed into a tree, then fell on its side. The Munchkin paparazzi slammed to the ground; their little bodies lay in the grass, unmoving.

"Do you think we pushed him too hard?" a Munchkin groaned.

"Dead, can't talk now," replied the second Munchkin. "Try again tomorrow."

Andy reached for the tire.

"Ah-Ah-Andy," said the stuttering Munchkin. "Wu-wu-where are you gu-gu-going? We need you, bu-bu-buddy."

Ignoring the Munchkin's protestations, Andy lifted his head. Not far ahead was his destination--a steep hill. He lifted the tire on its treads.

"Ah-Ah-Andy, don't lu-lu-leave us. Whose mu-more important? Your best bu-buddies or that stupid gu-girl?"

Andy rolled the tire over them, squishing them deeper into the grass.

"Ouch!" the other Munchkins moaned.

"Bu-but Andy. She's gu-going to get you ki-killed. Use the bi-big head, not the li-little one."

Andy rolled the tire over them once more as he headed down the road, leaving them behind.

"Ouch again," the other Munchkins grunted.

The stuttering Munchkin struggled to his little feet. "Bu-but Andy!" he yelled, stretching his arms wide. "Remember our cu-credo, 'Bu-bu-bros before hu-hu-ho's?'"

"SHUT UP!" cried the other Munchkins. They whacked the stuttering one with their boom poles, then dog piled on top of him, beating him with their little fists.

"SU-SU-SORRY!" yelled the first Munchkin, his voice muffled under the pile of angry, bruised little bodies.

The gnarly bark of a thick oak tree pressed hard against Rebecca's back. She could have relieved herself of the pressure, but she was in no mood to move away from the tree's concealing presence, not even a fraction of an inch. The woods outside the lumber mill were thick with murky shadows, but instead of feeling oppressed Rebecca was grateful for the dreary blackness, for if she could not see very well, surely her parents would be equally handicapped. Nevertheless, she wanted to stay there for the shortest time possible.

She was worried about the plan they had come up with to capture her mother and father so the Doctor could remove the devices in their foreheads. The *third eye* the doctor had called it, smiling that smug little smile of his that pontificated how much more *educated* he was than either of them. The sight of those lips, stretched thin with arrogance, made Rebecca sick to her stomach. She wanted to pull a secret lever that would open a trap door beneath his conceited feet, so that she could enjoy watching his narcissistic rear end drop into a bottomless pit.

That egomaniac is going to have a real bad wake up call some day. I only hope I'm there when it happens so I can see the shocked look on his self righteous face.

She recalled with a perverse feeling of delight when Andy tied the Doctor up to a chair with some rope they'd found because they still didn't trust him.

Oh, he was as mad as a hornet shot with bug spray.

At first the Doctor adamantly refused to be tied up. Rebecca threatened to hide his medical bag from him forever.

That really zinged him. I thought for a moment he might even cry.

In the end, he cooperated--very reluctantly. She remembered the look on his face as Andy tied him to a chair.

That man really hates me. I think he'd like to boil me in oil.

The thought filled her with satisfaction. That was ten minutes ago. Now, she waited behind a tree for Andy to return. Time and worry were becoming burdensome to her resolve.

What is keeping him? Where's the signal? Oh, please Lord, let this work.

She held a foot long pry bar they had found in a tool shop. She was supposed to hit her mother with it and knock her out, that is if the first plan did not work. Andy was going to trick her father into going one way while Rebecca got her mother to go the other way. That meant using themselves as bait.

Bait for bullets, she thought uncomfortably.

Once her dad was far away, Andy would sneak back and together they would jump her mother. When they had her tied up, they would deal with her dad. To Rebecca's distressed mind, the first plan sounded next to impossible and the second would need an act of God to succeed. Still, her steadfastness to rescue her parents from whatever it was that was controlling them was paramount to her. She looked down at the steel bar, realizing she might have to use it on her mother to protect herself.

What's a loving daughter to do?

Mr. and Mrs. Senicki searched about in a thicket, their flashlights stabbing around in the dark.

Andy snuck past them, carefully moving from tree to tree for cover. He observed Rebecca's parents didn't speak a word to each other. They acted as though the other person was not even there. This was further evidence to Andy that they were not in control of themselves. If they didn't know the other was present, he could use that to his advantage.

In fact, his entire plan depended on it.

He hid behind a tree, hoping the invisible what-cha-ma-call-its couldn't figure out what he was up to. Andy remembered his history lesson. *If I can just get them to divide, we can conquer them. At least it worked for the Roman legions.*

Andy wished he had a Roman legion to take on Rebecca's parents. He imagined them surrounded by his soldiers, wearing battle armor and metal helmets; their swords at the ready. Andy, their Supreme Commander, would give Rebecca's parents an ultimatum.

Surrender. You are surrounded by my elite troops.

Rebecca's parents would fire their guns; the bullets would bounce off the soldiers' armor. His soldiers would laugh the entire time until the shooters ran out of ammunition and were taken into custody.

Mission accomplished. Problem solved. Hooray for General Andy! Lady Rebecca will kiss you now.

A flashlight beam illuminated a leaf hanging down in front of his face. Andy jerked his head back. *Whoops! I better pay attention.*

He hunkered closer to the tree.

Now came the dangerous part, getting them to go to where he needed them to be for phase two of the plan to commence.

Sure, thought Andy. *I just have to trick both of them at the same time. This'll be easy.*

His mental lieutenant stomped in, combat boots squishing into his brain. *Commander, the enemy refuses to cooperate with your plans. What are your orders, sir?*

Yeah, thought Andy, discouragingly. *As easy as inflating a bicycle tire with a hand-held pump until it explodes.*

Being careful to remain hidden, Andy fished one of a dozen stones he had collected out of his pocket. The stones were about the size of a small jam jar lid, flat on the top and bottom, which made them excellent for throwing.

This should do the trick. I hope.

Waiting until Rebecca's parents backs were turned, Andy stepped out from behind the tree, then cast the stone towards the lumber mill. Soaring far away from the parents, the flying rock slapped through the leaves, landing with a dull thud. Rebecca's parents heard it and moved in that direction.

The troops were ecstatic.

Good going, General! You've got them on the run now!

Andy took a deep breath, exhaling silently. *Now it just has to work eleven more times.*

Holding another stone, he followed Mr. and Mrs. Senicki as they moved towards the lumber mill, taking great pains to not step on *anything* that would make a sound.

Twenty pain-staking minutes and ten stones later, Rebecca's parents were standing at the spot Andy wanted them to be at. He wished that everything would go this well.

Now to signal Rebecca.

Raising the bicycle tail-light out of his coat pocket, Andy turned it on. It flashed on and off with a soft, reddish hue.

Come on, Rebecca. Please be there. Please see the light.

Rebecca had not moved a muscle for what seemed like forever, until the sound of a stone landing through the brush caught her attention. Peering around the tree trunk, she saw two flashlights and jerked herself back out of sight.

Oh, gosh. It's my parents. They're really here.

Her heart beat faster. Her mouth felt dry with the taste of fear. Her parents were coming down a narrow path in her direction. She had no idea if Andy was alive or dead.

He must be close by. He'll find me. I know he will.

Rebecca had faith in Andy. He was always at the right place when she needed him the most. She trusted that everything would turn out for the best. Even so, her breath came out short and quick.

She glimpsed around the tree. Mom and Dad were in the general area where Andy wanted them to be. What was she supposed to do? She couldn't remember.

I'm supposed to look for his signal.

Rebecca peered around the trunk in the opposite direction. A weak red light flashed in the distance. She waved her arm in the moonlight. The light turned off.

The next time it blinks, I have to step out where my mother can see me and run like crazy before she can shoot me.

As she waited for the signal, she cupped her hands together and silently prayed.

After seeing Rebecca's arm wave in the pale moonlight, Andy turned off the flashing bike light.

She's still there. Way to go, Rebecca. Don't fall apart on us now.

He knew it had to be difficult, standing in the blackness, waiting alone, with only hope to comfort her. Several times that night, Andy had wondered just how much stress Rebecca could handle. When they had first discussed the plan, he tried to get her to go back to the Bronco. If her parents had left the keys in it they could simply drive away.

Rebecca wouldn't hear of it.

She was determined to help her mom and dad. Once that happened, he was committed to helping her. She needed him and, as scary as things were about to become, he needed her just as much. Still, he was glad the Munchkins weren't around. They had scared him with their questions, so he got angry and squashed them with the tire. They shouldn't have said that it was stupid to be in love. He only hoped that they were not right.

Once, as a boy, he had asked his mother what it meant to be in love. She told him, "Love is caring about someone else's needs more than your own." By his mother's definition, Andy knew he loved Rebecca. There was no other explanation for putting his life in danger like this.

Why are love and insanity so close together that it's next to impossible to tell them apart?

Popping onto a nearby tree branch, the Munchkins chanted, "The more you endure with patience and grace, the stronger you grow and the more you can face."

"What a crock," one Munchkin whispered to another.

"That's poetry for you," said the second one.

"Poetry is worse than having kids," replied the first.

"No. Where did you learn that?"

"In comic books."

"No way, prove it."

"Did Peter Parker ever have a kid?"

"Okay, you win."

"Spiderman was one smart guy."

"Do you think Andy can be like Spiderman?"

"Can a pig play the flute by sticking it in its woo-hoo?"

"We're really doomed, aren't we? We're going to die."

"Try to be positive. We're being all that we can be."

"Hey, you two," a third Munchkin said. "Quiet down. We want to watch Andy get his tail whipped. Right, fellahs?"

"You bet," the other Munchkins agreed.

"Pass the popcorn."

"Nachos for me."

"Who put a snack bar up in a tree?"

Andy peered his head just far enough past the tree trunk to see where Mr. and Mrs. Senicki were located on the path. Mrs. Senicki was closer to Rebecca and Mr. Senicki was closer to him. This was as good as it could get.

He reached inside his pocket for one of his special rocks, held up the bicycle light and gave the signal.

Seeing the flashing light, Rebecca crouched back behind the tree. Taking a deep breath of courage, she stepped out into the moonlight, fully revealed to her mother. Feeling like a dodo bird waving to a hunter, she raised her arms up and flapped them.

Mrs. Senicki saw her. She raised her gun.

Rebecca dashed behind the tree, running towards the lumber mill. She glanced back, her mother pursued her, struggling to find her way through the dense trees. She thought if dodo birds ever acted like she was doing now it was no wonder they were extinct.

Reaching the road, she ran. Her footsteps sounded thunderous in the chilly night.

Mr. Senicki searched the forest. Given a few more seconds, he would have seen Rebecca running away. Andy hurled a dirt clod that struck his pant's leg, turning his interest away from Rebecca and towards himself.

A second dirt clod hit him square in the chest. Soil spattered into his eyes, forcing him to try and blink the grit out. Through watery eyes, he saw Andy standing beside a tree. He raised his gun to shoot him, when another clod bombed his forehead, spraying even more dirt into his eyes.

Hiding behind another tree, Andy felt strangely thrilled. The plan was working perfectly. What had he been so worried for? He was such a good marksman he could keep Mr. Senicki at bay all night.

Time for another, Andy thought, stepping out from behind the tree with another dirt clod in his hand.

The Director knew exactly where Andy was the entire time. A dozen Eyes recorded the action and fed the data directly to his holo-monitors. He could see Andy's thoughts from a probe connected to his head with tendrils of energy. The probe sent images of confidence into Andy's brain.

"My cast is giving excellent performances. I have prepared them well for their roles. My acting method is so much better than Stanislavski. The acting is truly real."

At the same time Andy was feeling confident, the Director forced Mr. Senicki to visualize Andy slapping Rebecca's face. He slapped her hard again and again, raising ugly bruises on her pretty skin.

Rage ignited in Mr. Senicki's heart.

The Director smiled. "Being a Director is the best job in the universe. My job is my ego, and my ego is my God. Lucky me."

Andy stepped around the tree, dirt clod in hand, ready to throw another perfect hit. Mr. Senicki was in his sights, his head bowed towards the ground, wiping his eyes and growling.

Andy swung his arm forward, letting the dirt clod fly. It was a beautiful throw. He saw its trajectory as though it was moving in slow motion towards Mr. Senicki's head, about to explode at any moment. The thrill of anticipation rushed up his spine.

Kaboom, Andy thought, smiling widely, when Mr. Senicki snapped his head back at the last possible moment. The dirt clod sailed right by him, bursting harmlessly on a tree trunk.

Mr. Senicki turned his head towards Andy, his eyes blazing with hate. Lifting his hand, he wagged a finger at Andy.

Bad boy, the finger seemed to say.

Andy's confidence plummeted to zero.

The Director noted this on his instrument panel and smiled.

Crouching and raising his arms, Mr. Senicki emitted a blood-curdling snarl. Like a sumo wrestler, he took a thunderous step towards Andy … then another … and another, grunting like a beast.

Andy turned and fled deeper into the woods; a probe hovered before him releasing pheromones of fear in his flight path.

Andy sprinted like an Olympic champion with Mr. Senicki hustling after him.

Rebecca dodged through the thick forest, putting distance between herself and her mother. She had the advantage of speed in this race. It gave her a feeling of hope.

A bullet spanged off a tree beside her. Gasping, she ran even faster.

Coming to the edge of the trees, Rebecca crossed the road leading to the lumber mill. Passing through the chain link fence, she dashed across the yard, her legs aching with every step. She wanted to stop and rest, yet all she could think of was getting away from that terrible gun.

Running swiftly, the pry bar under her sweater felt hard against her ribs. She wanted to ditch it but dared not do so. It was her only weapon if things went wrong.

Rebecca reached the largest building. She and Andy had scouted it when they came up with the plan. It had a maze of rooms and corridors to get lost in. It seemed their best chance to sneak up on her mom and take her down without hurting her.

Rebecca swung the door towards her, just as her mother passed through the compound gate. She had to play the mouse to her mother's cat. Rebecca made sure the cat would know where the mouse went by leaving the door wide open.

Okay, mother. Here I am. Come and get me.

Summoning her courage, she stepped inside the shadowy building as a bullet slammed into the door.

A stout wind rose as Andy sped through the forest away from Mr. Senicki. A bullet whizzed by his head, encouraging his legs to quicken their pace. Dark masses of overhead leaves swung thickly to and fro, their quavering branches giving voice to Andy's terror.

Moonlight pierced the treetops with scattered beams of light, populating the dense, dark forest with frightening shadows. The vigorous wind forced the spotty lights to writhe in a nightmarish kaleidoscope. Shadows seemed to surround him, flitting about him as he ran.

Andy glanced back over his shoulder. Mr. Senicki barreled his way towards him, leaping over bushes and bounding by trees. His ability to negotiate the woods at night bordered on the uncanny. It made him seem like he was either supernatural or a cyborg.

Andy's terror gave rise to horrible imaginings.

It's John Conners, sir. The Terminator is after you. The troops are all dead. Run, sir, run! Tell Mom that I love her. Give my allowance to the poor. Transmission and life over and out!

The Director watched the action. He didn't like what he saw. "The Andy is too fast. The wind and swaying shadows are a nice visual, but it's too easy for him to escape. It needs more drama."

He hit the intercom button.

"Yes, Herr Director?" said the Production Manager. "What is your wish?"

The Director thought for a moment. "Have an Eye trip the Andy … and get me a good close-up of his face hitting the ground."

"Yes, Herr Director. Right away. Over."

Andy leapt over a bush; his foot hit something; he tumbled to the ground. Dirt found his tongue; he spat it out.

Where is that darn hill? I should have reached it by now.

He had been running for a couple of minutes. Had he missed it in the dark somehow? The thought filled him with apprehension. Was he lost? He had to find it before Mr. Senicki caught up to him.

Low on fuel and high on danger, Andy lifted his head off the ground. Beyond the low hanging branches was the base of the hill he was looking for.

Something trampled through the brush behind him; Andy turned his head. Mr. Senicki charged at him like a maddened bear.

Andy bolted to his feet and ran for all he was worth. He dodged past trees and crashed through bushes, desperate to reach the hill.

He wished that he was Superman and could fly.

Up, up and away. Kryptonite bullets! No fair! I want a rewrite!

Andy burst out of the trees; reaching the steep hill, he began to ascend it. Hands tore at grass, plants, anything he could grasp to keep his balance and gain altitude. He looked like an anxious crab scuttling upward in a frenzied race against the clock. He had to reach the top before Mr. Senicki cleared the woods and had a clear shot.

Ever helpful, the Munchkins sang him an inspirational song.
(to the tune of "Give My Regards To Broadway")
"Andy you better climb fast,
Or bullets will kiss your behind
(Kiss! Kiss! Kiss!)
Then for a thrill, you'll bleed, roll down the hill,
The trip down won't be kind.
(Ouch! Ouch! Ouch!)
Rebecca with no other,
Will have to make it on her own.
(Gosh! No!)
But it won't matter because when that happens
You'll be dead as a stone.
(Stone! Dead!)"

Thighs burned; lungs ached; feet scrambled. Expecting to hear gunshots any second, Andy battled his way up the difficult slope. He kept his head down, seeing only what he was grabbing at as his heart throbbed in his ears.

A gun fired; a rock shattered beside him. Andy slipped and fell against the hillside. Before the bits of fractured stone had ceased their bullied flight, Andy knew Mr. Senicki would kill him. He felt sorrow for Rebecca. He had failed to protect her. He was a loser after all … a hopeless clown … not a man.

It made him angry.

He pounded his fist on the ground above his head. The angle of the earth felt flat. He glanced up. Two feet away was his goal--the hilltop! How could he be so stupid! It was right there. Get a move on.

With a frantic burst of energy, Andy hurled himself over the edge as a crack of gunfire burst into the night. The bullet creased the back of his left arm in a flash of pain, drawing blood. He cried out.

Andy spun in circles on the grass, away from the edge where death could still reach him. Facing the night sky, he stopped rolling and took in lungfuls of cool air, grimacing from the pain in his arm. He felt the wound. The bullet had grazed him. He got lucky. The night above was filled with brilliant stars, a welcome sight to his anxious mind. It helped him recover his composure.

The enraged scream of Mr. Senicki shattered the silence.

That sounded pretty good to him, too.

Inside the lumber mill, a dozen anti-gravity, set decorating robots materialized in a large furniture making room. They looked like three oval shaped flying saucers stacked on top of each other, the center one being twice as large as the top and bottom. Surveillance antennae stuck out on top, while four arms appeared around each of their middles. Each saucer could rotate in a complete circle, allowing it to do multiple tasks at the same time: grasping, spray painting, hot gun gluing, forced air drying, stapling, nailing, building objects, carpentry, etc.

Following the directions of the set decorator back in the ship, the deco-bots got down to business.

They moved all the equipment away from the walls, spraying the entire room black with a non-smelling paint, then put everything back into place. Several decorative end tables with wilted flowers in thin vases were spaced about the room giving it a hint of color and decay. Lighting-bots changed the lighting and moved a light switch several feet further away from the exit at the back of the room. A love seat was placed in front of a wall framed by French curtains behind it. Three deco-bots quickly made a fake window and hung it on the wall behind the curtains; it was the most beautiful spot in the entire room.

The deco-bots had just finished hanging a chandelier when footsteps echoed in the distance. Huddling together, the deco-bots were transported out of the room. From within the adjoining room, a lone deco-bot shorted out a ceiling light bulb and raced to the spot where the others had vanished. Quickly scanning through its "smell" database, it sprayed the scent of hot buttered popcorn in the air and beamed back to the star ship.

The room was empty again, except for several invisible camera Eyes.

Footsteps clattered in a rhythm of panic. Rebecca tip-toed around a hallway corner making every effort to be quiet as she fled from her mother. In the room she had just left, the roar of a gun blast pierced the stillness, followed by a frustrated growl. Clasping a hand over her lips, Rebecca tried to stifle her fears, which came out in a long, high-pitched squeak.

Rebecca rushed past the large pair of open double doors, then returned sniffing the enticing air. A not too distant growl of frustration made her flinch. Her shadow hurried into the large room with Rebecca close behind it. Her shadow grew larger the further in she went, as a fixture from the hallway cast its yellowish light behind her. Ignoring her shadow's sudden growth, Rebecca hastened deep inside. She wanted to find a place to hide and fast. She knew the extra distance she had put between herself and her mother was only temporary, it wouldn't last long.

This "leading her on" business is driving me crazy. I should just let her shoot at me until she runs out of bullets, then hit her with the crowbar and hope that I don't kill her.

She breathed in some air. *Why do I smell popcorn?*

Half way into the room, the light from the hallway ended. The rest of the room was swallowed by blackness; she couldn't see anything in front of her. Gingerly, she walked forward, reaching out with her hand to test the darkness. For all she knew, she could smack into a wall or a piece of furniture. She needed more light and she needed it now.

Rebecca retraced her steps to the doorway, located a wall switch and flicked it upward. A single overhead lamp popped to life, sending a weak light into the depths of the enormous room. To her surprise, the walls were black, making the actual depth of the room hard to determine.

She looked for the popcorn, but could not find it.

A variety of large tools were present, but Rebecca didn't recognize any of them. Peering further inward, she saw some half-built chairs and unfinished tables by the far wall along with some denuded tree logs.

It's a wood shop. They made furniture here.

She saw a love seat framed by gorgeous French curtains and a fake window that hung from the black wall.

That's so cute. Mother would love that, she really would.

The love seat brought her back to reality. Mother … gun … death ... run.

Rebecca made a beeline for the far exit. Flipping the switch, she plunged the room into darkness. She leaned against the wall, taking deep breaths to slow her pounding heart, all the while wondering why the place had so many dead flowers and where the heck was that popcorn. Normally, she found the dark to be rather spooky, but at the moment it seemed like a good friend. Still taking deep breaths of air, she tried to assess her situation. The meeting place where she had arranged to meet Andy was still some distance away. If she wanted to get there in one piece she should probably keep going. Unfortunately, she had gone the wrong way and was lost; she needed to get her bearings.

A silhouetted figure with a huge head of hair appeared in the double-doorway. A gun pointed into the room, its dark outline stretching into the room's center. Lengthened by the angle of the light, the weapon looked sinister and enormous. Alexandra panned it across the room until it was aimed straight at Rebecca.

Rebecca froze, ants of fear climbed all over her body. She was certain the darkness concealed her, but equally certain that if she moved her mother would shoot her. Then reason asserted itself.

If I don't open the door I won't have a chance anyway. How did I ever get myself into this mess? Oh, why didn't I listen to Andy? And why is this light switch so far from the door?

Rebecca inched her way towards the next room. The knob reflected the barest amount of light. Her hand stretched towards the brass promise of salvation. She was going to make it. She was going to get away.

Her fingertips grazed the doorknob. The overhead light flared on. Instead of being feeble, it seemed to blaze with an alarming brightness.

Rebecca felt like a vampire in the sun, certain she was going to fry and die. Her eyes shifted back across the room where her mother stood by the light switch, gun in hand.

I take it back, Andy. Let's go to the Sheriff.

Alexandra fired. A bullet pinged off the wall near Rebecca's head.

Rebecca hustled into the next room, slamming the door closed behind her. The room was swallowed by an inky blackness. She felt for the dead bolt and locked it.

I'm safe, she reassured herself. *This door is solid wood. She can't get in. No way.*

Unable to see, Rebecca felt around for the light switch. She flipped it up, but nothing happened, the room remained darker than a lump of coal. Holding her arms out, she tried to find a desk lamp. A few seconds into her sightless quest, she heard a light scratching on the door.

Is that my mother?

The scratching changed into a mild tapping.

What does she expect me to do? Say "who is it?"

The tapping became an insistent knocking.

This is getting worse. I'd better find a light.

The knocking became a demanding banging.

Come on. Where's a light? A match? A candle?

The banging became a violent, double-fisted pounding.

Rebecca wanted to jump out of her skin. She bumped into something that felt like a desk.

The pounding kept on and on.

"Stop it, mother!" Rebecca shouted.

Her hands roamed over the desktop. Something crumbled under her fingers. She touched a cold metal object, felt some buttons and pressed one. A desk lamp shed a pale light, exposing an ashtray filled with cigarette butts. Rebecca looked at her fingers; the tips were black with ashes. She looked for something to clean them with while her hands fluttered about.

A door stood at the opposite end of the room. Rebecca rushed towards it. Opening the door she saw a large cafeteria. Good. She was not too far from where she should be. Then she realized the pounding had stopped. Had her mother given up and left? Did she dare unlock the first door before disappearing into the next room so she could lead her mother into their trap?

The pry bar under her sweater prodded her in the ribs. She wondered if she would ever have to use it.

How could I possibly hit my own mother? She's not a juggernaut, she's actually pretty fragile.

A tremendous blow struck the door. Rebecca yelped in surprise.

On the other side of the battered door, Alexandra picked herself up off the floor. The door had a slight crack in the center. With steely eyes and grunting with the effort, Alexandra picked up a five foot length of denuded tree trunk and held it on top of her shoulder. Screaming with wild determination, she rammed it into the door, falling down from the force of the blow.

The crack in the door was longer.

Rebecca could not believe it. She stroked her cheeks with her fingers, leaving traces of cigarette ash on her skin.

But Mother can barely twist open a jar lid. She can't break down a solid door ... can she?

A third scream and smash cracked the door down the middle. One more blow and the door would fly apart.

Knocking the ash tray to the floor, Rebecca fled towards the cafeteria. Before she could get completely inside, the cracked door exploded behind her. Her mother burst through the hurtling chunks of wood bearing a big log on her shoulder. Howling, she fell to the floor.

Their gaze locked on each other. Gritted teeth, feral eyes, and guttural breathing stared up at Rebecca with the animosity of a monster.

Moving quickly, Rebecca stepped backwards, slammed the door shut and threw the deadbolt.

She's like wild animal. What am I going to do? She wants to kill me.

Feeling suddenly weak in the knees, Rebecca stumbled through a large cafeteria with tables, chairs, and a service area where orders were taken and food was prepared. Several stoves lined a wall behind a counter on top of which two cash registers sat next to an empty rack for snacks. She desperately wanted a cookie, but didn't see any lying around. She always ate sugar when she was stressed. A dozen chocolate-chip ones sounded about right at the moment.

From behind the door, growls and footsteps dragged something heavy. Rebecca backed further away. She was glancing about distractedly when she heard a familiar scratching sound on the door.

Rebecca knew what was coming next. As her mother tapped on the door, she darted towards the next exit.

This place better have lots of doors. Where are you, Andy? I need you.

Ungh! Ungh! Ungh!

Hearing Mr. Senicki overexert himself, Andy rolled over onto his stomach. With careful consideration for the preservation of his cranium, he crawled to the hill's edge, expecting to see what he indeed saw. Mr. Senicki was climbing the slope and having a tough time of it. Older, heavier and less spry than Andy, he huffed his way up the steep slope like a clumsy turtle. Veins strained out on his forehead; his face turned red with the effort.

Andy scratched his chin with his finger.

His head looks it could erupt at any second.

Andy decided to wait a bit longer, to let Mr. Senicki wear himself out more so that he would be motivated to fall for his ruse. So he waited and watched and listened to the pop who looked like he might pop.

"Ungh! Ungh! Ungh!"

Mr. Senicki was halfway up the hill. Andy decided it was time to spring his surprise. He called down. "Mr. Senicki?"

Mr. Senicki stopped grunting and looked up at Andy.

"Can't we talk about this?" said Andy. "What have I ever done to you?"

Mr. Senicki reached for the gun in his back pocket, grasping it by the handle.

"Why are you chasing me?"

The gun circled around towards Andy.

"Why won't you talk to me?"

Mr. Senicki took aim when he lost his footing and slipped down the slope. He jammed the gun into the ground like a tent stake, halting his descent. The barrel filled up with dirt. He shook it vigorously to clear it out.

"That's it!" shouted Andy, thinking the time was ripe. "I'm running so far away from you you'll never find me, ever."

Mr. Senicki resumed his climbing with even greater effort.

"Ungh! Ungh! Ungh!"

Andy ran to where an old tire lay, the tire he had found at the mill and rolled all the way to this spot after squashing the Munchkins. He pushed it to the edge of the hill on the side away from Mr. Senicki. The slope ran down for a long ways with only scattered shrubbery here and there.

Cupping his hands, he yelled, "I'm telling the Sheriff. You'll never catch me." He pushed the tire over the edge. It crashed down the hill making lots of noise.

Andy hoped his scam would work. Rebecca needed him. He was worried that this was taking too long, and that her mother would catch her before he could get back.

Please fall for it. Please take the bait.

He tip-toed back to the where Mr. Senicki was, got down on his knees, cupped his hand to his ear and listened carefully.

Mr. Senicki shimmied down the hill. When he got to the bottom he rushed towards where the tire had fallen.

Andy watched Rebecca's father until he disappeared from sight, then crept down the hill as fast as he could.

Hold on, Rebecca. I'm coming, he thought, running as quietly as he could back to the lumber mill.

What a nightmare!

Rebecca stumbled down a hallway in her flight from her relentless gun toting mother. The sight of her malevolent stare had shaken her up inside. Her body was in shock; her mind confused; she could hardly think. The log battering ram bashed at the locked cafeteria door which she had also blocked off with some chairs and a couple of tables. She needed to find the meeting place and the quicker the better.

At least I'm keeping her busy. Hurry up, Andy. I don't think I can do this much longer.

She reached an intersecting corridor dimly lit by moonlight filtering down through a row of skylights. To her left was a room too dark to see clearly into, while further down was a door leading somewhere else. She entered the closest room, finding lots of tools.

I remember this place. This is where Andy found the pry bar. The meeting room is not far from here.

That meant that Andy would find her when he got back. She could just hide and wait for him to return. Her mind was so muddled, she needed to rest. Rebecca had never felt this alone or threatened before. The bullets, the narrow escapes, running about in the dark, fumbling for a light switch while her mother tapped on doors and bust them down; it was wearing her nerves thinner than thin. Trying to think positive, she hoped she was at least losing some weight.

Rebecca felt the ring that Andy had given her, with its beautiful turquoise stone. She closed her eyes and imagined Andy sliding it on her finger, asking her to be his girlfriend. She knew it was precious to him. It was given to him by his grandmother to remember her by before she died in Germany. That he had given it to Rebecca made her feel that he truly cherished her.

The ring kept her from drowning in a sea of despair.

He could have refused to help. He could have run away, but he didn't. He really loves me.

A crashing sound spooked her. She guessed her mother would be coming any time now. She needed a diversion and she needed it fast.

She took her key ring out of her pocket. It was made of plastic with an "R" upon it made of dozens of tiny fake jewels. Twisting the key ring, she broke off a bunch of the jewels and scattered them in a trail on the floor. She tossed the key ring further down the hallway, hoping it would trick her mother into going the wrong way.

Rebecca snuck across the tool room to a door on the other side. It led to a second workshop where chairs and sofas were upholstered. The glass window in the door had a wavy pattern in it that distorted light so she could barely see through it. This worked to her advantage, as she could hide behind it in the dark on one side and still detect any movement through the glass on the other. She rubbed her hands on her upper arms, trying to disperse her mental lethargy.

Finding a stool to sit on, Rebecca sat and waited, thinking about raspberry cheese cake and a tall glass of milk without any rat poison.

Alexandra's body blazed with rage and anguish. She had smashed through three solid doors with her tree trunk battering ram and was exhausted. Her body demanded rest.

The Director had to cool her down.

Plopping her down on a nearby bench, the Director had her close her eyes. Sending signals through her implant, he reached into her mind, flooding her with caring memories: the day on the tour bus when Andy called her his "shining star," speaking her wedding vows to Andy, the taste of his fingers when he put a bit of their wedding cake in her mouth, their nights of passion, Andy's lips raining hot kisses on her body, his manhood filling her with his love. The joyous memories made her flesh vibrate with new life, new energy. Her strength returned.

Having restored her energy, the Director tipped the scales of her psyche back to his malignant purpose. "Run motivational memory A-7," he said to his effects crew.

Alexandra imagined she saw Rebecca give Andy a poisoned glass of warm Brandy, his favorite nightcap. She imagined her trying to run him over with the station wagon, kiss him in the Butcher shop, and aim a gun at him as he stood naked in a warm Greco-Roman pool filled with rose petals. Herman dragged Andy across the lawn while Rebecca pistol-whipped him. Andy's face bled; he cried for mercy as they hauled him away in the trunk of a yellow Dodge Dart. The images stampeded through her consciousness, whipping her back into an emotional frenzy.

The Director turned the volume of her feelings up as high as they would go. Her yearning intensified to a burning need. The need became terror over losing Andy, the terror begat anger at those who would destroy their love. A pledge emerged from her enraged soul promising that those who dared to harm him would suffer the ultimate price at her hands.

She rose from the bench, renewed in strength, revitalized in resolve and determined to destroy the kidnappers. Her mind throbbed with a memory that echoed throughout her hate-inflamed flesh. She was at her wedding with Andy, speaking their vows to the Priest. The Priest turned to all present. "What God has ordained, let no woman rip asunder or she shall suffer the homicidal wrath of the bride."

Grasping the silver revolver, Alexandra trod along on her mission of love, death and vengeance.

What happened to mother? What is taking Andy so long? I'm so scared.

Rebecca hid behind the tool room door, waiting. She wondered if her mother had gotten lost or if Andy had escaped her father. She couldn't figure out what to do; her mind was numb. She hoped that Andy would arrive first.

She pushed the door open a few inches. It squeaked; Rebecca cringed. Nearby footsteps echoed softly. Rebecca recognized them. It was her mother. She left the door where it was, not wanting to chance it squeaking again if she closed it.

She wished she could vanish and take a nice long nap.

The pearl-handled revolver extended around the corners of the hallway. Her mother's head peered about as though hoping to catch her prey by surprise. Seeing it through the wavy glass, it reminded Rebecca of her cat, Mr. Meow, stalking a bird in the yard. Knowing she was the bird, it was creepy to watch.

Her mother twisted her head towards the tool shop. Rebecca held her breath. Her mother took a step towards her, crunching the jewels scattered on the floor. Her mother saw the key ring, glittering in the moonlight.

Please mother, take the bait. Do it for me.

Her mother proceeded down the hall.

Rebecca breathed a sigh of relief.

"Boring," declared the Director observing the scene from his hover recliner. "The scene is losing dramatic tension. I've created some exciting drama, but the beats of action are becoming repetitious. He picked up his latest martini with tiny shrimp swimming inside it. Tossing the contents into his mouth, he tilted the hover recliner to a vertical position and began to pace the floor.

"Genius," he muttered like a mantra. "I am a genius. What's wrong here? How can I fix it?" He stretched his arms above his head, took a deep breath and exhaled slowly, lowering his arms. Bringing his hands in close to his chest he repeated the process two more times. "Peaks and valleys," he muttered. "I know what to do."

He switched on his communicator.

"Yes, Herr Director?" the Production Manager said over the channel.

"The story is going flat," declared the Director. "Send in a probe. I need to bring this story beat to a climax."

Rebecca sat on her stool. Despite her genuine desire to rescue her parents, enough was enough. She was nearly faint with anxiety. *Let her go the wrong way. I can't take this any more. I'll just meet up with Andy and ....*

The fog in her mind lifted.

An invisible probe floated above her, forcing images into her brain. Andy was waiting for her at the rendezvous point. He was discovered by her mother. Cornered, with no place to run, Andy looked down her mother's gun barrel; his face contorted with fear. "Rebecca!" Andy cried as the gun fired, filling her mind with a flash of blinding light.

Oh, my gosh, thought Rebecca. *What have I done? She's heading towards our meeting place! What if Andy is there and thinks she's me? What if he exposes himself and she shoots him?*

Her pounding heart was becoming an all too familiar sound. She had heard a horse could run itself to death, run until its heart burst. She wondered if human hearts ever exploded from too much stress. Hers felt like it was being squeezed in a vise.

Tilting her chin down, she saw her hands painfully gripping her breast. No wonder it hurt. *Can I do anything else to scare myself out of my wits?*

Releasing herself from herself, Rebecca tugged at her sweater. She still had to do something about her mother. *Has she gone through the other door yet? How do I keep her from finding Andy? I've got to do something.*

Her ankle began to itch. She bent down to scratch it finding a penny lying on the floor. It gave her an idea. Picking up the penny, she slipped her arm through the crack in the door and tossed it high in the air towards the corridor.

The penny soared, flipping end over end. It almost hit the ceiling at the peak of its trajectory before diving down towards the wood paneled floor like a tiny bomb. Smacking the ground, it bounced, struck the far wall, then miraculously landed on its side and rolled down the hallway, spinning its way past dust motes, bits of paper, and Rebecca's ripped up key chain. It cruised along like it had a motor and a gallon of gas. Dipping into a slight crack in the floor, it wobbled, bumped into Alexandra's shoe and fell over flat.

Alexandra glared at the copper interloper. Like Gulliver to a Lilliputian, she silently demanded where it came from or suffer her 900 stories tall wrath. The very presence of the copper penny was sufficient to spill the beans.

Nimble as a panther, Alexandra charged into the tool shop. Her gun snapped this way and that as she stalked the shadows for a sign of her daughter. Finding nothing, Alexandra growled. She fired at the wall, cracking the peg board. Tools fell to the counter, knocking over bins of furniture nails. Alexandra shot at the far side of the room; a window shattered. Glass fragments fell, revealing one very surprised Rebecca.

Rebecca stood exposed to her mother, the gun aimed right between her eyes.

Rebecca screamed as her mother pulled the trigger.

Breathing hard from running, Andy reached the fence bordering the lumber mill. A scream and a gunshot filled the night. He froze in his tracks, listening with every fiber of his being.

Please, not Rebecca. Anything but that!

Andy listened intently; his ears gathered in nothing but the hoot of a distant owl. Imagining the worst, Andy raced across the dirt yard towards the warehouses in a blind panic.

The Munchkins helped him as best they could.

(To the tune of "Ding, Dong, The Witch Is Dead")

"Ding, dong, Rebecca's dead.

She'll never get to Andy's bed.

Ding, dong, Rebecca's really dead.

He'll never, ever get to feel her,

Unless he's into necrophilia.

Ding, dong, Rebecca's really dead."

Whether Rebecca had her dues with the Lord paid up in full or whether she was just plain lucky, the bullet missed drilling the top of her head by a few centimeters. The passage of the lethal metal through her hair sent a shock wave into her brain. Her muscles locked up. Her mother aimed again. Her life was over in the next three seconds.

Her last thoughts were of Andy gently holding her hand.

Sneering in victory, Alexandra pulled the trigger.

The hammer struck an empty chamber.

Both women looked at the gun, but for completely different reasons. Alexandra pulled the trigger again. Nothing happened. She pulled it again and again.

Wailing like a banshee, Alexandra tossed the weapon and charged. Arms outstretched, hands clawed, she flung herself at the closed door straining to reach her daughter's throat.

An instant before Alexandra's body struck the bottom edge of the window, the metal hand of an Eye swiped the jagged, broken glass away.

Alexandra lunged through the opening, her fingernails barely missed scratching her daughter's face. Slamming to a stop, her body slumped over the broken window. Hung over the door, half in one room, half in the other, she thrashed about.

Rebecca didn't wait for an encore.

Leaving her mother dangling and screaming, Rebecca took off through the upholstery shop. She didn't know or care where she was going as long as it was far away from her savage parent.

After Rebecca left, Alexandra became oddly still. Her lungs gathered large breaths of air as she hung limply over the window cill.

Enjoying some soothing classical music, the Director decided to cool the Alexandra down for the second time. There would be another confrontation. He would see to that. Time was on his side. Besides, her physical limitations created more conflict, more peaks and valleys in the story which gave it more depth and excitement. Harrowing escapes were big with Those Who Watch. Now he could start again with a valley and build it up. With lots of terrific footage like this, he could always fill in any minor gaps with his post-production team. "That is the beautiful thing about being a director. You can always fix it in post."

Snatching half a lemon wedge from a nearby bowl, he squeezed the juice straight down his throat, smacking his fishy lips in a satisfied "ahh."

Swinging her upper torso backwards, Mrs. Senicki flung herself off of the broken window, landing unsteady on her feet. Standing still in a trance, a floating robot materialized behind her. It spread its eight arms out like the legs of a giant spider with very strange hands, one of which held a violin. The spidery arms became active. Two hands played the violin, while two sprayed her body with a soothing, regenerative mist. Four other arms massaged her shoulders, back, legs and buttocks using sonic vibrating hands. Next, the robot primped her hairdo with a curling iron, a brush and hairspray, then freshened her lipstick and rouged her cheeks. It redid her fingernail polish, steam cleaned her dress, shined her shoes, cracked her back like a chiropractor, and powdered her underarms and face. Last of all, a hand gently opened her mouth, while another hand sprayed breath freshener inside it.

Having completed all its tasks, the makeup robot disappeared in a transporter beam.

Revitalized, Alexandra picked the silver revolver up off the floor. Coolly, she flicked it open and stared into the revolving cylinder.

Each chamber contained a brand new shiny bullet.

Without a thought as to how they magically got there, Alexandra primped her fiery hairdo, opened the door, and promptly resumed the hunt for her daughter.

Rebecca found herself at an intersection in a long hallway. Down the perpendicular passage, she saw five open doors with glass windows on the left side while the right side was a wall with pictures hanging on it. A sixth door stood by itself at the far end. Nerves shaking, she half-walked, half-stumbled forward, hoping she wouldn't pass out.

As she passed each door, she locked and pulled them shut, thinking her mother would ignore them and her hideout so she could take a collapse break.

Feeling woozy, she took refuge behind the sixth door, not bothering to look inside its interior. All she wanted to do was stop; nothing else mattered. She didn't want to move another inch.

Closing the door to her hideout, the room became as black as pitch. Her fumbling fingers found the deadbolt and twisted it in place.

This was not where she had agreed to meet Andy, but her nerves weren't capable of honoring that challenge just now. Stress threatened collapse if she didn't cooperate and heed its stern warning.

Rebecca leaned against the door, sliding down it until her rear end hit the floor. She tried to think about Andy, but all she could see was her mother trying to kill her. In the darkness that engulfed her, the image of her mother haunted her like a vengeful specter. She envisioned the flash of light from the gun barrel; her hair being singed by the bullet's passage; her mother's kamikaze charge for her throat. When her mother reached out to strangle her, Rebecca connected with her eyes. The pure malice she saw in them was like an axe blade to her heart.

She held onto Andy's ring, keening softly. Her whimpering moans echoed in the gloomy darkness.

In a way, the ring and Andy came to her rescue, for as tears poured down her cheeks she mercifully blacked out.

She's after me. She's going to shoot. No, mother, don't!

The gun fired. The tip of the bullet had her mother's screaming face.

Rebecca awoke with a start to discover that she still possessed body and soul. She had no idea as to how long she had fainted.

I've got to find Andy. I can't take this anymore. I quit.

Rubbing the wetness from her eyes, Rebecca smeared the eyeliner on her already cigarette-ash-smeared face. She prayed that Andy was safe. She had gotten him into this mess and she would just die if any harm came to him because of her.

Ignoring the black smudges on her fingers, Rebecca stood up and cautiously cracked open the door just in time to see a familiar shadow rear up on the far wall at the end of the hall.

Rebecca barely had time to close the door when her mother stepped into the hallway entrance.

Andy stood in a large woodshop with the walls painted black. He didn't know which way to go. He was supposed to have run around the back of the large building and meet Rebecca at a pre-planned spot, but upon hearing her scream he had rushed inside to help her. Now he was completely disoriented as to where he was and how he was going to find her.

Smelling popcorn, he floundered in his own thoughts.

How could I be so stupid? The building is huge. Rebecca could be hurt and I can't find her. What should I do? What would dad do? Be a man, that's what.

Andy marched back and forth across the floor. Should he go further into the bowels of the building or find his way back outside and run all the way around to the back? He figured that if he stayed inside the building he might run into Mrs. Senicki. If her back were to him, could he get the jump on her? Of course, she still had the gun. What if she heard him and turned around before he could grab her? Getting shot wouldn't help the situation. How could he ensure success without getting any round, bleeding souvenirs on his body?

The pain of his indecision was like wild stallions were tied to each limb, pulling him in four different directions.

He stopped pacing and stood still. A Munchkin with a fishing pole sat on his shoulder and cast the line out into Andy's mental pond.

Eight Munchkins appeared on the floor dressed like Egyptian slaves with big noses. Double lines of rope stretched out from Andy's shoe, which the slave Munchkins held over their shoulders.

On top of Andy's shoe, an Egyptian Pharaoh Munchkin sat on a gilded throne. His face was painted gold, his beard and hair were stiff like the mask of Tutankhamen.

"Bu-bu-bu-begin," the stuttering Pharaoh Munchkin ordered.

A Slave Master Munchkin stood on the toe of Andy's shoe. He cracked a whip. "Heave, ho, slaves. Pull."

Straining to drag Andy's shoe forward the slaves all chanted, "Rebecca's in serious trouble. Andy, make up your mind."

Andy continued to imitate a statute.

The fishing Munchkin's pole bent over. "Hey, fellahs, I got a bite."

Having given up on moving Andy's shoe, the Egyptian Munchkins played poker in a circle at Andy's feet.

"Yeah, yeah. Pig's fly," they muttered.

"I'll take three cards and raise you Ten Commandments."

Andy struggled to overcome his mental inertia. He imagined Rebecca dying in a pool of her own blood, weakly calling out his name (*Andy, help*), while her mother stepped slowly towards her, raising the gun to blast her out of existence. Like an unwelcome premonition, Andy visualized the last thing Rebecca saw in her life was him running by the windows in the moonlight (*Andy, save me!*), then Andy disappearing as the gun gushed forth its death-dealing payload (*Andy, you let me die. Act like a man you sniveling wimp*).

Andy gritted his teeth. Without Rebecca the world seemed gray and lifeless. He had to try to find her, no matter the cost to himself. It was time to act like a man.

Opening and closing his hands into fists, he pretended to defend himself by shadow boxing. He imagined punching Rebecca's mother in the chin and her eyes rolling around in circles. She collapsed to the floor, a bell rang, he raised his arms in victory.

The Egyptian Munchkins laughed at him.

"Andy thinks he's Rocky," commented a Munchkin.

"Forget him," another said. C'mon, let's play some poker. I bet the river Nile."

"I raise you a burning bush," another wagered.

"I call," a third Egyptian Munchkin said, "and raise you some fish and a few loaves of bread."

Andy's confidence deflated; he thrust his hands deep into his pockets. Still unsure about what to do, he noticed a door broken in half in the far corner of the room. Gathering his scattered thoughts, he scuttled off to find Rebecca.

"He's leaving, guys," the Slave Master said.

"He's leaving?" the slaves said in surprise.

"Hell froze over, guys. Let's go!"

The Munchkins ran after Andy, all but the stuttering Pharaoh.

"Bu-bu-but I have a ru-ru-royal flush!" protested the Pharaoh.

"SORRY," the others called out as they scurried after Andy.

Alexandra stood in the hallway of the six doors. Her eyes were transfixed; her body rigid. The Director had been waiting for just the right time to use a memory within her when she was 17-years-old, her role as famous opera character Princess Turandot.

"Opera music will make my story a timeless classic," the Director said. "Like that magnificent French movie *Diva*. And using flamboyant opera characters is much too rare an opportunity not to take advantage of. Besides, if the footage doesn't work in this show I can always use it in another."

The Director mixed Alexandra's memories and emotions as he prepared her for the role. He dressed her in her Chinese opera costume, a royal princess kimono of cold blue embroidered with beads the color of ice. Red hued tassels hung about her ears, suspended from a gem-studded tiara in the shape of entwined serpents that contrasted sharply with her flame-shaped hair. Her black fingernails, five inches long, were trimmed with claw-like tips.

She was an image of cold womanly fury.

"You are now the Princess Alexandra," said the Director, "passionately in love with Prince Andy, obeying the voice of your God, hell-bent on revenge at your daughter and Herman."

He appraised her appearance. "She looks wonderfully freakish." He put a scaly finger to his lips. "Maybe my theme should be 'Love turns you into a freak.'" He slapped his palms together, and drummed on the console several times in delight. "I really am brilliant." He smiled. "Come on you murderous Princess, show me what you got."

Princess Alexandra glared down the moonlit hallway. She spoke in a gravelly whisper that grew increasingly harsh and ended in a prolonged hiss.

"Re-be-ccaaaaaaaaaaaaaaaaaaaa--sssssssssss."

In the sightless darkness of her hideout, Rebecca felt about for a window when she heard her name uttered as though it came from the lips of a deadly snake.

Her spine tingled with dread. She wanted to leap out of her skin.

Her questing fingers found a window shade. Cautiously, she raised it up an inch. The shadow of the building extended several feet before her. Pale moonlight illuminated the forest, allowing her to see for the first time since she had entered the room. Rebecca had found her means to escape.

She silently drew the window shade up. There was a lock on top of the window. She flipped it open. Glancing briefly towards the door, Rebecca placed her fingers to lift up the window. The buildings shadow seemed different than she remembered. Then she saw the security bars on the windows. The bars were so close together, there was no way she could squeeze through them.

Where did these bars come from? I could have sworn they weren't there a moment ago. How could I have missed seeing them?

A moan threatened to rip out of her throat. The cat and mouse chase was over, the mouse was about to be caught.

Turning, she saw that she was in a storeroom. There was a small desk, shelves with boxes of office supplies, a mop in a rolling bucket, and other items. The only way out was through the door in full view of her mother. She was going to have to make a run for it.

Her beautiful knees trembled at the thought.

Outside the building, an Eye projected the image of security bars across the window.

Princess Alexandra's feral eyes took in the row of doors. Her daughter could be hidden behind any one of them. Rebecca was always hiding behind glass windows. This time she would finish the job. Taking numerous tiny steps, Princess Alexandra glided gracefully to the first door. Puccini's dramatic music thrummed in her ears. In her mind's eye, thousands of Chinese peasants sang *shoot Rebecca.*

She thought back to the moment she had that traitorous-bitch-of-a-daughter squarely in her gun sights. She wished she hadn't run out of bullets.

On the thought monitoring system, the Director overheard her desire. He transmitted into her the notion that she could fire the gun without ever running out of ammunition, then ordered the prop department to make it so.

He observed her reach first door … twist the doorknob … it was locked. She was going to ignore it and move on when she spied a strand of pink yarn caught in the doorframe. Her thoughts came over the speakers. Rebecca had to be hiding inside; somehow her sweater got caught in the door jam.

"The pink strand of yarn," the Director said, mentally patting himself on the back. "Another nice touch by moi."

Stepping back, Princess Alexandra kicked out with her Chinese shoe, breaking the cheesy lock. Swinging the door wide open, she rushed into the dark, firing wildly. Intermittent flashes from the weapon illuminated the room's interior in a freaky strobe effect. In the brief, intense flares of light, Rebecca's face popped up like a hyperactive jack rabbit: behind the desk, in a picture frame, on a computer monitor, a coffee cup, everywhere and reality be damned.

Pop … Hi, Princess mom … Pop … Shoot me if you can … Pop, pop, pop.

Alexandra's gun roared its tune of death at every Rebecca who came into sight. Each shot missed the elusive target, appearing somewhere else to taunt her.

Alexandra shrieked and fired as bullets slammed throughout the tiny room as the Chinese peasants sang *shoot Rebecca.*

The small accounting office became a shooting gallery for the Chinese Opera criminally insane.

In the storeroom, Rebecca heard her mother firing incessantly. Her mind unhinged. The objects breaking, her mother screeching, the gunfire ripping the air with terrible purpose; it was much too horrible to bear. Her mind collapsed back to the nightmarish place it had been before she blacked out. Her mother's face appeared before her, a grimace of rage surrounded by darkness. Her crazed eyes blazed with an evil fire; she was surrounded by a ten course turkey dinner.

Exposing fierce teeth, her mother growled, "Keep cooking!" Her face vanished. The ten course meal attacked.

"Excellent," the Director applauded. "She's as crazy as the Andy. Such is the power of love. I am such a winner!"

With a flip of a five inch fingernail, Princess Alexandra turned on the light switch. A picture of a smiling man hung at an odd angle on the wall, a hole where his nose should have been. Fragments of a Mount Rushmore coffee cup lay on the messy desk. Old coffee, green with mold, ran over the desktop, spilling onto the carpet. Bullet holes pockmarked the walls, but Rebecca's bleeding body was not there.

Growling, Princess Alexandra swiped at a red tassel that whipped at her face. Resuming her icy stare, she regally moved on to the next room where she savagely kicked in the door and started firing.

Rebecca crawled behind a desk while her mother's little revolver spat slugs of hot metal. Bent over, she rested her head on a chair seat and covered her head with her hands in an effort to drown out the source of her terror.

A moment later, Rebecca became aware of a thick silence. *Is she finally out of bullets? Did she leave? Should I make a run for it now?*

She tried to move; her legs were jelly; she had to escape; time was not on her side. Summoning her courage, she got up off the cold floor. Her left leg felt numb. She silently cursed. *I've got to run for my life and my leg falls asleep. Why is nothing ever easy?*

Rebecca rubbed her hands against her thighs to get the circulation back to normal.

Her mother assaulted the third room.

Rebecca rubbed her legs faster.

Ignoring the deafening bursts of death, Rebecca limped towards the door. When her mother entered the next room, she planned to burst out of the storeroom and run like a bat out of hell until she was miles away. Her fingers lightly gripped the door knob; Rebecca took a deep breath. Fear haunted her, making her tremble. This time it was do or die.

The Eye in the room turned on the ceiling light above the desk.

Gasping, Rebecca slapped at the wall switch, killing the light. *What was that? How did that happen? Did mother see it? Oh, I hope not.*

She wrung her hands in front of her chest.

The Eye flipped the light switch up again.

The meager bulb burned like a beacon announcing her presence to the world.

"I like it," the Director said. "She can be unwittingly telekinetic, like in the movie *Carrie* by Brian De Palma. Her emotions can cause her own downfall. It fits my self-destruction theme perfectly. Maybe I can figure out a way to drench her body in pig's blood."

He clasped his finny hands together. "Wouldn't that make a colorful poster?"

In the storeroom, the light came on again.

Rebecca gasped and slapped the switch down.

The bulb became brighter.

Stop it! Mother will see it!

Rebecca flicked the switch up and down again. The bulb's intensity increased with every motion, pumping up in brightness until it seemed to blaze like the sun.

As bullets pelted another room, Rebecca climbed on top of the desk to unscrew the bulb. She touched it with her fingers and burned them.

Kitty crap! That really hurts.

Blowing on her fingers, she saw an ashtray filled with cigarette butts and ashes. Rebecca snatched it up. The foul smelling remnants flung through the air as she smashed the light bulb.

On the holo-screen, the Director watched the light bulb explode in extreme slow motion. Thin glass fragments flew out in a circle, slicing through the ashes, striking the cigarette butts, and glancing off the ash tray. From the hot filament, light stretched out in all directions like a time lapse flower opening up.

"Beautiful," the Director said. "David Lynch, meet your master."

The light expanded several more inches when the darkness abruptly rushed in and swallowed it up.

The Director thought it was a remarkable arty moment. He was certain this shot alone would turn his production into a cult classic like *A Clockwork Orange*.

Blinded by darkness, Rebecca stood on top of the desk. Each time she blinked, bright spots swam before her. Still, she needed to keep moving. She bent her knees and touched the desk, feeling for the edge so she could climb down. The gunfire had stopped. She heard footsteps in the hallway. Rebecca knew there was but one more room between her and machine gun mommy–the corner office.

She slipped off the desk. Something hard pressed against her stomach.

The pry bar. I forgot all about it.

She tugged her sweater out from under her jeans. The foot long mommy-whacker was inside a hand towel she had found. She unwrapped it. The metal felt cold to her fingers. She decided when her mother entered the corner office and started shooting she was going to throw it her at and run.

The gunfire Rebecca expected didn't come. She leaned close to the door, straining to listen. Looking down, the shadow of her mother's feet broke up the slash of light coming in from under the bottom of the door. Fingernails scratched the wood in an all too familiar rhythm.

A chill raced up Rebecca's spine.

She clutched the pry bar, fearful she might have to use it after all.

"Re-be-ccaaaaaaa-sss," Princess Alexandra hissed.

Rebecca's skin became electrified.

The foot shadows retreated, restoring the light strip. To her horror, Rebecca heard a low growl. She knew what was coming. She couldn't believe it.

Alexandra used her body as a battering ram; she crashed into the door, bounced off it and fell. Growling, she got up and crashed into it again and again.

The fifth time the wood jamb splintered and broke apart. One more push and the door would swing open.

Rebecca's heart skipped a beat.

She moved to the side so she would be behind the door when her mother came inside. Clutching the pry bar, her every nerve burned with an anxious fire. She gritted her teeth.

Come on mother. Let's get this over with.

The door swung partway open; the hinges squeaked. The sound was like fingernails scraping across the chalkboard of Rebecca's soul.

A yellowish light invaded the room. A blob of shadow crept up the far wall. The tip of a revolver peeked beyond the edge of the door.

Her heart pounding, Rebecca raised the pry bar over her head. She was going to have to hurt her mother if she wanted to live.

The shadowy intruder entered the room. Rebecca's brain gave her the green light. Electric impulses coursed down nerves, giving the signal to attack.

I'm sorry, mother. Forgive me.

The pry bar started forward, backed by all the strength the frightened young woman could muster.

Andy stood in the doorway holding the gun. "Rebecca?" he whispered

A wild scream; an object slashed by his face. Andy yelped and crashed to the floor. The gun clattered into the hallway.

"Andy?" Rebecca said. At the last moment, she realized it was him. She had jerked the pry bar aside, barely missing his head.

Andy leaned against a bookcase. He appeared to be unconscious or dead. Rebecca's mouth was a circle of worry.

Andy opened his reeling eyes. Two Rebeccas looked down upon him. *I have two girlfriends. Sweet.* Andy smiled weakly.

Rebecca dropped the pry bar. She lunged to her knees and embraced him, pressing her cheek against his chest.

Oh, Andy," Rebecca babbled, "I was so scared. I thought you'd never get here."

As Rebecca kept on talking, waves of heat from her face penetrated Andy's chest. A heady warmth shot out through his veins. Rebecca rubbed her hands across his lower back. Her touch felt wonderfully intimate. Danger didn't seem so bad after all with rewards like this.

Rebecca hugged his rib cage higher.

Andy winced.

Rebecca pulled away from him, terrified of losing him now that they were reunited. "Andy. Are you hurt?"

The corners of his lips turned upward, his eyes glinted.

"I win," he said softly.

Rebecca threw the cloth she had wrapped the pry bar in at him. It hit Andy square in the face. "What's wrong with you?" she scolded. "I could have killed you. Don't ever sneak up on me like that again." She noticed dried blood on his shirt at the elbow. "Oh, babe, you're bleeding. Are you all right?"

Andy removed the rag from his face.

Time froze as Rebecca awaited his reply.

Andy's eyes refocused. He was now back to a single girlfriend. She looked so serious staring at him that he couldn't help himself–he giggled.

Straddling his outstretched legs, Rebecca watched her boyfriend chuckle. "What?" she said, confused.

"You called me babe." He giggled some more, smiling broadly.

Glaring sternly, Rebecca put her hands on her hips. She intended to chastise him, but before she could speak Andy's stomach rumbled.

"Got anything to eat?" Andy asked. "I'm hungry."

Rebecca slapped his knee hard.

"Ouch!" Andy said. "What did you do that for?"

"Next time say who you are *before* you come in. You nearly scared me to death?"

Andy thought a moment. He realized that she was right. "Sounds reasonable," he said, nodding. His stomach rumbled again.

Rebecca's mind raced ahead. They were still in danger. "My mom's here. We've got to hide. Come on." She grabbed his hands to help him up off the floor.

Andy resisted her pulling. "She's right outside." He glanced sideways. Mrs. Senicki lay in the hallway, unconscious.

Rebecca saw her breathing slowly. "How did you do it?"

Andy smiled. "I'm a tiger, remember?"

Rebecca's face was a mask of astonishment. Andy had captured her mother. His plan had actually worked.

Andy fished a smelly rag from out of his pocket. "It's chloroform. When I couldn't find you I ran back and took it out of the doctor's bag. I soaked this rag, jumped her from behind and presto, nap time. Pretty sweet, huh?"

Rebecca couldn't believe it; her nose wrinkled in feminine mirth. Then something else came unbidden to her mind.

"Andy, where's my father?"

Andy grinned. "Your father? I tricked him into going the wrong way. He's chasing a tire way over—"

Before Andy could finish his sentence, wood explosively splintered from the bookshelf above his head.

Mr. Senicki stood at the end of the hallway. Wisps of smoke curled out from the barrel of his Colt 45/pistol.

Rebecca and Andy slammed the door shut.

Andy and Rebecca knew the door could not be locked. They scrambled up against it with their backs, propping their feet against the desk.

Andy's stomach rumbled as footsteps pounded the carpet.

Taking advantage of his opera motif, the Director had the Herman see himself as Wotan, King of the Norse gods from the Wagner Ring Cycle Operas. Wotan wore golden Viking battle armor, horns curled up from his fierce-looking helmet. The Colt 45 was his magic spear. Bearskin sandals with little wings on them were laced up his hairy calves. The light from the hallway glinted off of his mighty frame.

King Herman marched down the hall towards his enemies, his footsteps thundering, knocking the pictures off the wall as he passed them with the help of an invisible Eye for additional dramatic effect.

The Munchkins saw him coming.

"HEY, WOTAN!" they all yelled.

"How's it hangin', God guy?" said one.

"What's the rush, Vi-King?" said another.

"HASTE MAKES WASTE!" they all chanted.

King Wotan charged towards them.

"He don't look too friendly, guys," a timid Munchkin said, moving away from his friends. "Maybe we should go."

The other Munchkins turned around, their backs to Wotan. Three of them spoke.

"Go?"

"What's the matter?"

"You afraid he might step on us?"

The Munchkins laughed with contempt.

King Wotan's foot stomped them hard, squishing their teeny bodies into living pancakes.

"Gee, guys. Does it hurt?" the timid Munchkin said.

"NAW!" they all lied.

"Could someone get a bicycle pump, please. I need some fresh air. I feel a little flat."

Andy and Rebecca braced themselves as King Wotan hurled himself against the door. A shockwave passed through their bones, lifting their bodies up, then crashing them back into their former positions.

At least we can barricade him out, Andy thought. *At least we're safe in here.*

King Wotan placed the tip of his Colt 45 magic spear against the solid wood door.

A bullet passed above Rebecca's head, right where her chest would have been had she been standing. She was too scared to scream.

A second bullet erupted above Andy's head; wood flakes sprinkled down on his unruly hair. A beam of light streamed out above him forming a spot on the far wall.

Andy grimaced. *I hope he doesn't think about shooting lower.*

The next bullet tore between them at eye level.

Andy and Rebecca screamed.

The Munchkins sang to the tune *"Everything's Coming Up Roses."*

"This is it! Run, no way!

There's nothing you can do now but pray.

Death is here. Death is now.

It's too late, to cow tow.

Screaming means that you are helpless!"

Breathing deeply in and out, the Director clenched and unclenched his toes in the massage grass, enjoying a foot massage.

"This show is go good it could get me promoted to an honorary Class 7 Intelligence, the Royalty Caste. Soon I'll be called *Sir Director.*"

Fantasizing about his promotion, he pleasantly sighed as the grass kneaded the soles of his feet.

"Herr Director?" the Production Manager said over the communication channel. "Please check your monitor. Something strange has happened."

"I was taking a quickie break. Did I miss something?"

When Andy's and Rebecca's screams died out, the place was eerily quiet. No more bullets invaded their besieged sanctuary. No more door bashing had them rising up off the floor.

Andy wiped the sweat off of his chin. His eyes locked on Rebecca. The two of them had the exact same question on their minds, 'Was Rebecca's dad still out there waiting to shoot them?'

A knock on the door gave them the gasping willies. They sucked air into their lungs so fast it sounded like they were wheezing.

"It's me. Open up," a familiar voice said. "Hurry it up. I haven't got all night."

Andy sidled away from the door and opened it a crack. The Mysterious Man lay on the floor. He was sandwiched in-between the Senickis, Herman on top, Alexandra on the bottom. Both of the parents were unconscious. Their arms and legs went every which way, making it hard to tell whose limbs were whose.

Andy grinned. *It's a parent sandwich. A three-human pretzel. Siamese triplets!*

The Mysterious Man held a hunk of cloth over Mr. Senicki's nose. "Get him off me. He's heavy, damn it."

Rebecca pulled the door further open. "How did you--?"

"You left this in the other room," the Mysterious Man said, holding up a bottle of chloroform.

Andy scratched his elbow, realizing for the first time that the Man was not tied up. "But how did you …?"

"You really must learn to tie better knots, young man. Weren't you ever a Boy Scout?"

Andy shook his head.

Rebecca stared at her toppled parents.

"I said get this man off me," the Mysterious Man complained. "My nose itches. I need to scratch it."

Andy and Rebecca pulled Mr. Senicki off of the Mysterious Man. Andy saw that the Man had knocked on the door by kicking Mr. Senicki's shoe against the wood.

Did he learn that in Boy Scouts? Andy wondered.

Four Eyes recorded the scene, capturing it from several angles.

On an old 3-d hover monitor, the Director watched an old television program with the Production Manager. It starred the Mysterious Man.

"So," the Director mumbled. "He survived this episode and found us. We must find a way to make his life interesting."

He faced the Production Manager. "Retrieve his psychological profile from the data banks."

"Right away, Herr Director," the Production Manager bowed, then left the control room.

Yes, the Director thought. *Interesting and dangerous. After all, he is our Guest Star.*

The log cutting shop was an enormous room with two massive doors that led to the courtyard. Forklifts carried huge trees inside its cavernous maw to be made into lumber. Along one wall, a power saw with a four foot diameter blade sat at the end of a long conveyer belt. Stripped of its branches, a tree was secured to the belt and sent to be ripped in two by the saw's sharp, jagged teeth. The raw lumber would be sent to another part of the facility for cutting into smaller boards or in making furniture.

The Doctor chose this room to perform the operation in as numerous lights hung down from the tall ceiling, washing the room with a bright, harsh light. He wished it was more sterile, but they cleaned the area as best as they could. It was just going to have to suffice.

Still unconscious from the chloroform, Mr. Senicki lay beside the conveyer belt on top of a big table they had dollied in from one of the furniture making rooms. Mrs. Senicki, also comatose with her hands bound tightly together, rested on a flatbed dolly used to transport Rebecca's parents to the log cutting room.

The Doctor was glad to see someone else tied up besides himself.

"They'll be out for hours," the Doctor said, scratching his nose with his fingers. "Now, young lady," he said to Rebecca, "would you mind showing me where you hid my medical bag?" He paused, smiling smugly. "Pretty please? So I can save your parents' lives?"

The Doctor waived his fingers as though to hurry her along.

Rebecca felt a sharp twinge of distress at having to trust him. If she didn't need his medical expertise, she would have sooner trusted the black plague.

She walked over to a steel cabinet with a rusty lock on it.

"Where did you find a key for that?" Andy said.

Rebecca took a sledge hammer from a nearby rack of tools. With a furious swing, she broke the lock off, then gave Andy a does-that-answer-your-question look.

"Oh," Andy meekly nodded as she swung open the locker exposing the medical bag.

The Doctor frowned. "Tie up daddy-o here," he said to Andy, strolling up to the table, "And make sure he can't get loose. I can't have my patients flopping about the operating table while I'm cutting their heads open, now can I?"

Andy took the rope he had tied the Doctor up with earlier and bound Mr. Senicki's feet together. He secured the rope to the table legs so Rebecca's father couldn't wiggle around.

Beaming with self-righteous delight, the Doctor waited for Rebecca to bring him his medical bag. Looking squarely at Rebecca, he thought to himself, *Now who's in charge here, you little pink sweater wearing bitch?*

Pulling the medical bag out of the locker, Rebecca carried it towards the makeshift operating table. She could tell the Doctor was enjoying this; it fueled her resentment. After all the trouble he had caused, she was certain he was at least half, if not all, crazy.

With a full-fledged smirk on his face, the Doctor calmly held out his hand to take the bag from her. Getting Rebecca to do his bidding was a moment of victory and he relished every second of it.

I'm the professional here. They should be grateful I'm even helping them at all, the ignorant brats.

Rebecca plopped the kit down on the table, making the instruments inside jingle.

The Doctor was not amused. Snorting, he opened the bag, removed a scalpel and set down on the table. "This is a surgeon's dream come true," the Doctor said, pulling out a stethoscope. "This is the first time anyone has had the opportunity to remove a mind control device from a living patient. Ah, here it is."

The Doctor raised a small electric bone saw out of the bag.

Rebecca saw the spinning wheel's razor-sharp teeth. She glanced at the lumber mill's serrated saw blade with its large, jagged tines, comparing what it did to the trees to what was about to be done to her parents.

She felt sick at the thought of what was to come.

The Doctor ignored her repugnance. Instead, he gazed at Andy. "What are you waiting for boy? … the second coming? … tie him up …."

Andy's and Rebecca's eyes met, sharing their mutual dislike of the Doctor's belligerent attitude in giving them orders. Andy to tie up Mr. Senicki.

"If I am correct, and I am," the Doctor boasted, "the implant is bio-electronic. That means there's a little critter attached to it. If I can capture it alive it would make me famous."

Grinning, he reached deep inside his medical bag as Andy secured Mr. Senicki's left arm. Taking a second piece of rope, Andy moved around the table away from Rebecca.

The Doctor pulled a false bottom out from inside his bag, removing an old German Luger. He pointed it at Rebecca's head. The gun was shiny, black and threatening.

Rebecca took a step back.

The Doctor cocked the hammer.

Andy froze.

"Unfortunately for you two," the Doctor said. "I would rather be alive and obscure than dead and famous any day."

Rebecca felt betrayed. "What are you babbling about now, mister?" she said, her voice low with resentment.

The Doctor smiled widely, his thin lips stretched out into narrow slits. "That is why I'm in charge, not you. Because I know what I'm doing," he said hotly. His voice was firm and confident, but his eyes betrayed his unease.

"And what exactly do you *think* you know that we don't?" said Rebecca softly.

The Doctor glared at her. Didn't they know he had been tracking *Them* for years? Didn't they know what he had sacrificed in all that time? How could they even *pretend* to question him? After all, wasn't he the *Them* expert?

"Listen here, child. I am certain that whoever is behind all of this knows exactly where we are. They'll be here soon. I know it."

"How do you know for sure that they're coming?" Rebecca persisted.

"Because you defeated them!" the Doctor shouted. His confident mask slipped away, revealing the frightened, sad person beneath it. "I never defeated *Them*," he said. "Not once in six years."

The gun dropped an inch lower. "It's just not fair," he whined.

Andy wanted to say, "But you captured Rebecca's father," when the Doctor pointed the gun at both of them, moving it back and forth between them.

"It's all your fault," he said to Rebecca. "You wanted to save your parents. You put us in grave danger," he hissed.

"What if you're wrong?" Andy said. "What if they don't come here at all?"

"Wrong?" the Doctor said. "Do you think that *They* are going to let me remove a device that will prove their vile existence to the entire world? Do you think I'm CRAZY?" His chest heaved up and down with his panicked breathing. "Oh, believe you me, they'll hate that worse than you'd hate a kiss from a cockroach."

Rebecca made a sour face.

"They're coming," the Doctor continued. "They *know* and they're coming here right now." His voice dropped to a whisper. "And when they get here they'll bring the white light."

At the mention of the "white light" the Doctor's entire body trembled. He had stepped on the bottom line and it sunk home in his psyche like a pointed barb, chilling his blood.

A mean look possessed his face. His eyes became intense.

He turned the gun on Andy. "The bracelet. Put it on the table. Now."

Andy was afraid to move.

The doctor swung the gun at Rebecca.

"Put it down or I will shoot her right between her pretty blue eyes," the Doctor threatened, taking a step towards Rebecca. "Hurry up, boy. I'm not kidding around."

Before Andy could move a muscle, the Doctor fired a round to the side of Rebecca's head.

Rebecca screamed; her hands flung up to her face.

The air in the warehouse rang with the echo of the gunshot.

The Doctor's eyes grew large and glazed; a madness welled up inside him. He glared at Andy, his stare a commandment for obedience.

Andy removed the bracelet, setting it down on the table next to the unconscious Mr. Senicki, hoping once the Doctor had it he would depart and leave them alone.

Rebecca's eyes were downcast; her hands clasped in front of her waist.

The Doctor pointed the gun at Andy, waving him away from the bracelet.

"You see I did some research," the Doctor chortled. "Strange events … documented … going back some 200 years. Bizarre murders in every country in the world."

He nodded his head in confirmation. "*Them*," he whispered tensely. "No one has ever escaped Them. No one except me."

Andy and Rebecca stood in shocked silence as the Doctor suddenly swallowed several quick sobs down his throat. His eyes watered; his faced scrunched up; painful memories assailed him.

Andy felt sorry for him. He was obviously a victim of *Them*.

"My real name is Carson Gray … I was a Doctor with a family and a good medical practice until *They* came. They controlled both my wife and myself with their implants. Then they made two other people kidnap my wife and son and hold them for ransom. I shot them with this very gun."

Carson stroked the black Luger like a lover.

"But my son died as a baby. They used his memory to manipulate us. Made my wife and I think that Eric was still alive." He paused for a moment, staring into space with infinite sadness. "I went to Alaska to save her ... I searched for two days out in the frozen wastelands." He faced Rebecca. "When I found her, she saw me as one of the kidnappers and shot me with that very same pearl-handled revolver your mother had. That was six years ago."

Andy glanced at the small silver gun lying on the table. He wondered if his story was true or if the doctor was a deluded psychopath.

"But luck was with me that day," Carson said. "As I fell my suitcase broke open. The ransom money, a hundred thousand dollars, blew into the air like so much confetti. I would have died, but my medical bag was still inside. This very one here." He patted the bag like a beloved pet. "I patched myself up and crawled back to the car. It took two whole days." He giggled maniacally at the memory. "I ate snow the entire way. At night I almost froze to death." His eyes grew large and scary. Madness lurked behind them. "But I survived. I'm the only one who has ever survived *Them*."

"But I thought you said the police discovered two bodies," Andy said. "Now you say that one of the bodies was you."

"I lied," said Carson truthfully. "I phoned the police anonymously after I got back to town. They only found my wife. The copper implant was removed from my own head. That's the one I showed you. I did the operation myself. I was ... a little disturbed back in those days."

Carson remembered his lovely wife and the misery they endured because of *Them*, his lower lip quivered. "Oh, Kimmy," he moaned. "I'm so sorry. You were the love of my life." Tears streamed down his cheeks as grief tore at his heart.

Andy was mesmerized.

Rebecca stared at her father. She was worried he and her mother would not get the help they needed.

Carson wiped his eyes and pointed to the two guns on the end of the table. "See that pearl-handled revolver? It's 75 years old. And this other gun? Take a close look at it."

Carson held up Mr. Senicki's Colt 45. "This pistol was used by the outlaw Jessie James back in 1852. You can see his name carved into the handle. Look."

Carson shoved the underside of the gun butt under Andy's nose.

Andy saw "J. James" scratched into the metal. He also saw that the gun barrel was pointing at the Doctor's body. He imagined himself reaching for the weapon, pulling the trigger, blasting a hole in the Doctor's chest.

Carson snatched the gun away. He began to rave; spittle spurt out of his mouth. "Our mystery guests have been using these guns to play their filthy games for over a hundred years!" He laughed through his nose, inhaling and exhaling quickly with his mouth tightly closed. Strange squeaking noises lived in his throat.

Andy hoped he didn't shoot them in a fit of madness.

"The Luger I found in Germany," Carson said. "It was used by Hitler himself. He was their victim, too. Now do you see how dangerous they are?"

Andy turned towards Rebecca. She was lost in her own thoughts. The Doctor's words were startling. *They started World War II? Is that possible? They turned a window washer into someone who almost conquered the planet?*

The implications of such power astonished him. Then reality took hold. The doctor was as dangerous to Rebecca and himself as Der Fuehrer was to the world. It was a matter of first things first. It was up to him to do something.

If I don't, we're doomed.

Carson continued in a shaky voice. "But they know I'm here now. They chased me through the forest tonight with the white light. That's why I have to have the bracelet back. It's the only thing that lets me know when they're around so I can avoid *Them.*"

Carson reached for the bracelet. "I'll just take it and go."

Rebecca whispered, "What about my parents?"

Carson extended a finger towards the bone saw. He grinned a mad grin. "Since you're so smart you just do it yourself. Try not to cut anything important," he chuckled.

Andy saw Rebecca become sullen. She looked like she was about to cry.

I have to do something, Andy thought. *But what?*

Carson reached for the bracelet. He placed it over his wrist. "Now I'm safe. Now they can never --"

Mr. Senicki's right hand flew up, knocking the gun out of Carson's hand.

Carson went ballistic. "No!" he cried.

The gun landed on the ground near the end of the table below Mr. Senicki's feet.

Andy and Carson lunged for it.

Carson reached the gun first. Andy gripped his wrists. They grappled over the weapon, shuffling their feet on the concrete floor. Their arms arced over their heads from side to side, twisting their bodies in a dangerous dance for dominance.

Rebecca came out of her mental funk and sprang into action. Seeing the small sledge hammer she had used on the rusty lock, she ran to the tool area to get it. Rebecca was mad. She wanted to give Carson a headache he would never forget. She was through messing around with this horrid egomaniac who came to his senses only after making a complete menace of himself. Blood pounded in her brain as much as she intended to pound the hammer on his lying skull. Her eyes glinted with righteous fury.

It was pay back time.

A gunshot sounded; Rebecca whirled around.

Andy and Carson fell down between the table and the conveyer belt. Andy's head struck the concrete floor. Pain erupted between his ears. He released Carson's wrists, unable to do anything but suffer.

Rebecca grabbed the heavy mallet and dashed around the table to clobber the evil son of a bitch.

Carson stood over Andy, watching him clutch his throbbing head with his hands.

"Sorry, kid. I like you, but I really have to go." Carson aimed the gun at Andy's head as Rebecca watched in horror.

The Director improvised quickly. It wouldn't do to have the Andy die so soon. His death must come from the parents, not from the guest star. He wasn't exactly sure of how this mysterious man fit into the story, but murdering the main character was definitely out of the question. He had just reached the second turning point. It would be the shortest Act 3 in the history of entertainment.

No, the Andy had to live … for now.

The Director made his next move.

A scream froze on Rebecca's lips. Andy was going to be executed. She was too far away to reach the Doctor with the mallet. She cried out to God for help.

Her silent prayer was answered when Mr. Senicki stabbed Carson in the upper arm with his own scalpel.

Carson shrieked, flinging the gun before him.

Rebecca charged around the table, mallet raised. *Take this you murdering little snot!* She meant to bash his head to his toes and make him pay through the nose. He tried to kill Andy. She was going to make sure he could never attempt it again.

Rebecca's mad rush was halted when something gripped the mallet and yanked it backwards out of her hands.

Grimacing, Carson clasped the scalpel in his punctured right shoulder. Turning to flee, he slammed into Rebecca, knocking her backwards on top of her mother.

Alexandra saw things differently than the others. To her alien-altered sight, Rebecca was about to make a mashed potato out of Andy's head, not the doctors, with a mallet. Despite her rope-tied wrists, she managed to reach out at the last second and catch the mallet's head with her fingers, wrenching it out of Rebecca's grasp. Tossing the mallet aside, she threw her bound hands around Rebecca's neck and pulled tight.

Herman also saw the things that he was programmed to see. To his point of view, he had not stabbed the doctor, but had stuck Andy with the scalpel instead. Andy pulled it out of his shoulder, dropping it on the table.

Snatching up the scalpel, Herman went to work on the bonds confining his feet. With a soft snap, the rope gave way to the sharp steel of the blade. He swung his legs towards Rebecca, who was making high-pitched gagging sounds as her mother strangled her.

The Colt 45 lay on the floor near the saw blade. Herman saw Andy stumble towards the gun. He had to hurry and stop him.

Herman raised his leg and kicked out at Alexandra, knocking her and Rebecca back onto the conveyer belt.

"Damn it all," the Director cursed. "I hate third act problems." He scratched the back of his neck with his fingernails. "I've got the wrong characters trying to kill each other. The Andy is on the floor, clutching his head, completely useless. I had to make the Herman think the Guest Star is Andy so he would attack him with the scalpel, so naturally I have to make the Alexandra think the Guest Star is Andy too or it will cause even more confusion."

He threw his hands in the air, yelling, "Agh! What a mess! Why is making a masterpiece never easy?"

Pacing the floor, the Director crossed his arms, his hands dug under his arm pits. "So now the Andy is not the Andy. So what am I going to do with the ANDY? And I still don't know how the Guest Star fits into the story. It's time for a cocktail."

The Director spoke at a nearby replicator. "Give me a clam martini with fish eggs … a big one." Waiting for the drink, he pressed his webbed hands to his fishy forehead and mumbled, "Form follows function … but what is the Guest Star's function?"

That he had no answer to his question greatly disturbed him.

"Bloody black holes, I'll have to fix it in post!"

The clam martini materialized with the fish eggs stuck on a toothpick. The Director swallowed it down in greedy gulps. "Ah," he sighed, banging the empty glass down. "That really gets the old synapses brewing." Sticking the fish eggs in his mouth, he pulled out the toothpick they were stuck on. He smacked his lips. "Ahh," he sighed. "Now back to business."

Turning back towards the console, he pieced together a temporary solution and dictated it to his special effects team.

Andy lay sprawled on the floor, completely confused, his head swimming. Dressed in a full-length white smock, a Munchkin popped into the air at eye level. A stethoscope hung from his neck; a reflector on a headband sat on his forehead.

"Hello, young man. I'm Dr. Munchkin. I'm here to test your reflexes."

Dr. Munchkin turned to his white lab-coat wearing assistants, who stood below Andy's knee, grinning and giggling like idiots and holding a rubber mallet above their heads.

"Okay, fellahs," said Dr. Munchkin. "Hit it."

An Eye zoomed in towards Andy. It shot an electric current at his leg as the Munchkin assistants whacked his kneecap with the mallet.

As Carson stumbled towards the Colt 45, Andy kicked him between his legs.

Carson fell to his knees, clutching his genitals and moaning deeply.

"Healing," Dr. Munchkin said. "It's such a great feeling."

The other Munchkins nodded and giggled.

Tears streamed from Carson's eyes. Lunging forward, he seized the Colt 45. He planned to kill everyone as soon as he could stand, starting with Andy.

Clutching the gun, Carson slowly got to his knees.

Herman crashed into Carson, slamming him towards the power saw. The barrel of the gun punched the saw's start button. The 40" inch blade came to life, rotating faster and faster as the two men battled beside it. Herman bumped a second switch with his elbow. The conveyer belt began to move.

The Director leaned on his elbows, glaring at the holo-screen.

"Comet crap! This is not working. I've got to fix these problems. I've got to think."

He decided to try a writer's exercise he often used to stimulate his creativity. He hit the intercom switch.

"Yes, Herr Director," said the Production Manager.

"How does this sound for the trailer?" The Director spoke in his best dramatic voice. "On planet Earth mother fights daughter, son fights father. Thus we see the horror that is family." The Director's tongue flicked out. "What do you think?"

"Your skill in bringing moral depth to your productions is what makes you stand out as an artist above all the rest," said the Production Manager.

"I thought so, too," said the Director, "but it's good to have confirmation."

"Of course the Andy is not the Herman's son."

"For the trailer who cares. It's a sales pitch."

An idea came to him. "Make a note to switch the Guest Star with the Andy in this scene in post."

"Yes, Herr Director. Anything else?"

"No. Over and out."

The Director smiled and shook his head. "The solution was so easy … switch them in post … all that worry for nothing … sometimes I'm so smart I even surprise myself." He shook his own hand, then returned to the job at hand.

"Hmm," he ruminated watching the action. By switching out the two characters, it wasn't as bad as he thought. Still, it needed something more. He decided to try using the new probes. "Let's see what going on inside their heads. Maybe I'll get lucky and come up with something fantastic."

Rebecca and her mother fell on top of the conveyor belt. Stunned, her mother loosened her grip.

Rebecca was able to breathe again.

Twisting around facing her mother, Rebecca freed her head from the ropes around her neck. As she raised her head, her mother grabbed her sweater and pulled hard. Rebecca's face was buried in her mother's bosom. As she struggled to get away her mother ripped off a lock of her hair.

Screaming, Rebecca landed a hard right to her mother's jaw. Pain shot up her arm from her knuckles. She cried out and arched her head back. The whirling saw blade loomed before, buzzing with a high-pitched whine.

Seeing the spinning saw blade, fear gripped Rebecca to the core of her being. She instantly went berserk. Her fists flailed out like clubs, but her mother still clung to her tightly. Rebecca bit at her mother's arms, but only got a mouthful of clothing.

All the time she fought, Rebecca felt her body moving closer to the saw blades deadly embrace.

Carson struggled with Mr. Senicki. The bracelet flew off his wrist. The clawed hand of an Eye materialized and snatched it out of the air and dropped it on Andy's chest.

Andy tried to focus on the object, but the confusion in his head would not go away. Something in the back of his mind was troubling him. He knew he should be doing something, but for the life of him he couldn't figure out what it was.

An Eye misted Andy with a chemical while a probe recorded his thoughts.

The substance made Andy hallucinate.

A puff of smoke enveloped the medical Munchkins. When it cleared their clothing was different. They wore gaily-colored rumba outfits and round flat hats with dingle balls hanging all around them. They shook maracas and beat on conga drums. They sang a bastardized version of *Cuban Pete*.

"Andy, what's on your chest?

Check it out baby, it's the best.

Hold it close to your breast and go

Chick-chicky boom, chick chicky-boom, chick chicky-boom."

The Director watched in stunned amazement at the images the probe recorded from Andy's mind. "Chick-chicky boom?" he said, his face contorting. "No. This can't be happening. This isn't drama … it's just … weird."

He struck his palms against the console. "This earth child has a diseased mind. Destroying him will be a public service to the universe. This is beyond alarming. This freak should not be permitted to reproduce."

The Munchkins danced in a samba line in the air above Andy's stomach. Several wore grass skirts, women's wigs and batted long eyelashes while Andy happily smiled.

On some deep inner V-lan level, the Director began to feel sick. "This is awful," he groaned. "What kind of pool do humans draw their genes from? … a cesspool? … Is this boy an imbecile? … Is my masterpiece about a dimwit?"

While the Munchkins pranced, the Director's mouth opened; a tear rolled down his fishy cheek. "The boy is mentally retarded," the Director pouted, his fingers splayed across his lips and chin. "How can I show this sordid nonsense to an intelligent person? I'll be a laughing stock. I won't be able to get a job doing starship travel commercials."

An Eye moved Andy's head back. Herman's fist narrowly missed hitting his face.

Carson and Herman rolled across the floor beside Andy, grappling and slugging each other. Andy didn't notice at all. The singing Munchkins had his complete attention.

The Director stared at the crazy action. He felt a headache coming on. He covered his eyes with his hand and muttered to himself, "List the elements. Check the story structure. Figure out what's missing." He thought out loud. "There is male violence over a gun, midgets in grass skirts having fun, brawling females about to get sliced by a power saw, lively music playing over it all."

He let his mind go blank, then put the images on the movie screen of his mind. The chaos reminded him of 3-ring circus. It suddenly struck him as very comic.

Removing his hand from his eyes, he swayed his body to the samba beat, letting the music and dancing move him while the fists of fury and screams were flying.

"On second thought," the Director decided. "I take it back. It's very Monty Python's *The Meaning of Life*. If anything could prove that being a family was socially absurd and intolerable this is definitely it."

With a roundhouse right, Carson punched Herman in the ribs just as Herman's elbow struck his nose. Pain exploded in Carson's head, Herman doubled over. The two men clutched their injured bodies, ignoring each other for the moment.

Herman was the first to recover. He grasped Carson's ponytail. Spinning Carson around in a circle, Herman flung him towards the far wall. The air-borne doctor crash landed, striking his head on a heavy wooden chair.

His eyes fluttered; he groaned; he slumped to the floor, unconscious.

Rebecca swung hard at her mother as they neared the whirling saw blade. Before her fist could connect, Alexandra smacked Rebecca's chin with her forehead, knocking her out cold. Rebecca slumped down on top of Alexandra. The loudly whining blade was now just a few feet away. Alexandra clung to her limp daughter in triumph, not seeming to care if they failed to move out of harm's way in time.

Herman swiped the bracelet off Andy's chest. He rushed over to the two women. They appeared to him in reverse order, Alexandra was on the top, unconscious, while Rebecca held her in a vise grip of hate on the bottom.

If they traveled a few feet further they would be shredded into ribbons by the saw.

"Rebecca, let her go," Herman whispered.

Alexandra saw Herman as Andy, his deep brown eyes blazing with heated concern. She unclenched her fists, letting Rebecca's body slide to the floor. Andy lifted her off the table, her white knight in shining armor. Using the scalpel, he cut the ropes from her feet and hands. Alexandra was thrilled when Andy pulled her into his arms.

Herman took Alexandra by the hand and led her towards the exit. On the way, he picked up the Colt 45 and the silver revolver. Their footsteps reverberated in the giant room with a pinging softness as they walked and cherished each other.

Reaching the exit to the courtyard, Herman pushed one of the massive doors open. Moonlight shown down upon him. On his wrist lay the glistening bracelet.

"Let's go home, Rebecca," said Herman, glancing at the bodies of the others, believing them to be dead.

Head throbbing, Carson opened his eyes just in time to see the bracelet on Herman's wrist and hear his departing words.

The door closed behind them. As the latch clanked into place, he realized the bracelet was gone.

A foreboding chill penetrated his soul.

Three of the five Eyes in the room zoomed in to Andy, Rebecca and Carson, one to each performer for a dramatic close-up. A fine mist wafted down to each human; vigor and alertness seeped back into their bodies.

The German Luger lay on the floor near him.

Carson grabbed it.

Andy blinked twice; his vision returned to normal. A small object sat in the palm of his hand. It was a black stone from the alien bracelet. He had no idea what it was or how he got it.

Rebecca stirred. Andy dropped the stone into his shirt pocket and crawled on his knees to help her. He stroked her arm lightly.

"Rebecca. Are you all right?"

Rebecca pushed her hair back with her hand. "I think so. Are they gone?"

Andy nodded.

"Good. I don't think I can take this anymore."

Andy nodded again, this time more emphatically.

"No-ooooooo," Carson moaned, staggering towards the main doors. His face was streaked with blood from being stabbed; his right arm was wrapped around his guts. He extended his left arm imploringly.

Andy thought he looked pathetic.

He wondered if he should do something when the ground began to vibrate. A tremor rocked the earth beneath them. The surgical instruments jiggled on the table, rattling as they banged against into each other. Before Andy could blink twice again, the Earth jerked hard to the side, tossing him on his back. The corrugated tin roof lurched, causing the overhead lights to swing to and fro. The surgical instruments vibrated off the table, plunging to the floor.

The building lurched again. A ceiling fixture crashed in front of Andy and Rebecca. They scurried away from it on their hands and knees, crawling under the large heavy table for protection.

Andy glanced at the doctor.

Carson stood and swayed, his cries stifled by an urgent need for balance. He lurched to the center of the room. Through the side windows, a searing white light seized his flailing form.

"No!" Carson howled, blocking the intense light with his one good arm.

Andy and Rebecca watched in awe as the doctor seemed to physically wither under the piercing beam, wailing and bawling as though he was being tortured to death.

Carson brandished the Luger in the air. "You can't kill me! I won't let you!"

He fired into the white light, then turned and rushed towards the two young people.

Andy pulled Rebecca close to him as the rampaging doctor leapt up on the table. Andy wondered what he was up to.

With a vigorous leap, Carson bound onto the moving conveyer belt. Turning, he rushed towards the deadly spinning blade.

To Andy the saw blade's high-pitched whining was as though it were screaming for the doctor's death.

With a manic cry, Carson raced insanely forward. He seemed intent on his own destruction rather than return to the white light's heinous embrace.

All along the ceiling, light bulbs exploded in their fixtures. Showers of thin glass and sparks fell like rain about the fleeing doctor.

The Eyes captured the action from every angle. The Director was on the edge of his seat. Those Who Watch love a good death scene. This was going to be a most satisfying cinematic moment.

Rebecca hid her face in Andy's shoulder.

Andy held Rebecca tight.

He watched the doctor's death charge. Three more steps and he would be a bloody corpse.

Shrieking, Carson took two steps and leapt, hurling his body at the saw.

Gasping, Andy shut his eyes tight. He couldn't bear to see the doctor cut into a gruesome mess.

Carson raised his leg at the last possible moment, barely missed the ripping blade. Soaring past the saw, he crashed into a window.

Glass explosively shattered.

Carson disappeared into the night.

The white light abruptly vanished.

The Director struck a table with his balled up fist. He had wanted the Carson to die a gory death. He was already well into Act 2 and he still didn't have a single corpse. That would have to change and quickly. He decided he would have to use one of his backup subplots.

Darkness dropped down like a hammer. The ground ceased lurching. The saw lost power, spinning slower, descending in pitch until it came to a grinding halt. The broken overhead lights stopped their crazy swaying. The table ceased to shake.

An eerie quiet prevailed. The sense of violence that had happened before seemed to evaporate and vanish.

Andy cracked his eyelids open. He could barely see in the pale moonlight. Rebecca seemed unhurt. He sighed in relief.

Is it finally over? he wondered.

Raising their heads above the massive table, Andy and Rebecca peered about the room.

Andy wished he had Superman's X-ray vision and invulnerability.

Rebecca wished she could take a nice hot bubble bath.

"I don't hear anything," Rebecca said. "Do you?"

A bead of sweat dripped off Andy's chin. His shirt was soggy with perspiration; his dark hair was matted to his forehead. "No. I think they're gone."

Rebecca swallowed past a dry throat. "I hope you're right."

They stood still, holding each other. She felt so good in his arms.

"We may not have freed your parents, Rebecca," Andy whispered softly. "But at least we're still alive."

Andy was relieved that it was all over. The parents were gone, the doctor was gone, they could take their time to figure out what they would do next. He contemplated spending the night in the lumber mill, when an eerie moan rolled over the silence. The unearthly utterance swept up his arms in a wave of frigid creepiness, raising goose bumps in its supernatural wake. Something was outside in the night. Andy wasn't certain he wanted to know what it was.

The two teenagers walked towards the tall double-doors. Three feet from the entrance, the faint sounds of distress drifted to their strained ears. The sounds had a wounded quality to them, as though something outside was dying.

Reaching the exit, Andy put his trembling hands on the cold metal latch and raised it up.

Creaking, the tall door slowly swung outward.

Andy and Rebecca peeked outside.

The courtyard was covered with fog, thickening the night air with a touch of the surreal. The grayness spread across their line of vision, making it difficult to distinguish the details of their surroundings.

Entering the murky haze, Andy and Rebecca left the imagined safety of the building. They craned their necks about, prepared to run back inside at the slightest hint of danger. Their hesitant steps took them further away from the open door as the fog surrounded them.

Two more ghostly cries floated through the concealing mist.

Rebecca clutched Andy's arm.

Andy cupped his ear with his hand to try to pinpoint the origin of the eerie sounds.

Rebecca tugged on Andy's sleeve. "Look up there."

On a hill bordering the lumber yard's tall chain link fence, Andy and Rebecca saw the figures of Mr. and Mrs. Senicki silhouetted by moonlight against the inky heavens. Their arms and legs were spread apart in the shape of an "X"; their faces seemed twisted in torment.

Riveted by their bizarre appearance, Andy and Rebecca clasped each others hand, when a second anguished moan escaped the parents' throats.

Rebecca's heart broke at the sound of their misery.

Andy wondered what had happened to them. They had won the battle and left with each other. They could have killed them, but they didn't. Now they appeared to be helpless and in pain, the victims of a bizarre Greek tragedy.

What was going on?

The Director watched Andy and Rebecca enter the fog he had ordered created. It added a certain environmental ambience. He thought it was a nice touch for the new subplot.

The communicator rang. "Speak," the Director said.

"Good evening, Herr Director," said the Film Student. "I'm at the lake filming the monsters and wanted to ask a couple of questions."

"Make it fast, I'm shooting."

"Well, I was just wondering. I wasn't given any notes on character development."

There is no character development," the Director said. "It's just a monster movie."

"But isn't character development important?" the Film Student said. "And what about profluence?"

"You mean the sense that things are moving both within and without the main character and that those two movements are inextricably linked?"

"Yes."

"Keep your radical ideas to yourself," said the Director. "Just give the committee what they want and let them do the rest."

"But --"

"I'm shooting," said the Director. "Just do it."

"Can I use --"

"Use anything you want. Don't call me again." The Director cut off the transmission. He set the communicator to block any more of the Film Student's calls.

"Humph," the Director smirked. "Even a student knows more about making a movie than that worthless Producer. Nepotism is ruining the studio system."

He glanced back at Andy and Rebecca as an Eye dollied into a close-up.

"Now let's show that loathsome producer what a real artist can do without his imbecilic interference. It's time to show why I'm a class 6 genius and he's a class 5 moron."

While inputting new instructions into his console, he ordered another martini from the food replicator.

Bound to two thick poles stuck in the ground and criss-crossed into a giant "X", Herman saw a sight that made his soul cringe. He was surrounded by a battalion of Nazi soldiers; he had been captured by Hitler's army. The soldiers appeared like phantoms, see-through enemies with a greenish tint.

Woven out of living tree branches, huge swastikas appeared high in the surrounding forest around the compound. Scattered torches burned, giving off an unnatural flickering light as the ghostly German army marched on the plain.

Tied to a pole held between their shoulders, two burly soldiers carried a prisoner. The prisoner's feet dragged in the dirt; their head hung limp. With military precision, the goose-stepping spirits snapped to a halt before two officers.

The prisoner was Rebecca.

The German officers were Alexandra and Andy.

"This Nazi motif is superbulous," said the Director. He pretended he was making a trailer and he launched into voiceover mode. "When haunted by their dangerous emotions will the two lovers survive the final conflict? Will love contaminate their rational minds? Is it the inner enemy, the Nazi army that will destroy them body and soul? If they choose passion over social duty will they pay the ultimate price?" He took a dramatic pause. "Find out citizens of Home World. Come and see my exciting new show!"

He jiggled his martini glass frightening the small octopus floating inside it. The octopus squirted a jet of dark ink that formed an inky cloud which the Director then swallowed, enjoying the salty, biting flavor.

"And since all true suspense is a dramatic representation of the anguish of moral choice you couldn't ask for better a television program."

The Director rubbed his finny hands together.

"Can I direct or can I *direct*."

Alexandra and Andy stepped forward. Andy coiled Rebecca's hair tightly in his fist. Rebecca's face was bruised; purple blotches discolored her flesh where she had been beaten. Alexandra spat on her.

Watching from the cross on the hill, Herman groaned.

Two ghost soldiers cut Rebecca's bonds. They dragged her to a stout post stuck in the ground where two stout chains ending in handcuffs hung down from the top. They chained her wrists above her head.

Alexandra and Andy smiled with contempt, highly satisfied with her helplessness.

Herman feared that this was the end for them both. Just as Jewish friends of his parents had died at the hands of Hitler's Gestapo, so he and his precious Rebecca were facing the exact same ordeal.

Alexandra shared Herman's predicament. Secured to a pair of crossed timbers, she watched in horror as Andy was tied to a post on the field below. Dressed like Adolph Hitler, Herman smiled as his Nazi mistress, Rebecca, pistol-whipped Andy across the face. During the Second World War, Alexandra had witnessed German soldiers in Rumania drag people out of their homes and shoot them in the street. She knew they would slay Andy and then come to finish her off.

The army of phantom soldiers chanted: "You have failed your God."

"And now we come to the true culprit," the Director said, improvising his acceptance speech for the Best Director Award. "The chief architect of their annihilation is this fictitious being they call God. Failure to comply with the so-called *divine being's* edicts causes rejection of the soul and subsequent persecution. Love is proven to be a false dictum, a misleading theorem of safety and blessedness. By choosing love over social duty, you condemn everyone and everything to violence, suffering and death." He took a deep satisfying breath. "Now watch as I prove my thesis with a fantastic visual metaphor."

The Director pressed several keys on his holo-console.

Using rifles, Andy and Alexandra murdered Rebecca.

Aiming pistols, Rebecca and Herman executed Andy.

The echo of the gunfire throbbed in the parents' ears as the bodies of Andy and Rebecca slumped down on the posts.

The Director pressed more keys on the console. A holy light from the sky pierced through the clouds, illuminating the lifeless bodies. The spirits of Andy and Rebecca emerged from their motionless flesh, glowing with a luminous aura.

Angelic voices sang, summoning the two spirits to rise into the light. They sang of God's love for them and how they were saved to dwell with the Lord forever.

Herman and Alexandra cried as the souls of their loved ones ascended towards Heaven. Despite their failure to protect them, the Lord still took them into his sacred bosom. Their hearts rejoiced; merciful and mighty was the Lord.

As the two teenager's spirits floated higher in the white light, the swastika trees burst into flames; an area of the foggy ground glowed with intense heat.

The earth below the spirits of Andy and Rebecca turned into a hellish bog.

Herman and Alexandra watched in horror as the holy light and voices vanished. It was as though the bog denied them the rewards of Heaven. The spirits of Andy and Rebecca became heavy; they drifted downward towards the fiery bog.

"And the Earth became as hellfire," the Director said, chuckling. "And love was destroyed by its true nature--evil."

He rubbed his forearms up and down, enjoying the warming sensation.

"Death," he said with passion. "It gives me such a lift."

He ordered the final special effects scenario to be put into play, eagerly wetting his fish lips by rubbing them over each other, top over bottom, then bottom over top.

Andy and Rebecca's astral bodies sank towards the unholy swamp. The grotesque pool bubbled and burned, spewing out thin trails of inky smoke. The tall back fins of hideous creatures cut through the bog like sharks circling their prey. Sucking sounds mixed with the teenagers' cries of despair as they drifted closer to the vile waters. When they were three feet above the bog, the hideous creatures rose up from the foul smelling muck. Hissing, they grabbed the ankles of the teenagers' spirits with their taloned claws, clinging to them in a vise-like grip.

Andy and Rebecca struggled to free themselves, kicking at the monsters in terror.

A whirlpool formed in the center of the bog, creating a deep funnel. Spurts of flame flared out from whirlpool's depths, accompanied by the voices of the damned, shrieking from the bowels of the underworld. The voices wailed with the spine-chilling sounds of agonizing torment which rang in the reeking wind.

The hideous creatures hauled the teenagers' spirits towards the ghastly, swirling orifice. Plunging themselves into the whirlpool, they dragged the two teenage sweethearts down with them.

With a final cry of despair, the souls of Andy and Rebecca were sucked into the depths of hell while Herman and Alexandra watched in horror.

"Welcome to Hell's toilet," the Director sneered. "Population: two more lovers."

The whirlpool quickly collapsed. The bog rushed in to fill the gap.

The last thing Herman and Alexandra saw was a noxious bubble rise from underneath the bog's murky surface. The bubble popped with a *blooping* noise.that included the sounds of Andy and Rebecca screaming.

The phantom soldiers chanted: "You have failed your God."

A profound wail tore out of Herman and Alexandra's throats. God had rejected them. Their souls were damned. They had destroyed themselves and the persons they loved the most.

The Director was spellbound. "This Judeo-Christian imagery is as fascinating as it is senseless. How do they make this stuff up? Heaven and hell? Sin and salvation?

Monster escorts for the damned?" He shook his head from side to side. "It's so irrational … it's so scientifically obscene … I admit it … I can't get enough of it … it's entertaining beyond belief!"

Extending his elbows, the Director merrily flapped his arms, whistling the tune *We're Off To See The* Wizard from *The Wonderful Wizard of Oz.*

Standing in the fog drenched courtyard, the real Andy and Rebecca had no idea that Rebecca's parents had just seen the two of them murdered and ferried into the underworld. They took a step forward, intending to aide them, when a creaking noise to Andy's left caught their undivided attention. A huge earthmover sat on a small rise by the side of the building. Its enormous headlights were directed towards the very windows through which the white light had appeared.

Could that have caused the quake and the bright light? Andy wondered. *What really happened here?*

Andy and Rebecca stared at the immense machine. From within the fog behind them a dark figure emerged carrying a length of 2 x 4. Creeping up behind them, it knocked them both out cold with the hard piece of wood.

CHAPTER 13

LIGHTS, CAMERA, DEATH!

Andy had a headache. His body felt stiff. Since he didn't feel much like moving, he opened his eyes instead. Blurry pine trees towered above him against a black backdrop of spotty stars in the heavens. He thought he must be dreaming. That would explain why his pillow felt like lead and his bed was as hard as a board.

A whistle shrilled for his attention. His alarm clock was telling him to wake up. Andy contracted his muscles to rise, but he met resistance and lay back down.

If it's time to get ready for work why is it so dark outside?

Feet crunched the ground. Groggy, Andy twisted his head. A tall figure stood above him.

Andy squeezed his eyes to see more clearly. "Dad? Is that you?"

Gunter Barulich loomed over his son. The harsh moonlight made his face appear craggy and menacing. He wore gray flannel pajamas and a fabric cap with a dangling tassel. Brown bedroom slippers completed the bedtime ensemble.

His lips uttered madness. "You were told not to go near her, Siegfried. You were warned. Now you will pay the price for your rebelliousness."

Siegfried? Andy thought. *That's the hero dude from that Wagner opera? What's up with that?*

The whistle sounded again. It definitely was not his alarm clock. Andy craned his neck up. He saw the bright headlight of a train a ways away. Heavy white smoke billowed up from its smoke stack.

He discovered why he couldn't move. He was bound to the railroad track by many loops of rope, forming a thick, hemp cocoon around his body.

Gunter held up a large meat cleaver; his eyes glowered down at his son.

Emma Barulich stood behind her husband. She was dressed in a flower print nightgown; rows of curlers adorned her head, covered by a heavy hair net; her feet wore fluffy, furry slippers.

They both were in a trance.

Oh, no, Andy thought as the truth slapped him hard in the face. *Mom and Dad are controlled by Them.*

A strong wind rose. Gunter and Emma's clothing billowed about them. The train's powerful light shone in their eyes.

Spreading his arms wide, Gunter shouted to the advancing train. "Take him, great Wotan. Take him father of the gods."

"Deny him the Rhine Maidens' fiery steeds," bellowed Emma.

Gunter hefted the meat cleaver. "Deny him the afterlife of a hero in Valhalla."

Andy's brow grew slick with moisture as his parents raged at the advancing train. He struggled against the ropes as dust blew all around him.

It was no use. The ropes were too tight. Escape was futile.

Unconscious, Rebecca was tied to the tracks beside him. Her hair was in disarray, her face spotted with dirt. Despite her disheveled appearance, she looked so lovely Andy could not believe anyone would dare destroy such gentle beauty.

The train whistled again. Andy saw her stir. "Rebecca," he called out softly.

Her blue eyes opened; her voice was weak. She stared imploringly at him, anguish written heavily on her countenance.

"Pagliacci," she whispered, blacking out.

The name struck him like a thunderbolt. Pagliacci. Her secret name for him. It was Andy's favorite opera. The clown who killed the woman he loved. The stirring melody of Leoncavallo's tragic music trumpeted in his mind, torturing him with its sense of dramatic catastrophe.

Steam erupted from the train's churning wheels like a snorting bull pawing the ground before a mad charge. Fire belched inside its coal-burning furnace. White smoke spewed forth through its chimney. Between its metal guides, the unstoppable goliath hurtled forward, its bright cyclopean eye burning through the dark upon its victims.

Andy felt the situation was hopeless. He had found the love of his life and now he was going to die with her. It was tragic.

I'm a failure, a loser, a clown.

A gusty wind blew over him. The opera music coursed through his mind, charging his cells with a fatalistic energy. Yet his thoughts were not of himself, but for the girl he loved.

Gunter and Emma howled in the wind.

"It's show time," said the Director, swishing a swizzle stick in a martini with tiny seahorses swimming inside it, scurrying to avoid being crushed. "Grab your popcorn, sip your drinks and let me entertain you."

Andy struggled against the ropes, hoping for a miracle. He desperately tried to free a hand, but the bonds were too tight. A whistle blew; he glanced at his parents; they continued to rage at the oncoming locomotive. Andy knew the wheels of the steam-spitting train would soon squash them with its crushing bulk. He racked his brain for answers.

He got none.

Looking at Rebecca, he saw the ring he had given her, his grandmother's ring, the token of his true feelings for her. It encircled her finger like a broken promise given by a lowly, no good clown.

An idea, barely formed, began to take root in his mind.

The ring ... the ring ... something about the ring.

His parents stepped onto the tracks in the path of the locomotive, ranting and raving into the howling wind. It reminded him of something. But what? The idea was on the tip of his tongue. *The ring ... my parent's rage ... the ring ... dad's fury ... the ring ... Wagner. Could it work?*

The idea clicked into place and Andy Barulich, son of Gunter and Emma Barulich, lovers of German opera, inhaled deeply and sang his father's favorite music theme from Wagner's *The Ride of the Valkyries.*

"Bom-bom, da-da bom-bom.

Bom, da-da bom-bom.

Power and glory.

Bom, da-da bom."

Andy's voice boomed forth, cutting through the raging wind. He sang it over and over as the 80-ton colossus roared towards them. Andy felt the train track's tremble. Time was running out; it would soon be over. He tried to break the evil hold on his parents so at least they would be spared a crushing death. He sang with all his might, praying to God to heed him in his dire need. His father's ravings began to falter, then his mothers as well.

Gunter and Emma starting singing along with their son. A fire burned behind their eyes. They raised their voices strong against the rising wind to the *power and glory* of opera.

Andy put his plan into effect. Like the Munchkins, he made-up new lyrics.

"Bom-bom, da-da bom-bom.

Bom, da-da bom-bom.

Defy authority.

Bom, da-da bom."

Gunter and Emma took up their son's challenge. The three rebellious singers crooned together with the Valkyries, defying the deadly authority of *Them.*

"Defy authority.

Defy authority.

Defy authority,

Bom, da-da bom."

The light of the train glared hot upon them. Andy heard the taunting steam; smelled the acrid smoke. He felt its unstoppable power through the vibrations in the metal tracks. In seconds it would be upon them.

Time had run out. Their lives were over.

His father stood at his bound feet, a defiant rage boiled in his eyes. Looking down at his son, Gunter drew the huge meat cleaver behind his head. Howling, he swung the heavy blade.

Andy believed the last thing he would see in this world was his father's enraged face as he chopped him up like a chicken.

With one swift stroke, Gunter sheared through the ropes connecting Andy and Rebecca to the track. As the locomotive pounced on them, Gunter dragged the teenagers out of its path, followed by Emma.

Andy felt the wind whip at his legs as the train sped by. It felt like it was sucking his soul out through his feet. Red lights from the back of the train grew smaller as it barreled down the tracks away from the humans.

Gunter cut Andy loose. Andy glanced at Rebecca, who stirred. It was over. Rebecca was safe. A burdensome ache lifted from his heart.

Kicking away the last bit of rope, Andy ran over to Rebecca. He tenderly stroked her cheek. "Rebecca. Are you hurt? Please, say something."

She opened her eyes. "Hi, babe."

Andy smiled; his eyes beamed with joy.

He cut her bonds with his father's meat cleaver. The rope parted under the razor-sharp blade. As the last coil parted, he scooped her up into his arms crushing her to his chest. With her in his life the world was a place of love and happiness, he felt whole and complete.

Rebecca wallowed in his warm embrace. She didn't ever want to let go. All night long he had come to her rescue despite the danger to his own safety. She knew that she would love him for as long as she lived. There could be no other.

Their eyes met, conveying their unspoken love for each other as though they stood at the altar of their souls. The realization of that pledge, sworn to by devoted hearts and validated by selfless deeds, inspired inside them an exquisite beauty. They leaned forward to kiss each other, when Andy heard his parents struggling to breathe.

Emma clutched her throat, her eyes bulging, as her lungs fought for air.

Gunter's hands clung to the sides of his face, his fingers spread, his lips stretched wide in a vertical "O." Tiny sounds of pain squeaked out of his constricted throat.

Blood dripped out of their noses dotting their bedclothes crimson.

Two small copper objects dropped to the ground at their feet. Thin, hair-like tails whipped about from within the tube-shaped objects. The creatures uttered eerie cries, like tiny babies untimely ripped from the womb. Flame and black smoke spurted forth. The creatures died, cremated into ashes.

Gunter and Emma recovered their senses.

Emma spotted her son embracing Rebecca. "Andy, what are you doing? Let go of Rebecca this instant! You have been forbidden to see her by her mother!"

Andy and Rebecca cast sidelong glances at each other, then released themselves from their intimate position.

Gunter scratched his chin. "What are you two doing way out here?"

Emma was shocked by her son's display of intimacy with a girl. "Answer your father, young man. The truth now. Out with it!"

A smile crept up on Andy and Rebecca's lips. It grew to full-fledged grins before bursting forth in a gale of laughter.

Gunter and Emma were speechless. The surprised looks on their faces provoked further mirth from Andy and Rebecca. It infected the reproachful parents until, confused, they too began to smile.

Gunter wiped his damp forehead with a beefy forearm. "What is so funny, Emma?"

"I do not know," said Emma, dabbing tears from her eyes. She noticed his garments. "Gunter? Why are you wearing your bed clothes outside the house?"

"I do not know," answered Gunter. "Why are you wearing yours?

"I can't imagine."

"Emma," said Gunter. "Your nose is bleeding."

"So is yours, husband."

Gunter and Emma wiped the blood from their noses and then took in their surroundings.

"Andy?" Gunter asked. "Where is the house? What is going on? How did we get here? Why do you have my butcher's cleaver?"

Andy ran a hand through his tousled hair. "Dad, you wouldn't believe me if I told you."

An image came to Gunter of him screaming at a one-eyed monster. It gave him a sense of gravity. "Son. If you swear that what you tell me is the truth I will believe you."

Andy gazed at Rebecca. She nodded her head.

Andy sighed. *Here goes.* "You see those copper things on the ground near your feet?"

Gunter picked up one of the devices. He rotated it before his nose. Ashes flapped out of a hole. The cylinder smelled of death. "What is this?" said Gunter.

Andy set the record straight. "That thing came out of your nose when it bled."

"Impossible!"

"I swear it's the truth," Andy said.

His father deliberated a moment. "But how?"

Andy girded himself. "We think you've been under the control of hostile invisible beings, sir."

"Andy!" his mother snapped. "That's crazy talk. Stop lying to your father or I'll wash your mouth out with soap this minute."

Gunter inspected the device. Flashes of nightmarish memories intruded on his conscience.

Andy could tell his dad was trying to recollect the recent past. "Do you remember anything, Dad?"

"I do," said Gunter, nodding. "I remember driving to the old mill … and hitting you in the head with a two by four. I tied you to the train tracks," he said with sorrow, the truth weighing heavy on his heart. "Do you remember helping, Mama?"

Emma remembered. She wrung her hands in shame. "Oh, Rebecca, son. I am so sorry. How could I do such a terrible thing. Can you ever forgive me?"

"It wasn't your fault, Mrs. Barulich," Rebecca said, shaking her head. "Your minds were ruled by those things in your head." She pointed at the copper tube beside Emma's shoe.

Emma flinched away from it as though it were still alive and capable of harm.

Gunter stared at the charred device in the palm of his hand. "It seems we have been like the puppet on the string, Mamma. Yes, it is coming back to me now. The hatred, the terrible hatred."

Gunter stood still, a stocky mountain of a man, trembling with an inner fury. He thought of the homeland he had fled from after World War II, and the leader who had led Germany to the brink of annihilation. And now something was here in his new homeland, something that could do these terrible things to him and his family. He vowed that they would never be given the chance again, so long as he could raise a fist or take a breath of life to defy them.

Gunter dropped the copper device to the dirt.

He stomped down hard on the tube, cracking it loudly. Moving his slipper aside, he saw the device crushed into powder.

Rebecca stepped forward and held his hand.

Gunter felt her touch, so feminine, so gentle, her face kind and compassionate.

Tenderly, Rebecca spoke. "It was Andy who saved you. He found a way to break their power over you."

Gunter had never thought his son was more than a boy until this very moment. He gazed at Andy, noticing the change in him. He held out a burly hand.

"You have acted like a man today, son. I am proud of you."

For the first time in his life, Andy shook hands with his father as man to man. Clasping his free arm around Andy's back, Gunter fiercely hugged him while Emma and Rebecca proudly watched.

Gunter broke off the embrace. He slammed his right fist into the palm of his left hand. "Come Andy. We must warn the town about this terrible threat. The people and their families must be protected."

Gunter marched alongside the train tracks towards a nearby access road. His Volvo could be seen in the pale moonlight, parked not far from the tracks. Andy, Rebecca and Emma hurried after him, crunching gravel under their shoes and slippers.

They marched in silence, each caught up in their own thoughts. Andy was thinking in terms of manly responsibility, rather than his own boyish desires.

Dad's right. The people must be warned or more will suffer at the hands of Them.

"Why that toxic little upstart," fumed the Director. "He got the control chips out of their heads. That's never happen once in 200 years! HE JUST RUINED THE CLIMAX OF MY STORY ... THAT NERDY LITTLE TWERP!"

The Director stomped on his massage rug, twisting his foot in anger. Grass blades tore apart from the sudden pressure creating a dead spot on the rug. Not only was his preplanned ending ruined, but the humans knew all about them.

They had to die. They all had to die immediately.

His webbed hand went to slap the intercom when he stopped himself midway. He still had a story to finish. No human was going to deny his genius that. They had broken the sacred commandment of alien reality television acting--they knew they were being watched.

The Director scratched his neck scales with his fishy fingers. "How can I use this to my advantage? Those Who Watch will be angered by what they have seen. What could happen to take that anger and turn it into righteous vengeance?"

He slapped the intercom's hail button.

"Yes, Herr Director," the Production Manager said.

"Prepare the white light--I need all phases."

"But, Herr Director, we're coming up to a shift change."

"All phases," the Director insisted. "Keep the technicians from both crews at their posts as well."

"But Herr Director, I will have to open the second production bay. Think of the cost!"

"I'll authorize the overtime. Just do it."

"Are you sure, Herr Director? You know what the Producer will say."

"Listen to me. They know about us. They found the jellyfish."

The intercom went silent. "Yes, Herr Director ... of course ... right away."

The Director tapped his face with a scaly finger. No other production had ever shown the actors discovering the Cortex Control Devices. Such a thing was taboo. The Director knew that if he broke such a taboo, he had better give Those Who Watch the retaliation climax of a lifetime.

He was determined to do so, so help him George Lucas!

Andy, Rebecca, Gunter and Emma marched towards the little green Volvo when a rumble swept beneath them, causing bits of gravel to shake.

This doesn't feel like an earthquake, thought Andy. *It feels more like being surrounded by angry giants stomping their feet.*

"What is it, Andy?" Gunter whispered, continuing to hike forward.

Andy swiped his hair with his hand. "I can't be certain, father, but it happened once before in the lumber mill. I think the invisible beings are up to something."

A sudden flash caught Andy's attention. Two hundred yards away, an immense white light flared down from the sky onto the train tracks surrounded by slowly moving cloud-like streaks. It was three times as tall as football field was long and had no visible source of origin. It was simply, hugely, there.

"Holy kitty crap," Rebecca whispered in awe.

Andy's pupils grew wide. Dr. Weirdo had spoken the truth. There really was a white light. He also believed Doctor Weirdo when he said that it was exceedingly dangerous.

"We have to get out of here, now." Andy told his father.

Gunter heard the seriousness in his son's voice and knew that it came from someone who had more knowledge than he himself possessed. "To the car, everybody. Run."

They dashed to the sedan as the ground trembled. Fear drove them on with worried concern.

Marching on top of the Volvo, wearing monkey guard uniforms from the *Wizard of Oz*, the Munchkins chanted: "Andy's in trouuuble. Better move your ass on the douuuble."

Invisible eyes lurked near. They locked the Volvo's doors.

"Hey, who did that?" the Munchkins said. "Something sneaky's going on here."

They humans reached the auto. The white light was 100 yards and closing.

Gunter fished the keys out of his pocket, flipping several out of the way.

"Hurry Gunter," Emma said, twisting her nightclothes.

"Emma, go around," Gunter commanded.

Emma bustled about the front of the vehicle towards the passenger side, cringing with every fluffy, furry slipper step.

"It's almost here," Rebecca whispered to Andy, gripping his arm tight.

Gunter found the proper key and rammed it into the lock. A quick twist and the lock popped up. Opening the door, he reached around, unlocking the back. Andy and Rebecca scooted inside, unlocking the passenger door for Emma.

Emma slipped inside. "Hurry, husband. It's coming."

Gunter twisted the key in the ignition. The motor gunned to life.

Andy's spirits lifted as his father rammed the stick into first gear.

An Eye caused the engine to die.

Gunter twisted the key again. Strong vibrations rumbled as the engine turned over.

The Eye killed the motor again.

Andy leaned forward. "Dad. What's wrong?"

Gunter wiped the sweat from his brow. "I don't know. It's as if something is keeping it from working."

Andy twisted his head. The white light was almost upon them. Andy and Rebecca gaped at the dazzling brightness looming above them. Luminous, black bands of energy slowly spiraled inside; silver and red sparkles twinkled everywhere.

Mesmerized by the deadly beauty, Andy and Rebecca froze.

Look at the size of it! Andy thought. *It's bigger than Godzilla!*

On and on the white light came. Forty yards … thirty … twenty.

Rebecca gripped Andy's arm. The two sweethearts clutched each other.

The Volvo's engine roared to life. Gunter shoved it into gear.

Andy and Rebecca were hurled back in the seat as the tires spit dirt and rocks. Hope blossomed in their hearts as the Volvo raced to safety.

They were halfway across the railroad tracks when the white light swallowed them up. The black bands twisted downward, pinning the car to the train tracks, restraining it from moving forward.

Spinning tires dug into the soil, flinging the earth and rocks beneath them high into the air until the car's bottom touched the train tracks and the tires could burrow no more.

The turbulent wind outside the car was deafening. The rolled up windows barely kept its ear-splitting volume at bay. The black bands crackled with ominous energy. The white light became visibly thicker, taking the shape of dense storm clouds.

Andy and Rebecca watched in amazement as the monstrous forces formed around them.

With a prayer for a miracle on his lips, Gunter floored the gas pedal. The engine ripped the air with a whining, futile sound. Gunter kept on with his prayer and his pressure on the pedal.

The roof began to buckle. Hairline cracks scurried across the windshield. The outer rear view mirrors tore from the side of the car. Striking the soil, they shattered.

Andy saw the glass fragments forced into the hard earth as though shoved there by an invisible boot.

"Andy," Gunter yelled over the din. "What can we do? How can we stop it?"

Everyone turned to Andy, hoping he could come up with a way to save their lives.

Andy had no idea what to do. He was completely clueless.

He saw plants, rocks and pieces of broken mirror mashed into the soil. If they left the car and made a run for it, that would happen to them, too.

More cracks on the windshield appeared. Glancing at Andy, Emma frowned, her hazel eyes betraying her panic.

Andy struggled for a solution. *Blast a hole through the floor and dig until we reach China. Tear off the roof and use it as an umbrella. Shoot out the bulb! Flip the "off" switch! Don't pay the power bill!*

His chest felt like it was caving in. Now that his father acknowledged him as a man, he felt the appellation crush him. *I'm just a guy. I don't have the answer to everything. I'm just Andy.*

Even the Munchkins were no help at all. Together, they sang: *The time has come to bend over and kiss your ass goodbye.*

The roof punched in a foot; everyone screamed.

Andy and Rebecca hunkered down in the back seat, their faces were inches apart, they thought they were going to die. The dark storm clouds twisted downwards like a corkscrew, squashing the car like a trash compactor.

A second shaft of intense, white light abruptly appeared inside the darker stormy one. Spotlighting the Volvo, it expanded, pushing the storm clouds back off the vehicle.

The pressure on the roof. was lifted.

The menacing noise abated.

The roof ceased to collapse on top of them.

The humans stopped their screaming. Cautiously, they peered out of the low-roofed vehicle wondering what had just happened and why they were still alive.

Reclining in his hover chair, the Director munched on some dried fish eye candy.

"Every good show has an obligatory moment of quiet before all hell breaks loose," the Director said, chewing his snack. "You have to start from a low place so that you have room to build to the climax."

Licking his webbed hand, he put it in the snack bowl. A dozen fish eyes stuck to his flesh; using his tongue, he wiped them into his mouth.

"Its basic storytelling technique," he said, crunching the fish eyes loudly.

Andy cracked the door of the Volvo open.

"Andy, don't go out there," Rebecca said, clutching his arm.

Andy considered her request, but someone had to do something. He pushed the door open and swung his legs outside.

"Andy!" Rebecca blurted.

Andy stuck his hand into the light. He felt no power, no breeze, nothing that seemed threatening. Sliding outside the Volvo, he stood on the ripped-up ground seeking a means of escape. Gazing about, he could see two distinct areas. The inner beam of white light had a diameter of about 30 yards. The outer storm cloud layer was a good 20 yards wide, but it was barely moving and seemed to be at rest.

He speculated if they could get the car off of the tracks maybe they could ram their way out of here.

The problem was how to test his theory.

Andy felt something hard in his jacket pocket. It was the last throwing stone he had collected when he led Rebecca's parents back towards the lumber mill.

Hefting the stone in the air, he caught it and threw it as far as he could. The flattish rock soared across the inner circle without resistance. When it reached the dangerous outer ring, the stone was dashed to the ground along with Andy's hopes.

Looking at his shoes, he fumbled in his mind for other options.

"Andy, look out!" Rebecca shouted.

Andy lifted his head. The inner ring was reducing in size with the dark clouds right behind it. The enormous tower of death sped directly towards Andy. The awesome sight overwhelmed him. He froze, unable to move.

Dumbstruck, the Munchkins stood at Andy's feet gazing upward at the approaching storm of death. "Crisis in progress," they cried in panic, covering their eyes with their tiny hands. Blind, they ran around in circles, smacking into each other. Five pairs of little bodies fell down like dominoes, one right after the other.

"Is it safe to look?" a Munchkin queried, his hands still keeping him sightless.

"Okay, fellahs," another Munchkin said. "We played dead. That should do it. We're safe now."

The Munchkins removed their hands from their eyes. The angry storm raced towards them.

They screamed their little hearts out of their mouths, then swallowed them back inside.

Several Munchkins ran towards Andy-the-giant's shoes and started to scale them.

Others pulled knotted ropes with grappling hooks out of their clothes and flung them at Andy's pants. The hooks bit deep into the fabric. The Munchkins scaled Mount Andy sniveling in terror.

"Achtung, fu-fu-fellahs," said the stuttering Munchkin. "Cu-cu-climb for your lu-lu-lives," he shouted.

"We want to move back to Germany," the others said out loud. "Right now."

Rebecca snagged Andy's belt and pulled him back inside the car.

Andy ducked down and swung his legs in, jerking the shrieking Munchkins through the air on the ends of their ropes. The Munchkins crash landed, rolling like dice on the carpet.

"Dang," a Munchkin said, holding his head to keep it from spinning. "If this keeps up I'm going to need therapy."

The white light shrank in size until it covered just the car. The storm clouds didn't touch the vehicle, but surrounded it with a passive menace.

Andy wondered what was going to happen next.

The storm clouds started spinning; the air became thick with power; the howling wind returned.

Rebecca grabbed Andy's arm as the storm clouds surged over them, slamming into the car, rocking it on the railroad tracks.

Before anyone could blink, the metal roof was yanked violently upward.

The windshields exploded outward; shattered glass flew before Andy's eyes; a deafening wind rushed inside the Volvo.

The front and rear hoods of the vehicle sprang up with a loud clang. The sheets of metal tore off the car streaking upward into the sky.

The black bands crackled with greenish energy; dirt and gravel propelled upward. Grass was ripped out of the soil; railroad track spikes were wrenched out of their moorings.

The roof of the Volvo was savagely ripped off.

The Munchkins were sucked up into the heavens, shouting *We're off to see the wizard!*

Andy grabbed the door handle, expecting to be catapulted into the atmosphere. Instead the air became still. The black bands rumbled to a halt. The silver and red sparkles passively floated.

They're playing with us, Andy thought. *Why are they playing with us?*

A humming sound, low in pitch, became a high-pitched warbling. A dot of vivid ruby light flared high in the brilliant whiteness.

Andy's instincts told him that something really bad was going to happen.

The ruby light stabbed down from on high, inundating them with pain.

Rebecca felt herself pierced by a thousand tiny needles. The shock of it stunned her senseless. Losing control of her limbs, she collapsed unconscious.

Agony ripped through Andy's flesh. He reared up in the seat, his muscles contracting hard. His parents were out cold, their skin was turning pale.

Andy wanted to see Rebecca, but couldn't make his head move; he strained with all his might.

He fell back down; his eyelids closed; a pitch-black darkness enveloped him. Losing consciousness, Andy slipped into a nameless void.

"Comet crap. This is far too easy," the Director said, cracking his knuckles behind his back. "Dramatic tension is maintained by not resolving the conflict but by stretching it out. The humans must fight back or Those Who Watch will find it boring." He glanced on a holo-monitor at a list of the show's subplots finding one that he liked.

"Hope," the Director said. "Perfect. I will give the Andy hope before I destroy them all. That always works."

His fingers flew across the holographic console assembling his next story idea for his technicians to put into play.

"Execute the execution," the Director said into the intercom. "Alliteration," he sighed. "A good rhyme is a good time."

In the blackness that was Andy, the edges of eternity became lit by a distant light. His life unfolded before him, flashing through the movie screen of his dying mind. The beauty, the sadness, the joy, the sorrow, every scrap of memory was his. The very best came at the end, for he was united once again with Rebecca. Then she faded away and he was back in the void where he started.

That was my life. He got busy dying again.

A silvery voice whispered his name.

Andy could not believe his ears. *Grandmother? Is that you?*

His grandmother appeared before him, her wrinkled face and tender eyes glowed with a radiant light.

Go back, Andy. Rebecca needs you. It is not your time to be here. Go back and have a full and happy life with her.

Rebecca is dying, Andy said. *Help me, Grandmother. Please.*

A smile spread on her shimmering face.

I can send you back to her. But to save her you must do what I say.

Do what? Andy said. I'll do anything.

You must hold her hand and give her your love, even to the point of death. Can you do that, grandson?

Yes.

Then you both have a chance for life.

Raising her hands, Grandmother placed them above Andy's heart. Her afterlife force flowed into him.

The feeling was pure rapture.

The Director pursed his lips. "Give her all your love," he sneered. "These creatures are so sentimental it's disgusting. The Andy wants to be a man, yet he defines his manhood in terms of protecting a woman." The Director shook his head. "Human women claim to be equal to men. Let them fight their own battles. They should all be destroyed for having babies and raising families."

He made a rude gesture at the holo-monitor. "Don't you humans get it? Love is a crime. It's only for crooks and losers!"

Andy sucked air into his nearly lifeless lungs. Oxygen and his grandmother's spirit strengthened both his body and his resolve. Clutching his shirt pocket, he twisted his head towards Rebecca. Her skin was bloodless, she was not breathing. He willed himself to reach out and touch her.

The red ray pummeled him senseless.

Rebecca's hand hung limp. Her palm was down; her fingers were uncurled.

Andy could tell she was barely breathing.

Determined to fulfill his promise, he pushed his fist across the back seat. The crimson agony stabbed at him like knives, draining his strength, bleeding his life away. From somewhere deep inside him a loving power restored what the death ray stole.

Andy battled on. His hand crept forward. His grandmother's ring was on Rebecca's finger. He was determined to fulfill his promise to his grandmother by taking Rebecca's hand and giving her all of his love.

The ring seemed to call out to Andy as his fist slid another inch forward. The red light blasted his body; his nerves burned with an excruciating fire.

Andy thought only of Rebecca, how he ached to touch her, how much he cared. He would gladly trade his own life if it meant that she would live.

The red light intensified. Prisms of pain exploded inside Andy's skull. His sight blurred; his lips drew back, exposing gritted teeth. Andy willed himself to carry on; there was just a few more inches to go.

He touched her fingertips with his own. He could feel that she was alive. Joy flooded his soul, giving him an extra surge of power.

He slipped his hand over her fingers. He tried to speak her name, but his lips would not function.

Intense pain ripped at his body.

Andy lost all his energy; he went limp.

"Dying for love ... how noble ... how sickening," said the Director, his eyelids narrowing into thin slits. "No V-lan would ever sacrifice his life to save another. The very idea is morally offensive." He looked at the holo-monitor at the unconscious Andy and Rebecca. "Wake up stupid humans. One last disgusting family hurrah and then you all be joining the organic rot festival."

Rebecca opened her eyes. The red light drenched her body, sucking the life out of her like a wet sponge left in the sun.

Andy's face was pale, his eyes dark and sunken. The skin of his hand was bloodless. His hand slid off the top of her fingers, exposing the ring. Rebecca saw the stone was different. It was smooth, shiny and black.

It also pulsed with power.

Rivulets of amber energy lapped up her arm. The scarlet death bounced off of her flesh as though it was protected by a force field. Rebecca covered Andy's hand with her own. The tawny energy swept over him. Color returned to his cheeks. He took a quick breath.

Rebecca sobbed at the sight.

Getting stronger, Andy awoke. They each put a hand on Andy's parents, Andy on his father, Rebecca on Andy's mom. The amber rays surged over the parents; their blanched skin became pinkish. Gunter and Emma opened their eyes to the sight of two smiling youngsters.

"Isn't that touching," the Director jeered. "Humans are such emotion criminals. Those Who Watch will love to hate you. You deserve what happens next!"

He spoke into the intercom. "Give me full power."

The ruby beam intensified; the death ray's strength was doubled; it bashed the humans apart. There was no time to even blink.

Andy caromed into the back seat so hard his breathe burst out of his chest.

Rebecca was flung into a corner.

The parents collapsed in the front seat.

The red light smashed them all.

The pitch-black ribbons united, turning into thick bands of convulsing shapelessness. Electricity crackled about its edges.

Crimson lightning struck the train tracks in four places, bending them up above the vehicle. The metal became red hot.

The air about the Volvo began to bake.

Andy toppled towards Rebecca; his face landed on her lap. The amber power swept over him, but it was feebler than before. He reached out to touch his dad. A wave of brutal heat enveloped him. The sudden shock of it forced him to stop.

The sudden rise in temperature was so overwhelming it made Andy's vision dim. He closed his eyes. He could hardly breathe. Oblivion beckoned as his next port of call.

In desperation, Andy covered Rebecca's hand with his own. Coming into contact with the ring, he wished with all of his heart that he could protect her. Memories surged through his mind as their lives connected as one … watching the moon through a telescope … holding hands … Andy as a tap dancing spider miming cutting her head off … sitting on the rocks, sharing their feelings … Mr. and Mrs. Senicki shooting bullets at them … racing bicycles in the night … passionately holding each other after escaping the deadly train. Fear, suffering, pain, anger, caring, joy, tenderness, hundreds of moments from their lives passed between them as their souls connected together as one.

The black stone in the ring bubbled like a cauldron of orange and black lava. A beam of amber shot up from the molten mass, blazing upwards against the brutal red weapon. Ten feet above the humans, the amber force spread open until it covered them all with a bell-shaped shield.

"What in Jupiter's moons is this?" the Director said, seeing the force field protect the humans. He checked the software system monitor. The display showed vectored lines and power status. The readout showed the humans had more power than his death ray.

"Not again!" the Director howled. "I will not be defeated by a bunch of lowlife actors."

He hastily typed on the holo-console trying to fix the problem. When nothing happened he banged his fists against the keyboard.

"I will not be denied my masterpiece."

He tapped the intercom switch.

"Yes, Herr Director," said the Production Manager. "What is your wish?"

"Transfer all power from the engine's warp core into the death ray."

"But, Herr Director, we've never done that. It could be dangerous."

"Don't talk back to me. Make it happen. Do it now."

"Yes, Herr Director, immediately" said the Production Manager.

The ruby beam contracted, becoming smaller, tighter, stronger. Violent flames engulfed the humans, giving their shield form by its scorching presence.

The inferno boiled them like lobsters in a pot. The towering train tracks sizzled. Hot metal ran down the twisted, blackened towers like wax off a burning candle.

"Yes!" the Director screamed, projecting his thoughts on the walls with the thought pen. "More power. Kill them all!"

Sweat ran down Andy's face in rivulets; his dark brown hair was soaked. He felt like meat being grilled on a barbecue. They needed more help and fast.

Hoping for a miracle, Andy grasped his father's shoulder.

Andy plummeted deep into his father's life. He saw Gunter as a child in Nazi Germany, six years old, at a rally where crowds screamed "death to Jews." Mobs of teenagers broke into his house, searching for Jews to murder, frightening young Gunter. German armies marched through Berlin; Gunter's older cousin, Wilhelm, went to war. He died in battle for the fatherland.

Andy was transfixed by his father's life.

The memories of his father as a child living through years of war surged through Andy's being. Russian planes flew over Berlin ... long trails of bombs cascaded from their bellies ... anti-aircraft fire blackened the sky ... buildings burst open, collapsing around them ... people screamed. Gunter's father was mortally wounded by a bomb blast. Young Gunter watched his mother wailing over his father's lifeless body.

Germany was defeated. Gunter toiled to help his mother, who worked in a garment factory. Many years later, he met Emma. They got married. The family struggled, barely making ends meet.

Andy was born.

He saw the countless sacrifices his parents made, both large and small. He learned that his parents cared that his life would be better than their own. They did it all for Andy, their son.

Greenish black lightning shot out from the thick black bands, striking the shield with abandoned fury. A thin jolt of painful energy crackled through the shield, striking Andy, making him reel. Andy's connection to his father weakened. The images became sporadic. He felt himself slip away.

"I am the greatest A.R.T. director in the universe!" gloated the Director. "Kiss your animal, Christian, low life, useless class 2 butt cheeks goodbye. Su-su-su-sorry!"

More lightning struck the shield. The amber shield fractured like an egg shell cracking. Flaming blood-colored hail stormed down from the sky, striking the protective barrier. The superheated cubes smacked the engine, bashing through the dense metal like wet paper. Hot steam sprayed, tires burst, the bumpers melted into slag.

Andy opened his eyes. His father and his mother had slumped together in the middle of the front seat. Rebecca had flopped forward, touching his mother.

Andy felt hot and dizzy.

"Love is destruction!" the Director yelled. "Your deaths will make me famous!"

The amber barrier cracked. The red light leaked inside. Andy saw his father, mother and Rebecca's clothing erupt into flames. He heard them shriek.

Andy's clothes burst into flames.

His flesh began to burn.

Crying out, Andy fell forward, falling on top of Rebecca. All four humans were now connected, their bodies ablaze.

Images from his parents and Rebecca surged through Andy's mind: his mother baking apple strudel … Grandma's funeral … the family moving to America. Gunter learning to be a butcher … Andy struggling to learn English. Bullies at school picked on him … he hid the bruises from his parents. He withdrew into himself, only the Munchkins gave his life any joy.

Gunter taught him the butcher trade. Andy saw that the cruelty his father had suffered under Hitler was what made him excessively strict. Andy saw himself through the eyes of his parents. He daydreamed, he was irresponsible. When the three old ladies waited for their orders, he ignored them to play with the Munchkins.

He met Rebecca and her beautiful knees. They rode up to the lake. He was the frost giant Schnozola. He gave her his grandmother's ring. Love blossomed in his heart. He felt outraged that it was all going to end.

Somewhere deep inside him, Andy turned a corner. This was wrong. He needed to live. He was determined that his loved ones would survive. Reaching out with his will, he demanded life for them all.

The ring obeyed his summons.

A surge of power roared through his spirit. Energized by the combined might of four human souls, the black power stone responded to Andy's consuming desire--life!

Suddenly Andy's body glowed from within with a powerful silver light.

The potent light filled the chamber. It extinguished the flames that consumed them. It healed them all in an instant. It kept growing, stronger and stronger, building up indescribable pressure.

Andy was just getting started.

The Director stared at the holo-screen ... he gawked at the power gauges ... he could not believe his eyes. "This can't be happening. This is impossible. I can't be defeated by a brain damaged boy. What movie does he think this is – *Rainman*? You're not Dustin Hoffman!"

He raised his finny hands, clenching them into tight fists.

"I am not a loser!" he yelled as the thought pen projected his words on the storyboard wall behind him.

Andy lifted his head; his face glowed; his eyes blazed with determination. Leaping to his feet, a mighty silver light shot out from his eyes. It burst a hole through the amber shield and jetted through the fiery hale like an unstoppable comet.

It streaked directly at the red cone's zenith.

The death ray violently exploded.

A thick ring of silver energy surged downward, decimating the red and black storm clouds from existence. The dazzling wave slammed into the earth with a tremendous roaring blow. The ground heaved; the humans were tossed about like rag dolls in the Volvo.

A shockwave crashed into Andy, stretching the skin back on his face, knocking him over.

Within a mere few seconds, the chaos vanished, leaving only silence.

Lying flat on the back seat, Andy gazed upward at the night. Silver snowflakes drifted down through the pitch-black sky. Andy held out his hand. The twinkling particles touched his skin, rippled like a pebble tossed into a pond, then winked out of sight.

Stars peeped out from the heavens, glistening like sugar. It seemed to Andy as though some of the snowflakes had found a new home in the velvet black night as twinkling stars.

Four human beings climbed out of the wrecked Volvo, pinned between four smoking, half-melted, upright train tracks. Steam rose from the slag that was once an engine block and two bumpers while the snowflakes covered the ground.

"We did it," Andy whispered, bits of ice clinging to his hair.

Rebecca shook her head. "You did it Andy. It was you."

Andy raised Rebecca's hand up, exposing the ring. "No. It was this."

Rebecca smiled. "No, it was this."

Leaning forward, she kissed him passionately on the lips.

Feeling like a man, Andy kissed her back with all of his heart.

Gunter and Emma smiled. They hugged each other tight, sweat-soaked bedclothes and all.

The Munchkins returned, dancing and singing (*to the tune "Hooray For Hollywood."*)

"Hooray, Andy's a man.

He kicks a villain's ass like no one can.

He won the heart of his girlfriend– Rebecca,

Oh yeah, you betcha, her kisses taste real good.

(Real good!)

His actions saved their lives.

Invisible beings gave them the hives.

But sacrifice and effort conquered their strife, they'll be man and wife.

He did the best he can,

Now Andy is the Man!"

While the Munchkins sang, Andy and Rebecca pulled away from each other's lips. In their eyes they saw only love for each other. They had bonded closer than any pair of human beings ever had or ever would. Immersed in the power of the ring, they experienced each others lives as though they had lived it as their own, not only feeling the love they had for each other, but undergoing each others' crucible of fear and hardship. They understood how precious this was and loved each other all the more deeply for it, for within that knowledge was the unalterable truth that by themselves they were nothing, but together they made a world.

A loud cracking sound pierced the night. The top of a pine tree crashed down to the ground. Another treetop fell, followed by another, and another ....

Andy, Rebecca, Gunter and Emma looked upward as an invisible *something* scythed a wide path through the tops of the forest. Hunks of branched, leafed tree tops peppered the ground like a bizarre harvest of Christmas trees.

The humans heard a sonic rumble. A warm breeze blasted them as their unseen foe streaked away.

"We win," said Andy, beaming. Rebecca smiled and kissed him again, sharing another stream of powerful memories between them that made their spirits soar with love.

As the Munchkins watched the lip-locked sweethearts, their tiny eyes grew large, their little mouths dropped opened and their small hearts pounded in their diminutive breasts.

"Wow," the Munchkins whispered in awe. "Would you look at that. Wow."

"Guacamole is life," a Munchkin whispered. "Girls are fantastic kissers."

Suddenly energized, the stuttering Munchkin ran in front of his fellows. He stretched his arms out wide; his feet were dancing in place.

"C'mon fu-fu-fellahs. Le-le-let's have some fu-fun!"

"O-ku-ku-kay," the other Munchkins agreed. "Yu-yu-you're it."

They plastered the stuttering Munchkin with mud, covering him from head to foot. He looked like a dirty snowman with two blinking startled eyes.

"Hey," the stuttering Munchkin said, putting his hands on his hips. "The snow is still frozen. Wh-where did you get the wa-wa-water to turn dirt into mu-mu-mud?"

In response, the nine other Munchkins zipped up their pants.

The stuttering Munchkin glared at his friends. "Why you conniving rogues.

I ought to wash your mouth out with soap. I ought to make you bathe in skunk stink. Why I ought to …. Hey, I'm not stuttering. Rebecca's kisses have cured me. Holy wow! Love is the best medicine of all! What do you think about that fellahs?"

"SNOW BALL FIGHT!" the Munchkins shouted, pelting each other with balls of ice.

The no-longer-stuttering Munchkin shouted "Whoo hoo" and started tossing snowballs with the others, while the littlest Munchkin sculpted snow all over his head until he looked like an icy Santa Claus.

The Munchkins shouts of laughter filled the night as they playfully warred together. It was a time for celebration and they indulged themselves to the hilt.

Holding their arms around each other, four humans gazed at the star-filled night.

The black stone on Rebecca's ring vanished.

A stone of turquoise materialized in its place.

CHAPTER 14

THE MARTINI

Three hours later. The Senicki residence was as dark as a buried coffin. The station wagon sat parked in the murky driveway. The Bronco was missing.

It appeared that no one was home.

Tires crunched the ground. A car crept closer to the silent abode, coming to a halt in the shadows under an Oak tree. The dented radiator slowly dripped fluid; one of the headlights was busted; a mangled daffodil was stuck in the grill.

The door to the Dodge Dart opened; car keys dropped on the ground, one of them broken.

Ready to bolt at the slightest sign of danger, Dr. Carson Gray stepped out into the shadows, watching the residence with grave intensity. Biting his fingernails, images of hot-wiring the car and driving through the forest like a demon danced in his fevered brain.

He waited fifteen minutes. He chewed the tips off all of his fingernails in three.

Satisfied the house was empty, Carson snuck across the lawn. He left the car door open and the engine idling in case he needed to leave in a hurry.

The living room window slid up an inch. Carson peeked between the narrow space. The floor was littered with opera records: Mozart, Bizet, Wagner, and others. A record was stacked on the turntable. A single taper candle--less than an inch long--sat on a wooden coffee table. Its flame was so weak, Carson couldn't detect it when he surveyed the house from the road. Wax had spilled onto the glass, creating a small, hard puddle. Beside the candle lay the silver bracelet.

The center stone was missing.

Carson blinked to clear his eyes before scrutinizing the bracelet again. No. He was mistaken. The black stone was there after all. Nothing was missing, all was as it should be. The only problem as he saw it was that the bracelet was not on his wrist.

He was concerned the Senickis were home, but he heard no sounds of life. He listened intently for the creak of floorboards, a murmur of a voice, the click of a flashlight ... there was nothing.

Perhaps they lit the candle before they first left ... the house seems empty ....

His desperate need for the bracelet finally overcame his extreme sense of caution. Slipping the window up higher, he slowly wriggled his body inside.

Carson's feet touched the carpet. He hugged the floor, moving crablike. He wanted to grab the bracelet and run--run and never come back. This was it. This was the last time he was going to traipse after *Them*. Six long years of difficult wandering and all he knew was that *They* could not be defeated. *They* were far too formidable a foe. How much did he really know about *Them*? The answer was simple--next to nothing. It was time to quit. Time to go back to the city where *They* would never find him. Time to become a doctor once more; to lead a life without constantly dreading discovery and death.

Ah, normal. What I wouldn't give to be normal.

Crawling across the floor on his hands and knees, Carson pushed the scattered records out of his path. His eyes darted about, seeking betrayal in every shadow. His heart beat so loudly it seemed to be located between his ears.

Carson slinked to the table; the bracelet was almost within his grasp. Rising slightly, he leaned in towards it, his mind filled with conflicting emotions. Sweat bled from his pores, making his face glisten in the candlelight. The bracelet was his badge of safety. He felt naked without it.

Carson's fingers gently enfolded the precious alien artifact. Lifting it off of the coffee table, he rolled onto his back, clasping it to his wrist. As the bracelet contacted his flesh, relief washed over him like a healing balm. He put three fingers on the stones, slowed his mind and asked the all-important question.

Are they here?

The bracelet gave no response, not even a tingle. That was excellent, for no news was good news. It meant that *They* were gone. It meant his war was over.

Carson relaxed. Tension drained out of his body like someone had pulled out a plug. It felt so good to finally quit. He should have done this years ago. He couldn't imagine why he hadn't.

A snick of sound caught his attention. The record player started spinning as the record dropped onto the revolving turntable; the needle descended in the middle. Puccini's Opera *Turandot* starring Alexandra Senicki started to play.

Carson's guts knotted hard in his belly. He knew this opera. This was the famous question scene.

It was a death scene.

He rolled over into a half-crouch, pulling the Luger out of the waistline of his pants.

The room flooded with light so bright Carson was momentarily blinded. When his vision cleared, he saw Mr. Senicki off to his right with the Colt 45, while off to his left Mrs. Senicki held the pearl-handled revolver.

Through bloodshot eyes, King "Wotan" Herman Senicki saw the Nazi officers, Andy and Alexandra, before him. Pain flared in the palms of his hands and feet from the spikes they had driven into his flesh when they hammered him to the cross. They had killed Rebecca. He burned with vengeance. Protected by his golden battle armor, he vowed the evil Nazis would pay with their lives.

Princess "Turandot" Alexandra Senicki glared at the Third Reich Gestapo officers, Rebecca and Herman. She couldn't decide whom she hated more, her Hitler-loving husband or the daughter who betrayed her by killing her true love, Andy. Holding the silver revolver in her five-inch fingernails, she was determined they would die by her hands.

Carson's eyes flitted back and forth at the two parents. His brain raced with confusion. *How can they be here? The bracelet should have warned me?*

His brain cells sought an answer, when his nose began to bleed.

The blood trickled slowly at first, just enough to catch his attention, then came out in a gushing burst. Pain exploded in his forehead. Something wiggled under his skull, shoving, pushing, writhing. The jellyfish squirted out of his nostril and fell out onto his outstretched bloody hand.

Carson stared at the copper device. Tiny hair-like tentacles whipped about, tickling the palm of his hand. His eyes grew huge. *No. It can't be. I cut it out. How did it get back in there?*

The implications staggered him.

I've been used like a puppet! How long have they known about me?

The bracelet sent an image to Carson. The Director seemed to appear before him and yet not be truly there. He looked like a cruel and ugly fish, glowering with round, hate-filled eyes.

"You've been extremely entertaining," said the Director. "But we're canceling your performance contract. This is your final scene."

Stumbling backwards, Carson slapped the jellyfish off of his hand. Rejecting the truth, he uttered a quivering moan.

The five Eyes in the room filmed Carson's torment. Probes recorded his agony into the computer memory banks.

The Director smiled; his teeth stained red from the prune juice and Metamucil. "When you jumped out of the warehouse window, we caught you and put it inside your head."

Carson tore the bracelet off his wrist. Tears welled up in his eyes; an icy chill ran down his spine; he strummed his lips with his fingers.

"I escaped you in Alaska ... I'm the only one who ever beat you at your own game ... leave me alone ... I promise I won't tell anyone ..."

King Herman raised his magic spear at Andy the Nazi.

Princess Alexandra aimed her gun at the Gestapo officer Rebecca.

They pulled the hammers of their weapons back with a loud *click*.

Together, they softly whispered, "You are my shining star and I will never let you go."

Carson screamed.

He fled towards the window.

Gun muzzles flared.

The room filled with the sound of thunder.

The last thing Carson saw in his life was his get-a-way car traveling away with a huge yellow Eye behind the wheel, driving, and waiving goodbye with its strange mechanical hands.

Carson collapsed; a stream of bright, red blood pooled out on the carpet; the end of his pony tail dipped into it like a quill into an ink well.

"Death at last," the Director sighed, drying his cold, clammy face with microwaves from an electric handkerchief. "I almost thought it would never happen. After all the frustration I've been through today, death is truly a joy to behold."

Stretching his hands in front of the holo-monitor, he cracked his knuckles. "Besides, what good is a murder mystery if nobody kicks the bucket?"

He laughed out of a sense of relief.

Herman and Alexandra aimed their weapons in each others direction. The Director waited for them to shoot each other. He was vexed that the other humans had lived and needed to increase the body count in the production. His masterpiece was a mess. He had gone way over budget. The main characters survived. He only hoped he could find a way to salvage it in post-production.

Staring blankly at the holo-monitor, he wondered what Francis Ford Coppolla would do.

The star ship violently lurched, knocking the Director off of his feet. He landed flat on his face, pinning one arm under his chest.

What in the great Galactic Eye was that? An earthquake?

A blade of massage grass wiggled inside his nose, irritating his sinuses. With a wave of his free hand, he slapped the green reed aside and raised himself up.

"Whatever is going on here, I demand it stop this instant."

The ship lurched again. The Director banged his chest hard against the console panel. "Damn it to Krypton!"

Before he could swear again, the ship brutally rocked back and forth.

The Director pitched forward, falling into his anti-grav director's chair. As the spacecraft heaved, the chair bounced about like dice being shaken in a cup before a roll.

The holo-monitor went blank, showing only static.

The chair crashed into the console. A half-sucked lemon struck his eye, stinging it fiercely. The anti-grav chair sprang about the room like a pogo stick as the Director clung to it for dear life.

Seconds later, the rumbling ship came to a shuddering halt.

The Director got to his feet, his sight blurry from his soapy tears. Squinting, he noticed the energy display panel showed a major power surge had come from inside the ship.

The holo-monitor picture came back on. Herman and Alexandra were still pointing their guns at each other, but they stood stiff and unmoving.

"Why don't they shoot each other?" the Director mumbled. "What in Orion's belt is going on here?"

Turning his head, the Director saw the cortex control power indicator was blinking on and off.

"There's a short in the power supply. That's just great. This is the worst frelling day of my life."

Pointing the Colt 45 at Alexandra, images flickered in Herman's mind--sitting with Alexandra on an opera tour bus in Romania … professing his need for her … the anger in her eyes melting to confusion and finally wonder ... at their wedding on a small performance stage in Gdangst, he spoke his vow of unending love, then kissed her ... his entire life flashed before his eyes … Alexandra was the cause of all the best parts.

The hatred he had felt for her for the last several hours flashed on and off. His muscles froze; he could not pull the trigger. This was his wife, the woman he loved, the source of his happiness.

Why was he pointing a gun at her?

A dam burst inside Alexandra; memories flooded her soul – Herman proposing marriage … the opera company throwing flowers as they walked down the aisle of the theater while the orchestra played at their wedding … putting a slice of cake in Herman's mouth as he playfully licked her fingers … their wedding night of passion … the birth of Rebecca … her baby sleeping in her arms as Herman embraced them.

Her revolver was aimed right at him.

How could she kill the man she loved?

"The computer is fibulating, Herr Director," said the Production Manager over the intercom. "Their memories are going back to their original settings."

"Well, fix it," the Director shouted.

"Yes, sir. We're working on it now."

On another holo-monitor, the Director saw a human memory. The Herman and the Alexandra were hugging each other, rejoicing over the birth of their daughter.

"Love and family," the Director frowned. "It makes me sick to my stomach."

He popped a couple of antacids into his martini glass. Tiny seahorses scurried about trying to escape the rising bubbles.

The communicator buzzed.

"What is it?" the Director said irritably.

"The monster movie is finished, Herr Director," the Film Student said. "I just completed shooting the second climax at the lake. It took a lot of power, but it came out quite superbulous."

"Took a lot of power?" the Director said putting two and two together. "It was you. You overloaded the ship's power grid. You short-circuited my special effects generators. Because of you I lost control of my actors. You've ruined my masterpiece you fecal lump!"

"But you said I could do whatever I wanted," the Film Student said lamely. "I was just following the committee's orders."

"Get back to the ship immediately."

"But I have to do a few pickups …"

"GET BACK TO THE SHIP BEFORE I TURN YOU INTO WHALE GRUEL!" screamed the Director, turning off the com channel. He pounded his fists on the tops of his shoulders, beating himself, groaning shrilly. "Why is this happening to me? I don't deserve this. How can I be an artistic genius when I am surrounded by incompetent fools!"

The Director looked at the storyboard wall. He had forgotten to turn off the thought pen. Phrases like: I AM A GENIUS, KILL THEM ALL, LOVE IS FOR LOSERS, I WILL NOT LET A BUNCH OF DUMB ACTORS DEFEAT ME encircled his private production quarters in the bold, emotional strokes of a criminal madman.

His body trembling, the Director gulped down his alcoholic stomach medicine. Sitting at the console, he switched it to manual override and typed in his final program.

Herman felt his finger exert pressure on the trigger of the Colt 45. He struggled to gain control over himself. He couldn't shoot Alexandra … not the woman he loved.

A battle raged inside Alexandra as she slowly squeezed the pearl-handled revolver. Her body would not obey her. The force on the trigger increased.

Herman and Alexandra realized that something evil had taken control over them. Their eyes filled with heartfelt tears at what they were slowly being forced to do. Locking their eyes upon each other, their souls reached across the living room, speaking of their eternal devotion to each other and how they would be reunited again in the afterlife to live forever in love.

Crickets sang outside the Senicki house. Two bright flashes of gunfire briefly lit up the living room curtains from the interior. The sound of two bodies thudded to the floor.

An eerie silence prevailed.

The crickets resumed their singing.

The Alien Reality Television camera crew and the Director materialized on the Senicki's lawn in a transporter beam.

"We're on the martini," the Production Manager shouted to the crew. "Let's shoot the closing credits and we're done."

Sitting at the outdoor picnic table, several its manipulated their portable camera control boards with their four-fingered hands.

Inside the living room, three dead bodies bled on the tan carpet.

The Eyes phase shifted, becoming visible. One went to the record player and placed the needle towards the end of the album.

The finale of Turandot, a majestic love song between the Prince and the Princess, swelled out of the tinny speakers. Two Eyes filmed Mr. and Mrs. Senicki on the cold carpet as blood pooled out from under their bodies. The Eyes slowly dollied in until the actors' faces were framed in a tight close-up. Copper cylinders squished out of their noses, plopping into the crimson puddles. The organisms inside squealed, then incinerated in a puff of fire and smoke. Their demise was artfully lit and photographed as a reflection in the Senicki's lifeless eyes.

Another Eye shot a low angle of Dr. Carson "Weirdo" Gray, his face awkwardly twisted towards the silver bracelet that lay inches away from his outstretched hand. Even in death, he seemed to crave the alien artifact with its smooth, black stones.

The piece of alien jewelry, so invaluable to preserving his existence, dissolved into a stream of atoms that rose upwards in a vaporous trail until they vanished into thin air like *poof.*

"That's a wrap," the Production Manager said. "Let's strike the set so we can all go home."

An Eye opened a window with its mechanical arms. Five cameras flew outside. The cameramen, like a bunch of twelve-year-olds, directed the Eyes to zoom above the house. They did loops, barrel rolls, precision flying, barely missing each other; colored smoke trailed behind them in a dazzling display of aerial tomfoolery.

It was all great fun.

The Director gazed at the Eyes, zipping around in front of the full moon. Things had not gone the way he had wanted them to. He chewed on a webbed finger.

"My masterpiece is ruined," he mumbled. "The Andy, Rebecca, Gunter and Emma were supposed to die horribly in a train wreck. The Andy did something with his voice that saved them before the train squashed them to a pulp. Then the white light failed as well."

He shook his head. "This is outrageous. I am humiliated by these lesser creatures."

Two cameras raced by the Director; Iggy and Glop trotted up to him, smiling, wanting to congratulate him. Noting the Director's intense, brooding gaze, the cameramen quickly went in another direction.

The white light would also have been a sensational finale, the Director thought. *It is the most advanced special effects generator in the universe. When the white light changed to red, it would act as a metaphor for social retribution and justice. It should have burned the humans alive, consuming their bodies in a raging fire, purifying their immorality for Those Who Watch to see. The show could have been a stunning morality play on the destructive power of love and societies righteous anger in eradicating its treacherous existence.*

The Director cracked his knuckles. The joints snapped loudly, one after another.

"THE CRITICS WOULD HAVE LOVED IT," he bellowed, startling the rest of the crew.

Closing his fishy eyelids, he bowed his head upon his scaly chest.

Love leads to destruction. What a great theme. It could have been a masterpiece, now it's a joke. And it's all that damn, baby-faced Film Student's fault! I'm sorry Steven Spielberg. I failed you. It wasn't my fault.

He overheard a Production Assistant report to the Production Manager that the Film Student had returned to the ship so frightened he put himself in cryo storage without seeing the Director first.

He'll be stuck in cryo for a very long time, the Director thought. *Forever, if I can arrange it.*

The Production Manager ambled over. "Congratulations, Herr Director. That is the finest piece of reality TV I have ever seen--the mind mixing, the Nazi memories, the opera characters, the triple climax, giving them one of the black stones, even the grandmother — simply amazing."

"All that effort wasted," the Director mumbled distractedly. "What power stone?"

"Don't worry. I put it back in the locator," the Production Manager said. "And switching the theme at the end to a different character. Absolutely brilliant."

The Director's eyes dilated. Had the Production Manager seen something he hadn't?

"You noticed that, did you?" the Director said. "What did you think about it?"

Air wheezed into the Production Manager's lungs. He misted his throat with throat softener spray before he spoke, emulating the Director's fine narrator voice over voice. "The story begins with the coming together of two families and their offspring, which Those Who Watch will find repugnant and highly illegal, deserving the death sentence—"

"Yes, yes, get to the point," the Director interrupted.

The Production Manager continued without his narrator voice. "The guest actor was more dangerous than the Andy and Rebecca, Herr Director. Once you rewrite some of his speeches explaining that, using the locator, he can track down the V-lan Home World and decimate our planet with A-bombs, he could be like that emotion criminal Hitler back in the 1940s. We could use footage from the World War II show we shot here decades ago and intercut it with computer generated interstellar warships attacking our planet with him in charge of the fleet. Those Who Watch will be so horrified, when you kill the Carson you'll become a planetary hero."

The Director pondered the Production Manager's words. "You have deduced my intentions correctly. Prepare a list of footage modifications. We'll go over them on the flight back home."

"Yes, Herr Director, I am honored. One day you will be awarded the medal of high intellect."

The Production Manager sauntered away.

"Wait," the Director said.

The Production Manager stopped.

"What is your name?" the Director said. "What is your *birth* name?"

The Production Manager blinked twice. Such a request was unheard of. Everyone on Home World had a birth name, but they were addressed in public by their job description. It weeded out emotional closeness. Asking someone's birth name was considered rude. Still, the request came from the Director, whom he admired. How could he refuse?

"Nambie," the Production Manager said. "My birth name is Nambie."

"I am Thor," the Director said. "You are doing an excellent job, Nambie. You put the jellyfish back in the Carson's head very quickly. I value your services. Carry on."

The corners of the Production Manager's lips twisted upward in a restrained smile. He saluted with both of his right-side hands. "Thank you, Herr Director. It is an honor serving your genius in the important task of sustaining the virtues of civilized behavior on our planet by sublimating our peoples' genetic heritage of aggression through the use of violent entertainment."

Finishing his salute, he smartly turned and left.

Watching the Production Manager leave, the Director put it all together.

Nambie was right.

If he gave the Carson some emotional rantings and ravings Those Who Watch would see him as a menace to the rational universe, a psychotic brute with destructive emotion and a legion of star ships on the attack. It was a unique concept, bold, outrageous and entertaining.

It's fresh and I will get all the credit.

The Director ran his tongue across his jagged teeth. *It was a good thing I reimplanted the jellyfish in the Carson after he fled the warehouse. It led to some interesting acting at the finale. Of course, he had to die, but all actors must suffer for their craft. It's what they do.*

The Director envisioned the Producer and his story committee being fired because of their awful monster movie. The Director would ascend into their place, a power unto himself. With the prestige and increased income, he could carpet his entire home with massage grass. He imagined squeezing his toes in the wiggling lawn. He would never wear footgear at home again.

Now that's what I call superbulous. This calls for a celebration.

Extending his ears to maximum perception, the Director held a remote controller and depressed a crystal on it.

The production star ship materialized above the house, over twenty times the size of the two bedroom domicile.

The Director depressed a second crystal. Gigantic speakers rotated into view from within the craft's hull. The finale of Turandot played.

The cameramen stopped horsing around with the flying Eyes. They stopped to listen to the music. The speakers drenched the crew with a composition so moving it brought a tear to each one of their four eyes.

As Puccini filled him with rapture, the Director recalled how he first found this planet by taking a wrong turn at Alpha Centari some 400 years ago. It was peopled with class two beings, so he brain-tapped some and made his first picture with minimal equipment.

It was a big hit at home.

Years later, he returned to Earth with a production team. The human creatures provided a plentiful source of acting talent. It earned him a reputation as brilliant. Planet Earth became one of the most popular V-lan reality television shows ever.

He quickly optioned the entire planet, obtaining all the legal cinematic and merchandising rights in perpetuity. Over the years, he had done well for himself, but some bad investments back home had nearly wiped out his entire nest egg. He needed a masterpiece to put his retirement solidly back in the black.

He still hoped to make a killing on action figures. Young V-lans especially enjoyed evil characters. Maybe he would put an eye-patch on the Carson and a sinister looking goatee.

Despite their inferior minds, the Director gave humans credit for their music. It was rich in beauty and grandeur. What did they call it? Opera. He thought of this world as planet Opera. That it was created by an race of mentally defective beings was irrelevant.

Opera music was the best music in the entire universe.

He remembered how he first discovered opera through Adolph Hitler, who knew the famous German composer Wagner.

Poor Adolph. I should have let him win the Second World War with the atomic bomb ... but it would have killed too many actors for my other productions. Still, I admired Hitler. He was the boss and no-one defied his orders. Too bad I made him insane. But what great artist isn't?

Inside the living room, the props were beamed out by the transporter--the copper devices, the pearl-handled revolver, the Colt 45 that belonged to the outlaw Jessie James and Hitler's Luger.

The Director and his crew beamed up to the star ship. Interstellar engines throbbed with a growing power. The ship's external speakers rotated back inside, making its exterior smooth and space worthy. On the hull of the great ship was the production company's logo--a black swastika in a white circle on a red rectangle, in honor of the man who introduced an alien planet to the glory of opera music.

Thank you for that, my Fuehrer, thought the Director. *I'm sorry it had to end with your death. What can I say? That's show biz.*

As the music of *Turandot* reached its grand finale, the star drive engaged. The mighty vessel thrust forward, catapulting itself into outer space towards Home World in the wink of an alien eye.

The murder mystery was over.

The following morning, the rising sun cast a golden light over the forest. Near some melted and twisted railroad tracks, an eagle flew above some unusual shapes carved out of the treetops.

The shapes formed the letters A-R-T.

In a strange sort of way, it looked as though it had been made by a giant cookie cutter.

EPILOGUE

(Compliments of the singing Munchkins)
(To the tune of "The Wonderful Wizard of Oz")

Your life is an adventure,
So give to it all of your heart
Its thrills, its chills, even if it fills
With aliens and opera stars.

If you want to live then you must dare
Your creative side, to share, to share
To share, to share, to share, to share, to share
Your uniqueness is what's truly rare.

Your life is an adventure,
So give to it all of your heart.
Ha-ha-ha-ha-ha!

"Hey fellahs. Are we still figments of Andy's imagin-nu-nu-nation?" the stuttering Munchkin asked. "Oh, kitty crap. I'm stu-stuttering again."

"Shut up. We're playing poker," the other Munchkins said dismissively.

"I bet a burning bush," a Munchkin gambled.

"I'll see your burning bush and raise the dead," wagered another.

"Hey fellahs," the stuttering Munchkin wondered. "Do you thu-think I could gu-get Rebecca to ku-ku-kiss me again?"

"NO!"

"I'll match your walking dead," another anted, "and raise you the Apple of Forbidden Knowledge."

"I call and walk on water," a fourth Munchkin said.

"Bu-bu-but fellahs," the stuttering Munchkin insisted. "Love is the cu-cure for everything bu-bad."

"SHUT UP OR WE'LL DOGPILE ON YOU!"

"Su-su-sorry," the stuttering Munchkin said as the others continued their gambling. Feeling sad, he looked around the card table. "Hey fellahs," the stuttering Munchkin sighed. "Did anyone bu-bu-bring some guacamole?"

Send us your comments about THOSE WHO WATCH

E-mail them to: ThoseWhoWatch@GalacticEyePublishing.com.
Let us know your name and the city you live in.
Like to read a sequel? Tell us that too!

Download our free flyer!
Help us promote this wonderful story!

A free flyer is available at: www.GalacticEyePublishing.com/TWW_flyer
Please e-mail it to your friends and help us spread the word
about this unique story.

Visit our website

www.GalacticEyePublishing.com
Read an interview with author Jon Henn and see photos of him with sci-fi actors
from: Battlestar Galactica, Farscape, Star Trek Enterprise,
and the movie Lord of the Rings.
Check out our Science Fiction t-shirts, posters and other great items under
The Alien News. Free t-shirt drawing every month!

Read our <u>FREE</u> comedy newsletter!

**Join the paranoid adventures of reporter GODFREY OPERA
as he uncovers alien shenanigans happening on planet Earth!
Send an e-mail to: Comedy@TheAlienNews.com**

E-mail me all about it.

<u>Coming soon by author Jon Henn</u>

Stranded On Earth (science fiction) – a race of 400 alien healers crash land on Earth in an interstellar hospital ship. Dr. Tanner, a metallurgist by trade, finds himself chosen by the aliens to be the *Waholin,* their sacred human blood brother who will guide them to their future on Earth. With their incredible healing abilities and super-technology, the aliens could turn the planet into a paradise for all. But who should control all this wealth? How can one man know what is best for both the aliens and humanity?

Plagued by forces that will stop at nothing to impose their will on the religious, peace-loving aliens, will Dr. Tanner keep them safe from harm? Or will a war be started that could destroy the entire planet? And how will the healers' mystical religion influence humanity forever?

The Adventures of Flippy the Magic Frog (a story for grades 3-8) – Flippy is a young frog who lives in the country village of Pineville with Johnny (a 14 year old boy) and Peabrain (a telepathic brain who lives in a glass jar). They are his best friends and life with them is good. But unknown to the three young beings, high upon the mountain a storm of evil is brewing in a magic castle. It is Christmas day and an evil magician named Count Boo wants Baked Hawaiian Frog on the Christmas dinner menu. Will Flippy, Johnny and Peabrain survive their encounter with dark magic? Will Flippy save the lives of the other young creatures trapped in the Count's magic dungeon? How will Flippy deal with hypnotic spiders, angry bats, monsters, a fire breathing dragon, and a Sorceress who is a pair of eyeballs. Why is the Count's mysterious prisoner a deformed girl named Lumpy? And what is the secret to a magic book that could destroy them all?

And most important of all, how can a young frog stop an evil magician who commands a magic pirate ship with a ruthless crew from ransacking the world … starting with Flippy's home town!

Very cool.
Contact me when it's ready.
I'll send you my e-mail address.

Like to wear something different?

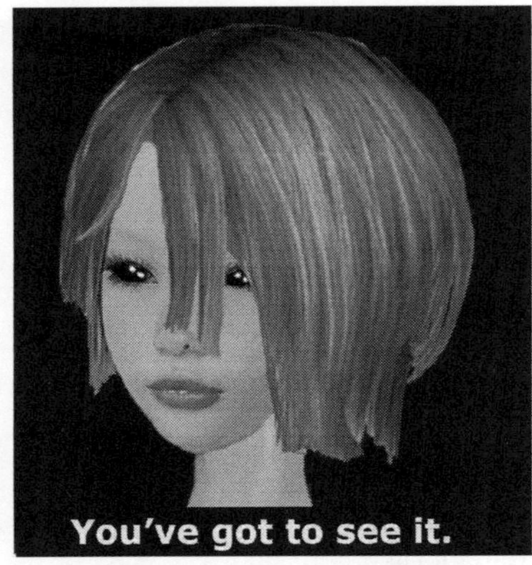

T-Shirts, Posters & more!

**Science Fiction & Fantasy,
Animals, Sayings, etc.
for Children and Adults.**

www.TheAlienNews.com

DISCOVER
TheAlienNews.com

Your Internet Sci-Fi clothing store!
(Here's just a few of our wonderful designs.)
(And wait until you see them in color!)

Alien Guard

Royal Guard

Alien Skateboarder

Doggy Abduction

1948856

Made in the USA